THe
GHOST OF
MIDSUMMER
COMMON

GORDON
MC BRIDE

WINDSTORM CREATIVE
PORT ORCHARD ✦ WASHINGTON

The Ghost of Midsummer Common
copyright 2008 by Gordon McBride
published by Windstorm Creative

ISBN 978-1-59092-689-5
First edition August 2008
9 8 7 6 5 4 3 2

Design by Blue Artisans Design.

Printed in the United States of America.

For information about film, reprint or other subsidiary rights contact:
legal@windstormcreative.com

Windstorm Creative is a multiple division, international organization involved in publishing books in all genres, including electronic publications; producing games, videos and audio cassettes as well as producing theatre, film and visual arts events. The wind with the flame center was designed by Buster Blue of Blue Artisans Design and is a trademark of Windstorm Creative.

Windstorm Creative
7419 Ebbert Dr SE
Port Orchard, WA 98367
www.windstormcreative.com
360-769-7174 ph

Windstorm Creative is a member of Orchard Creative Group, Ltd.

Library of Congress Cataloging-in-Publication data available.

For my wife Kari who shares
my Anglophile's love of Britain
and especially of Cambridge.

ACKNOWLEDGMENTS

Many works were consulted in preparation for the writing of this novel, some over many years and in other contexts—both historical and theological. Special mention goes to Marc Ian Barasch, *Healing Dreams* (Riverhead Books, 2000) and, for the words of Julian of Norwich, *Julian of Norwich: Showings (Classics of Western Spirituality)*, ed. Edmund Colledge, James Walsh and Jean Le Clercq (Paulist Press,1977). Thanks to my wife, Kari Boyd McBride, and friends Elizabeth Gooden, Pat Dickson, and Pamela Decker for reading the manuscript and making valuable suggestions. To the people of Grace St. Paul's Episcopal Church who supported my writing while I served as their rector. To Frederick and Rebecca Masterman who led me to Windstorm. To Cris K.A. DiMarco and all the folks at Windstorm Creative who made the publication possible. All errors remain mine.

THE GHOST OF MIDSUMMER COMMON

GORDON MCBRIDE

chapter one

The 1:32 from King's Cross slowed and jerked to a halt at the Cambridge station. Brian leaped out of his seat and danced around inside his skin like a kid on his birthday. He searched for familiar landmarks: a little coffee and pastry kiosk, the newspaper stand, a distant spire. Everything was where it should be and looking the way he remembered it. He straightened up from bending to look through the car's window. He had missed this place so much that it was all he could do to choke down the lump in his throat. Had it really been ten years since his last time here? Such a lapse was wildly out of character for an Anglophile like Brian. Today he felt like the returning prodigal.

So where was the fatted calf? No clouds parting with rays of golden sun falling on tousled fair hair? No strains of *Jerusalem* swelling in crescendo?

Right.

He wrestled his bags off the train and strapped the small cases on top of the two large wheeled ones. Other departing passengers darted around him as he dragged it all down the platform. Another wave of fondness and familiarity swept over him; he loved this little city with all its tradition, vitality and energy, its twisting old streets, grassy expanses and spired buildings.

The shoulder-to-shoulder crowd swept him with it through the ticket machine-lined reception hall like a river at flood. Bumping. Jostling. "Sorry." "Sorry."

The past, both the impersonal centuries and his own stories, unwound into the present in Cambridge. Colleges and bookstores, churches and pubs, libraries and archives—all formed a central place in his life. It was here that he learned to do real research; here that the tentative first chapters of his dissertation were written; and here that he and his young first wife conceived the child who grew to become his only daughter. It was to Cambridge that he returned over the years to find renewal and refreshment. But all that was before Emily, the second wife. Emily didn't like England, didn't like any foreign country, and he had given up fighting with her about it. Now she was divorcing him to live with her Chevrolet dealer. Chevrolets. Couldn't the guy at least sell Volvos? As if her infidelity hadn't been insult enough. Had the rejection and the loss not felt so humiliating he might really have been amused by her bad taste.

No doubt his own self-absorption had made him a lousy husband, and he had to admit that Emily and he had never been a good match. It had been a second marriage for them both. They had just fallen into it. Once their animal lust had evaporated like spilled water on an August sidewalk, their life together had settled down into a dull routine. Still, he would be sorry to end that chapter and lose his comfortable life. He had been cozy with Emily, and he loved that big old house: three stories on a tree-lined Evanston street just across the Northwestern campus from the lakefront. He adored those attic rooms with their dormer windows and his book-lined study. Whose contents were now languishing, captives in cardboard boxes, in a rented storage shed. He thought about the many mornings when he would crawl out of his warm bed in that house, throw on some clothes and head toward the lakeshore for one of his solitary walks. Or runs. There would be no more morning walks. No more cozy bed. No more study. No more Emily.

After sabbatical he would have to find himself a new place as close to the lake as possible, perhaps a little nearer to the heart of the city. He fantasized about an apartment high atop one of the old brick buildings along Lake Shore Drive: high ceilings and dark wood trim. Suddenly he craved the rush and rhythm of Chicago's heartbeat. He felt very alone and a little frightened here in Cambridge. He missed Emily.

Brian took his place in the taxi queue and sat down on one of the large suitcases. There had to be fifty people in front of him.

A wash of sadness nearly swamped him. He thought about the things he would miss about Emily. She could be smart and savvy. She could think through ten complex subjects while the average person was wrestling with one. She was funny. He hadn't seen much of that wit recently, but he knew it was still there. Her sarcasm must now be turned against Fords and Toyotas instead of his departmental colleagues. A Chevrolet dealer? The very idea. Maybe it was inevitable that an accounting professor would be drawn to car sales. Was this the business world's measure of success— a Chevy dealership?

Even he recognized his academic snobbery.

Cambridge was a home in need. Now, maybe a year in Cambridge would give his academic life a kind of kick start. It certainly needed something. The mollusk minds, usually called university administrators, would be thousands of miles away. The tedium and monotony of classes and committees would soon grow remote. He would restore life as he had known it before Emily came into it. Maybe he could get back to his real work in earnest and be productive again. Maybe even write something.

But he felt another jab of emotion, of fear. After everything that had happened on his last visit to this island he had a right to be fearful. His second marital disaster, the aura of failure that seemed to hover over everything else in his life right now and the return of his fear: Brian was a mess.

He watched as city busses, taxis and private cars moved in a ritual dance around the circular drive in front of the rail station. Every few minutes he pushed and pulled his cases ahead as the queue shrunk. The young man in front of him was eating a Donar Kebab. It smelled spicy and tempting. Watching and sniffing brought back memories of meals just like that one, caught on the run, moments when some interior drive was more compelling than stopping to taste and sample something really elegant. But he was no longer in his twenties. Even his thirties and half of his forties had slipped away.

An impeccably turned-out older woman stood impatiently behind him. She was dressed in mauve and black with matching hat, purse and shoes and had a green Harrods shopping bag on her arm. She felt to him as imperious as she was obviously impatient.

Glancing across the street, Brian saw a field of parked bicycles. Making a quick calculation, he estimated that there had to be something approaching five hundred of them. Appraising quantities inside containers or enclosures was a kind of hobby of his. How many grains of rice could be gotten into a jar? How many people could you cram into a railroad car? How many strings of spaghetti fitted in a pound package? Or he could use the subject matter of his work as a historian and ask how many angels could dance on the head of a pin? Obsessive? Probably so. But there seemed little real harm in it.

The Kebab eater polished off his sandwich and flashed a grinning mouthful of sparkling white teeth. The snooty woman gave him a disdainful look, much as if he had been a distasteful and embarrassing growth on her bum. Finally, it was Brian's turn to get into a taxi, a minivan that gave him lots of room for both his long legs and his bags. "Lord's Hostel," he said.

The driver grunted something cheerful but unintelligible, pointed the van into the roundabout and careened around it onto the narrow road.

Brian leaned back in the seat and looked out fondly at the familiar town as the minivan scooted between parked cars and moving busses. He was charmed and amused afresh by the orderliness of the buildings and the chaos of the traffic. Long rows of attached brick houses lined the way. In the distance, the spires of medieval churches and college buildings jabbed into the sunny afternoon sky and gave him a little thrill. He soaked up the antiquity of it all, feeling better already.

Ten years ago Brian's first marriage had finished unraveling, and he was on the mend. Where else would he go to nurse his wounds but England? He had been with Alison, one of his graduate students. She had pursued him until she caught him. Then she ministered to him in the ancient way of younger women. He had been having the time of his life, a time of sexual extravagance. But that was before Alison decided to throw him back. Until, quite frankly, she had grown tired of him. Or had thought he was just too weird. He remembered how she had looked with her riotous blonde hair atop that unblemished young body. A Camelot existence. Then the strange things started happening.

It wasn't so much that he had begun seeing things, though that had been part of it. Mostly he had felt them. Vivid emotional encounters with the past, especially the violence of tragic events. Ultimately he had gotten an explanation about it all. Enough to convince him that he wasn't going nuts. But it still seemed pretty bizarre. The Chicago shrink called what he was having *place memories*. According to the theory some people are susceptible to lingering residues of the past in physical locations—rooms, houses, battlefields. "It says much about haunted houses and such like," she had said in her quiet way. With gray hair tumbling over gold-rimmed spectacles and a tendency to mumble something very like tut-tut, she had reminded him of an eccentric grandmother. "The Church of England even had a commission a few years back to look into the rash of strange occurrences that broke out right after the Second World War," she had explained. "Their theory held that the bombing stirred up some unsettled old stuff from the past." She shook her head. "No, really, that's what they said. Susceptible people started seeing, hearing and feeling things." Susceptible people. Apparently Brian was one of those susceptible people.

Alison had wanted to see Coventry Cathedral, so they made a little detour in the day's plans and took it in. A World War II Luftwaffe attack on the evening of November 14, 1940 had left the medieval building in ruins. It remained that way as a reminder of the horror of war. Brian walked amidst the roofless partial walls and began to feel strange. He became aware of the new cathedral looking down on them through its wall of etched glass, turning the ruin into a terrible cloister. He tried to imagine what it would have been like watching the old church burning out of control, the firefighters doing what they could about it, but being helpless. Meanwhile the bombs continued to fall.

Then something changed. He had felt the accumulated pain and fear of many people. He heard quite clearly the rough uneven drone of German aircraft, the whine and buzz of British Spitfires and Mosquitoes, the whistle and concussion of the bombardment, and the rapid report of antiaircraft guns. He became terrified. Ghostly shapes of people were screaming and running around in what seemed like aimless circles. Shattered glass littered the ground. The sight of bloody wounds and missing limbs filled him with horror. The whole place began to burn. He had even felt the heat of the flames. It had been as if that massive attack were going on right then. With him standing in the middle of it. For a time the pain of those killed and maimed was staggering. Then his mind stilled and the quiet of the morning returned, leaving only the present moment. Tourists wandered in and out of the gift shop. Others went around the walls of the roofless building or into the new cathedral. Alison was looking at him as if he had lost his mind. She later told him that he had been ducking and wincing, and, even worse from her point-of-view, people had been staring at him. The whole experience must have lasted less than a minute and was over as quickly as it had begun. But he had been left shaking and in a cold sweat. That may have been the beginning of the end with Alison. It certainly raised questions in his mind. What could he tell Alison? He didn't get it himself.

That was only the first, if the most dramatic, of those strange experiences. On the field of Culloden Moor in the Scottish Highlands, he had felt the thrill and horror of eighteenth century conflict. For a moment he heard the clash of swords and the explosions of cannon and musket. He left there terrified. A few days later, the ring of hard steel against stone had shattered for him the serenity of Winchester Cathedral as statues were smashed and the clomping of Cromwell's horses echoed in the nave. He came to feel like a frightened child every time they visited some ancient monument. His relationship with Alison didn't survive their return to Chicago.

Brian hadn't had the nerve to go to Britain since. Emily

had provided a convenient excuse. But now, well, now he wanted to get away. He needed to get his work back on track by doing some research in the original documents and having the uninterrupted quiet to write. He needed to be in a place that had always renewed his spirit. He would just have to take his chances with the place memories.

Lord's College's historic buildings sat just off Trumpington Street near St. Catharine's and Corpus Christi colleges. Right in the heart of the medieval town. Brian's year in Cambridge would be spent as a visiting scholar of Lord's. Several lunches and dinners a month at the high table and full rights to use the university library were tops among his privileges. But he wouldn't be living in college. Instead, he had a flat at the Lord's Hostel, or Lo-Host as he had learned the locals called it. Situated half-a-mile west of the college, Lo-Host was convenient to the history faculty building and the university library. Otherwise a brisk fifteen minute walk along Sidgwick and Silver streets or across the grassy college Backs would bring him to the heart of the medieval city. It was a perfect location: quiet and yet close to everything.

The taxi stopped in front of a Georgian red brick house that, according to the information he'd gotten from Lords, must contain his flat. He paid the driver, tipped him and stood for a moment looking at the place. Not bad, he thought, though the building's original integrity had been spoiled at the rear by a thirty-year-old addition. He pulled his bags around to the left side of the house where an opening led into an inner courtyard. A door bore the label, "Residential Office." It opened to his touch, but the room was unattended. In the interior clutter, he spotted an envelope waiting on the counter with his name, "Prof. B Craig," printed on it in heavy black ink. He tore it open to find two keys, each with a piece of string attached to a tag. A single sheet of official notepaper said, "Welcome to Lo-Host," and was signed, G. Firth. One of the key tags said "outside." The other had the number "5" written on it. Back on the sidewalk, Brian soon found the entrance door at the rear of the Georgian house and tried the first key. It opened onto a flight of stairs.

Number five was two flights up. Making three trips with his luggage, panting and huffing—and muttering "shit" and "damn" as he banged his shin against a low table—he finally closed his own door behind him with an emphatic sigh. He was glad to be done with it and to have the trip behind him.

He took an appraising look around. The flat's interior was unlovely and painted a shade of off-gray. "Charming," he mumbled in vague disappointment. It had an interior hallway with doors on either side. First on the left came the sitting room; it doubled as a dining room. "And now for elegant relaxation, the living room suite," he said in a cynical tone and bowed. The room had one wing chair, a desk and chair set with lamp, and a small end table beside the wing chair. A sort of dining table with two mismatched straight-backed wooden chairs rounded out the room's furnishings. Everything looked well seasoned. A bare bulb hung from a cord in the middle of the room. He noticed a string dangling beside the door and remembered this as a common way of turning on lights in England. He tried it out and flooded the room with a harsh glare. Not a single print, calendar or any other kind of decoration broke the monotony of the scarred dull walls. He resolved to do something about the look of the place. He would, after all, call this home for a whole year.

Across the hall a kitchen the size of a closet had a small cooker, an even smaller Fridge stuffed under the counter, and a single sink. The lingering rancid smells of frying eggs and bacon grease hung in the air. He found the bedroom and bath up a half-flight of stairs at the end of the hall. The bedroom had a pair of twin beds. He would have his usual challenge stretching his six- foot-two frame from end to end without hanging over at the bottom. A two-headed lime-green goose-necked lamp sat on a small table between the beds. A chest of drawers and a large wooden wardrobe were ready to take his things. The bathroom made him wince. "Bath" meant exactly that, a bathtub. No shower. He was supposed to fold himself into that thing? He looked at the deep narrow tub with disdain. It was an unattractive prospect. Oh well, it was home.

Other than this unlovely place, Brian Alexander Craig,

full professor and visiting scholar, author of books and articles and historian of some modest note, had just joined the ranks of soon-to-be-divorced men ejected from their comfortable lives. He pictured himself homeless in Chicago, a street person with a five-day growth of beard on a pleasant enough face. His still full head of boyish light-brown hair in disarray, tattered once-fine suit pulled tight against the wind, and a look of hungry despair in his hazel eyes. The disreputable Chicago alley of his imagination was littered with broken wine bottles, garbage, piss and puke. He struggled with a former executive for a refrigerator box as a shelter for the night. All the while the famous Chicago wind howled off the lake and down the man-made canyons. Was that what Emily wanted to see? Why do people who have lived with each other for years, sometimes without any passion whatsoever, become nasty and hostile toward each other upon the decision to break-up? Suddenly they exhibit levels of emotion that the marriage itself never evoked. Brian felt no animosity towards Emily. Not really. She was the one who wanted the divorce. Why did she have to be so rotten to him?

Oh well, at least he had his year in England and this bare, unadorned flat. Despite what it lacked in decor, it provided what he hoped would be a warm and cozy place to tie up for the winter. Still many months off. He might have been stuck with a single room with bath down the hall. That had been his initial expectation. He decided to like the place, bathtub and all.

He left one of his large bags and his laptop in the sitting room and carried the other one up the four steps to deposit it along with the overnight in the bedroom. That was where he collapsed, shoes kicked off but otherwise fully dressed face down on the bed nearest the door. A nap would feel just right.

What is this place? It looks familiar, and then again it doesn't. Everything is so intense. Greens are greener and blues are bluer. Light is brighter and shadows are deeper. A beautiful June day dotted with the brilliance of a thousand flowers and aromatic from the musty warm scent of the water. And quiet—it's so quiet.

But where are the people?

I'm standing in a little flat-bottomed boat, like the punts in the River Cam. Standing? God, I'm going to fall into the water. I steady myself with the pole I have in my hands. Pole? Where did that come from?

I know this is Cambridge. Lush vegetation, plain trees and willows, long grasses and wild flowers. They all could be anywhere. Even the buildings beyond the trees look pretty generic. But I just know I'm in Cambridge.

I pull the pole up from the bottom of the riverbed and thrust it down again as if I've done it a thousand times before. The little boat vaults ahead. This is fun. Now it's slowing again and drifting with the current, turning slightly on its axis. I lift the pole and push it down again, and it straightens out.

I laugh out loud. I'm having the time of my life.

I thrust the pole down, grinning for the sheer joy of being here. The boat acts like a live thing and leaps forward.

Now I see another punt coming around a bend in the river and headed my way. I let my boat drift as I wait for it to draw near. It's good to be sharing the river with the punter and his lone woman passenger. She's looking toward the punter and away from me. Something about her seems official somehow. There's a stiffness to her spine that shouts, "I am important. Ignore me at your peril."

And she seems familiar in some way. Her dress seems a bit eccentric.

By some intuition I know that the punter is her servant.

Suddenly the woman turns around. A shiver of recognition passes through me, and I nearly fall over. I stare at her and confirm with astonishment her regal identity as Gloriana. Or at least someone who looks very much like the fabled Virgin Queen. This Elizabeth is in early middle age and reminds me of how she looked in a portrait I once saw of her, dancing with the Earl of Leicester and laughing. Elizabeth Tudor. Brilliant. Loaded with talent.

Dangerous. But this Elizabeth isn't laughing. She turns back around and looks the other way again.

I remember that actors sometimes dress in Elizabethan garb to promote local Shakespearean productions. Is this someone drumming up business for As You Like It *or* The Taming of the Shrew? *But riding in a punt? And looking this much like the real thing? Feeling this much like the real thing?*

Surely I wouldn't bother to dream about a fake queen. Cool.

I pole my boat along with the current, anxious now to draw near to the other one. I go under a bridge. The two punts meet. We pass. The woman—the Queen—is glaring at me. Can that stare possibly be for me? What have I done? Her look gives me a quake of fear. Might she send me to the Tower?

But this isn't real, is it?

Still, I'm uncomfortable. I look away for a moment, and then back again. The other boat carrying the last of the Tudors has vanished. I have the river to myself once more. Where have they gone? There's no place for them to go.

I'm nearly knocked from my perch by a sharp pain. It comes without warning and radiates through every limb in my body. My legs and arms ache. I feel as if I'm falling into the water. The scene in front of me is fading. Am I going blind? My legs are weak. I'm going to fall after all.

Brian woke to find himself curled up in the wing chair of his new flat's sitting room. His legs were pulled up against his chest in a fetal position and clasped in his arms. How'd he gotten there? He was shaking. He remembered falling asleep in the bedroom. "The dream," he muttered. Why did he feel so bad?

Brian had dinner in a little Indian restaurant on Regent Street. Later he explored some of the Cambridge pubs. He finally settled in at his old favorite just off King's Parade. The Eagle. It hadn't changed in twenty years. Mellowed and comfortable, he sat there, surrounded by old wood and laughing people, and thought about the dream he'd had that afternoon. Bizarre. It lingered, as vivid and present still as if he were continuing to dream it. What an imagination. Connected to the place memory stuff? Not necessarily. There hadn't been any strong feelings connected to it—except his oddly fearful reaction. But that wasn't the same as sensing pain and other feelings lingering in a place. Still, he got a little thrill thinking of the image of the Queen. In some odd way he felt as if he had actually seen her. He shook his head, got up from his table and went back to his flat, knowing he would toss and turn before he would be able to fall asleep.

Now I'm standing alone, looking across the River Cam. I recognize the Clare College Bridge, lighted only by a waning moon. The bridge arches over still water. Stars reflect off the river's surface. I lift my foot to step with trepidation onto the bridge, feeling a vague uneasiness. The worn-smooth texture of the handrail against my palm and fingertips reassures and steadies me. I wait for something to happen. A little shiver of dread passes through me. Shadows of trees with branches weeping toward the ground, and structures, some boxy and some pointed, sculpt the horizon. Night flowers in the garden behind me spray cloying perfume into the breathless air. The riverbank smells of mud and rotting vegetation. On my right the unmistakable shape of the King's College Chapel soars to a sharp line of buttress pinnacles. Soldiers standing guard over Perpendicular Gothic walls of glass and stone.

I strain to listen, and I hear the river's gentle sighing against its banks and the rustle of a new breeze high in the trees. But no sounds of roaring motorcycles or sirens wailing in the distance. No tires squealing in complaint against hard asphalt or even harder cobblestones. No typical sounds of a city intruding on the quiet of this night. Not even the barking of a dog or the buzzing of a motor scooter. I listen through the stillness as I try to hear something, anything, beyond the river and the trees. Even the breeze has stilled.

Now an indistinct band of horsemen, perhaps a dozen strong, rides superimposed into my line of sight. Some have swords drawn. Others brandish old-fashioned firearms. Their leader waves and gestures with his sword as he urges his followers on. But no matter how hard they ride, they get nowhere: immobile, silent and opaque. They fade and disappear. Something about them frightens me.

I look back at the bridge and see a man perched on a short stool. His body is round and looks soft. I recognize him instantly. He's a scholar, one of the greatest ones of his age. He's accustomed to endless hours at his books and manuscripts, writing his treatises and his letters. I wonder if his fingers are as ink-stained as I imagine them to be. I look at him hard. His robes are gathered about his torso and legs. A Canterbury cap is pulled over his ears and brow. His vein-latticed nose peeks out from beneath the cap. I've seen every known portrait of him; have read all of his published works and much of his voluminous correspondence. I used to think that I knew his mind as well as I know my own. But I've rarely thought about him in years. Now here he is.

"Evening," I say. My voice startles us both, breaking as it does into the near sound vacuum that surrounds us.

He looks up. Pale eyes stare unwaveringly at me, "Ja?"

"You are Master Erasmus?"

"Ja. To be sure," he says in accented English. His face brightens, and he grins at me as if he knows who I am.

Now he begins to fade before my eyes. He's gone. The bridge and everything around it disappears. I am left empty and alone. My whole body aches. My stomach hurts. I think I might throw up.

Chapter Two

"Jeannie, are you there? I'm on-line. At least I think I am."
Brian glanced at his computer screen and hit "Send." He
had just connected his laptop to the hot-spot in his Lo-
Host room.

Jeannie Mautner was his friend. He liked having a
woman friend. Someone who would join him for runs along
the lakeshore and sometimes talk with when one of them was
having a crisis. It was his turn to have a crisis. He was in luck.
Her reply came in a minute. "I'm here, Brian. You're safe and
sound, then? Good. You managed the computer mysteries?
What a good boy you are. Was that hard to do?"

He crowed proudly to her about his computer prowess.
Then he keyed in a change of subject, "Something else has
happened. Something weird." He told her about yesterday's
two dreams. "Both times I woke up in a chair in the front
room. I don't remember getting there from the bed. Sleep
walking, I guess. I've never done that before, and I felt like
crap." He clicked on "Send."

"Jet lag can do some strange things," he got back a
couple of minutes later. "Sorry you felt bad. But what cool
dreams. It must have been your official greeting. You know,
the arrival of the great historian. Visual signs. A kind of royal
audience with your queen of choice :-). And old Erasable—
who was the other one?"

"Are you being a smart-ass?" He fiddled with papers on
his desk while he waited for her reply.

"Guilty."

He smiled and read on.

"Everything's good here, though it's still hot and muggy.
Typical Chicago summer. I'm up early so I can have a run
along the lake before I go in and start my summer class on
the twentieth-century novel. I really love that stuff. I can't
wait to get started. I can't believe that they pay me to do this!

"But I'd still change places with you in a heart beat. I'm
envious, you creep. Anything new from Emily?"

He wrote back, "We're going to have to get instant messaging. This takes too long.

"There's nothing new with Emily. I have no sense that she will change her mind. I don't really think I want her to.

"And good luck with Lawrence and Joyce and the rest of the gang. Speaking of work, I'm headed over to the university library myself right after I grab some lunch. Maybe I can get started with my research project. Get something done for a change." He sent the email.

"I know you've been feeling unproductive," she wrote. "But don't work so hard that it makes you weird. Maybe Candy and I should come for a visit? Thirteen-year-old girls and their mothers definitely fill up lots of emotional space. Might be good for you. BTW, we are having dinner tonight with my mother. Mother wants to know when I'm getting married again and providing HER GRANDDAUGHTER with a father. Know any good prospects?"

"How about me?" he wrote. A wide clown's grin dancing across his lips. "I'm single. Or I soon will be."

"And spoil a good friendship?" she replied.

He laughed and wrote, "I was thinking the same thing."

"Hey, maybe there's something in that instant messaging stuff," she wrote before shifting the subject to a previous one.

"Candy and I both have time, and we could get away the last week in July or the first part of August. How would that be for you? For a visit, I mean. Do you have room for us or could you find us a place to stay nearby? I'm real serious about this."

Brian had to think for a moment. Did he really want to have visitors? He wasn't sure he did. But then again he wasn't sure he didn't. This was Jeannie, after all. "That would be great," he wrote half-disingenuously. "Wish I could put you up, but it wouldn't work too well. You'll see. Besides you're as rich as Donald Trump."

"Donald? Since when am I a Donald? But that's cool. Find us a place and I'll get the tickets. Watch out for those dreams."

Jeannie certainly was no *Donald*. He sat staring at the screen and thinking about his friend Jeannie Mautner.

"Hmm?" he asked aloud. They always flirted with each other, and she certainly was cute—if a bit healthy and outdoorsy looking. Smart, too. But she was probably right. They had a good friendship. Shaking himself out of his reverie, he turned off the laptop, unplugged it from the wall socket and tucked everything into its leather carrying case. With a determined expression on his face he spread some peanut butter on a piece of bread and headed out the door. He tucked his folded umbrella under his arm. Shifting to thoughts about getting down to work,

The ice crystal-bearing Chicago wind had been slashing across the bleak Illinois landscape, making the walkways slippery and the footing treacherous. Breathing the air was like inhaling needles. Brian had been drinking a latte at the Starbucks on the edge of campus when Jeannie came through the door in a rush of cold air. She dropped an armload of student essays onto the table next to him, pulled off her parka and stuffed it onto a chair. All in a single disdainful motion. The sweet smell of her perfume blended with freshly ground coffee beans to make a heady sense-arousing combination. Brian had already been hiding out in the Starbucks for an hour, downing his second cup while his eyes passed over the third draft of a dissertation chapter. Anything seemed better to him than braving that bitter cold again, just to slip and stumble all the way across campus to his office. He had been longing for a little companionship.

She ordered a tall mocha. His eyes had already been dazzled by color that shouted defiance to the drab day—high furry boots, tight blue jeans, maroon turtleneck and loosely tied bright blue scarf. All this color was eclipsed by a bundle of wild red hair and an equally vivid set of matching fingernails. Even the air around her seemed to be charged with electricity.

Soon she was back sitting in a chair five feet away from him. Her perfume came in gentle waves again, more like a spring day than a Chicago winter afternoon. Brian had begun to look for something to divert him from his dull work. He studied her as she put on a pair of dark-rimmed glasses, picked up a paper from the stack of essays she had previously dropped with such disdain, and started in reading. He guessed she was in her late thirties, at most six or seven years his junior. She sipped on the steaming mocha. Soon her red ballpoint began to bleed all over the paper. Brian watched her from his chair and from behind the student paper he pretended to read. She continued grading. Her mouth formed a tight thin line as she emitted a sigh of something very near misery.

He dropped the chapter in his lap and said, "That bad, huh?" without consciously knowing he was going to start a conversation.

She started and looked over at him, pulling off her reading glasses and holding them in her hand. "Terrible. What's it to ya?" she asked and then smiled. It was a wide smile, and warm. "Want a few of 'em?"

Brian's chest constricted as he looked into her deep blue eyes. He noticed that her lipstick matched her hair and nails. What a sexy woman. He very much wanted to get to know her.

"Sure. Why not?" He stretched out his arm and picked up his red pen from the arm of the chair. "See, I'm all ready. Must've been fate. Meant to be."

"Yeah-yeah-yeah. What qualifications do you have for reading freshman comp essays?"

"English composition? Offer withdrawn." He put the pen into his pocket with a flourish. "My name's Brian." He leaned forward and stretched out his hand toward her.

She stopped and seemed to think before she reacted. Finally, she said, "Jeannie Mautner." She took his hand with a firm clasp and looked him in the eye. She didn't waver. "Hi Brian. Brian what?"

"Craig. Hi, Jeannie. Mind if I join you?"

"Two first names? Isn't there some kind of warning about men with two first names?" She laughed and pushed out a chair with her foot as a response.

That flustered him. "I'm in history," he said, slipping into something comfortable (his work) and taking the chair. "Tudor period. The Renaissance."

"Cool. I do English Lit. Early twentieth century. World War I poets and all." She fixed those blue eyes on him again. "Actually, I'm just an adjunct. You know: the academic sub-species." She gestured toward the stack of composition essays on the table. "I hope to get on a tenure track in the next year or so. Maybe have to do a few less of these."

They chatted. Finally he glanced at his wristwatch, saw that the time had flown and said, absently, "I have to get to a meeting. At church." He grinned sheepishly. "What I wouldn't give to duck that."

"What church? Where do you go?"

"When I go," he grinned again. "St. Michael's Episcopal in Evanston.

"You're kidding. That's where I go. How come I've never seen you there?"

"I have a little confession to make. I don't really go anymore. Haven't been in, oh, it's probably been two or three years. Except maybe Easter. This meeting's the rector's way of trying to get me back. Ostensibly it's about me offering a class on the Reformation."

"My daughter loves the program they have there for kids her age. Journey to Adulthood."

"Yes, I've heard of that. I do read the newsletter. You have just the one daughter?"

"Yes, and at the moment that's more than enough. She's twelve. I have to admit that Candy and I don't make it to church every single week. Most weeks, but not every one." She grinned. Then her expression turned serious. "My husband never goes."

Brian felt the atmosphere change, as if mention of the unnamed spouse had sucked the air out of the room. He had to wonder with suppressed interest if there wasn't a bit of marital discord there. "I also have one daughter," he said. "Bobby. For Barbara. She's a sophomore here at SU. An art major." His heart warmed at the mention of his only child: his forthright, independent and self-reliant little girl; his six-foot-tall little girl. Brian checked his watch again and realized sadly that he had to leave. They promised to meet for lunch two days later, ostensibly to talk about St. Michael's and the

Episcopal Church's controversy du jour. He cast one lingering glance at her and wondered if this might just go somewhere. He asked himself whether or not he wanted something to happen with this gorgeous redhead. Actually, he rather liked holding the moral high ground with his cheating spouse. He had already concluded that she was having an affair.

On Thursday a full-fledged December snowstorm had descended. Wind gusts scattered the light dry flakes into every crevice, and a treacherous blanket covered otherwise gaping potholes and filled keyholes and cracks around car windows and doors. Snowy shadows were appearing on the windward sides of storefronts and plate glass windows. Already an accumulation of about four inches had built up. Tender skin was protected from the biting sting of blowing ice crystals, leaving bundled mounds of wool scarves and parkas-with-eyes to shamble and slip their way along sidewalks and around corners. That number included Brian as he trudged across campus from his office in the ridiculously named J. P. Dingle Building. There was no way he was going to miss meeting her again. He'd been thinking about their chance encounter in the Starbuck's all week. And wondering what it might be like to have something new and exciting in his staid emotional life. He took a table at the Hog and Head and waited for her to show.

The pseudo-English pub had a sign outside bearing the face of a fierce-looking razorback porker gazing at a frothing mug of brew. That same hog's face and glass of beer appeared on menu fronts and just about everywhere else inside the remodeled clapboard house. The rough-and-tumble campus favorite smelled of beer, grease and frying burgers and offered up any food that could be served with French fries. The specialty of the house.

He waited for nearly twenty minutes while a sinking disappointment settled into the pit of his stomach. Each time the door opened he looked up expectantly. Finally she came through it. But she lacked the same electric charge she had carried on Tuesday. Her affect seemed flat.

"Hey," she said. "Sorry to keep you waiting."

"Hey, yourself," he answered. He stood to greet her. "No problem. I was afraid you weren't coming."

They pressed cheek against cheek in a quick almost absentminded gesture.

"I said I would. Actually, I've been looking forward to it." She smiled weakly and sat down on the edge of her chair, still wrapped in her heavy coat. She looked small and vulnerable.

"You okay?" he asked.

Tears filled her eyes. "I admit I had a pretty bad night. Richard—my husband—uttered his final threat to leave. So I told him to get the hell out. And he went."

Brian looked at her carefully, trying to read behind the words as more tears came and ran through the freckle forest on her cheeks. He smoothed his blazer and tugged on the collar of his white turtleneck, uncomfortable with her show of emotion. His parka had been thrown loosely over an extra chair at the table. She stood up and shrugged out of her heavy coat then dumped it on top of his and sat back down. Her red sweater of last Tuesday had been replaced by a multicolored one of red, yellow and blue, but it was over the same sort of blue jeans as before. Brian felt many things for her at that moment—compassion and tenderness, certainly—but he could not ignore the undeniable sexual effect she continued to have on him.

"He'll be back," Brian said without conviction.

"No, he won't," she answered with a certainty that surprised him. "He has somebody else, one of his colleagues. I've finally had it with him. I've already called the Super to change the lock on my apartment door. I've often suspected him. The arrogant bastard hasn't even tried to hide it. When I would get pissed at him I'd end up feeling like a fishwife."

"I'm so sorry," Brian said.

"Thanks." She stared through still-wet eyes before flashing a feeble smile. "It's funny really. All my friends seem to think my life is perfect. Married to a handsome bright doctor. The perfect match. I worked quietly away at my own graduate degrees at Yale and then at Northwestern after we moved back home. Richard did his neurology residency and then began his practice."

She toyed with her water glass that the server had just brought. They both ordered burgers and fries.

She looked wistful. "It *might* have been the perfect marriage. One child, two careers, North Shore lifestyle. But Richard . . . I'm sure he always had something going. He was so self-absorbed that he never seemed to care whether I knew or not—nurses, patients, other doctors. As if it was his right to screw anybody he wanted! The fights have become terrible, and now it no longer seems worth it. He's a jerk!"

Brian winced. He too had been called self-absorbed. Especially by his two wives. It was always his work, his work, his work. Never them, or so he'd heard. He'd had a couple of little flings—and those a long time ago now—but mostly he'd been faithful. Still, Emily seemed equally caught up in her work, and she was the one with a lover. At least he'd thought she had one. Those suspicions were ultimately confirmed. He reached over and gave Jeannie's hand a little squeeze.

"Thanks for being there," she said. "I need a friend right now. Someone who doesn't know Richard and can just, well, be my friend." She pulled her hand away.

From that moment on he had understood her. No words had been spoken, but there was not going to be some kind of tawdry affair—any kind of affair—between them. He settled instead for being friends. They met for lunch from time to time and served together on the student life committee, occasionally attending a disciplinary meeting for dorm students or fraternity boys who crossed the line of acceptable behavior. They ran together a few times along the lakefront near her high rise home on the North Shore. But she never invited him up to her apartment, and they never so much as kissed. He had helped her work her way through her divorce. Now she would be there for him in his. Even if several thousand miles separated them.

Brian couldn't ignore the vague feeling of loneliness that kept creeping into his gut. He didn't understand it, but something was missing. For weeks he had been impatient to get to Cambridge. Now that he was there it didn't feel like

quite enough. Was he grieving Emily? He didn't really think
so. Pissed? Yes he was pissed at her. But he didn't ache for
her, at least not yet. Perhaps he never would. That certainly
wasn't what was happening. Instead of thinking about Emily,
he found thoughts of his friend Jeannie popping into his
head. Snatches of conversations he'd had with her and
images of her smiling freckled face and red hair kept rising to
the surface. That's odd. He rarely ever thought about Jeannie
back in Chicago. So her mother wants her to get married
again? He wasn't even aware of her seeing anyone. Just
thinking about that possibility made him feel even more
alone.

The University Library was a red brick monolith only a
few blocks away from his flat through a quiet mostly
residential neighborhood. A copyright library, it housed at
least one of everything published in Britain since the 1930s
when it was built. He climbed the outside stairs, counting as
he went. Eight steps. More of his little hobby. He went into
the reception hall and followed the signs to the credentials
room downstairs. It seemed not to have changed at all in a
decade, and gave him that odd feeling of familiarity and
strangeness that places known but not seen in a long time
often gave him. The dark and crowded little cubbyhole
smelled like freshly brewed tea.

"Actually, as it says in my letter from the dean, I'm
mostly interested in the collection in the Western
Manuscripts room," he said to the registrar of credentials in
response to her question. "But, yes, it would be convenient
for me to have circulation privileges. If that's possible." Why
did encounters with officialdom always make him feel like a
self-conscious ten-year-old?

The registrar was one of the no-nonsense bureaucratic
types. Graying blonde hair pulled back in a bun. Horn-
rimmed glasses perched on the end of her long nose. "Of
course it's possible. Let me see now." She peered at him over
the glasses. Then she looked down again. "I see I have your
letter of introduction from Lord's and from your Dean, a Ms.
Friendly."

"Yes, I think she takes a lot of ribbing for that name."

"I don't wonder." The registrar adopted a firm set to her lips.

Brian doubted that this woman would be making any jokes about the dean's name or anything else anytime soon. Joking didn't seem to be her style. He almost smiled at her, but thought better of it. That might have been taken as a challenge.

She studied the papers in front of her again. "Everything seems in order," she said at last.

"When will I have my reader's ticket?" Brian almost found himself hoping he wouldn't be permitted to get right down to work today. Would feel much like a last minute reprieve from the dentist's chair.

"In about two minutes. Please stand just there for your identification photo." She pointed to a spot beside where he stood.

"That's terrific," he said and did as she instructed.

He walked out of the room five minutes later, his reader's ticket stowed in his jacket pocket. "A fresh start tomorrow," he said under his breath. No rush. He didn't have anybody to report to. He stepped outside. The weather was perfect for wandering around Cambridge. Seventy degrees, twenty-one Celsius, and clear with a light breeze. The earlier clouds had vanished. Somebody had just finished mowing a lawn nearby and the fresh scent of cut grass was still in the air.

He returned the laptop to his flat and then struck off down the street and across the Backs toward King's College's ornate black and gold rear gate. He would walk through the grounds and check out the time of Evensong in the chapel. At the gate, he mumbled, "Member of the University," and was admitted to the grounds. Inside he walked into a wooded section. Branches of trees joined each other above his head like intertwined fingers. Manicured gardens lined the path on either side. Beds of flowers spread a carpet of bright oranges and reds, blues and yellows. Cheerful colors that sent shimmering imaginary reflections in the warm sunlight. He felt as if he had acquired a new freedom. He passed on out onto the broad lawn that led past Georgian college buildings and into the King's quad. He took in the spectacle of the chapel. The beauty of it all brought tears to his eyes. "Emotional twit," he muttered and remembered his look at the chapel in last night's dream, the one that included the scholar Erasmus. He thought about the two dreams. They interested him. Maybe they were a mild form of place memories after all. He could handle that much.

Evensong would be sung at five-thirty. He promised himself that he would be there for it, remembering that he couldn't be late if he wanted to sit in the quire. Passing through the main gate, he went out onto King's Parade and into the middle of a dense throng of people moving in all directions at once. Pushing, jostling and laughing. The street felt like a carnival. He wandered through the open market and looked at fresh fruits and vegetables, had coffee and a snack at a sidewalk café, and looked into some of the shops. Killing time until he could return to Kings for Evensong.

The service drew him in. With the exception of the lessons and a few of the prayers, everything in it was sung. Both the musical setting and the anthem were Tudor. Even the readings came from the King James Bible. It was as if he had stepped backwards in time. He sat in the quire just a few feet from the choristers and, relishing the moment, leaned into the carved wooden stall. The fan-vaulted ceiling nearly took his breath away. He studied the towering stained-glass windows. Little by little he slipped backwards into that earlier century. Into his own chosen world. He had a momentary fear that being in the chapel would trigger something abnormal in him. But it didn't. The Thomas Tallis *Magnificat* filled his ears. Stone walls sent the descants of the boy trebles dancing back and forth between them like small birds. He was perfectly, blissfully, ridiculously content.

His mind turned again to his two dreams: Elizabeth the Queen and Erasmus the scholar. He recognized how their lives spanned more than a century and framed the Tudor era at its beginning and end, summarizing in their persons two of the century's main themes: religious turmoil, which Erasmus helped to inaugurate; and the burgeoning statecraft of the emerging national monarchies, of which Elizabeth was a monumental example. The Queen was both the head of state and the Supreme Governor of the Church of England. How intertwined the two motifs of religion and politics were in that era. Perhaps they always had been. So much the worse for politics, he thought.

After Evensong, he walked around the corner from King's to the Eagle for a pint of the local ale. He sat beside the cold hearth and thought back twenty years to when he had first been in that pub and in Cambridge. He had been a penniless graduate student with a freshly pregnant wife. Thoughts of Kathleen, the mother of Bobbie, his only daughter, filled his mind for the first time in months. Beautiful, vivacious and slightly crazy Kathleen. Learning that she was bi-polar and her getting medication came too late for their marriage. Though by no means was she the only one with a problem in that union. He shook his head as a wave of affection for her washed over him. Then he thought about Emily. For some reason, he was unable to call up many feelings for her. How odd that the memory of his first wife overshadowed the current spouse who was divorcing him.

He finished his second pint of IPA and went out into the evening.

What the hell? He rummaged once more through the carton of documents spread out on the table in front of him. Like all the rest of the furniture in the manuscript reading room the table was made of some open grained wood and stained a uniform blonde color. Between the furniture and the large windows that dominated two sides of the room, the place had an almost over-bright cheerful look. There must be more than this, he thought.

He had gotten to the university library first thing that morning, his third day in Cambridge, and began sifting an archive of late sixteenth- and early-seventeenth century estate documents. His laptop computer sat at the ready on the table in front of him. This cardboard carton—his third of the day—held original papers of all sizes and shapes. In it he had run across something that surprised and intrigued him. Most people would not have been so surprised at the discovery of an obscure and unnamed Jacobean landowner. But Brian had made such people the focus of his work for half-a-dozen years now. This was no ordinary landowner. He decided to check it out. He also really needed to stretch his legs, and it was lunchtime. He would head for the main bank of catalog computers downstairs. Then he'd get some lunch. He took the carton back to the desk to hold and went downstairs to the broad hallway leading into the Main Reading Room. He soon discovered that he could not unravel the codes for the locations of books in the stacks. It had been ten years since he had last been there, after all. There had been no single computer system available to the public then. The longer he stood there clicking at the keyboard and hitting "enter," the more his aggravation mounted. He looked around for some sign of help. Only one other patron stood in front of the computers at that moment, a tall slender man about Brian's age. He wore blue jeans, a brown corduroy jacket and a pressed shirt with a button-down collar open at the neck. His long thin fingers seemed to fly over the keyboard in front of him. His pony-tailed dirty-blonde hair bobbed and shook as he worked at making notes on a small pad at his side. Something in his professional demeanor encouraged Brian to ask for help.

"I hate to bother you," he said, "but I'm having trouble figuring this out."

"Let me have a look." His accent could only be American. "What are you trying to do?" He took the three steps that brought him to Brian's side.

"Well, I've stumbled across something in my manuscript research." He pointed at the ceiling, vaguely in the direction of where he had been working. "Sort of by accident. Kind of a mystery. On my first day. Now I want to check it out. But this system," he shook his head and pointed at the computer screen, "It means nothing to me. I found the reference I was looking for; still I can't unravel the code for how to find it in the stacks." He gestured toward a string of numbers on the screen with a lower case letter "c" in the middle.

His rescuer laughed. "I get it, man." He grinned at Brian and explained the system "Kind of odd having the first thing you need appearing in the middle of the call number, isn't it?"

"That's one word for it. I could think of a couple of other choice adjectives. Okay, but how do I know where to go to find the right section in the stacks?"

He explained. "And to get there you just follow the signs. Get it?" He pointed toward the long corridor where Brian had come in.

Long hallways lined with carved Georgian bookcases stretched in either direction perpendicular to the catalogue passage. Enormous and classically decorated, they had been moved there from the former University Library when this one was built some seventy years before. The building appeared to Brian at least in part to have been designed to house them. In the middle of those impressive shelves and cabinets he could just see an opening, presumably to a stairwell leading into the stacks. Now he started to remember where things were.

"Thanks," he said. "I do get it." He was feeling less stressed and grateful to his helper. "I'm Brian Craig. Sterling U."

"Hi Brian. Jeff Barringer." He stuck out his hand. They shook solemnly. "How long have you been here?"

"Just a few days. Still having some jet lag," Brian answered. He felt himself relax. He liked this lanky man on instinct.

"Like to catch some lunch? I don't really recommend the food here, but we were going to make an exception today."

"We?"

"I'm meeting Charlie, Charlene actually. My partner. She's a musicologist."

"Sure," Brian answered. "If I wouldn't be intruding." It was good to be interacting with another human being. "Where are you from?"

"Tennessee. Vanderbilt. But I'm really a Californian."

"They chatted as they walked along a corridor of ceiling to floor stacks of venerable leather-bound volumes. Brian remembered the little tea, coffee and sandwich room.

"I need to step outside for a breath of fresh air first," Jeff said, pointing to a doorway.

Looking through the wall of windows, Brian saw a rooftop courtyard on one of the low wings of the building. He followed Jeff, who had a cigarette going within seconds.

"Fresh air is it?" Brian quipped.

"Nothing quite like a little carbon monoxide mixed with oxygen. Sort of thins the effect—of the oxygen." He grinned and looked up at the gray sky.

A gust of damp air had Brian shivering. England in June? He pulled his jacket around him and flipped up the lapels, pacing and almost wishing he had a cigarette of his own. Almost. After several deep drags Jeff smashed out his butt in a sand-filled bucket. They went back inside and into the restaurant. The air was filled with the scent of coffee and tea mingled with the smell of something cooking.

Jeff's partner, Charlie, soon came in. She was a short energetic woman—a dynamo. Her strong-looking compact body, very short dark brown hair and intense manner gave the impression of somebody who could focus for hours without tiring. Dogged and determined.

"I'm a music historian," she said. "Working in the music manuscript room."

"That's what Jeff said."

"Mostly I'm in the main reading room," Jeff interjected. "Not much use for all that old stuff that you two are so taken by." He laughed at what Brian recognized as an old joke between them. She pushed him away with her hand in mock rejection.

They didn't seem like a natural match for each other. But why not?

Brian got himself a big bowl of bean soup. Jeff and Charlie selected some rather thin toasted sandwiches. They sat and began to eat.

"You've heard of Bess of Hardwick?" Brian asked after a long silence. "The enterprising Elizabethan who founded the great wealth of the Cavendish family?"

"Can't say that I have," said Jeff.

"He wouldn't admit it if he had," Charlie said, pointing at Jeff. "Of course I've heard of her," she said, casting Jeff a verbal challenge and sipping at her tea. "Countess of Shrewsbury and builder of Hardwick Hall."

Brian grinned. He liked Charlie even better. "Among a string of other titles and constructions," he said to Jeff. "She was notorious for making profitable marriages and surviving all four of her husbands, accumulating their wealth and passing it on, ultimately to her children and those of her fourth husband, the Earl. She was quite a phenomenon, usually thought of as unique. Men controlled wealth of all kinds in those days. Period."

"Sounds like a dangerous lady," Jeff said.

"Dangerous or not, she was really something. She's always raised a lot of comment." Brian paused for a moment and looked around almost as if he were hatching a conspiracy. "Well, I've found another Bess. Not the name, but the behavior. This one had some of the success. But on a smaller scale. Just a bit later. So far, I've located only oblique references to her in the original documents. You know," he said for Jeff's benefit. "Papers contemporary to the events and people. In this case very puzzling ones. It's almost as if there's an attempt to erase her from the record. Apparently she had disposed of mates left and right and kept their property for the enrichment of her matriarchal family. A real Black Widow."

"Matriarchal?" Charlie asked.

"Yes. Her daughter and granddaughter seem to have been involved, too."

"She's the one you were checking out in the catalog a little while ago?"

"Well, not exactly her. I don't even have her name. But that book I looked up, that whole section of the stacks, has about everything that's known about property ownership in East Anglia during that period. There must be some reference to her there."

"And that will solve your mystery? Good luck. I'll be interested to hear," Charlie said.

"I'm sure I'll find something. Surely she wouldn't have gone entirely unnoticed until now. It is intriguing though. I'm puzzled how she's escaped my attention." He grinned and then turned more serious. "I'm really interested in the woman and her daughter and granddaughter. Their extraordinary flouting of the social conventions of their day." He swallowed the last spoonful of his soup. "I can't believe I wouldn't have heard of them before. I've been working on this topic for years. In their century women just didn't control property the way they did. Separate from men. Not even Bess pulled that one off. The couple of references I've found in the sources were—well, they were cautious. Kind of strange." He laughed uncomfortably.

Charlie seemed to wait smilingly for him to finish. Then her expression sobered. "Strange? How so?"

Brian's smile faded, "Maybe this is the find I've been looking for. Make my reputation." His mood shifted and he laughed, full-bodied this time. It felt good to have people to laugh with.

"This I've got to see." Charlie grinned, but he could tell she was interested in the Black Widow. Jeff looked bored and seemed impatient to get back to his own work

Brian sat in the stacks, more puzzled than ever. He had scanned through book after book and in indexes and specialized works on early Stuart property ownership, looking for female landowners of any sort. He glanced at every book he knew that might include something vaguely like what he had stumbled onto, even looking into the index of one of his own books on a related subject—an act more out of vanity than in the expectation of finding something there about the Black Widow of East Anglia, as he had come to think of her. He grinned at himself. Then he set about widening the search and skimmed and scoured works on all the counties around Cambridge. He could find no instances of female enclaves anywhere in East Anglia. He decided to go back and look further in the original sources. Maybe he would find something more there.

He retrieved his carton of estate papers from the desk and scoured through it without finding anything more about this puzzling discovery. Finally, he got tired and, shrugging his shoulders, decided to call it a day.

CHAPTER THREE

Brian wandered the streets of Cambridge. From time to time thoughts of the three East Anglian women popped into his head. Mostly he reveled in being there. He strolled past ancient churches and college chapels, sat outside King's College and listened to street musicians in the square between King's Chapel and Great St. Mary's Church. Finally, unable entirely to avoid a productive purpose, he decided to shop for some prints in the Street Market. Those empty walls of his flat cried out for him to do something about them. He made some choices. Maybe he would even take some of them home with him after sabbatical. In the meantime pushpins would do an adequate job of it. It all gave him the sense of nesting: settling in and establishing a regular life for himself. Orderly and purposeful. As he left the market, he calculated how many people were crammed into the busy block of open stands. He grinned. Maybe he was getting back to normal.

He resumed his walk, rolled up prints tucked under his arm. Finally he dropped onto a sidewalk bench outside St. John's College, diagonally across from the ancient Round Church. The soft warmth of the afternoon sun felt good on his face and bathed the primordial stones of the church until they seemed to glow. Once more he puzzled over the Black Widow he had discovered earlier in the day. It was a real puzzle. Brian liked puzzles.

Mellowed by the setting and his own lassitude he watched people walk along the medieval street, now mostly a pedestrian precinct. One young woman caught his eye. Tall, slender and sophisticated she had a mass of curly black hair over a crisp white blouse and a short black skirt. Her legs were long lean and shapely. She stood gazing in a shop window. Only a distorted reflection of her face showed. She looked so familiar. Painfully so. He strained to see those haunting blue eyes he remembered so well, but he couldn't. Perhaps it was the way she held her body or the angle she cocked her head. But she set off internal alarms as she moved her head back and forth looking in the window. His stomach jumped and his heart skipped a couple of beats.

"Mary Beth?" he exhaled under his breath, disgusted with his foolishness. Why did he always do this? Always jump to such ridiculous conclusions? Still he couldn't avoid letting the memory of his long-lost college love flit briefly across his consciousness. It had been nearly twenty-five years since their break-up and a decade since he had last laid eyes on her. Then only at a Kentonworth College alumni dinner. Still, Mary Beth was always popping up like this: in crowds and on street corners. At least in his imagination she did.

Finally the young woman turned and walked toward him. He saw that she was pretty and looked sexy enough, but that her face was nothing like the girl he remembered from college. He shook his head, stood up and crossed the street to walk past the Round Church and down Sidney Street toward central Cambridge's main shopping district. On the whole, it had been a good day. Intriguing even. Now he had both Mary Beth and the Black Widow to obsess about.

I'm standing in the quad of King's College. The chapel's buttresses claw the sky above me. Manicured grass spreads out like an immaculate green carpet. I like this setting very much. Suddenly I see a man in typical Elizabethan dress— ruff, doublet and hose, black from head to toe except for the white ruff—walking directly across the grass, a privilege usually reserved for the master and fellows of the college. He has a full dark beard over swarthy skin and an intelligent look in his eyes. Something about him looks familiar. He seems not even to notice me. Now I hear him call out to someone.

"Is that you, then, My Lord?"

"Aye, Sir Francis. What delays thee?"

"No thing important. I wanted only to visit my old Master. He's suffered grievously with a flux. I confess myself sore worried for his life, and I give thanks to God that he did not die before I set eyes on him the one last time. The body's rottenness can damage the mind and the whole man, but—

*God's eyes!—he still knows me. I owe him much for his many
kindnesses. But I fear his life is lost." He pauses, apparently
in reflection, and then continues, "Enough of this sentiment.
'Tis the Spaniards we've come to talk about." He looks
around and lowers his voice. "I have heard from my man in
Madrid. King Philip is up to no good. A great villainy, God
knows."*

*I think I recognize this man. He'd be hard to miss. Sir
Francis Walsingham is the Puritan spymaster and head of
an infant Tudor domestic secret police. Elizabethan
England's FBI and CIA all rolled into one. His spies search
out Jesuit priests and any signs of "Papist" plots at home or
abroad. He looks much like his 1587 portrait and this
conversation fits that time. Am I spying on the spymaster? I
feel a jolt of fear. What if I'm caught? But I'm on his side. Or
at least that's how I think of myself. Not on the side of Spain.
But I'm not really on any side, am I? I'm not here.*

*"Surely God will not prosper their schemes,"
Walsingham continues.*

*Now indistinct movement in the distance catches my
eye. The same opaque hard-riding horsemen I saw before
are thundering silently across the quad. Like the last time I
saw them they don't seem to be getting anywhere. Their
gesturing leader keeps turning around. Perhaps he is
shouting orders to the others. Something about the way he
brandishes his sword makes him seem extra fierce. But
what are they doing here? Surely they have nothing to do
with Sir Francis or with King's quad. I feel a little shiver
pass through my body.*

*Now the scene is fading before my eyes. I'm afraid I'm
going to be sick.*

Brian awoke as before in his sitting room, shaking and
clammy with nausea. For a moment he had trouble
separating the dream from reality. He thought about
Walsingham. Would the Spymaster be looking for him? Was
he in danger then? Where could he flee to? Should he fly to
another country? His chest tightened up. He began to feel as
if he couldn't get his breath. Finally, he shook his head and

pulled himself into the present. He wasn't in any danger from a sixteenth century version of the FBI.

He started to think like a historian and analyzed the dream. Though he knew nothing about this particular meeting of Sir Francis's, everything he knew about the year or two before the Spanish Armada in 1588 fit with what he had overheard. Apparently Walsingham had once been a student in Cambridge. Brian had no specific historical memory of such a detail. But why shouldn't he have been at King's? And who was the other person, the one Sir Francis called "My Lord?" He had no idea. Probably this detail came from some memory fragment that Brian had been able to recall in his dream state. But it remained a waking mystery. Maybe a little checking would help. But what were the chances that he would ever locate that fact from among so many? Pretty slim at best. If it ever happened. He smiled and thought about all the "God talk." Walsingham was as tough-minded a character as Elizabeth I ever had working for her. But in the sixteenth century he would use that kind of language as a matter of course. It wasn't about being pious. That was the temper of his times and the norm in discourse. Walsingham the Puritan was a deeply political man, and his Puritanism was at least as much a political position as a religious statement.

But what about those mounted riders? What on earth could they be about? Brian had no idea. They were really strange. Even after he had stopped worrying about Walsingham, he still found them frightening somehow.

Brian tried to keep busy, partly to ward off having more dreams. He was almost afraid to fall asleep. The historical characters he encountered in the dreams had been interesting enough—intriguing even—but the intrusion of those fierce-looking horsemen felt ominous.

Every night that week he took in the Cambridge Summer Music Festival scene. He heard a string ensemble at Trinity College, the Clare College Choir in its chapel, and a memorable organ concert at Queens'. At the Guild Hall he basked in a famous tenor giving a performance of popular

Verde arias. During the interval as he was mentally estimating how many people were crammed into the vestibule (at least two hundred!), he spotted an older woman he had seen at several other events. Like him, she had always been alone. She made Brian think of a stereotypical Miss Marple right off the pages of an Agatha Christie mystery. He imagined her as an amateur sleuth skulking behind closed doors and solving complex mysteries about proper upper-middle-class murders.

Acting on an impulse, he made his way through the cheek by jowl crowd, raised his glass of wine rather formally in salute and introduced himself.

"I'm Brian Craig. I can't help but notice that we often seem to be in the same places."

"Is this a pick-up, young man?"

"I beg your pardon." Had he heard her right over the noise and confusion of the crowded room?

A noisy group of enthusiastic drinkers nearly swept her away. Regaining her balance after they had passed, she smiled with a memory of coquetry on her lips. "I'm very flattered. But don't you think I'm a bit past it?"

Brian was rarely at a loss for words, but this time nothing would come to his rescue except, "Uh, you see—it's, hmm, you know. Of course not." He stood there, dazed and breathing in the pungent odors of the packed humanity around him.

Her gray hair was pulled into the tight bun he always saw her wear. She had on a modest light-blue suit with a frilly white blouse and the kind of sensible shoes that suited an English woman of her vintage. Tall and angular and looking brittle enough to break, she nonetheless radiated an extraordinary resilience. She gave him a beaming and slightly wicked smile. "Now in my day I might have been up for a cuddle. But too many squalls have ravaged this old hulk for anything like that." She laughed, apparently at the nautical metaphor. "I'm Mrs. Heppel. Mrs. Carol Heppel. I have also noticed you at some recent concerts." She thrust out her hand for him to grasp.

This feisty opening marked the start of a regular

friendship between Brian and. Carol Heppel.

Carol was a living cliché: a dauntless volunteer who worked for any worthy cause that came along; a concert-goer who went to just about everything in Cambridge; and a retired librarian who arranged flowers at St. Bene't's (for Benedict's) Church. Tiny St. Bene't's was part medieval and part Victorian and sat right across the street from the Eagle, Brian's favorite pub.

"St. Bene't's is a C of E parish church, you know, not a college chapel," she said on one occasion. "It's part of the patrimony of Corpus Christi. So is the Eagle for that matter. A community of Anglican Franciscans cares for the church. We all look after the Eagle." She flashed him another one of her wicked grins. Brian learned that Carol was a long-time widow and a tough uncompromising daughter of the Church of England. He guessed she was about seventy-five, but he wouldn't have dared ask. Brian sometimes teasingly called her "Caramel Apple."

Brian regularly joined Carol for concerts, even meeting her now and then for an early supper. She always charmed him with witty little asides during the programs. "How do you imagine he plays that oboe through such a bushy mustache?" she asked in wonder one evening. "He looks like the walrus in that Disney film." She could usually be trusted to make such exclamations of untrammeled delight as, "Oh, oh, I've never heard anything so beautiful!" while she clapped her little hands rapidly together.

"I've formed a kind of community for myself," Brian assured his friend Jeannie Mautner, who had called about some travel details. She had expressed some concern about his being alone too much. He told her about Jeff and Charlie and Carol Heppel. "I manage to have just about as much human contact as I want. No more, no less."

"The perfect life. So I won't find you being some kind of hermit when Candy and I get there?"

"No. Not a hermit. Not at all. Just comfortable. So you're really going to come, then?"

A moment of silence followed. "You—you still want

visitors?" she asked. She seemed uncertain.

"Absolutely," he said.

Sounding as if she had recovered her composure, she said, "And the dreams? Are you still having them? What about women? You are eligible you know."

He smiled at all her questions, "No. No women, thank-you-very-much. Just the three dreams. I told you about that last one"

"Yes. No more since then?"

"None."

"And your work?"

"It's pretty dull. But then I knew there was a monotonous aspect to it. No reason why I can't finish scouring the documents though. Maybe even get the book drafted."

"What's the topic? I've forgotten."

"That great land grab of Henry VIII's: the Dissolution of the Monasteries as it spins out over the following century."

"That doesn't sound dull."

"Partly I'm struggling with the handwriting. It's something called secretary hand, and it often feels like a weird foreign language. I'd almost forgotten how tough it could be. In denial I guess." He laughed. "The writers usually didn't lift their sharpened quills off the paper or parchment as they went from word to word. Made it faster for them. It's a nightmare for me. It all just runs together. Even worse, most numbers are in lower case Roman Numerals, and they all blend together. X's and v's end up looking pretty much alike when the writer hasn't lifted the quill to write them. What a pain. Ultimately I'll get past this dreary stuff and on to the lifestyle implications of it all. That's what I'm really interested in. Or at least it's what I've set myself to do. What a massive transfer of property it was."

"And that meant wealth?"

"And power."

"Then I don't get your boredom. That all sounds pretty interesting."

"I might once have thought so. But most of the time I'm really just looking for something more on that Black Widow I told you about. But no luck. At least not so far."

"Well, Candy and I will distract you."

He thought for a moment. "Why don't you stay with me after all? For maximum distraction?" He realized that he'd forgotten to look for a place: forgotten or decided-without-deciding not to. As he talked he became excited at the prospect, "You and Candy could have my bedroom. I can easily get a cot put in the sitting room for me. It'll be a bit cozy. One bathroom and all. But who cares? It would be more fun. For me certainly. I hope for you, too."

"You sure? We'd love it."

"I'm sure.

After hanging up the phone Brian sat for a moment, looking out his sitting room window into Lo-Host's back yard. The last rays of the evening sun hit the border garden. Oranges, reds, yellows and blues of the primroses and the white alyssum gave it all an electric look against the lush green of the lawn. Suddenly Brian was excited about Jeannie's visit, even though it was still a month away. Just for a moment the restlessness that had been haunting him since his arrival in England slipped away. It would be very good to see his friend. To be with someone he already knew and who knew him.

Jeannie had come to be important to Brian long before he left on sabbatical. She helped to keep him from taking himself too seriously. He smiled to himself as he thought about a time when they were having lunch in one of the campus spots at SU. An undergraduate had chased him down. She had an old problem with a new twist.

"Oh, Dr. Craig, Dr. Craig, I'm so glad I found you," the perky little sophomore had gushed. She combined a charming innocence with a nubile voluptuousness that was hard to miss. She had turned up that day with made-up face, sporting a single nose ring and wearing a light cotton tee shirt that obscured little of her high jiggling breasts and pointy nipples. "It's been oh-soooo very difficult." Her eyes smiled through long dark lashes below very blonde hair.

Jeannie had whispered a quiet cynical aside, "Either the dog ate her paper or her grandmother has just died."

Brian put a hand over his mouth to mask the grin he couldn't entirely suppress. He stood up. "Yes, what is it, Stephanie?" He adopted a tone of annoyance, a familiar timbre these days when speaking with students.

"Well, you see, like, I meant to take the history test, like, yesterday. But—but, you know, like, I, well, I thought I might be, like, pregnant. I was—I was sooo scared." She rolled her eyes and dropped her hand on Brian's forearm in a helpless female gesture. He could feel Jeannie shaking with repressed laughter.

"Oh, ahem," he said, feeling discomfort both with Stephanie's exaggerated expressions and Jeannie's barely stifled mirth. "Is everything okay?" He frowned in a lame effort to seem concerned, a wave of annoyance with Jeannie passing over him as he felt her begin to shake again. A similar wash of embarrassment followed soon when he realized what he had just asked.

She compounded his discomfort, "Yes. Everything turned out fine." The girl's innocent smile confirmed that her period had started. This was knowledge he would just as soon not have. He felt himself blush: Look out world: this adorable sexually-active child is ready for whatever new adventure awaits her.

"Well, don't worry yourself," he said, feeling the awkwardness that he assured himself most men would feel under similar circumstances. See me in my office tomorrow, and we'll arrange for a make-up."

At that Jeannie lost it and laughed out loud, pretending to be connecting with someone in a remote corner of the restaurant.

"Thanks, Dr. Craig." Stephanie flashed him a coy smile. She cast a curious glance toward Jeannie and bounced away.

"'Don't *worry* yourself?'" Jeannie asked after the girl had gone and she had stopped laughing. She sipped at her glass of iced tea. "That's an imaginative use for an classic dilemma. You really fell for the sexual manipulation bit." Giggles won out over her attempt at seriousness.

He guessed he had fallen for it all. Then he caught her infectious laughter, managing to squeeze out a pinched, "Yes,

I guess that worked better than the dead grandmother."

Their howls were so loud that people began to stare at them.

"You can be such a dweeb," she said, imitating her adolescent daughter.

And that set them off again. No doubt about it, Jeannie helped him not be so stuffy.

Brian never stopped being attracted to Jeannie. But he had repressed the attraction. Mostly. He always looked forward to when he would see her next, and he enjoyed being with her. Then why had he initially resisted the idea of her visit—and the notion that she and her daughter might stay with him? Would it spoil a good friendship if something more happened between them? That was something to think about.

chapter four

Brian stopped at Lord's nearly every day to check his snail mail. Usually after lunch. He often found something from SU waiting in his cubby at the Porter's Lodge He always hoped for one of Jeannie's amusing little notes or comical cards. Like the one that had said, "Having a great time. Wish you were here," as if she were the one who had gone away. Another postcard of the Chicago skyline had two little stick figures drawn on the reverse side. They were shedding fountains of tears. The caption read simply, "Candy and me. We can't wait." But neither University mail nor light-hearted cards from Jeannie came today. Instead, though he had been in Cambridge barely two weeks, he found lawyer's papers from Emily. She must have already had the process well advanced before telling him of her intentions. He laughed cynically to himself as he tore open the letter. She demanded the house and half of everything they owned, minus his inheritance from his father. Not entirely unreasonable, he knew. But generosity of spirit eluded him just then. He loved that big old house and would be sorry to lose it. He had no intention of giving in so easily. Going outside, he dropped heavily on the wooden bench beside the Porter's Lodge and read through all of the legal verbiage.

"So be it," he muttered. "Bitch!." He angrily scrawled his name on the form that referred all negotiations to his attorney. He stuffed the letter in the enclosed envelope and left it with the porter to post. Let the ambulance chasers work it out between them. His walk back to Lo-Host was brisk and gradually siphoned off some of his anger. Three fingers of single malt whiskey helped even more. Now he was drinking in the afternoon?

Emily had often been there for Brian during times of crisis, and he had felt they were close then. Like when his father died three years before.

Hiram Craig, a bull of a man, could hardly have been more different from his bookish son in appearance, attitude or habits. Active and physical he had powerful arms and torso and a nearly bald-head by the time he reached forty. He seemed hard-wired with tireless energy. Always impatient with reading but good-natured about it as in everything else, Hiram claimed that radio and television and the sound bite were invented for him. He was trained as an industrial engineer, and crawling under machinery was an occupational and temperamental obsession. He never went anywhere without a pair of coveralls so he could get his hands as greasy as he wanted without damaging his clothing and raising the ire of his fastidious wife. His idea of a good time usually meant drinking a Bud and watching sports on TV. It didn't seem to matter which one. Brian and his mother always accused Hiram of being a cliché of the all-American male. He would just smile and go about his business. Brian had never known a more good-natured human than this person who masqueraded as his flesh and blood. Brian's wrenching only-child grasp onto adulthood fell under the guidance of his father.

Brian grew up in Peoria. His English-teacher mother's cancer, ultimately metastasized widely through many organs, resulted in her painful lingering death. That was during Brian's freshman year in high school. His adolescence was thus filled with anxiety and grief. Her disappearance from his life devastated Brian. Had she lived until he managed to get through his teen years they might truly have become the great friends that mothers and sons sometimes can be. Occasionally he wondered if his relationship failures stemmed from a search for his mother. But this kind of thinking struck him as too Freudian.

Hiram's death at age eighty-six came with no warning. Rarely ever having had a sick day in his life, he had suddenly been struck down by a cerebral hemorrhage. He managed a fleeting grasp on consciousness just long enough for Brian, Emily and Bobbie to get to Peoria from Chicago. They sat around his bed in the ICU keeping what they knew was a deathwatch but pretended to each other wasn't. Emily had held Hiram's hand and wiped his forehead with a cloth. She had also been very attentive to Brian. Finally Hiram slipped quietly away in his sleep. The contrast to Brian's mother's death twenty-five years before could not have been more dramatic. Brian had grieved his father, but he also celebrated a life lived well. Emily had truly been helpful to him in getting through that time.

No, he couldn't say goodbye and good riddance to her and their years of marriage.

Brian sat there in his flat, trying to let go of his shock over the divorce papers and the sadness over this definitive mark of Emily's departure from his life. After sending a quick email to Jeannie with the details, he turned to thoughts of work. That had always distracted him before. Perhaps it would help him get his mind off Emily and away from his brooding. He pulled up some notes he had taken that morning on his laptop. But he couldn't concentrate on them. Every little distraction seemed to draw him away from his work. His wife was divorcing him and his ability to focus was shot. Whatever had become of his devotion to work regardless of what else might be going on? Thoughts just wandering all 'round Robin Hood's barn.

That was a strange phrase—'round Robin Hood's barn. He wondered about it as he typed the homey idiom into the Google search engine and read what he found. The legendary Robin Hood's home was Sherwood Forest and hence the whole neighborhood was his barn. Whenever he needed something he just picked it up wherever he might be. Meaning that going all the way 'round it meant traversing the entire forest. Brian closed the window on his computer screen.

"Now I've done it again," he muttered. He'd chased an extraneous thought and been diverted from something that really mattered into something trivial. And he was talking to himself. What was his problem? Had he acquired ADD? What had become of his famous concentration? The phone interrupted his solitary conversation.

"This is Brian Craig."

"Hi. I'm on my cell in traffic." It was Jeannie. "I got your email before I left home to pick up Candy at Water Tower. Sorry about Emily. The house and all."

"What's Candy doing at Water Tower? And thanks about Emily."

"Candy? Some friend thing. Did it make you very sad? You know—getting the papers and all."

"I guess I'm kinda bummed. Mostly 'cause I really don't care a lot. I should care more, but I just don't. At least not about Emily."

"I know. By the time Richard and I finally cut the cord, all I felt was relief."

"I remember. But I don't even feel that."

"It's too soon. Any more dreams?"

"None. I almost wish I would have another." He changed the subject. "I'm really looking forward to seeing you and Candy."

"You really are lonely."

"You're my friend."

Brian heard the sound of a horn honking through the receiver.

"You idiot! Watch out. Sorry about that Brian. This traffic's freakin' horrible."

He laughed. "You have such a passionate relationship with cars." It felt good to be talking to her. He clicked the computer mouse on the solitaire icon and began listlessly playing a game as they talked.

"You know, Brian, I've been thinking. Not to get all serious, but I've felt pressured by mother wanting me to get married again. My reaction really puzzled me. At least for a while. But now I think I get it. The reason for my reaction. For the first time in my life I understand why so many competent women over the centuries have become the mistresses of married or otherwise unavailable men."

"That's a big leap, especially for a feminist. Old-fashioned thinking isn't it?" He laughed, his first genuinely light moment in hours.

"I suppose so. But, I have this new insight. I'd always thought of mistresses that way, too. Pitiful demeaned women, martyred to gendered inequality. But now I'm not so sure. I can't imagine myself getting married again anytime soon, maybe ever. But I've been feeling lonely."

"Just lonely?" he said and laughed.

"That, too. I'm just not a one-night-stand kind-a girl. Seems too desperate. Anyhow, it dawned on me. All those women who were mistresses of rich or powerful men had actually found a comfortable way to live. They could see their lovers mostly as often as they wanted. And have the rest of their lives pretty much to themselves. When they're tired and simply want to go home alone and curl up in bed with a book they can do it. They can have the freedom of not sharing their space with another person. Perhaps the life of a woman of independence with both a profession and a lover strikes an acceptable balance between dependence and loneliness. At least that's how I've been thinking about it."

"So you're looking for a suitable candidate?"

"Not exactly. But I'm open to the possibility. I probably shouldn't make any sweeping generalizations about this." She paused. "But I'm going to do it anyhow." He imagined her grin: impish, playful. "Maybe the whole idea of marriage is outmoded. What if instead of trying to rebuild the mythical family unit into those life-long relationships between one man and one woman and a clutch of kids we were to find ways to keep women and children from being the permanent underclass? Valued as real human beings with a shot at having a decent life. With or without there being a man around."

"Sounds as if you're working up a whole social philosophy. Are you thinking of going into politics? Didn't Che Guevera go through a similar dawning of conscience?" He felt himself grinning as he said the words, but he began to get an uncomfortable feeling in the pit of his stomach.

She must have picked up on something in his voice, "Sorry. I didn't mean to sound threatening. But I've lost my illusion that marriage is the antidote to either poverty or loneliness. Or that it's the true source of happiness. I admit that I don't have all the answers. I'm a very privileged person with both a career and financial security. Most women don't have either. But I think I'm finally looking in the right place for meaning. Contentment in life. That's inside me. Not somewhere else."

"I don't know what to say."

"That wasn't very helpful of me was it? You're the one down in the dumps, and I just ramble on and on. Really I am sorry."

"No—no. It's okay."

She chuckled a little. "You're so sweet to listen to my stuff. All I mean is that my mother can forget about looking for the right marriage prospect for me. A lover is one thing. A husband is something else."

He realized that he had entirely lost interest in playing solitaire. He minimized the program, aware of the uncomfortable feeling in the pit of his stomach. Jeannie was in the market for a lover? That would certainly get in the way of their friendship.

Jeannie laughed out loud. Clearly she was having a great time. "Out of my way you creep!" A horn honked again. "Sorry, but that jerk tried to cut me off. Advanced testosterone poisoning."

"You're sounding like a real ball buster."

"Now-now. As I was saying. You know, before. Candy and I are getting really excited about our trip. I hope we won't be too much trouble."

"Not as long as you don't expect me to cook. Really, I'm looking forward to it. A lot."

"There's Water Tower. But I can't see Candy. There's some kind of construction. Oh there she is. Gotta go. She gives me a lot of lip when she catches me driving in traffic and talking on the phone. Ciao."

"Ciao? Where'd that come from?" But no answer came from Jeannie. She had broken the connection.

He returned to the solitaire game, feeling more like himself. Less gloomy. Glad she had called. But the uneasiness? He tried to imagine her in a relationship. Where would that leave him? Without noticing it his life had suddenly come to be defined by Jeannie Mautner. By her visit. That made him uneasy all over again. He finished his game and shut down the laptop. Picking up a book, he curled up in his wing chair.

I am sitting in a large college chapel. The wood paneling of the walls and the classical motif of the decoration give the place an eighteenth-century look, though I assume from the outlines that it is much older than that. Probably Tudor Gothic. Beautiful and simply carved choir stalls blend in with the wall paneling to give it all a seamless appearance. I glance around and see on one end a magnificent choir screen topped by organ pipes and console. Beneath it a passageway leads into the narthex. Opposite the choir screen an equally massive reredos looms over a broad wide chancel. It looks like the Trinity College chapel, which I have been in, but with which I have little real familiarity. Somehow the place makes me feel puny and insignificant. I'm sitting in one of the stalls. The place is deserted except for me and one other person. He sits directly across from me in the top stall on the opposite side of the chapel.

My lone companion is rather odd looking. Beneath a large black skullcap is a great unruly mop of fine-looking stringy brown hair. His long face has a pointed chin and a prominent hooked nose. Sunken cheeks and pasty complexion suggest serious health problems. He is dressed in a black robe of some kind. Not exactly a cassock or an academic gown as I know them, but a tailored garment topped by a huge flapping white collar. Probably made from Irish linen. He is not a poor man. The dress style suggests he is a clergyman living in the first half of the seventeenth century. Before the Civil War and the Puritan triumph reduced many of his kind to poverty.

In the quiet of the otherwise empty chapel I can hear my solitary companion muttering something as he looks down at the prayer desk in front of him. I can't hear the words, but I can catch the rhythm. He appears to be reciting poetry. I strain my ears. I still can't make out the meaning.

There is something relaxing and hypnotic about the cadence of his words. I sit content even without knowing what he is saying, reluctant to disturb him by moving closer. Finally I become restless. I want to know the words. I move over to his side of the chapel and climb the stairs in front of him to the second stall. He doesn't seem to notice me. Now one stall only separates him from me, and I can hear him clearly. His breaths come in short painful gasps. I listen to his intense passionate words as he reads.

> Kill me not ev'ry day,
> Thou Lord of life; since thy one death for me
> Is more then all my deaths can be,
> Though I in broken pay
> Die over each hour of Methusalems stay.

He isn't reading from a book but from a manuscript, and his expression of faith seems very deep. Is he a poet? Donne or Herbert or Marvell perhaps? It's not Shakespeare, whose work doesn't convey this same religious passion. Not Lancelot Andrewes either, though his prayers often carry a poetic power.

Movement in the corner of the room catches my eye. Is it the horsemen? I look hard in that direction, but I don't see anything.

My presumed poet shuffles papers, pauses for a moment, as if resting, and begins again.

> Joy, deare Mother, when I view
> Thy perfect lineaments, and hue
> Both sweet and bright.
> Beautie in thee takes up her place,
> And dates her letters from thy face,
> When she doth write.

Another coughing spasm interrupts him. Gradually the hacking subsides to be replaced by agonized wheezing breath. Is his life threatened? Is there something I can do for him? The labored breathing calms. I wonder if he knows I'm here. Does he even see me? Am I even visible to him?

Now the room around me begins to fade. I feel pain:

first in my legs and then in my arms. My stomach begins to churn. Once again I feel as if I'm being dragged from a place I really don't want to leave.

In a reversal on his previous dreams, Brian awoke in his bed. He was even undressed and seemed to be waking from a deep sleep. None of the usual symptoms of withdrawal were in evidence. But hadn't he fallen asleep fully clothed in the wing chair? He looked around. "Fucking bizarre."

Brian took less than an hour identifying his poet and finding the incomplete poem, "The British Church." The portrait he found of George Herbert bore an exact likeness to the man he saw in last night's dream. Why shouldn't it? What other basis could there have been for the dream except some image he had seen before? After all he dreamed about people whose portraits he had seen and about whose life he already knew. He found something comforting in that.

Herbert always appealed to Brian, especially his poignant sacramental poem, "Love III." He puzzled over that realization for a moment. He had come to doubt all things religious and had stayed away from Holy Communion ever since he had been in England, and for many months before that.

Still his attraction to Herbert's statement of sacramental faith remained magnetic. Or was it to the sense of forgiveness that was also in it? What did he, Brian Alexander Craig, really believe about God's grace and the Eucharist? Herbert understood that the presence of the sacred was all around him, infusing and animating everything. Not even the difficulties of church politics and the rising strife between different confessions during his lifetime seemed to discolor his vision. Each word was oddly fresh and each insight into the human spirit lively and potent with energy.

Even the chauvinistic poem about the English Church, which had had such a prominent place in the dream, carried surprising power. Why might he have dreamed that poem among all the others? He had no longer thought that the church held any importance at all. Either to him or to the world. He would have to buy himself a copy of Herbert's posthumous single volume of poems.

Brian looked around the well-worn back room in the Eagle. Carol Heppel sat across from him, sipping her half pint of Shandy. Brain drained his bitter in large swallows. Many of the great figures of English history these last few centuries had passed quiet moments here, drinking pints of ale and having deep thoughts. Or perhaps quiet assignations. Brian especially liked the inscriptions on the tin ceiling above his head. World War II pilots and flight crews had written their names or initials with lipstick, candles or Zippo lighters during times when they were unwinding from the air war and waiting for the next call to man their aircraft. Something about those moved him deeply.

Brian had just told Carol about his dreams.

"Don't you ever daydream about visiting the past so you can know what it was really like? Don't you historians do that all the time?" she asked. "Is this something like that?"

"Right. Like becoming a fly on the wall when Adolph Hitler plots to conquer the world." He laughed, his voice laced with irony. "Or how about King John? Was he really cowardly?"

She waved her hand dismissively.

"No, I never have done that. Not really. I've wished I had a way of knowing more than I do but never anything like that."

"All of these people once lived in Cambridge, didn't they?" she asked.

"That's right. That much I've figured out." He paused for a moment. "Have you ever heard of place memories?"

"Actually, I have," she said.

"I've wondered if the dreams aren't something like that."

"Well, I once heard a story about some people who built a new house in the country," she mused "Each year the local hunt from hundreds of years before, horses and hounds and all, are said to come riding right through their front parlor. Through walls and everything, you know. It happens on the very same day each year as predictable as a bank holiday. The local Vicar offered to come and exorcise the ghosts." She looked playfully over her glasses at him and grinned. "But the owners of the house refused, saying that they had come to like the whole thing. Instead, they made that day an annual event when they would invite their friends. It became a big occasion. Hunt Day they called it. They have a big brunch and then wait for dogs, horses and riders to go through the room just to see which ones of the guests can see it and which ones can't. So far as I know they never found out the cause of the disturbance. I imagine they still do it."

Brian thought about his own place memories and also the mysterious horsemen who intruded on his dreams.

As if reading his mind Carol said, "What about your mounted men? From what you say they aren't going off on some peaceful country hunt."

"They're more deadly than that, especially the fierce looking leader. But I think this has to be different. The horsemen don't seem to be connected to any one place. At least so far as I can tell."

They were quiet for a moment. Carol broke the silence. And the tension, "Well there's certainly one thing you could do. You might read up on dreams and place memories. Isn't study what you do?"

"Oh, I've read plenty about place memories," he said, draining his own pint. "But I haven't looked into dreams as a subject. Not yet I haven't."

Brian began his research with Freudian dream theory. How could repressed sexual energy or even the fact of his mother's early death be somehow implicated in all this bizarre stuff? Jung wrote about archetypes and symbols in dreams. Okay, so how did these particular historical personages or their conversations connect him to something archetypal? He spent a couple of hours on that one and got nothing but frustration to show for it. Not much help in Jung. Nor did he find anything very interesting in other psychological takes on dreams, except to note that most dreams as vivid as his usually tended toward the fantastic and the bizarre: wild colors and horrible murders, blood and

gore. But not Brian's polite and—except for the horsemen—
rather sedate fantasies. He had to chuckle at himself when he
thought about how orderly and tame his dream life seemed
in comparison to others he read about. A comment on his
life? He didn't even have the intense emotion accompanying
those earlier place memories. Still, something about the
dreams remained upsetting to him.

He examined his life carefully for clues. He wasn't
dreaming about anything current in his research. None of the
issues of his life seemed to be addressed: divorce, frustration
with the university and his students and colleagues, or a
mounting ambivalence about his research. Nothing washed.
He was becoming obsessed with this fuzzy semi-reality and
without any resolution to it on the horizon. Not even the
obsessively painful dreams he had had during college over
his breakup with his first real girlfriend, Mary Beth, rivaled
these for intensity.

"The key to your dreams has to be what's going on in
your mind," Carol began after his report to her about his
dream research. They were walking along King's Parade after
a choral concert at Claire College's chapel. "Aren't you some
sort of workaholic? I gather that everything else in your life
gets pretty short shrift."

"Yeah, I guess I am. Or at least I have been. But nothing
I've been working on lately includes Erasmus. I used to be
interested in him. But that was years ago. I haven't done
anything with Walsingham since my dissertation and then
only peripherally. I've never worked on George Herbert."

"Maybe you need to see if you can take charge of the
dreams in some way," she said after a moment. "Why not try
to control what happens? You know, pile on some heavy
reading. A biography, say. Make it somebody really
interesting." She sat down on the low wall in front of King's
College.

He joined her on the wall. They watched people walk
past. Finally he turned sideways to look at her and so he
could also glance over his left shoulder at the brilliantly lit
facade of King's chapel. There must have been some event

going on inside because the exterior spotlights found their rival in the interior lighting that shone through the brilliant blues and reds of the Perpendicular Gothic windows. He remembered that Henry VIII had put his indelible mark on the college.

"You're right," he said. "This has been uncharacteristic of me." He had always taken pride in his ability to manipulate the world around him, to meet his needs and to control the details of life. These dreams made him feel like a victim. Maybe that was what troubled him most. "I'm going to do it. Try to manage these dreams and see if I can make something happen."

Brian tried drinking heavily for three days and then abstained completely for the next three days. He ate rich food, loading up on carbs and veggies. No dreams. He even experimented with brief periods of fasting, but that just made him hungry. He tried following Carol's advice and read a new biography of Henry VIII to see if he might dream about the second Tudor. Could there be a much more colorful historical character than Henry? But he had no dreams of Bluff King Hal. Finally he decided that the dreams were over. Maybe they had been the product of the jet lag, or just a reaction to being back in Britain again. They did seem similar to the old place memory thing. Perhaps he had been coming a bit unglued over getting divorced. He didn't know. But since there were no more of them, hadn't been any for over two weeks, and his work seemed to be going okay, he decided to forget the whole thing and get back to normal. He had managed after all to get control over the dreams in one way—through ending them, hadn't he? Why not leave well enough alone? Right. Then why didn't he feel as if he had regained control over his life?

chapter five

Brian sat on the low wall outside King's and let the afternoon sun warm his back and fill his cold places. He often stopped there in the cultural shadow of the chapel to think—and just be. A large group of young tourists talked rapid fire in some Asian language as they followed a tour guide who held a loosely furled huge red-and-white umbrella overhead like a flag. Brian began to feel grumpy. Just for them being there. Even the flashes and little red eyes of their cameras annoyed him. Soon their high-energy antics melted his attitude and he was smiling in spite of himself. A group composed of older Americans passed by. One tiny little lady with snow-white hair wore mixed expressions of wonder and of terror as she struggled to keep up. He felt a kind of affinity with her fear and confusion. Nearby a pair of street musicians played Baroque music on an electronic keyboard and an antique fretted string instrument. The man's fingers flew across the neck as he picked out intricate melodies and counterpoints. His female partner played accompaniment on the keyboard, set to sound vaguely like a harpsichord. Something about them attracted Brian. He got up and walked nearer before sitting down again. King's chapel loomed tall behind him and Great St. Mary's glowered from across the street. At that moment it felt as if he had never heard anything so beautiful as what those two street musicians were playing. An instrument case salted with a clutch of coins lay open before them. The two musicians seemed oblivious to the noise and confusion of the street or the pungency of the fast-food discards in the garbage can beside them. Their faces radiated an ecstasy that he began to share, feeling a little giddy. Strange. When he became steadier, he stood up, reached into his pocket for a pound coin and dropped it into the open case. He paused, then reached back into the pocket and came out with a five-pound note, crumpled it and dropped it in the case as well. He turned and walked toward the Eagle.

"A double whiskey," he said to the bartender, pointing at a bottle. "Glen Morangie." He pulled out his wallet for money to pay.

With drink in hand he worked his way through the crowd to an empty table in the outside courtyard. A wide gate opened onto the street. It had once been the carriage entrance that welcomed passengers to the establishment in comfort and safety. The lower portion of the porch at St. Bene't's Church and other parts of its Victorian addition showed through the open gate. He could even see a small section of the Saxon tower. All around the Eagle's courtyard hung colorful baskets overflowing with bright flowers. Bees darted in one flower and then out again only to disappear into another. The sweet perfume mingled with the scent of spilled beer. No wonder the bees were so active. As he sat staring at the drink in his hand, the golden translucence catching the light of the afternoon sun, his thoughts passed to his dreams. It wasn't so much that he had had them that troubled him but the sense of loss he felt since they had ended.

He shook his head slightly, aware that he had been sitting almost transfixed looking into the whiskey glass. He took a sip of the single malt. It warmed his throat and stomach as it flowed wonderfully through him. He leaned back in his chair and enjoyed the moment.

"You're looking mighty pleased with yourself."

Brian looked up to see the lanky frame of Jeff Barringer. Jeff was in uniform: soft-soled shoes, blue jeans, tie loosened at the blue button-down open collar, and comfortably rumpled tweed sports coat in various hues of brown.

"Hi-ya, Jeff. What's not to feel pleased about?" He held up his glass of Scotch in a vague salute.

Jeff folded himself into a chair and set his sloshing-full pint glass on the table in front of him, creating as he did a newly spilled puddle of what must be Young's Special Bitter, his usual.

Jeff was one of those transplanted Californians who feel like a captive when obliged to live anywhere else. He praised Nashville and his Sociology job at Vanderbilt, saying, "It's a great school with interesting colleagues. Nashville is lots more than Elvis-land. The country around the city is beautiful and green. But it doesn't have the Southern California beaches. I hate the cold winters. And I hate the hot and humid summers."

"And you like California a lot?" Brian had asked.

"Not really. It's superficial, shallow, materialistic, racist, dominated by the automobile and hence hopelessly corrupted with the exhaust of the internal combustion engine," Jeff had answered without skipping a beat. Jeff was a deeply committed critic, living his life in perpetual opposition—to everything. No place ever met his exacting standards, no groups of people (races, classes, occupations, genders) ever mustered up to the expectations that Jeff had for them.

But Jeff's negative attitudes didn't stop Brian from liking him. Despite his sweeping criticisms Brian knew that for Jeff every individual human being was a gift to explore, to get to know and to love. At the abstract level Jeff was Attila the Hun; personally, he was Barney.

"My work," Jeff had once told Brian, "explores the decay of symbols in contemporary culture, both religious and national. Though I have no religion to speak of myself, you understand. And I despise all the patriotic stuff as fostering nationalism and its horrific bloody consequences in the twentieth century."

"What on earth brought you to the subject, then, if you dislike everything the symbols stand for?" Brian had asked.

"I value these old images—crosses, flags, Stars of David, eagles, the Statue of Liberty—as symbols because they reveal the heart of the culture. Their decay is a mark of the crumbling of the society and its values. The symbols that have replaced red-white-and-blue bunting, church steeples and menorahs are even worse than they are. These are the standard bearers of materialistic culture. The Golden Arches, the Coca Cola logo, the Shell Oil scallop and the Toyota symbol—ovals within ovals capturing world, universe and the fertilized egg. Ha! These logos have come to define contemporary life. Don't you see? Values and symbols are intimately connected. If the prime symbols carry, for example, a spiritual message, then there are strong spiritual elements. If the prime symbols are material, then the culture's values would be found there. If the only symbols we can relate to are trying to sell us something, then we aren't left with much."

"And the religious and patriotic symbols weren't selling something?"

"I think you're onto something." Jeff flashed his widest toothy grin.

But this all came from earlier conversations. Today Brian was feeling playful so he asked a facetious question. "I've been thinking about your research—symbols and all. So which came first, the symbol or the value, the chicken or the egg? Or were they products of simultaneous generation?" Brian grinned at his new friend.

Jeff didn't even take a breath, "I expect those questions to provide the subject of my next two or three books and probably twenty-five or thirty articles. They might even see me all the way to retirement." Jeff drew a long swallow from his pint glass and gave Brian a mock serious expression.

"So, what's up, Jeff?"

"SHE said that if I ran into you, I should invite you to dinner for Saturday night. You free?" Jeff always spoke of his partner in caps. Brian often wondered if this arose out of some combination of respect and fear. With Charlie he could understand both possibilities.

"Sure, I get pretty tired of eating alone." He thought quickly about what he had said and the expression on Jeff's face. "No, I don't mean that. Not just like that, anyhow. I really would like that—being with you and Charlie."

Jeff's face brightened. "Our flat is just the other side of Midsummer Common. You know, past the Drummer Street bus station. You follow the path straight across the park, Christ's Pieces, then on to Butt Green and the Common. Makes for a great walk. Just watch out for the cows on the Common." He laughed and gave Brian the address. "Seven okay?"

"Perfect."

Brian left the Eagle, thinking about religious symbols and what Jeff had been saying. He walked past St. Ben'et's, where Carol arranged flowers for Sunday services. He thought about Carol and Jeff, realizing that in his own way Jeff was professionally preoccupied with the symbols of religion though he rejected what they stood for. Caramel Apple's life revolved around that little church and all of its Christian symbols. But he suspected that he himself better represented the times in which they all lived than either Jeff or Carol. He was the normal one. Church membership was just something a person from Peoria did. It wasn't anything particularly spiritual. In the academic world even such nominal church membership was something of an anomaly. Then there's God? He often asked himself what he really thought about that quaint concept. The big-guy-in-the-sky didn't mean much to him. But he was surprised to find himself asking the God questions at all. The effect of the dreams perhaps? Hmm. Maybe being in Cambridge amidst so many physical reminders of the Church of England and the historic Christian faith. Perhaps it would help him to resolve once and for all his ambivalence about religion and his nominal Episcopalianism. Whatever had happened to the intense spiritual feelings that had poured out of him during his divorce from Kathleen? That emotional wandering had brought a brief rebirth to his slumbering search for spiritual meaning. He had even taken up church attendance again for the first time since he was in high school. But rather than following that fresh new quest, he had gradually taken the easier course and settled for the antique eight o'clock Sunday liturgy at St. Michael's in Evanston. It was formally methodical rather than passionate or compelling. That language and theology seemed to fit how he had gradually come to see life: a harsh God passing judgment on everyone and everything. Yes, he did think that the world was filled with "miserable sinners" as the text he had repeated each Sunday affirmed. The spirit of it had seemed to fit his professional life too as he wallowed at church in the same antiquated language that he saw in his research. In both he encountered a sense of imminent cosmic disaster common in all kinds of sixteenth-century European texts. Something about using that old language had seemed permanent and affirming of an unchanging absolute truth. That was what he had been looking for. For a few years he had dutifully sat, stood and knelt in the orderly and predictable way of Episcopalians, surrounded mostly by empty pews. Feeling little or nothing, he had seemed to revel in the very blandness of it all.

Sometimes Brian had defended his church attendance to his intimates by the cynical assertion that Sunday Mass was as necessary to his well-being as a bowel movement: essential, even pleasurable sometimes, but not something you wanted to talk about or waste much thought over. So long, that is, as nobody tried to upset the apple cart by changing things. He had fiercely guarded the impregnability of that historic service. Emily had goaded him about what she called his lukewarm religion. But church attendance had made a comfortable beginning hour to his Sunday, much as his thirty-minute run did most other days. It had made scant intrusion on the rest of his morning spent by himself reading the *New York Times* and drinking café lattes at a neighborhood Starbucks. Little by little he had stopped going to church at all. Instead, he worshipped at Starbucks' altar and made his communion on coffee and croissants. He hadn't even made his nominal church pledge the last couple of years.

Brian rarely ever thought about his religion or his spirituality anymore—topics that for a time had mattered a great deal to him. Except to wonder at his disinterest. He had come to puzzle over why he called himself an Episcopalian. Or a Christian, for that matter. As nearly as he could tell, God, if any such Being existed, remained persistently remote from and unconcerned about life. At least life as he experienced it. More and more he laughed at the pie-in-the-sky-by-and-by god as well as the cosmic scorekeeper god—"gonna find out who's naughty or nice." The warrior god. The tribal god. The exclusive god who demanded particular rituals as entry requirements into paradise. The social revolutionary god. How many gods lived in this so-called monotheistic faith called the Judeo-Christian tradition? The god of vengeance, the god of love, the father god, the mother god, the triune god: gods, gods, so many gods. Maybe he should dump the whole thing as most of his colleagues had already done.

Eventually his mind turned to thoughts of his present work project. Mostly, he wasn't terribly interested in it. The one exception to this general boredom had to do with the intriguing hints he had found about his Black Widow. Three women managing to marry several men and accumulate their property: a situation more than mildly interesting to him. He was always on the alert for fresh references in the manuscripts. The one new thing he had discovered since that first day as he sifted through many cartons of estate papers was a name—Jane. He knew it was the same woman, because the same person who had put him onto her in the first place had written the letter where he found the reference. This second letter also contained mention of a daughter and granddaughter. That seemed fairly conclusive. Maybe with a name, if only a first one, he would have more success finding something about her.

He avoided a young man on a bicycle as he turned in at Lord's to check his mail. Nodding to the man on duty as he stepped into the Porter's Lodge, he walked on into the mailroom. Two letters stood upright in his little cubby. Pulling out the first one, he saw that it came from Jeannie. He tore it open and laughed out loud. Just like her, he thought as he looked at the lavender heavy-bond envelope holding a single sheet of matching paper. Classy. In the middle of the page in tiny blue-ink printing he read the words: "August 2, 11 a.m. Gatwick. American 1055." Only three more weeks to wait.

He looked at the other letter. It was from an Elizabeth Schumann in Buffalo, New York. He didn't know any Elizabeth Schumann, much less one in Buffalo. A former student? Probably. But usually he could remember the names of the ones likely to write him, even if he couldn't connect a face. Maybe her name had changed when she married. Probably wanted a letter of recommendation. He tore it open. The letter began in the familiar way, "My Dear Brian." Too familiar for a former student. He looked at the signature on the bottom of the second sheet, and his heart stopped. It said, "Love, Mary Beth."

chapter six

Brian stumbled out of the Porter's Lodge into the Lord's private garden and dropped with the buoyancy of a stone onto one of the wooden benches. This felt like receiving the papers from Emily's lawyer all over again. Only this was more shocking—more unexpected. After all these years Mary Beth's name and even her handwriting still had the power to stop him cold. How long had it been since he had actually seen or even heard about Mary Beth? At least a decade. When had he last thought about her? A week ago? Yesterday? This morning? Her memory had never entirely faded. Even now his heart leapt when he thought about that raven-haired nineteen-year-old girl.

Brian prided himself on being sensible and analytical, but where Mary Beth was concerned his rational mind had never worked very well. That had been true when he was a college freshman, and it was still true today. Mary Beth remained the image of perfection for him: an object both of sexual desire and near-religious adoration. She was also the bitch whose rejection had made his late adolescence a nightmare. But even knowing all of this failed to account for the breadth and depth of her emotional hold on him. Her representation of the ideal and the unattainable, the obsessive perfection of first love, had made her all the more desirable than she might have been as mere flesh and blood. Compared to Mary Beth's sudden real intrusion into his life his recent dreams seemed a pale haunting indeed.

Brian had long since concluded that carrying a torch for Mary Beth had doomed his first marriage. Even with their wedding day fresh in his memory he would wake up with Irish spitfire Kathleen beside him, dreaming about Mary Beth. Now that he thought about it, those dreams rivaled his current ones for being obsessive and intense.

He remembered one night when he and Kathleen had been married about a year and he woke up terrified and soaking wet with sweat.

"Brian honey, what's the matter? Are you okay? You were screaming."

For a moment he couldn't remember where he was or who this woman lying beside him might be. He remained emotionally trapped in the world of the dream. Mary Beth's car had been tumbling down a steep precipice. Bouncing, rolling and crashing against trees and boulders. Above in the night sky a full moon played an eerie game of hide and seek through mostly wispy cirrus clouds. Mary Beth was screaming in terror. He stood watching the car fall, laughing hysterically. That had shifted to a feeling of horror. He woke to his own screams of fear and torment.

Kathleen had put her arms around him to comfort him. But he pushed her away.

"Don't, Kathleen," he practically shouted at her. He remembered feeling as if his flesh might actually burn at her touch. He leapt out of bed.

Kathleen shouted after him, "What an asshole you are! What's the matter with you?"

He had pulled on his clothes and burst out of their apartment. The rest of the night he had spent walking, finally ending up in Harvard Square where he got coffee and Danish before going back home and apologizing to Kathleen.

That dream had started up a new round of yearning for Mary Beth. He longed for her during the day and dreamed about her at night. And cursed the very memory of her all the time. For over a month his work suffered, and he could barely stand the sight of Kathleen. Poor Kathleen. She had been deeply hurt by this unwarranted rejection, asking over and over what she had done. He could only deny that anything was wrong and say that he was worried about completing his degree. He certainly couldn't explain the real source of his pain. His inability finally to let go of Mary Beth stalked his emotional life. Even now he could get that familiar longing when he saw a curly pile of black hair atop shoulders tall and straight. Like outside the Round Church a couple of weeks ago. At the heart of his continued obsession with her was what he saw as her total rejection of him. Not only had she refused to have an exclusive relationship with him, she would never agree to sleep with him. The omission of sexual union left him feeling inadequate and humiliated.

On the tenth reunion of their college graduation Brian and Mary Beth and their partners were seated at opposite ends of the same dinner table in the crystal ballroom at the old downtown hotel. Brian always blamed that so-called coincidence on the joking malice of one of his old friends. He made some polite conversation with her and got through the evening somehow. But all the pain and longing flooded back. Years passed before he could push her back down again into his subconscious. Now, here comes this letter. Brian looked again at the envelope and saw that the departmental secretary back at SU had forwarded it. The chatty handwritten letter came as if from an old friend who had lost touch and wanted to reconnect.

"I learned by accident where you were teaching," she wrote, "and decided to drop you a note to find out how you've been." She showed no awareness of their painful history. Painful at least for him. He felt treated to Mary Beth's cool detachment. She wrote about her work as a research chemist for an international corporation, her home in Buffalo and the raising of her kids. Finally she dropped two bombs that sent him reeling. The first one read simply, "I'm almost completely over my divorce," but those six simple words carried a shock wave equal to the report of a frigate's broadside. Mary Beth was newly single. Once he got over the initial impact of that little sentence, he nearly snarled in cynical response, "So Little Miss Perfect's had a failed marriage just like ordinary mortals." The second explosion in Brian's brain came from her equally simple sentence, "I can't tell you how often I've thought about you since our freshman year."

Brian sat there on the garden bench at Lord's surrounded by manicured beds of roses, the air filled with their sweet scents and the buzzing of bees. He ignored it all. A swirl of emotions more cloying almost suffocated him. Would he never be rid of her? Must she dominate his mind and heart forever? He crumpled up the letter and threw it in the garbage can beside the bench, envelope and all, and stalked out of Lord's. He had reached Silver Street when he stopped abruptly, shook his head and turned around. He hoped no one saw him fishing both letter and envelope out of the trash.

Brian dragged himself out of bed. He had tossed and turned all night, sleeping for short periods and then wakeful and fretting again. He kept thinking about the crumpled letter he had left on his dressing table. Maybe a really juicy dream of murder and mayhem in the Tower or somewhere might have rescued him. Anything to get his mind off that letter. But he knew that escaping into the refuge of a remote past, even into his dream world, could not protect him from the danger Mary Beth's letter represented in the present.

He pulled on his robe and stuffed his feet into his fuzzy house slippers, stepped over to the dressing table and grabbed the balled-up letter and envelope. Shuffling down the hallway and into the kitchen, he lighted the kettle for a cup of instant coffee. Across the hallway in the sitting room he slumped down in his chair. The digital clock read 4:13. The dark figure of a knight loomed over him. Memory of buying that print in the Market flitted across his mind. He smoothed out Mary Beth's letter again and reread it. How many times had he made those same preparations and forced his eyes to take in the words on the wrinkled paper? He still didn't know what to do about it or even what he wanted to do about it. The invitation, though subtle, was clear. She was "almost over her divorce." Mary Beth had always employed that kind of subtlety and would never come right out and say, "I want to see you again," or "I'm available. Are you?" No, she had always left the risks to him. Well, maybe not all of them. She did write after all. He went round and round in his head. What did he want to do about this? How did he want to reply to her? Did he want to reply at all?

He looked down at the wrinkled letter and envelope on his sitting room desk and picked them up, wadded them up again and tossed the paper ball toward the corner wastebasket. It bounced off the rim and onto the floor. He turned off the whistling kettle and went back to bed.

Brian scoured the Cambridge bookstores, among other things searching out and buying an aged leather-bound copy of Herbert's poems. He left G. David's, tucking the book lovingly into his computer bag. For some reason it had been important for him to buy just the right copy. He hadn't gone to the library at all. For lunch he went to a riverside pub on Silver Street and sat at an outdoor table with a mound of Shepherd's Pie on his plate and a pint of bitter beside it. He leafed lovingly through the book and sat wistfully for a time over his favorite poem, "Love, III."

> Love bade me welcome, yet my soul drew back,
> Guilty of dust and sin.
> But quick-ey'd Love, observing me grow slack
> From my first entrance in,
> Drew nearer to me, sweetly questioning
> If I lack'd anything.

He read through the entire poem several times, stopping finally on the concluding stanza, "'You must sit down,' says Love, 'and taste my meat.' So I did sit and eat."

At last, strengthened in some odd way by the poem, he put down the little leather volume and withdrew Mary Beth's crumpled letter from his pocket where it had threatened to burn its way out all morning. Reading it again, he made a decision and, after several false starts, got off a note that he hoped looked quickly and casually scribbled, "Dear Mary Beth," he wrote. "Your letter came as a great and welcome surprise. As you can see from my return address I am in England—on sabbatical. I'm here alone. My wife (the second one, alas) has left me for her Chevrolet dealer. The divorce is in motion. But that's, as they say, another story. It would be great to be able to renew acquaintances, and I could really use a pen pal." He chuckled silently to himself at the old-fashioned term, but welcomed its stiff protection. He went on to tell her about his work and of his hopes for this sabbatical. He also praised his artist daughter and her talent and asked about Mary Beth's children. "I'm really not surprised to learn of your major research job," he wrote. "And I'm sorry about your divorce. I know how painful that can be. Please do write again." He signed it simply, "Yours, Brian."

Quickly folding and sliding the letter into an envelope, he addressed and stamped it. The ten-minute walk to the post office made him feel a little like a condemned man taking his final steps to the gallows. "Dead man walking," might have been the call from observers as he walked by. A complex of feelings left him almost dizzy in reaction: excitement, anxiety, fear, wariness and a return of the old longing. But he also excavated a piece of the anger he had held onto for so many years. This time he would not come out the loser in any engagement he had with Mary Beth. Should there be one.

That night he had a new dream.

I'm standing in an open courtyard facing across Jesus Green toward the Cam. The buildings of Jesus College are on my right and Wesley House is on my left. It is very quiet, as if there are no living things about. I'm excited and impatient for the dream to unfold. Who am I going to meet? I pan to the left and to the right and see that I share this wide grassy and wooded place with an ox cart. It's the kind that has high, solid and heavy wooden wheels rising well above the cart's low sides. The tongue reaches toward the sky, unattached at the moment to any draft animals. The cart's rear edge sits against the ground. The bed of the cart is empty except for what looks like a bundle of rags on top of a pile of straw. Then I notice that the rag pile moves as if it's breathing. It stirs itself. The rags assemble themselves into a human form. The head of a woman well into middle age emerges and appears above the wheel of the cart. As I look closer I see a plain face. It has a kind of glow, the sort you sometimes see on people who have recently been very ill, perhaps at death's door. The woman's black garb, which I think might be a nun's habit from the look of it, is rough-woven, dirty, rumpled and torn.

What do I know about the history of Jesus College? Not much really: founded sometime in the late fifteenth or early sixteenth century on the property of a former nunnery—defunct even before the Reformation brought an end to all of the monastic houses. I can't remember the order.

The woman is now sitting upright on her pile of straw and gives me a weak gap-toothed smile. "Are you God's sending?" she asks. "The gracious gentleman who helps this poor woman to her new home three days and more travel from here?"

"I'm sorry, Sister, but I'm just a visitor myself," I answer. "Where are you going?"

"A very great distance, I fear. A journey to the grand cathedral city of Norwich, where a place has been found for me to recover from my ague and to tell the story of the strange things I have been seeing. For my soul's sake—and for my poor body—I am to stop a few nights at the convent in the Isle of Ely. In this, the Good Lord Jesus will me keep in the faith and truth of Holy Church."

"What is it that you have seen?" I ask. What could this strange old woman have to tell that would be of interest to me or anyone else?

"I have seen a revelation of love that Christ, our endless bliss, made of His precious crowning with thorns—many faire showings of endless wisdom and teaching of love." She sinks back on her cushioning pile of straw, wearied apparently by the effort of what she has said, but still she continues, "Me thinks I would have been, at that very time when they crucified My Lord, with Mary Magdalene and with others that were Christ's lovers, and therefore I desired a bodily sight wherein I might have more knowledge of the pains of our Savior, and of the compassion our Lady and of all His true lovers that seen that time, His pains, for I would be one of them and suffer with Him."

I know those words and that story. Who is it? Suddenly I know. Julian of Norwich. Could this be the woman known to posterity by that name?

"This simple creature cannot read a letter or write," she continues. "I must find a clerk who can write down these showings I have seen of Our Good Lord. Be you such a person, sir?"

"I'm afraid not," I say, but I think to myself: yes, this might be Julian.

Just then a very old man wearing a shapeless tunic comes around the corner of one of the buildings. He has a pair of oxen in tow that are bound together by a massive wooden yoke. He apparently doesn't see me, but gestures to the woman. She crawls to the front of the cart. He reaches up and pulls down on the tongue with one hand and backs the oxen on both sides of it with the other. He fastens the yoke to the tongue with what looks like a pair of metal rings. The woman lies down again, propped on one elbow, and the driver pushes aside a small cloth-wrapped bundle and pulls a long stick from the cart to prod the two oxen. He nods to me. The oxen begin to lumber toward the river, dragging the wagon behind them. The woman gestures to me in a combination of excitement and resignation. They leave me standing here watching them move slowly away.

The cart disappears from view and in its place, as if they have waited politely for the right moment, come the mounted horsemen led by the same leader. As before they don't fully materialize into this present. They ride hard several feet above the grassy green field of Jesus College. They make no forward progress. But I'm still frightened of them.

The pain comes over me suddenly. My face is bathed in sweat. The dream is over.

ChapTeR seven

The next morning Brian sat in the university library, troubling over three women. All of them out of the past. Mary Beth was a part of his personal past. The mystery woman, Jane, and the one known as Julian of Norwich, were both in the remote historical past. All three had suddenly been thrust into Brian's present. He had done some checking on Julian of Norwich. She had died nearly a century and a half before the monasteries were dissolved and hence were well outside his research area. He couldn't imagine anyone less likely to connect him to issues of land transfer, debt management and estate building than a fourteenth-century mystic and theologian. Far from dealing with landed estates, she had spent the bulk of her life physically walled in as an anchorite in rooms attached to the side of an English parish church. And she described Jesus as her "mother." Good grief. But he'd do some more research about her. Then there was the mysterious Black Widow, the woman named Jane. Plain Jane. There she was, accumulating property in violation of all understood contemporary standards of how landed wealth was controlled. So what happened to this striking experiment in female enterprise? That's the real puzzle. Why isn't she known? Bess of Hardwicke has always been the subject of much interest and comment. But Jane and her progeny simply disappear. It's as if they never existed. Almost. As if they were meant to disappear. At least she fits within his larger research goals. Sort of.

He went back to pulling out pieces of parchment and heavy paper one by one from the carton he had been working on. After an hour of gathering detailed information on the closing of the Cambridge monasteries, he happened onto the records of the defunct convent of St. Mary and St. Radegund. Its saintly patrons were the Blessed Virgin Mary and a sixth century Thuringian princess. He instantly recognized the convent as the predecessor of Jesus College, the site of his last dream. He sat for a moment remembering Julian, the presumed central figure in the dream. What made him so certain that she had been Julian? He recalled two vivid impressions that had led him to that conclusion. The woman he met possessed a gentle intensity and an intellect undiminished by a self-effacing humility. These are ways that history has known the anchorite. Besides, what she said to him fit so well with what he knew about the woman called Julian. Still, St. Mary's and St. Radegund's? He scoured the carton for more about that particular convent, his interest aroused. Hoping to figure it all out, he kept his eye open for reference to Julian in the process. Any number of names showed up on ledgers and convent rolls, but he saw nothing that connected to Julian either by name or by a similar story: a serious illness accompanied by a vision of Christ on the Cross. Mostly he had lists of names and resources.

In the library's stacks he soon learned that Jesus College's predecessor, an early twelfth century foundation, had been suppressed in the latter part of the fifteenth century with only two resident nuns remaining. That left the way for Jesus College to be founded on the site. While he was there he read up on Julian of Norwich. Nowhere in his reading did he find any suggestion that Julian had ever been at the Cambridge convent or in Cambridge at all. Nobody seemed to know anything about her origins or even what her actual name might have been before she took up residence in her anchorhold in Norwich. An anchorite, the solitary kind of monastic Julian became, was thought of legally as having died. Normally there would even be a funeral for the former person. The anchorite would then assume a new name as a way of leaving personal identity behind. Julian had taken the name of the parish church where she was attached and where she lived for the rest of her life. In effect she had no name, but was simply called by the place. He looked at two versions of her *Showings* and, indeed, recognized similar vivid language and expressions he had heard in the dream. Everything seemed to confirm Julian as the dream subject.

Then where did he get the idea that she had been at the long defunct Cambridge house? He had to have gotten it from somewhere in order to dream it. After all, his dreams had all been about people and events he already knew, and all the figures had been connected absolutely to Cambridge. Likewise, he had previously only encountered characters whose portraits he had seen and with whom he was familiar. There were no portraits of Julian. But he had dreamed about her anyhow in that particularly vivid and lingering kind of way that he had been dreaming recently. He had no previous idea of what she looked like. How could he? Nobody else did. No Julian expert Brian could find suggested that she had ever been in Cambridge at all.

But why shouldn't she have been there? "Julian" was not her actual name and nobody knew what she had originally been called. Her real name could be all over the scanty records of St. Mary's and St. Radegund's without anyone, including Brian, knowing it. She could have been a member of the convent community, or a guest while recovering from her illness. One writer suggested that she had been afflicted with anthrax. During that illness she had had her mystical visions, "showings" or revelations. There was no more reason to think that she had been in Cambridge than to think that she hadn't. Still, Brian's dream had unambiguously placed her there. The more he thought about these conclusions the more uncomfortable—and excited—he became. Perhaps he should write a speculative paper, maybe even identify names in the records that might have been hers. Maybe the records would show a particular woman who was recovering from anthrax in the years before Julian turned up in Norwich. He began to get more and more excited. He checked it out. The thin records listed a number of possibilities but revealed nothing conclusive. If he did write such a paper and anyone should ask where he had gotten the idea, "Oh, I dreamed it," would certainly do a lot for his reputation as a serious scholar. He laughed out loud.

Brian stepped out of his flat to walk to Jeff and Charlie's place for dinner, realizing that he had missed crossing Midsummer Common at the solstice by only a couple of weeks. A light rain was falling. It seemed to turn his umbrella into a cozy extension of his arm. The gray overcast largely obscured the evening sunlight and left a dim and darkened daylight that had prematurely brought lights on all through central Cambridge. Hunching under the umbrella, he felt alone and comfortably separate from other walkers. Soon he passed the Drummer Street bus station. From there he struck out across Christ's Pieces, a historic allotment belonging to Christ College. The city streets were much quieter than usual, and the open park was mostly deserted—a space surrounded entirely by city and university buildings and homes. It had straight paved walkways, rows of plane trees, benches, beds of brightly colored flowers and a bowling green. It had the musty smell of freshly-cut wet grass.

As he walked he thought about sidewalks in parks and on college campuses in the US, concrete footpaths put where some engineer or designer had decided people should walk. Worn grass showed the places where they did walk. But people had been hoofing it across public parks in England for centuries. He imagined Christ's Pieces over the years with the grass being mowed by grazing sheep, cattle and horses, and not by machines. That was long before any kind of paving had been laid down. So well established had the pathways become that when the concrete or asphalt was installed, workers could put it where people actually walked and make dry footpaths in places a person wanted to go. It seemed a small point, but for Brian it was a metaphor for living in a place that had been long-settled and established. Everything around him breathed continuity and enduring stability, like the Cam itself: rich in custom and tradition, fecund. Lovers loving; dreamers dreaming; and feet walking the paths. Like the one beneath him. What with so much stimulation everywhere around him, and all of his years of immersing himself in this particular history, why should he chide his subconscious for running off in its imaginary flights and conjuring up spectral inhabitants of the past?

From Christ's Pieces he negotiated a couple of blocks of city streets and then went out into open grass again. This time onto Butt's Green, so-called because it was the place where archery butts were once placed for practice. It's now actually a corner of Midsummer Common. Abutting the Cam, the Common is a wide expanse of undeveloped grassland and is even grazed by a small herd of cattle. Brian remembered Jeff's quip about the cows. What a remarkable slice of nature it makes, sitting there the way it does in the middle of the city. As he set out across it he imagined, in the ordinary way of imaginations, the medieval fairs of Midsummer that gave the vast open space its name and created its identity. That would have been right now, exactly at this time of year. He thought about the tents and displays of Italians and Spaniards, French merchants and Frisians, Germans and burghers from the Hanseatic League—all bustling with their wares on sale to other traders. Echoes of bargaining and changing coins seemed to hang on the air. It was one of the largest medieval fairs in Europe, held annually at Midsummer. Such fairs were more like wholesale buyers' conventions than places of entertainment. The original merchant fairs gave way to so-called funfairs in subsequent centuries, typically attracting all sorts of different entertainments. He remembered reading somewhere just recently about the huge fete that was celebrated at the coronation of Queen Victoria. That was Midsummer 1838. He was glad to be crossing the Common at that same time of year. He looked ahead at Midsummer House, a restaurant in a Victorian villa that sits nearly at the edge of the Common, and at the public house not far away. If he tried very hard he could just make out the roofs of the tied up houseboats lining the Cam beside the Common. At the moment the whole expanse was devoid of life. He didn't even see the cattle.

About two-thirds of the way across the Common in this reverie Brian felt waves of dizziness and nausea suddenly hit him. He felt vulnerable. Defenseless. It was as if he were standing at the edge of a precipice that wanted to draw him over its edge. He crouched down, sitting on his hams, and rested both hands on the wet grass, wishing it were dry so he could sit right down. Instead he propped himself up, palms down. He could feel perspiration breaking out on his face. He was afraid he would be sick. Shaky legs felt as if they might crumble beneath him and leave him in a heap on the ground.

Finally the vertigo passed, and he stood, trying to figure out what had happened and wondering if he had been slipping into a dream. He looked around. He was entirely alone. This was certainly not a dream. At least now it wasn't. The gentle light rain and the shroud-like protection of his umbrella created a comfortable little world. Would lingering outdoors result in triggering another dream? He wished he would have one, despite how bad they made him feel afterwards. Perhaps he had become addicted to his fantasy life. With regret, he hurried on toward the bridge ahead, crossed the Cam and soon found Jeff and Charlie's street.

"So, Brian?" Charlie greeted him. "You made it." He removed his windbreaker and stood his umbrella beside the front door. "Still doing the usual round of concerts with your Miss Marple?"

"Carol? Some." Looking around the room, he saw that it had been carved out of a larger one. Ornate crown molding ran along two sides, hinting at what the room must originally have looked like. The two additional walls, clearly a division of the former room, were unadorned where they contacted the ceiling. None of the naked plaster-and-paint walls told anything about either the flat's current or any previous occupants. Like Brian's flat, it was just one more aging rental largely devoid of personality and charm in a university town filled with places just like it.

Charlie had covered her compact and energetic body with a checked shirt, blue jeans and very white tennis shoes. She might have been mistaken for a man, but for the shape of her hips and rear and her narrow waist. They marked her as indisputably female. As usual there was something matter-of-fact about her. She walked and talked in direct ways. Her strong hands showed the scars of nicks and cuts, presumably from repairing musical instruments. She always insisted that she was a musicologist rather than a performer but admitted that she could sight read most anything. "I sing a little, play a little piano, some violin, a bit of flute and can find my way around a mandolin and a guitar," she had said. "Mostly I like to fool around with Renaissance period instruments, especially viols." Charlie's claim to a serious academic reputation came from a sweeping musical knowledge about late Medieval and Renaissance music on its own terms.

Charlie, like Jeff, was a born critic. If she decided that she liked a concert she would lavish praise on it. But more commonly if she didn't like something she'd heard her critique could be brutal. Brian's one experience of hearing music with Charlie and Jeff had led him to resolve never to repeat the experience. He had learned more about the composers and their technical musical skills and flaws that night than he had ever wanted to know. Her caustic critique of the performers left him imagining a pile of random musical notes heaped on the floor like trash. Brian much preferred taking in the Cambridge music scene with Carol Heppel, someone who simply loved it all.

Jeff was in his usual uniform, minus only a jacket. Brian couldn't help wondering if his wardrobe had anything in it besides button-down-collar Oxford cloth shirts.

They ate Indian takeout, drank icy Taj Mahal lager and, for an abrupt change in national cuisine, finished up with huge bowls of hot apple crumble covered in fresh cream. "We don't really cook," Jeff had admitted. "So many takeouts; so little time!" They laughed at almost everything. Brian couldn't remember the last time he had had such fun.

As they cleaned up a turn of the conversation brought up tales of odd occurrences and what it felt like to live where people had been settled for a thousand years and more—piles of human experience building layer upon layer. Much as he had been doing earlier, and that brought Brian's dreams and place memories to mind. Especially the centrality of both physical location and antiquity in all of them. He had never before told Jeff and Charlie about what was happening to him. "I don't want to be completely boring here," he began, "but something kind of weird has been happening to me." He laughed but found it hard to keep a serious edge out of his voice. "I do always find it enormously boring and self-indulgent when someone prattles on about their dreams. But mine lately are so— well, so bizarre."

"Go ahead. I promise to let you know if it gets dull," Jeff

said. "Got woman trouble? Dreaming delicious fantasies?" He grinned broadly.

"If only," Brian said, though it dawned on him that he did have some interesting complications with women. "Well, maybe some small issues there," he added, grinning self-consciously. "But these dreams are different." He sobered up and related the details of the dreams and what little understanding of them he had come to.

"Hmm," said Charlie. They sound so matter-of-fact and, well, expected. Dreams are usually pretty bizarre. These aren't. What makes you think of them as dreams?" She looked intently at him. "Aren't there other ways to understand them?"

"Like what?"

"Well, what about visions? Those are not exactly unheard of in these parts."

"Right-right. Now I'm having visions. They'll lock me up." Visions indeed. The whole notion made him very uncomfortable. Deciding that he had made enough personal revelations for one evening, he steered the conversation away and onto less threatening subjects. They talked for a time about their current work. Finally he said goodnight, grateful for their friendship, "You've really given me something to think about," he said to Charlie as he was leaving. "Visions?" He laughed. Inside, deep in his gut, his discomfort returned. Almost as if he were having a premonition of something about to happen.

The rain was beating down so hard onto the street that nearly everyone else had been driven indoors. He thought for a moment of calling a cab but decided against it. He liked the solitude and the quiet. Besides, it wasn't cold. The sound of the rain made for a pleasant companion. He walked, mulling over the conversation and the suggestion that he might be having visions. He rejected that. But there must be some pattern in the dreams that revealed something about his life and what was going on inside of him. Normally, this was exactly the kind of intellectual game he relished. Though he had to admit he was more comfortable with riddles when they happened to someone else and not to him. He was somewhere midway across Midsummer Common, the indirect light of the city bouncing off the cloud cover and bathing the open field with an eerie glow, when he began to feel strange again. Like what he had experienced on his earlier walk across the Common.

I am hunkered beneath my umbrella and drawn inside my windbreaker against the beating rain and the wind. Sudden gusts blow the rain horizontally across my way and send spray in my face; my umbrella shakes and vibrates with each new burst as I hold it like a windbreak. Shadows of remote tree branches dance over the ground from distant street lamps. I realize that I have slipped into a dream when I nearly collide with a solitary man. Neither of us speaks, though we stop very close to each other, eyes locked. I wonder about him. But nothing about his appearance suggests an identity. His clothing marks him as not a contemporary of mine, but I can't guess which century might be his. Perhaps he is the visible echo of one of those medieval merchants who used to ply their wares on these grounds.

There we stand, he and I, looking at each other. He is silent. Thoughtful. Wrapped against the rain and chill in a nondescript rough-looking garment, perhaps woven of unbleached wool. His hair is dark and long-cropped just above shoulder length and matted and wet from the rain. He looks wild and unkempt. But compelling. His full but patchy beard and dark heavy eyebrows frame a swarthy rough pockmarked complexion. I don't find his square-jawed face handsome exactly. But it carries strength and is oddly appealing. Dark eyes peer at me with an intensity that I find magnetic. And frightening. I reach out to touch him. I don't seem to be able to resist. Perhaps I want to see if he's real. I find the sodden cloth of his garment as coarse to the touch as it looks, and I can feel flesh and bone beneath. He shows no reaction to my intrusion on his physical space. Then to my surprise his face lights up as if in sudden recognition, and he smiles at me. He has a wonderful smile, one that makes me feel warm and confident all over. I'm no longer frightened of him.

Now I'm alone again, looking toward the end of the Common and the street beyond. I can feel the rain seeping through my jacket and onto my skin. No apparitions rise up to keep me company. I find relief in that. Still, I have the nausea and aching limbs that I've come to think of as my dream withdrawal. I lose my dinner. The bile of partially digested curry and apple crumble leave a sour taste in my mouth. I feel half in and half out of the dream state. I'm shaking, and I'm sure I must be as pale as a ghost. Ghost? Is that what I've seen? Something more fantastic than all of the other characters from my dreams? I can't even find a comfort in his historical identity, because for me nothing has suggested one. I have no clues whatever to go on. I return to feeling frightened by him. I'm also drawn to the thought of him. I realize that I miss him now that he's gone. Am I losing my mind?

chapter eight

Brian's morning run took him out into a bright July day. He went south of the town center along the Cam, through Lammas Land, across the Fen Causeway and onto Coe Fen where fat cattle grazed on tall grasses. Ducks and geese rode the river or sunned on its banks with their young. Small pieces of bread tossed onto the river would bring waterfowl from all directions to pounce on the crusty dry bits. A lone black swan swam elegantly among the others. A family of two white swans and their signets seemed to have outlawed it; they were nowhere to be seen this morning. That elegant black creature (he or she?) was a lonely figure on the river. Brian could relate to that swan. Like him (Brian decided it had to be a male.) no other living being shared his immediate world with him. Each of them seemed doomed to inhabit a lonely universe.

That sense of his aloneness struck Brian especially as he entered a stretch of path that wound through a forested area where ferns and thistles, stinging nettle and willow trees presided. The riot of plant life threatened to overrun the walkway. Insects buzzed. Scents of decomposing vegetation mingled with the perfume sent out by low flowers and shrubs.

In that quiet space his thoughts returned to the ghostly figure from Midsummer Common. That spectral image, though friendly enough, didn't seem to fit into Brian's recent experience at all. Nothing anywhere in his past suggested such an encounter. Only the phantom horsemen of his recent dreams had lacked a definable place in historical fact. Even they could be pinned down from their dress and weapons to the early sixteen hundreds. Brian always assumed that they would also have identities once he could figure out who they were. Even Julian had historical substance, however troubling and exciting his conclusions about her might be. But he could find no way to connect this new image with the solid world of data, events and people. Living or dead. There were no clues. No research projects or speculations suggested themselves, and he seemed to see the ghostly apparition everywhere. In long corridors at the University Library. Lurking in the stacks. Was he hiding behind the tall grass beside the river? Brian turned to stare. Nothing. How ridiculous. Yet that coarsely handsome face, patchy beard and penetrating eyes seemed to stalk every quiet moment, dancing before his mind's eye and leaving him feeling uneasy and a little frightened. Brian could find no avenue for retreating into the comfortable world of historical data and research to pin down the Ghost.

He left the woods and continued his run along the edge of a sleepy suburban neighborhood before returning to the open pasture along the river. This route led to Grantchester, the village Rupert Brooke immortalized in his poem about its vicarage. He thought about a place there where a person could get tea and scones and sit among the fruit trees while wallowing in Brooke memorabilia. The poet made him think of Jeannie and her fondness for the war poets. He made a mental note to take her there when she arrived.

Jeannie had instantly recognized what he found so disturbing about his latest dreams and, in one of her emails, offered a fresh twist, "I once read somewhere that dreams can have healing powers. It's not so much that you're suddenly cured of something overnight, but that gradually your psyche dumps stuff out of your unconscious and you become more ordered and untroubled. Maybe that's what's happening to you, even though it may not seem like it. At least not yet, it doesn't." Brian thought she might very well have a handle on something of what was happening to him. He hoped she had.

He finished his run back through Lammas Land, where laundresses of past centuries had laid out sheets and drawers to dry. A gaggle of geese had taken over the place on the river where the black swan had been before. Brian thought a lot about that swan these days. What crime had the bird committed that he had been rejected by the other swans and cast into an isolated and lonely life? The creature simply reeked of alienation. Perhaps the beautiful animal was prideful of his difference from other creatures. Or maybe it was simply a matter of nature: an unconnected male and therefore a threat to the signets. Whatever the cause, Brian thought a lot about the swan's dilemma.

Mary Beth surprised Brian nearly as much with her second contact as with the first one. He had settled in at the desk in his sitting room after finishing his morning run. He straightened some papers, booted up his laptop and checked his email. While the computer pulled in his messages he went out to the kitchen to pour himself a cup of freshly brewed coffee. He stirred in milk and sugar, shrugged and then put a piece of Lemon Slice, a tasty sweet citrus-flavored cake from Tesco's Superstore, on a small plate. "Not the best breakfast fare," he admitted to himself. He carried them both back with him to the sitting room and looked at his inbox. Mary Beth's note waited there along with a dozen other ones, mostly spam. The "from" column read "eschumann." At first he simply exhaled aloud, "Who the hell is eschumann? More spam?" and picked up the piece of Lemon Slice and opened his mouth to bite into it. Then he remembered, "E" for Elizabeth, and his heart stopped. He dropped the piece of frosted yellow cake onto the floor. Probably just as well, he thought as he clicked on the message. Suddenly the room filled with Mary Beth.

"Surprise," she wrote. "If you're reading this, I must have been successful in getting your email address off my search engine and reaching you. If not then it just doesn't matter, does it? I was so excited to get your letter! I even checked you out. You have really written and published a lot. How did you find time to do all that and have a child, let alone assorted wives? Sorry about that. You asked about my children, and I have three, all boys: Jason is sixteen, Jeremy is fourteen, and Jared is nine. Yes, I know, their names all start with "J." Their father's vanity, I'm afraid. His name is James middle initial "L." Corny as it sounds, all four are JLS. JLS senior founded and runs, you guessed it, JLS Pharmaceuticals. Rich bastard. All kinds of bastard."

Mary Beth married a rich guy? "Figures," Brian muttered

aloud before reading on.

"James is dull. My boys are anything but. At the moment I have a budding quarterback, one who wants to play trumpet, and a dreamer who always seems to have his nose in a book. He loves Harry Potter. They are great kids. I'll stop now and make sure this is actually reaching you before I get too carried away. Let me know if you get this, and I will write more."

She signed the email, "Love, Mary Beth."

Brian sat staring at the computer screen and then reread the email more slowly. Still he stared. "Shit," he finally said aloud. "Shit. Shit. Shit." He reached down and picked up the Lemon Slice and dumped it into the wastebasket beside the desk as if it had been the vilest thing on earth. Then he got up and stomped around the room, alternately frowning and then smiling as he tried to adjust to yet another intrusion of Mary Beth into his life. Finally he exploded into the kitchen, slammed the frying pan onto the hob and popped in a wide slab of butter. Far too much butter. He struck a wooden kitchen match against the side of its box and lit the burner. "Shit," he said again, lighting the broiler with the same match. "'Love, Mary Beth,'" he muttered in disgust. Where did she come off saying *love* to him that way? Why had he ever responded to her first letter? He placed two thin slices of brown bread under the broiler to toast and dropped two eggs into the hot pan and watched them sizzle. The edges of the eggs began to crinkle. He flipped them over. He liked his eggs cooked hard. Mary Beth. Just what the hell did he do now? He knew what he wanted to do, what he couldn't resist doing. Reaching into the oven, he quickly turned the toast, feeling the searing heat of the broiler on his hand. They were still too light; he would let them brown well on the second side. But the heat on his hand almost felt good. A self-destructive wish? It seemed to fit his present frame of mind. Mary Beth had always been that for him. An exercise in self-destruction. What now? It couldn't hurt to write her back. Could it? He had to face up to the truth: he wanted to answer her, damn it.

He stomped purposefully back into the sitting room. Mary Beth's email still showed on the screen. He clicked "reply" and keyed quickly, "You found me all right. Good piece of detective work. Impressive. But you always were impressive. Three kids, huh? I seem to remember that you had at least two. Still impressive. Sounds like their old man is a bit arrogant. I remember having met him. At the tenth anniversary dinner. Self-possessed. That's what I thought of him. Doesn't fit the Mary Beth I knew. How did you ever come to be married to someone like that?

"As for my marriages, both were busts. The present one should never have happened. The first one might have done better, but I just couldn't stop working all the time—as you noticed. There was also some unfinished business that got in the way." He wondered if she would recognize herself as the unfinished business. Probably not. He would die rather than let her know how he had carried a torch for her all those years. There was no way he would let Mary Beth disrupt his life again. No way.

A nasty odor suddenly broke into his thoughts. Something burning? "Oh, my God. My eggs. My toast." He ran into the kitchen. Smoke poured out of the oven, and a horrid stench rose from two blackened round blobs in the frying pan. He turned off the gas and opened the broiler door. More smoke. He grabbed for the frying pan to put it in the sink and run cold water over it. "Ouch." The hot pan clattered to the kitchen floor. "Shit." He thrust his hand under the tap instead. Then, realizing how many times he had used that expletive already this morning, he said, "What an excremental day," and began to laugh with a hysterical edge that even he could hear. "Better get the pan off the floor before it burns a hole in the linoleum," he sputtered, still laughing and, at the same time, feeling like an idiot. Mary Beth had done it to him again. He pulled a dishtowel from the rack beside the sink and used it to pick up the frying pan. This time he made it to the sink and drowned the disgusting stink with a flood of cold water.

Climbing the stairs to the bathroom, he rummaged around until he found a tube of salve for his hand. It felt better immediately as he rubbed it in and went back down to the sitting room. Mary Beth. What was it about her that brought such chaos into his life? He sat down at the laptop once more and wrote, "Just burned my eggs and toast. What a smell. I guess I'm still the dumb ass I always was. Damn, but it's good to be writing to you." He signed off with a simple, "Brian."

After he had clicked on "send," he sat staring out the window off across Lo-Host's inner courtyard and its green lawn. Without actually seeing anything and laughing at himself with the absurdity of it, he imagined a nineteen-year-old Mary Beth and the Ghost dancing across the grass together.

Brian wondered what Mary Beth looked like after ten years. Twenty-five, really. In his mind she hadn't changed since he first laid eyes on her at the beginning of their freshmen year. Had child-bearing and the years put weight on her? Did she still have a mass of curly black hair as she did in college? Or was it turning gray? Salt and pepper maybe? Had she dyed it some other color entirely? He tried to remember how she had looked when he saw her at their college reunion. Somehow that image always faded and the old freshman one, the original one, returned. For him she remained the tall raven-haired goddess of 1977. He couldn't wait to get home to see if he had another email from her.

But no messages awaited him. None came the following day either. Instead, an email from Jeannie brought him back to earth. A scant few hours remained before she and her daughter left for O'Hare to catch the plane to Britain. "Don't forget," she wrote, "you promised to take me running along your favorite route and to visit Grantchester and all those Rupert Brooke places. I remember when we ran together along the lakefront and how much fun it was."

He wondered if he should tell Jeannie about Mary Beth. No reason he shouldn't. But what would he tell her?

Brian reread the lavender note that he had been holding onto for weeks. It still read "August 2, 11 A.M." as he knew it would. He looked at his watch. Jeannie and Candy would soon be over the Atlantic. He looked around critically. The flat was clean, and the pantry stocked. The bedder had made up a single bed for him in the corner of the sitting room. That's where he would sleep tonight to keep the bedroom fresh for his guests. Downstairs, a rental car sat waiting to go to Gatwick early the next morning. What would it feel like having Jeannie and her daughter under the same roof with him? Would they be self-conscious and awkward with each other? Why should they be? He and Jeannie had always been comfortable together. The thought of having her to talk to and to do things with after nearly two months alone gave him a little stir of excitement. Had he ever before been excited about the imminent arrival of houseguests? Probably. But he didn't remember it. He finally fell into a fitful sleep, repeatedly interrupted by the fear of oversleeping.

The next morning he was up early, excited about the day ahead. Thoughts of Mary Beth had been expunged. He checked a dozen times to make sure that he had his maps and all the details of the trip straight. The planning was complete, right down to the final turn into the airport parking lot. That was his way. Always careful about the details. Life kept under control. He looked at his watch. Nearly time to leave. He decided to check his email one last time before getting on the road.

The usual litter of departmental business and spam also included notes from Mary Beth and from his daughter, Bobbie. He quickly disposed of the spam and dealt with the work, impatient to read what his daughter had to say and unable to deny the conflicting feelings that Mary Beth's waiting email raised in him. He called up Bobbie's short note. She asked if she could come to visit the first week of September, right after she finished with her summer internship and before classes began for the fall semester. He wrote back an enthusiastic affirmative. Then he turned with mounting anticipation to the note from Mary Beth. It was the first one to come since what he thought of as the morning of the burned eggs.

"Sorry it has taken me so long to get back to you," she wrote. "Work and kid stuff. The only time I've had to myself has been late in the evening, and I haven't had a computer at home to use. James took the old one when he left, and I can't really use one of the boys', especially in the evening. Anyhow I've been wondering how you are coping with your divorce. You said that it isn't a big deal, but I suspect you are being heroic. There's no way something like that can feel good. Let me know how you are doing so we can commiserate with each other."

The thought that Mary Beth might empathize with him over anything seemed absurd.

"I have been thinking," she continued, "about when we were in college. You were always so sweet and attentive. I did appreciate it. Our breakup made me so very sad, but you wanted a much more serious relationship than I was ready for. Did you know I was a virgin? I was, and I knew that if you and I ever crossed that line I would probably never finish college. You made me really scared.

"Sorry, I didn't mean to rake all that up, but I thought you ought to know after all these years why I was so determined to keep you at a distance. Have to run now. I'm going to go out and buy a new computer. Lots more later."

She signed it as before with "Love."

Brian reread the email. Then he read it a third time.

All the way to Gatwick he thought about Mary Beth's new email. She had shut him out in college because she cared too much? Or at least that seemed to be what she meant, even if it wasn't exactly what she had said. What if he had not been such a dumb ass, if he had been more patient with her, then what might their lives have looked like? Maybe no divorces. The perfect life? Or would their relationship have suffered from the same obsession with work that the marriage with Bobbie's mother had done? Then he remembered Bobbie. She wouldn't exist in that scenario. All the rest of his life would be different. He rejected thoughts of turning back the clock, even if he could. One change would have huge consequences. He thought about Jimmy Stewart's character in the movie *It's a Wonderful Life* in which that very scenario had been played out. Silly stuff. The English countryside sped by outside his car as he circled around metropolitan London to Gatwick Airport.

Jeannie and Candy came dragging through customs and into the central reception hall, travel-worn but excited. He felt the tears on his face. It wasn't like him to cry. He embraced Jeannie. They lingered.

"Damn, it's good to see you," he said at last. "I—I guess I've been pretty lonely."

She seemed to study him with her clear blue eyes. Had he ever really noticed the expressiveness of those eyes? All thoughts of Mary Beth and ghostly apparitions were driven from his mind.

"I've missed you a lot, too, Brian," she said.

They stood looking at each other for what seemed like a long time. He began to feel awkward, and to have feelings he didn't normally associate with Jeannie. His friend, Jeannie.

"Hey? What about me?" Candy said. "Don't I get any hugs?"

"You certainly do, missy." Brian reached out an arm and gathered her to them in a three-way clinch.

On the Motorway they negotiated the heavy midday traffic. "When do I get to see a castle?" Candy asked. "I can't wait." She seemed to effervesce as she bounced up and down on the seat.

"I've promised her many wonders," Jeannie said, laughing.

"I'll find you a castle real soon." Brian grinned back. "There's lots of old stuff in Cambridge. Churches and things. But only a bit of a ruined castle. Sorry, but mostly it's just a mound of earth."

Candy's fast-talking reply was, "It's so weird driving on this side of the street."

"You'll get used to it," her mother promised.

They drove quietly.

"I have an idea," Brian said, breaking the silence. "Just up ahead is the turn-off for the M4. We could take that and be in Windsor in a few minutes. I know a place on the High Street that used to do a pretty good lunch. Are you hungry?"

"I could eat," she said. "How about you?"

"Do they have fries?" Candy asked.

"To die for."

"Windsor has the granddaddy of all castles. It's one of the Queen's residences," Jeannie said. "I think that would be perfect, Brian. What a good idea." She reached over and touched his forearm. They shared a moment's eye contact. Her expression formed a curious combination of playfulness and something else he couldn't quite place.

Candy soon crashed on the back seat. That left Brian and Jeannie to talk

"I was afraid we would feel like strangers, hardly friends anymore," Jeannie said.

"I was a little unsure, too." He concentrated on his driving.

"But relax. You're no stranger than ever."

"Thanks a lot."

"How are the dreams?"

"Speaking of strange?" He took a deep breath and changed the mood. "Nothing I haven't told you about. Just hints of that unidentifiable man. It's as if I'm always expecting to see him everywhere. So I kind of do. Nothing substantial, though."

A little snore came from the rear seat.

"She really is asleep."

"She's a tired girl."

The Braised Beef was an ordinary provincial restaurant with pretensions to being more. But it served up Angus beef in any number of acceptable ways. Candy got a plateful of English chips that, along with her beef burger, drove away all cravings. Brian and Jeannie had steak frites and salad. The castle is Windsor's real attraction. It stands noble and glowering. High walls, battlements, state apartments and the massive round keep more than satisfy any child's romantic notions of what a castle might be. Indeed, it may have been, if anything, bigger than Candy had imagined—or so the expression on her face suggested. Brian thought it would be fun to show her one of the old Welsh castles, like Caerphilly, something really rough and wild. In the meantime Windsor's liveried attendants did not disappoint. They strutted back and forth and kept their formal watch over the goings on in this, the source of the royal family's surname. They walked with a crowd of tourists through St. George's Chapel, the banners of the Knights of the Garter offering faded splashes of color.

Candy exclaimed in disbelief, "You mean there are *dead bodies* under there?" She acted as if she didn't want to put her feet on the paving stones. "Not *even*."

Brian laughed and said, "And lots of them are kings, too."

"Sick!"

Spending an hour as tourists was about all they had in them. Soon the Ford Focus resumed its way around London and on to Cambridge. This time both of Brian's passengers napped. He looked over at Jeannie as a lock of red hair curled in rebellion over her forehead. It was all he could do to stop himself from reaching over and setting it right.

It might have been a well-rehearsed routine. Brian fussed about in the kitchen washing up a few glasses and snack things while Candy got ready for bed down the hall in his bedroom. She quickly fell asleep. Cambridge had done its work in charming her, specially the street full of fashionably dressed young people. He and Jeannie's early awkwardness with each other had evaporated, leaving them as companionable as before. Jeannie took a leisurely bath while Brian read. Finally, she joined him for a promised nightcap. His heart leapt when he saw her. She wore a night dress and robe of pink cotton, making her look like Candy's sister, instead of her mother, soft, vulnerable and lovely. The perfect combination of mature femininity and soft freshness. He put down his book and went to the little makeshift sideboard on a bookshelf.

"What can I get you?"

"How about a glass of red wine? I noticed there's an opened bottle there."

"You've got it." He poured glasses for them both. "It's a good thing there's only the two of us. That's how many wine glasses I have." He laughed. The awkwardness returned.

She took the glass and touched it to Brian's in an otherwise silent gesture. A breeze coming through the open window rustled the curtains and felt cool and fresh. Jeannie sat in the wing chair while Brian perched on his desk chair. They made small talk. He told her more about his research project and his interest in Plain Jane. She told him about her class on the war poets that had just ended. He began to think about what it would be like to kiss her lips. Then he noticed that her eyes were drooping and her head had begun to nod. He finished his wine. She put her unfinished glass down on the end table beside the chair.

"You look as if you're going to fall asleep right there," he said.

"I guess I am. Sorry."

"No need to apologize." He stood up. "You'd better get yourself off to bed."

"You're right. I'd like to sit here and talk with you, but . . . well, perhaps I should." She stood up."

Tension filled the room.

Finally she stepped over to where he stood, put her hand on his forearm and kissed him lightly on the cheek. It felt like the gesture of a sister, though he'd never had a sibling by which to judge. "See you in the morning," she said lightly.

"Sleep well."

She turned and walked to the door, stopping just long enough to throw him what felt like a wistful smile. Perhaps he read more into that smile than was meant. But that unspoken and perhaps unintended meaning was exactly what he wanted to read at that moment. It carried conclusions he wished to draw, promises he wised to infer, whether or not the smiler had intended them.

After she had gone, he fussed around a bit getting ready for bed, acutely conscious of her presence behind the closed bedroom door across from the bathroom. Finally, he settled into the bed in the sitting room with his current light reading. In the morning, he left a note for Jeannie and Candy telling them that he was going to work in the library for awhile, and that he'd see them for lunch.

chapter nine

God, I love this town," he said.

"Even loaded down the way it is today with students and tourists?" Jeannie asked.

"A typical weekend. Part of its charm." Brian leaned back in his chair and looked around the sidewalk café. On their table lay a china teapot and matching cups, saucers and plates: white and ringed by wreaths of tiny red and blue flowers. A few telltale crumbs and a couple of renegade currants remained on the plates. Little white ceramic tubs of clotted cream, mostly wiped clean, and ones with bright red strawberry jam sat in a jumble of cutlery. Brian loved a proper English cream tea. He looked out at the clusters of chattering people and listened to snatches of at least half-a-dozen languages being spoken. They too seemed to be enjoying the bright August afternoon. "Ah, yes, summertime in Cambridge," he sighed.

Jeannie smiled.

"But isn't there anything to *do* in this place?" Candy asserted her age-appropriate contrariness. Her eyes followed an apparent class of French students about her age, seeming to take in every movement of the group as it moved along like an undulating centipede. Each member held a notebook in hand and seemed to listen to the guide with rapt attention.

"What would you like to do, Sweetheart?" Jeannie said to her daughter and then, grinning, asked Brian, "Is it always this crowded?"

"I wish I could be with one of the groups," said Candy.

"At least on summer weekends it is," said Brian. "It's always pretty busy around here." He didn't know what to say to Candy.

Directly opposite the café on St. Mary's Passage loomed the stolid Gothic pile of the University Church, Great St. Mary's. Twenty yards to their left and across King's Parade visitors clustered outside the Perpendicular entrance gate to King's College. On the corner of St. Mary's Passage and

King's Parade, beside the rising bollards that regulated vehicular traffic into the pedestrian precinct, stood a handful of university students in brightly colored period costumes singing Tudor anthems. Brian stretched with contentment.

"Isn't that Orlando Gibbons they're singing?" Jeannie asked, a tiny frown playing across her brow.

"Could be," Brian said, sitting up straight again. "'Fraid I'm no expert. If my friends Jeff and Charlie weren't away on the Continent, Charlie'd straighten us out in a minute." He gave Jeannie a mock inquiring look, "And speaking of music experts, what do you know about Orlando Gibbons?"

She looked enigmatic. Their eyes smiled back at each other.

"You guys are ignoring me. Okay if I go over to the market and look around?" Candy said, standing up from the table.

"No problem," her mother answered. "See you in a few minutes?"

The girl tossed her head, grinned, and moved away like a slalom skier, dipping and maneuvering through the bunched masses of milling people toward the street market a block down St. Mary's passage. The singers ended one piece, accompanied by a ragged scattering of applause, and started another.

"And who's the composer of this one?" he asked, smiling.

"I think it's something Spanish, but I'm afraid it fools me."

"They're pretty good, though, don't you think?"

Jeannie nodded, cocked her head to the side and smiled in agreement. "This place is absolutely alive. I have no trouble understanding why you like being here."

"It's lots more fun, though, sharing it with you." He reached out his hand and squeezed hers for a moment. That felt comfortable and normal, but the energy soon changed into acute discomfort. They disengaged. The tension that had haunted them since her arrival, if anything, had grown. Again he surveyed the scene before him. The warm sun felt good on his face. He listened to the singers.

Over the last week, they had wandered the town's streets

together and enjoyed each other's company, without ever leaving Cambridge. Often they bumped into each other as they walked, sometimes lingering. From time to time they caught each other's eye and a silent communication, mostly unintentional, passed between them. But neither of them spoke of the tension that hovered over them like a fragrant cloud. They both seemed to know that if the words were ever spoken there would be no turning back. Each night they would say goodnight, and Brian would fall asleep in his sitting room thinking about Jeannie's nearness: the red halo around her head made by her hair; the freckles that danced like elves across her nose and cheekbones; the swell of her breasts; her slender waist and rising hips.

For her part Candy had skipped from one exciting discovery to another. "They have *dead bodies* under the floor here, too?" the girl had demanded one day when they were visiting a medieval parish church. "Sick." Another time they had been riding lazily down the Cam in one of the punts, and she had exclaimed, "I want to try. Can I try to make it go?" The handsome young Cambridge student who guided them relented. Candy clearly wanted to impress him. He showed her how to propel and steer the boat with its long pole. "Oh no! Oh no!" she had cried as the little craft headed directly into the bank. The guide laughed and resumed his duties.

Jeannie's voice broke into his thoughts. "I've been waiting for an opportunity to talk with you about a problem I'm having with the SU English Department, or more accurately, with its new head. I didn't want Candy to be part of the conversation."

Brian gave himself a mental shake to refocus his attention. "Oh?" he said.

"Francis—that's the chair's name—well, he has some rather trite ideas about how a recently divorced female junior faculty member might behave towards the head of the department. Towards him in particular."

"You mean that he's been making sexual advances?" "Advances?" She laughed out loud. "Where did you get that from? What a charming word, dated but charming."

Brian grinned. But he still felt uneasy. He didn't want to

hear about people putting the moves on Jeannie.

"But that's exactly what I do mean," she said, a serious expression settling on her face and the tip of her tongue poking out between pursed lips. She continued, "I hate that kind of sexual pressure. He makes me feel so vulnerable and insecure. Not being on a tenure track and all. For weeks now he's been getting more and more explicit, trying to get me to have drinks with him. He hasn't come right out and said he thinks I should sleep with him 'for the good of my career.'" She formed little quotation marks in the air with her index fingers. "But I'm sure that's where he's headed."

"Oh, come on. Surely that sort of thing doesn't really happen anymore. I know people are having affairs on campus all the time. But demands like that? The department head using his position in that way? Are you sure? Didn't that stuff go out with Clarence Thomas and Anita Hill?"

"I'm sure about this." She looked at him inquiringly. "Pull your head out of the sand." Her glance turned into a glare. "You be the judge. Here's what happened a couple of weeks ago. I ran into him in the hallway outside the departmental office. 'Drinks after work today? At the faculty club? Say around five,' he said. It felt more like a command than an invitation. 'Just the two . . . just the two of us?' He has this annoying habit of repeating his words. Anyhow, I had already turned him down so many times that he'd begun to develop a pinched expression on his nasty thin-lipped face."

"Ferret-faced, right? Isn't that the usual look for this scenario?"

She scowled back at him. He tried to feel chastened.

"You're as bad as Conrad, the old sweetheart in the department who's kind of taken me under his wing. When I mentioned my suspicions about Francis to him, all I got was, 'Oh, you must be mistaken. Francis wouldn't do anything as unprofessional as that. Besides, he's a happily married man.' I decided to go ahead and give-in to what might only be an innocent invitation to have drinks."

A bolt of jealousy passed through Brian, giving him real pause as he assayed his feelings. "And . . .?" he asked. She didn't seem to notice his discomfort.

"Oh, I thought of saying something like, 'I'm really not looking for a relationship just now.' But I knew that might be too risky to Francis's fragile ego. The problem is that without his active support, I have no chance whatever of getting on a tenure track. I don't want to give up my job at SU. I like it there, and I don't want to stay an adjunct forever. So I considered some other lines: 'Living with HIV gets so lonely, you know.'" She laughed. "Or, 'I think you and I could hit it off; my daughter really needs a father.' That would have scared him silly. Or, 'Yes, Lois and I were talking just the other day about what to do with husbands who wander.' To my knowledge I've never even set eyes on Lois Cardham, Francis's high-rolling wife. Or, I might have said, 'Are you kidding? You miserable little dweeb!' None of it washed."

Brian was relieved to laugh along with her.

"So, as I said, I marched off like a good little trooper to have a so-called quiet drink with the department head. I got to the faculty club just after five. You know the place. It's dark and cozy-feeling and has the friendly smell of old tobacco smoke and spilled beer." She grinned sarcastically.

"You make it sound so appetizing." Brian realized that he had been estimating how many individual pieces of flatware were on the table as he rearranged it, lining up spoons and knives like building blocks. Was that a sign of his being nervous? What was the matter with him? He looked back up at her.

"The club was nearly deserted when I walked in. The only people there were the bartender, Francis at one of the tables and another lone man on a barstool near the front door. You know, I do actually rather like the place. Its indirect lighting on shelves of books casts an academic ambiance and kind of lulls the likes of me into a receptive mood. He had chosen well."

Brian's anxiety increased.

"I once spent a dull cocktail party looking over the titles of the books. Mostly the discarded library of some former literature professor. All classics. Not a bad collection actually, considering how dated the criticism is. When I got to

Francis's table he stood up from his chair. It all seemed pretty natural. I let myself be embraced. That's when I knew I had a problem. He gave me this little smile—I swear his teeth looked pointed—and pushed his things, you know, his genitals, against my hip."

"He did what?"

"I'm not kidding. He had already ordered me a gin and tonic. How do you suppose he knew that G 'n T's what I usually drink? The more I thought about that the more it pissed me off. How dare he assume such familiarity with me? But I sat down and picked up the drink. My only interest at that moment was how I was going to get the hell out of there. Just then a beam of light from the ceiling caught his graying slicked-back hair. I'm not kidding." She flashed Brian an intense and humorless stare. "He reminded me of a sinister character in an old film. Add a white dinner jacket and he could easily have been in wartime Casablanca. Peter Lorrie maybe? I almost lost it." She grinned.

Brian fidgeted a bit, surveyed the scene in front of him, listened to the singers on the street corner opposite, and let what she was saying settle on him. It sounded like a typical seduction scenario. But surely not Jeannie.

"I sipped at my drink and tried to make casual conversation. Finally, Francis said, 'So, you must be wondering about your tenure track.' He toyed with his drink for a minute before he went on, 'You know that it's mostly up to me. To get the ball rolling and all.' He looked at me in a very direct and utterly unambiguous way."

"What an asshole!" Brian exploded and then realized that everyone was looking at him. He grinned, feeling stupid, and returned his attention to her.

"You said it. I must have answered him a little sharply. I don't remember exactly. But he looked surprised. I'm not sure about this now, but I think he glared at me. I felt threatened by him and began to say, 'You don't honestly believe . . .' Here I risk stretching my credibility, but that was exactly when my cell phone suddenly rang. Really, it did."

Brian realized that he was sitting on the edge of his chair.

"Isn't that amazing? If you put that in a movie, nobody

would believe it. It felt as if that silly little tune had saved me from opening my mouth and ending my career at SU on the spot." She grinned. "There was no question about saving me from Francis. My virtue was never at risk." She laughed again.

Brian suddenly felt better.

"At least not from him."

Brian's stomach began to knot up again.

"Anyhow, I excused myself. No doubt I sighed with relief. I rummaged through my handbag. I was really steaming by this point. It was Candy on the phone. 'Oh, hi Sweetie,' I say. She tells me that she's at a friend's house and doesn't want me to worry. That's our agreement. She calls on the cell and tells me where she is. But I say, 'Of course. Now I don't want you to be afraid.' Clearly, she thinks I'm nuts. 'Afraid of what, Mom?' she says. 'I'm just letting you know I'm at Ginny's.' I go on for Francis's benefit, 'I can be there real soon, honey. It's not all that far. I'm at SU. Just go inside and wait for me.' 'What *are* you talking about?' Candy demands. Poor child. 'Don't be nervous. Okay?' is what she gets back from me. But she's real quick on the uptake. 'Oh, I get it,' you're trying to get away from somebody. That's pretty funny. Then you're not coming for me right now?' 'That's right. I'm leaving immediately,' I say. 'You're wicked,' she says. 'You have no idea," I say. 'See you soon.' I closed the phone and put it back in my purse.

"'I'm sorry, Francis,' I said with all the innocence I could muster. 'My thirteen-year-old daughter has a problem. Needs me to rescue her.' I got up, sipped a little more of my drink and said, 'I hope we can finish talking about my tenure track another time. Real soon. And thanks for the drink.' I absolutely refused to flirt or be suggestive or show that I understood his real intentions. I wouldn't give him the satisfaction. A naive pose seemed better. Besides, I was still pretty mad. Francis looked a little startled and almost speechless. 'Sure,' he says. 'We can . . . we can talk about it.' But he said the last words to my back as I fled from that place and from him. I really owed Candy one."

"My God," Brian said. "I can't believe you have to put up

with crap like that." He meant to sound outraged to Jeannie, but he felt relieved at the way the story turned out.

He looked over at her as the singers began a familiar sacred piece, *If Ye Love Me*. "That's Thomas Tallis," he said in mock pride, aware of the deflection.

"The time really is flying by. I'm going to be so jealous of you being here while I'm back at SU duking it out with Francis."

"Maybe you should give up the job." He grinned. "You don't really need it to make a living, do you?" He acted as if he were joking, but he realized he was quite serious.

"No, not really. My trust fund mostly takes care of that. But I love my field, and I like what I'm doing. Those late Victorian and early twentieth-century British novels and the antiwar poets really get me. They have done since I first read them in High School: D. H. Lawrence, Elizabeth Bowen, T.S. Eliot, Siegfried Sassoon, Virginia Wolf—all of them. They seem like old friends. Besides, I need the university job as a research platform, entree into libraries and the like. While it might be unfashionable to admit in some circles, I also like my students: all their identity searches; the excitement they feel when they finally get a complex new idea; their scrambling grasp at adulthood. The whole teaching thing. They are very transparent—and so dear." Her eyes began to tear-up—such lovely eyes, so deep and blue—and one of her hands dropped on his forearm. Her fingers played a silent, absent-minded tune on his skin and sent mini electric shock waves to his brain.

"I'm going to miss having you—and Candy—here." He was sorry when she took her hand away.

She returned to the previous subject, "I can't imagine living the life of the leisured class. I'd get so bored. I want to work, and to get on a tenure track. I really do. Then I would finally begin to move up the career ladder. It's something everybody understands, and I really need to have that. I know how shallow it all is, but I want those marks of professional success. Otherwise, I'm just some kind of drone. Or a little rich girl playing at professor."

"Of course," Brian said, remembering when he had had a

similar professional ambition and commitment. What had happened to his own fondness for students and his engagement with their learning and their lives?

"But what about you, Brian?" Jeannie was saying, as if reading his mind. "You're the one who's having strange dreams. You seem so unsure, so unlike yourself. I'm worried about you."

"Oh, I'll be okay. I have so much work to do." He rubbed his hand over his eyes and across his forehead. He didn't know what else to say. So he fell back on his old standby of his work when he felt at a loss for words. Between the dreams and the reappearance of Mary Beth, to say nothing of what he thought of unfairly as *Emily's* divorce, life had become so vague, so unpredictable. Brian liked his life to have predictability. "Actually, would you mind if I went in to the library tomorrow morning. See if I can get a little work done?" Where had that come from? He hadn't actually thought about saying anything of the sort. He had no desire whatever to get to work. But suddenly there it was.

"Of course I don't mind," Jeannie answered. "Candy and I can find any number of things to do." But the look on her face registered surprise at his sudden change of direction.

My heartbeat quickens when I look at them. No mystery about the identity of at least one of the two men. Tall Elizabethan hat, formal black clothing and staff of office, long carefully groomed beard. All of it just as he appears in portraits. There's no mistaking William Cecil, Lord Burghley. Among Elizabethans only the face of the queen herself is more familiar to me than that of her Principal Secretary. But the other man is a stranger. I can tell by his clothing that he knows the good life of a high-ranking nobleman, but his face is unfamiliar. Nor does his arrogant bearing and manner identify him particularly. A great aristocrat, certainly. I can feel his power, both his physical strength and his apparent position in the world.

I look around and realize that Burghley, his companion, and I are all sitting on benches in what appears to be a college forecourt, my bench about twenty feet from the one where they sit together. Which college? I look around. Imposing Gothic buildings surround us on three sides. It looks familiar, but at first I can't place it. Then, glancing in the distance, I see the familiar shape of the Round Church, St. Sepulcher, and I know I'm in St. John's College. Not all of these buildings were here in Burghley's time. What do they see around them? Does it look the same to them as it does to me?

But, of course none of this is happening. Not really.

"And Sussex, then," Burghley says, "can we depend on him? God's eyes! He will return soon from Ireland."

"Aye. He has no fondness for the Favorite," says the other man, looks of arrogance and disdain painted on his face as if he had suddenly gotten a mouthful of something disgusting. "You can depend on all the Howards. Most particularly where Dudley is concerned." He seems to puff up with self-congratulation.

This conversation, then, occurs between representatives of two of the main factions at Elizabeth's court. The great aristocracy, of which the Howard family is among the most ancient and powerful; and the "meritocracy," the Cecil family clearly the most important among that group of Elizabethans. I know these two parties often side together against the shallow lineage and thin accomplishments of court figures like the queen's favorite, Robert Dudley, Earl of Leicester. It occurs to me that the other man in front of me, apparently a Howard, might very well be the Duke of Norfolk himself, the titular head of that family.

"And what of the Queen, then? Will she accept an Austrian match?" asks the haughty aristocrat.

"She smiles yet on our negotiations."

I'm getting very interested—and excited. Most of the information about the intrigues designed to marry off the second and final Tudor queen come from little more than the surmise and guesswork of historians. I remember the dream about Julian of Norwich. Maybe I'll be let into some of the secrets. By some means.

My attention shifts abruptly to the figure of another man in the forecourt, beyond the two men and outside their

line of vision. There's no mistaking his identity. My ghostly
companion from Midsummer Common is standing there
watching the whole scene and taking it all in. My focus
shifts again to the sudden appearance of the hard-riding
horsemen from previous dreams. The courtyard is
becoming positively cluttered. Here they come, riding
directly across the St. John's quad, except that they are still
not really there in their translucent semi-reality, or at least
what passes for reality in this never-never land of mine. The
same fierce-looking leader is urging his followers on as they
rush to get wherever it is they are going. As always, though,
they make no progress and get no closer. I am struck as
usual by their grim determined expressions.

And the dream begins to fade. It's as if the horsemen
have driven away all the other characters and leave me
with nothing but uncertainty. I am no longer there.
Everything hurts.

"Where did you go?" Jeannie broke into his thoughts
from the sitting room doorway.

"Have I been gone?" Brian noticed that he was fully
clothed and sitting in his wing chair. His stomach was
churning. He felt mildly disappointed at the dream's end,
wishing he could overhear more of that conversation and get
a line on something that might satisfy his historical appetite.
The whole experience was narcotic as never before. He
resented the phantom riders for seemingly ending it, but he
was glad to have seen the Ghost there. Somehow his presence
gave him confidence.

"What do you mean by, *have you been gone*? Don't you
know?" Did sharp words cover worry?

"I've had another one of those dreams. Do you mean that
I've not actually been here all the time?"

"Well, you're dressed, aren't you? I don't know what to
think."

Brian looked down at his clothes as if he had never seen
them before: the same polo shirt, khaki pants and brown
oxfords he had taken off the night before and left beside the
bed when he got undressed. He had gotten undressed, hadn't

he? Yes, he had clear memories of getting ready for bed and going to sleep. He felt disoriented, like a stranger in his own flat.

She stepped over to him, perhaps sensing his confusion, bent over, reached out and grasped both of his upper arms in her hands. "My God, Brian, you're shaking all over," she said. She reached out a hand and touched his cheek. "And you feel so cold."

His skin did feel cool, but he wasn't cold—at least not unpleasantly so. But, on second thought, maybe she was right. He began to feel chilly and noticed that, as she had observed, he was trembling. Cambridge may not feel exactly like the Bahamas this August, but it was hardly frigid. "It's sometimes like this afterwards—after one of the dreams," he said through chattering teeth. He stood up.

Jeannie pulled him to her and held him, petting his head as she might have done a small animal or a child. "What is this strange thing that's happening to you, Brian? I'm trying to understand it, but I just don't get it. Have you driven yourself too hard for too many years? I'm worried about you."

Gradually his trembling subsided. "I think it's okay," he said. "I really do." His gaze passed from the shadowed figure of Jeannie before him to the open window. It was an odd moment. He had gotten up, dressed and gone God-knows-where. The St. John's College quad? He looked at the illuminated digital clock on the VCR. 2:18. He knew he ought to be troubled by all of this, but for some reason he wasn't. Maybe having Jeannie there settled him. Or was it because the Ghost had appeared inside one of his historical dreams? With the phantom riders there too, it put everything together in one place. Or maybe only his brain unified the disparate parts. But his brain was what it was all about, wasn't it? And the conversation in the dream was so interesting. Now he was feeling mellow and optimistic. Jeannie continued to hold him. The trembling had stopped. And as it did the thought occurred to him: there might just be some purpose to the dreams. With the mounted men, the Ghost and specific historical people coming together perhaps he only needed patience and the pieces to the larger the puzzle would all fit.

Then he became aware of Jeannie as never before, of her arms around him, of the faint scent in his nostrils of her hair and soap. She felt soft and warm against his body. A breeze blew the curtains so that the light from the full moon outside cast its silvery light into the room. He looked at her eyes, glowing darkly, and at her freckled nose and cheeks. The curtains closed, and it became dark again. He put his arms, hanging until that moment limply at his side, around her and pulled her against him. He still gazed on her face and into her eyes. They kissed. It was natural that they should. He looked at her as the curtains parted again. The kiss repeated, hungry and eager this time. Then, with mutual desire and unspoken consent, they ended their supportive friendship and moved on into a new space with each other, one made more poignant perhaps in the time it had taken them to get there.

Everything that followed came slowly and deliberately like a string quartet playing Ravel, holding the passion only just in check so that the tension might peak and then move on to even greater intensity. The melodies and harmonies came rich, the counterpoint light and delicate. Plucked strings formed a rhythmic pizzicato. The resolution in the final chords left them vibrating. The quartet finished, they gradually and almost without noticing it drifted off to sleep in each other's arms, drawn together on the narrow bed, content and relaxed at last.

chapter ten

Brian packed up his laptop and stuffed it and some accumulated papers into the leather carrying case. After carefully arranging the carton of documents he had been working on and leaving a piece of low-acid paper to mark his place, he returned it to the manuscript librarian on duty. "Please keep this in reserve for me," he said. "I'll be back in a few days. Some other things I need to do." What he needed to do was be with Jeannie.

"Indeed," said the archivist, a wiry little man about Brian's age. He had seen the librarian almost daily since he had been in Cambridge, but he didn't even know his name.

Brian's attempt to get back to work had not been a success. He had had little enthusiasm for it. His powers of concentration had already been feeble at best. That was before last night. Mostly he wanted to think about what had happened between Jeannie and him. How he felt about that and about her. That warm friendship had instantly been converted into burning passion, at least for him. Mary Beth never entered his mind. Mysterious seventeenth-century women, dreams and ghostly apparitions were gone like yesterday's trash. His primary employment in the reading room that morning had been staring off into space. He wondered if he had a vacant expression on his face to match what was in his head.

Nodding to the archivist again and hefting the computer bag onto his shoulder, he got out of the library as fast as he could go. What an idiot he had been, thinking he might want to spend time away from Jeannie. Especially today. He thought about last night as he walked—delicious memories, sweet and warm. Every minute that lay before him seemed bright and filled with possibilities. He would catch Jeannie and Candy at Lo-Host before they left to go into the town center. He had no appetite today for a solitary meal, especially when he might share it with her. He had no desire for anything solitary. He climbed the stairs two at a time and opened the door expectantly. "Anybody here?" he called. But he had arrived too late. The flat echoed its emptiness. He was even less interested in a solitary lunch at home than in getting one on his own in town. So he put down the computer bag, turned and went back out the door. With luck he would find the others somewhere in the city center.

He was walking briskly along Silver Street when an idea crossed his mind. He and Jeannie had been talking about renting a car and getting out of Cambridge into the countryside. Why not today, this very afternoon? And why not visit sites associated with his dreams, maybe even a couple of cathedrals besides? "Yes, that's it," he said aloud. Norwich would be a good choice. It had it all. He knew that the castle was largely a ruin, but at least it was a spectacular ruin. Candy would love that. Then there was the cathedral; it was one of his favorites. Surely Jeannie would be charmed by it. The little St. Julian's Church would be his personal destination. Something about chasing his dream subjects to sites where they lived their lives, other than their old colleges in Cambridge, appealed to him.

He made an unsuccessful pass through the crowded Eagle Pub's courtyard, looking for mother and daughter. That was the only place at the Eagle where someone Candy's age could have lunch. He soon returned to the street feeling less and less like being alone and wishing he knew where to look for them. He made a quick circle around the market square, ignoring the produce, the tee shirts and the other assorted wares. The scents of fresh baked goods and fruit gave him a pang of hunger. He ignored it. The crowd held no fascination for him as he scoured the faces looking only for the familiar ones. Nothing. He glanced in a couple of the nearby restaurants before giving up. Finally he went into the Tourist Information Office to get some help renting a car. His impatience mounted as he stood waiting at the counter while the clerk, a pleasant enough young woman in a checked blouse, peered at her computer monitor and made some phone calls.

"Sorry, nothing this afternoon," she said at last. "Few of the major rental companies have offices in Cambridge, you know. Hertz has a small office at the rail station, but they're out of cars. You might find one in Peterborough. But as for Cambridge, tomorrow morning is the best I can do."

"That's fine," he said, feeling disappointed. "Please reserve a car with one of the local companies for tomorrow, then."

"Very good," she said and began clicking away on her keyboard again, finally printing out details for him. He handed over his credit card to secure the rental.

After making one more pass around market square, he gave up and decided to go back to the Eagle and at least find a liquid lunch. A pint of lager? Or maybe Guinness? That's the ticket. Didn't they call the dark Irish beer liquid bread? Might actually cheer him up.

The Eagle had become even more crowded than when he had been there nearly an hour before. He edged his way up to the front bar through laughing drinking people: a group of businessman in shirt and tie; a gathering of American students in jeans with backpacks; apparent shop and university workers; couples who were clearly there together. They made him feel suddenly very lonely and eager to be with Jeannie. How was he going to tolerate it when she went back to Chicago in a few days? But he wouldn't think about that now. He managed to order his pint, definitely setting aside the possibility of solid food for the moment. All of the tables were occupied, so he settled for his place at the bar. He watched as the bartender drew his pint of the Guinness —a unique ritual among beers. The head settled in the glass while the bartender got drinks for other patrons; he filled it a second time. Still, the glass sat settling as the dark part at the bottom gradually moved up to take over the light-colored head at the top. The cold stout finally came to rest on the bar in front of him. He paid for it, rested one foot on the brass rail in front of the bar and took a long pull from the glass. At about that moment he got the feeling that someone was watching him. Shaking off the creepy sensation that had him wondering if his Ghost were peering at him from one of the little alcoves at the side of the room, he turned and looked for an ordinary source of the intuition. He soon spotted Jeannie and Candy standing at the doorway to the courtyard, both of them grinning from ear to ear. His heart skipped a beat. The frustration of the morning evaporated as he let his face dissolve into a smile of pleasure. He walked to them.

Jeannie gave him a light kiss on the lips that sent his heart racing. She said, a look of inqiry in her eyes, "Do you think we can get a table?" She looked around at the courtyard as she dropped her hand onto his chest.

Candy gave them an inquiring look. This child was no dummy.

"Sure. I looked all over for you, and now—and now here you are."

"Got one!" Candy said suddenly as she pounced, beaming, on a small round table with an umbrella over it. In that instant all seemed right with the world.

The next day they began to explore outside the town. While Brian mostly still wanted to visit places connected to the subjects of his dreams he found an unexpected pleasure in seeing the historic sites through Candy's eyes. Ely Cathedral, a genuine medieval marvel, seemed to stun her. "How come it's so big when the town is so small?" she asked perceptively. But all things being equal she clearly preferred the shopping outside the close of Peterborough Cathedral to anything that the ancient buildings had to offer. She wasn't even impressed that girls were part of the Peterborough choir. "Well, duh!" seemed to cover that landmark innovation. Besides, they had already seen scores of ancient churches in Cambridge. On Wednesday, they searched out Little Gidding, the location where, early in the seventeenth century, Deacon Nicholas Ferrar and his extended family had created a kind of monastic community. On their drive down the country lane leading to the site, Candy kept voicing her disdain and lamenting what must have felt to her like a hopelessly lost driver and his hapless passengers. "Nothing could possibly be at the end of such a narrow road," she complained in an adolescent whine. "Besides, how do you know you have the right Gidding? What about Steeple Gidding or Great Gidding?" she asked referring to road signs they had passed. "Or is it *Stupid* Gidding? How many *Giddings* are there? What's a *gidding* anyway?"

"I haven't a clue about giddings, myself," Brian responded, "and I don't really know what's there . . . if we find it, that is." He laughed, genuinely enjoying himself and feeling more light-hearted that he had in years. He knew this was the euphoria of a new sexual relationship. A phenomenal new sexual relationship. Still, he reveled in the fresh new feelings. The excitement. The hope for the future. "Be patient and I promise something you'll really like after we finish here," he said. "How about lunch in one of the great old country houses?"

"Oh, sure. *Right.*"

"No, I mean it."

They finally came to the end of the narrow lane. He stopped the car beside a modern house that doubled as a Ferrar museum, gift shop and hostelry. They got out. The rolling hills of western Cambridgeshire spread before them: a patch-work quilt of cultivated fields, some bare and dark others light and yet others verdant with fresh growth. Distant steeples of rural churches poked their noses into the sky. Miniature villages with clusters of cottages dotted the hillsides. Even Candy's attention focused on the spectacle. The Little Gidding chapel stood weather-stained, tall and alone in front of a grove of trees. Surrounding it was an overgrown churchyard where weeds and tall grass and the inevitable headstones made up the sole occupants. Still, it looked not so much neglected as solitary.

"This is it, then? We came all this way to see *this*?" Candy's disdain was unambiguous.

But her tune changed the second she stepped inside the chapel. Something about the place seemed to inspire her into a mood of quiet and awe. A sense of mystery clung to it like a thick coat of dust. They wandered through the dim musty-smelling interior, lit by late morning sun streaming through stained glass and spilling across an interior of opposed choir stalls of carved old wood. Through a door off the small chancel they found what once must have been the sacristy. The room was absolutely bare except for a single candle ringed by a circle of pillows in the middle of the stone floor. The candle had spilled wax out onto the floor, but it was cold now as if waiting in anticipation for the kindling of a new flame.

"What's that?" Candy asked in a subdued voice.

"I don't know," Brian said.

"It looks like a meditation circle to me," Jeannie said. "Certainly nothing Nicholas Ferrar or George Herbert might have wanted to use." She stepped back into the chancel and then down into the quire. Brian followed behind. He began examining the wood carving on the stalls. Jeannie and Candy were similarly occupied.

"George Herbert. He's the reason I wanted to come here," Brian said, remembering his dream encounter with the poet. At that moment he had a strange sensation standing in a place where Herbert once stood. He wondered if he might be having a gentle place memory. Right here with Jeannie and Candy. As he thought that, he felt a breath of air on his neck. He smiled and turned around, expecting to see Jeannie. No one stood behind him. His smile faded and a chill climbed up his spine. For a moment he thought he saw the face of the Ghost in the corner of the chapel. But no ethereal figure finally materialized in the gloom. What an imagination. He shook it off.

"That is very cool. Is it for reals?" Candy's exclamations on her first view of Burghley House.

That brought smiles to the faces of Jeannie and Brian. "Oh, it's real all right," he said.

The Elizabethan mansion was one of the great country homes of William Cecil, Lord Burghley, and his descendants the Earls of Salisbury. Lord Burghley had been the central figure in Brian's most recent dream, one he would always associate with their first lovemaking. Closing his eyes, he could still see the scene in the courtyard of St. John's College as clearly as if the dream were happening now. Dreamlike, Burghley's turreted house sat on a hill in the middle of a park. It more than met the romantic expectations and fulfilled the dreams of an American teenager weaned on Walt

Disney and romanticized versions of the past. Cattle grazed and a lone hawk soared gently on the breeze. The scents of summer, of freshly mown grass and honeysuckle, drifted on the air. Candy ran ahead to get a closer look at the facade as they walked around to the front of the house from the car park. Brian and Jeannie strolled, arms around each other's waists, in delicious and companionable silence. They kissed lightly. It was a perfect day. He thought about the last three nights when they had been together on his single bed. Not even a fleeting memory of his dream about the house's builder interrupted for long those tender memories.

"This is how a person is supposed to live," he said, breaking into the stillness.

"You mean in a mansion and surrounded by all of this?" She waved her free arm in an arc.

"That would be okay, too, as long as you were there." He squeezed her. "No, I meant I could do this forever." He kissed her.

"Me, too," she said nestling against his side.

Candy turned and ran back toward them, "Are you two becoming boyfriend and girlfriend?" she asked.

Jeannie laughed.

Brian said, "Something like that."

"Cool." She ran off again.

They finally caught up with Candy, who could barely wait to eat lunch before touring the house. They ate steaming chicken pies with light flaky crusts and mounds of broccoli and peas. Sponge cake covered in fresh cream followed. Laughing tourists and day-trippers filled a room that had bright sun streaming through an entire wall of glass in this, the former orangery. Later as they joined a guided tour through the mansion Brian kept expecting something unusual to happen in this indisputable site of many of Lord Burghley's latter years. He certainly felt the presence of the great principal secretary—the usual kinds of historian's feelings. And he thought about the interrupted conversation over matrimonial designs on the queen held by her advisers. But nothing out of the ordinary came of his visit to Burghley House.

The following day they drove northeast to Norwich where they shopped in the pedestrian precinct and visited the cathedral and the Mustard Museum. "Another museum! Do they have an entire museum about *mustard*?" demanded Candy, incredulous, but was soon mollified when she got to see the ruined castle. They walked to St. Julian's, the presumed location of Julian of Norwich's anchorhold attached to the modest parish church. Brian already knew that the building had been rebuilt after heavy bombing in the Second World War had largely destroyed the original one. Despite that, he had a sense of actually being on the spot where the medieval mystic had spent much of her life. He looked through the window where she had adored the altar and waited for the Elevation of the Host. Had he expected the odd woman he had seen outside Jesus College to materialize—and he more or less did—he was disappointed. No Julian showed up, and there was no confirmation of his surmises over her identity and origin.

The drive back to Cambridge was mostly silent as Candy slept in the back seat and Jeannie dozed beside him.

A fresh email from Mary Beth threatened to burn a hole in his computer monitor. Brian had been about equally worried that one would come and that one wouldn't. Being in contact with her now seemed not quite right somehow. Still, he read with a familiar eagerness as she asked ordinary questions about what he had been doing. She wrote about herself, "I've been thinking about going to church again, and that's something I've not done in years. You remember what a good little Presby I used to be? Now I've been churchless for, dare I say, decades?"

Brian began to tap out a quick reply, "Why don't you just give in and go to the Episcopal Church? You know, the music and the poetic language, the brocade vestments—all of it. Ah, you know what I . . ." He stopped abruptly. Trying to persuade her to change to his church had always been one of their bantering jokes in those long-ago college days. But he couldn't pick up the game. He realized that he lacked a persuasive argument for her. Maybe he's the one who should try something new? He scrapped the email he had begun and instead expressed his best wishes that new and interesting things would soon appear in her life. He was bored by his own banality.

But he was shocked by his inability to resume the old joke. What had happened to his passionate attachment to the Episcopal Church? To the Church of England? Somehow in trying to resume the decades-old jest he was brought face to face with the uncomfortable admission that he had changed and that what had once mattered a great deal to him no longer carried any power whatsoever. He sat in front of the computer, playing the inevitable game of solitaire and wondering if it had only been habit that had driven him out of the house most Sunday mornings, except for a couple of periods of lapse, since childhood. Almost without his even noticing it church attendance had ceased to be a part of his weekly routine.

And what about this continuing obsession with Mary Beth? How can you continue to obsess over someone you haven't seen in years? He knew what he felt for Jeannie was the first throes of infatuation, but he suspected that something deeper might very well lie beneath that exciting surface. Yet in the quiet and private of his solitary hours, he still thought of Mary Beth.

The fun of being with Jeannie tended mostly to supplant those random thoughts during the day, only to have them return again in the quiet moments of the night. Brian hungered for a life of emotional clarity uncluttered by so much ambiguity. An impossible hope at the best of times, he had always heard. But why must that be so?

Despite all of the reasons why he shouldn't want to do it, little by little Brian was coming to face the uncomfortable truth that he wanted to see Mary Beth again, even despite what had happened between him and Jeannie. Whatever held him in bondage to his college flame its persistence was undeniable.

He was startled out of these thoughts by Jeannie calling from the kitchen.

"Do you want some eggs this morning? Done how? Our

time's running out. There's some stuff I want to do today. Before it's too late."

They celebrated Jeannie and Candy's last night by going to Brian's favorite Italian eatery, the Pizza Express in Jesus Lane. Housed in a defunct Victorian men's club, the place still held memories of black cigars, port wine and dozing patriarchs under tents formed from pages of the *Times*. One central room still retained its wood paneling, crystal chandeliers, rows and rows of leather-bound books and portraits of stout Victorian Tories—all from its heyday as the Pitt Club. Even Candy was impressed.

"This isn't like any pizza place I've ever been to," Candy said. Strains of the solo jazz piano in the combination bar and entry hall could be heard beneath the talk and laughter of the cheek-by-jowl crowd.

"You like it?" Brian asked lightly without expecting a reply. A little smile danced on his lips. Inside, sadness was welling up and threatening to choke both him and his appetite.

Jeannie saw through his pretense. She reached for his hand under the table, squeezing it encouragingly, and showing him that she shared what he felt. The truth of their impending separation could not be denied. Jeannie and Candy would be leaving the next morning, and Brian would soon be on his own again with the solitude and freedom to read and research undeterred by someone else's needs. That was an experience he had always welcomed before. But now he wasn't so sure. He would miss Jeannie terribly. So many personal uncertainties tore at him, ones he would rather not face alone. Jeannie had become like a part of him.

Later that night they lay in each other's arms on the narrow bed. Their loving had been sweet and even a little sad. Her tears left damp reminders on his chest of their time together and of its imminent end. The bright Cambridge moon spilled through the window into the room, illuminating their faces in a pale glow.

Brian's confusion grew as his emotions tugged at him. What was it about his relationships with everyone in his life?

He seemed to be looking through a sheet of plate glass at the people closest to him. He could see them, appreciate their strengths, respond to their beauty or their flaws, but still he couldn't reach them. Oddly, they could touch his body and he theirs, but their souls and his remained disconnected from each other. The one exception had been Mary Beth. She had touched and then torn at him as no other person had ever done before or since.

And now there was Jeannie. God, he was enchanted by this beautiful brainy woman. He kissed her lightly on the forehead and ran his hand up and down her arm. She tucked into him at his touch. More tears dripped onto his chest, warm and wet, shocking his flesh with their sweetness.

"You're awake, then, Brian?"

"Yes."

"The thought of leaving you alone here really troubles me."

"I hope you'll miss me. But why should it trouble you?"

"Oh, I'll miss you for sure. I hope it's not some kind of premonition, but I'm worried." She was silent for a long moment. "Oh, don't pay any attention to me. I'm probably just feeling bummed about our being separated now that we've finally found each other. Promise me that if you get too unhappy—or whatever—that you'll hop on a plane and come home."

"I promise." But his voice was small and weak like hers. "I love you, Jeannie."

"I love you, too, Brian."

Brian could not escape the conviction that the next time he saw Jeannie it would not be with such uncomplicated joy as on this visit. He did not believe in premonitions—or at least that was what he had always told himself. But something seemed final and uncompromising about their parting. He felt alone and very unhappy, almost as if he were grieving a death. At times he would choke up and fight back the tears that threatened to fill his eyes.

That night, ordinary but unsettling dreams troubled his restless sleep: of Jeannie's departure accompanied by an

empty longing; of email cluttering his in-box demanding
something of him; of Mary Beth as she had been over two
decades ago, taunting and laughing at him; of the square-
jawed Ghost, expressionless but intense. Even his new
friends Jeff, Charlie and Carol seemed more scornful in his
dreams than helpful, more derisive than supportive. Asleep
or awake, Brian felt very alone.

*I am walking south along the Cam through the Backs
toward Silver Street. Queen's Road is on my right and
King's College on my left. Ahead and across the river is
Queen's College. The path under my feet is made of carefully
tended packed earth, and on it I can see ahead to a low spot
where rainwater tends to gather and form a puddle.
Alongside the path some quiet pools in a small rivulet of the
Cam have become the home of a family of moorhens living
among a hodgepodge of lily pads.*

*Except for the moorfowl, I see only my companion. He
says nothing. He just walks silently along with me, looking
neither to the left nor to the right. His angular jaw is set and
fixed. I remember my first encounter with him on
Midsummer Common and the way he seems to be—or at
least I feel him to be—lurking everywhere I go. I realize that
I don't feel alone or lonely. Nor do I feel especially
threatened by him. Perhaps he is my friend after all and
doesn't pose some fresh danger to me.*

*I notice the oddest thing. Walking at my normal relaxed
gait, my walking partner keeping pace beside me, I seem to
be on some kind of weird invisible treadmill. We walk, but
we don't get anywhere. Queen's College remains just as far
away as when I first noticed it. King's still lies just slightly
behind me. The muddy low spot in the path is just as far
away as ever. Why can't I get anywhere? Thank God for the
moorhens. They alone seem genuinely able to move about.*

*Now I remember the horsemen who have intruded so
often into my dreams. They, too, have seemed unable to get
off their treadmill. The dream's end leaves me sitting alone
in my empty flat. I'm shivering like someone with a fever.*

It was late. The digital clock on the VCR read 12:13. Had
he fallen asleep in his easy chair after the end of the dream,
the one about his life being a treadmill? How long ago was
that? An hour? More? Getting up, he went outside and began
wandering toward Queen's Road, walking through cool dry
night air. Walking with neither aim nor purpose. Too restless
to sleep.

"Fuck!" The word exploded between his teeth. "What the
fuck?" A kind of panic gripped his chest and ran down both
arms. Had he needed to lift an object as light as a pencil, he
feared he wouldn't have had the strength. But his legs
seemed normal enough. So he walked.

He walked north along Queen's Road. It was dark and
quiet. An occasional car passed him by to confirm that he had
not slipped into one of the dreams. Unless, of course, the
rules had changed as they certainly had done before—and
with no warning. How, after all, did he know dreaming from
waking? The floodlights on King's College Chapel made its
pinnacles glow against the dark sky, while square lumps of
darkened buildings and the rounded shapes of trees filled the
foreground. Immediately before him the Backs opened
broadly. But if he looked at any of it, he did so without really
seeing. It was all more felt than observed. The dark shadows
of trees overhead shrouded him protectively and also seemed
vaguely threatening in some eerie way. Almost as if they
might be harboring something dangerous to him, their sense
of protection illusory. Picking up his pace, he passed Clare
and Trinity and Garret Hostel Lane. He was nearly running
by then. He stopped suddenly and tried to get a grip on
himself, but the panicky feeling soon returned. He started
walking again, this time holding himself in check like a coiled
spring. He tried to force a calm that he didn't feel. He soon
came to Magdalene Street and decided to turn right and
enter the medieval city. He stood for a long time on
Magdalene Bridge, staring down unseeing into the dark river
below.

"Fucking lunatic!" he said aloud.

Gradually he began to relax inside. The weight on his
chest lifted, and his arms felt alive again. He noticed that he

shared the street with a handful of other people, and a wash of relief passed over him. He was not having a dream. But had they heard him or seen him acting strange? He looked around to see. No one was staring at him. When he resumed walking, now into the twisting narrow streets of the old city, he felt more like himself.

But the self that reemerged was a troubled one. One that knew that the panic, the fear and the disorientation could return at any moment. He remembered reading somewhere about how fragile patients felt after the ordeal of open-heart surgery—fearing that at any moment the heart would suffer a sudden jab of pain. Or go into fibrillation. Or stop altogether. He knew how they must feel: fragile, out-of-control, weepy, scared. Tears began to form in his eyes, but he squeezed them away and kept walking through the darkened quiet streets. Now he had the clear purpose of completing the circle of his journey by turning on Silver Street and aiming himself toward his flat at Lo-Host. Once he was inside, he slammed the door behind him, poured a stiff Scotch and drank it as he dialed Jeannie's number in Chicago. She picked up on the second ring.

"Hi," he said simply.

There was a pause on the line.

"Aren't you up kind of late?" Quiet resumed for a long three seconds. "I'm glad to hear from you, of course. But is something the matter?"

"Oh, not really. At least nothing I could put my finger on."

"What does that mean?"

"I guess I'm just feeling lonely and maybe a little jumpy. I miss you."

"I miss you, too. Have there been more of the dreams?"

"Yes. One."

"Tell me about it."

He told her about the walk along the Backs with the moorhens and his silent companion.

"And that made you feel what? Alone? Threatened?"

"Not exactly. But as I was thinking about it later, I realized that my life seemed so pointless. Going nowhere.

Exactly like walking along that path, but staying in the same place. Then it occurred to me that nobody, including myself, cares whether I finish another article or not. Or get another book published."

"Of course you care. I care. Your work matters."

"Right! Still, I've never said those things before. I don't think I've ever even thought them. I—I'm no longer sure that any of it matters anymore. But thanks for saying that it does. What am I going to do about it all?"

"I don't know. But you did the right thing to call me. Remember, I'm always here."

"I know that, and it helps. It makes all the difference. Really it does. Thanks."

"Why don't you come on home? Maybe you've had enough of this aloneness. It doesn't seem to agree with you.

"I don't exactly know what's keeping me here. Something is. It's—it's as if there's something I have to do."

They talked for a few minutes and then hung up. His heart ached at the breaking of the connection. He picked up his empty glass, poured another generous measure of single malt into it and went up to his bedroom where he stood drinking and looking out across the Lo-Host lawn. Was that the Ghost he saw in the shadows? He shook himself and let go of his imaginary apparition. His agitation gradually disappeared along with the amber liquid in the glass. He began to feel a little dizzy from the liquor. When he got into bed he gave in to the urge to curl up, fetal-like, grasping some minimal comfort from that. Finally he slept.

chapter eleven

The next day Brian had an email from Mary Beth. She told about traveling to conferences and working at keeping up with her field. "Now I'm back in the lab for the immediate future, and life is becoming more settled." She said she had been thinking about Brian and their college days. "I've thought about you so many times wondering what life would have been like if it had all turned out differently between us."

He spent a couple of days fretting over his reply. What he finally wrote felt more revealing than he really wanted, "I've been thinking about you, too. Especially how important you were to me back in college. I guess in some ways I never have entirely gotten over our break-up. I really cared about you. While I wouldn't want to relive the months after we parted, I don't regret a minute of the time we spent together."

He sent the message. Then sat staring at the screen wishing he hadn't. How could any good possibly come from revisiting those old feelings? He looked at his watch. A quarter past nine. He'd already had his run. Now it was time to get dressed and try to get some work done. He had an idea of where he might find more about his Plain Jane. He ran water into the tub and lowered himself in, thinking about the puzzle of that unknown woman whose story, what little he knew of it, had so sparked his interest. Why on earth had she never been the subject of historical comment? Maybe this was the new find he had secretly always hoped he would make. In spite of himself, he savored the warm water and this new puzzle. He almost missed the chime that told him he had received an incoming email.

He sat for a moment thinking he would let it go, at least until after he'd finished his bath. But curiosity got the better of him, a real measure of his loneliness. He got out of the tub, toweled himself off, pulled on his robe and padded his way down the half-flight of stairs into the sitting room. He had mail from eschumann. It was the middle of the night in

Buffalo. What was Mary Beth doing up at this hour? Whatever the reason, they had managed to be on at the same time.

She asked if he was still there. He responded that he was. In less than a minute he had a response from her.

"What you said is very sweet. I remember how angry you seemed at me back in college. It really hurt to see you go out of your way to avoid me. I tried to understand, but I guess your anger did make it easier for me to keep my distance from you."

"Being angry was better than feeling the pain," he wrote.

"I'm sorry, Brian. Really I am. If only I could live that year over again. But of course that's never an option, is it?"

"No, it isn't. BTW, what are you doing up in the middle of the night?"

"My youngest has a cold. I'm sure you remember what that's like. Right now I've got to try for a bit of sleep. Enjoy your day. Wish me some uninterrupted zzzs."

Brian sat there and let his mind spin as he stared unseeing at the screen. He felt as if he had been reduced to that broken-hearted freshman again with little more than a jumble of feelings and raw nerve ends. The emptiness in the pit of his stomach mingled with remembered waves of longing for the Mary Beth of his memory. He struggled to restore his studied posture of analyzing and sorting what happened to him instead of merely responding with uncontrolled and unbidden emotion. Suddenly the computer screen reverted to the digital photo of Jeannie and Candy he had installed a few days before as a screen saver. Waves of tenderness and then guilt passed over him as he stared at Jeannie's happy smiling face. He clicked on the start button and then began the "shut down" sequence. A door had been opened into his past this morning that he might find difficult to close again.

"See, I've found it. I know where she lived," Brian said under his breath as he dragged Jeff from the main reading room's sanctified quiet, waving a sheet of copy paper in his hand.

"You've found what? What are you going on about?"

"Are you due for a cigarette?"

A big smile broke out on Jeff's face. He followed the excited Brian.

"Look. Here." Brian pointed at the sheet of paper as they stepped out into the rooftop smokers' area. Jeff reached for a cigarette. "Plain Jane. Remember? I told you about her."

Jeff looked puzzled for a moment. Finally he nodded.

"She lived in a little place called Stichen-Walling somewhere near Bury St. Edmunds. I need to see a map." The freshly lighted cigarette smelled so good that for a moment Brian was tempted to ask for one himself. He shook off the temptation.

Jeff looked down at the photocopy in Brian's hand. "That looks like . . . well, like the footprints of a small bird. What exactly do you see in that mess?"

Brian laughed. "Sorry. It's called secretary hand. Takes a little getting used to." He pointed at the paper. "See here. It says, 'And Jane, with her daughter and granddaughter, thou rememberest, hath been buried beside the parish church at Stichen-Walling. It is well over. Thanks be to God.'" Brian looked up from the paper. "How do you imagine that the three of them came to die at the same time? It doesn't say." He looked Jeff in the eye. "I feel like Sherlock Holmes."

"Congratulations, Sherlock. They could have died from some epidemic."

"That's possible, but I don't think so. I don't know why I don't, but I don't.

"You sure it's the same Jane? And what does 'It is well over' mean? What is 'it'?" Jeff drew deeply on his cigarette and exhaled.

"I wish I knew, but I'm sure these are the same women. I just know it. I can feel it."

"That's a solid scientific protocol, all right," Jeff said with a sarcastic grin. "Given that, I still don't see how it helps you much."

Brian caught the much less appetizing odor of Jeff's exhaled smoke and was glad that he had resisted his momentary urge to light one up himself. Ignoring Jeff's implied criticism he went on, feeling an enthusiasm he hadn't known in months. "Oh, it does help. It makes all the difference. Now I know the parish where they were buried, at least I think I do, and that means that I know what parish register to look at for their full names, birth, marriage and death records, and what local record office to search in for land transfers and other papers. This Stichen-Walling place must either have an archives office of its own. Or there's some local repository where their records are stored. Perhaps the county town. Ultimately it will all be available online through the Public Record Office in London. Not yet though, I checked." Brian's excitement mounted. "I can't wait to go there."

"What's the name of that place?"

"Stichen-Walling"

"That's it." Jeff took a long drag on his cigarette and glanced up at the dark and threatening sky. A few drops fell. "I think we'd better get back inside or you and your theory are going to get all wet." He grinned, buried his cigarette in a bucket of sand, turned and in his loping gate headed back inside.

"I did have one other thing I wanted to tell you," Brian began to say, thinking about his correspondence with Mary Beth, but he said it to Jeff's back.

"What's that?" Jeff called over his shoulder.

"Oh nothing. It'll keep," he said, surprised at how relieved he felt at not having to come clean about Mary Beth.

Brian walked into his flat after lunch to the phone's ringing. It was Carol Heppel. "I have a big favor to ask of you, dear boy," she said.

"What is it? I can't imagine denying you anything."

"You're very sweet. Well, when the Proms—you know the concert season, mostly at the Royal Albert Hall, every summer—anyhow, when it first opened up for reservations I saw they were playing the Saint-Saëns organ symphony. Don't you just *love* that? And they've done a complete rebuild of the Albert Hall's organ into the bargain. Dame Gillian Weir is playing. Anyhow, I bought two tickets months ago. My friend, Sally, was planning to go with me. But she's been ill.

And, well, she's canceled. It's for tonight. Would you be willing to come along and use that second ticket? I wouldn't want it to go to waste. I don't really like coming back alone on the train at night."

"What a wonderful offer. I've never actually been to a live Proms concert. I listen to the broadcasts, of course. They're terrific. But wait, don't people actually stand up the whole time? Isn't that why they call it the Proms—because people promenade?"

"Quite. But I'm a bit old for all of that. I have two box seats."

He could feel her imitation of a wicked little grin coming over the phone line. "I'd love to go," he said. When do we leave?"

"Well, I've checked the train schedule."

"I knew you would have."

"Hmm. If we leave on the 16:32 we'll get to King's Cross at 17:21. That's 5:21. I do get annoyed at that twenty-four hour clock, don't you? Then we can take the Tube to South Kensington. I know a little Indian restaurant right beside the Underground station. You do like Indian food don't you?"

"I certainly do."

"Good. From there we can get a taxi to the Albert Hall in plenty of time. Do you want to go?"

"Very much."

Brian hung up the phone and looked at his watch. There seemed no point now in going back to the library and starting in on another carton of documents. Instead he picked up his road atlas and studied the area around Cambridge until he found Stichen-Walling, the presumed burial place of Plain Jane. He just knew he would learn more there about Jane, her daughter and granddaughter.

Brian had been to the Royal Albert Hall one other time years ago: for a performance of Beethoven's Ninth Symphony. He and Kathleen had been married just under two years at the time and in England for six months. Kathleen had been pregnant with the fetus that would become Bobbie—four months gone, in the local lingo. She was showing enough to look overweight, but not enough to look like the cute little pregnant girl she would soon be. He had been working on his dissertation, and they had gone up to London from Cambridge for him to spend a few days looking at documents held at the Public Record Office. They never would have gone to such an expensive concert had the tickets not been the gift of someone he had run into at the PRO—a freebie like tonight's concert. The evening had begun auspiciously. The Ninth was a favorite of Brian's in those years. Brass explosions, singing strings and the powerful solo and choral voices in the fourth moment had practically brought the house down. Even Kathleen, who didn't like classical music, had been thrilled at the spectacle.

But the otherwise wonderful evening turned dark when he glimpsed someone outside in the departing crowd. "Mary Beth?" he muttered under his breath to himself. Kathleen looked at him inquiringly.

"Did you say something, honey?" she asked.

"Not really," he said.

It had been four years since his college graduation. The last time he had seen his old flame had been the day they received their diplomas. Then he saw in that departing concert crowd a pair of milky white shoulders topped by luxurious black curls. The owner of those shoulders was walking away from him. His heart nearly stopped beating, and then it started up again at a furious pace. They crossed the street to catch a bus back to Bloomsbury. Standing between the Albert Memorial and the Alexandra Gate, he found himself about twenty feet away from that same young woman and her party of two laughing couples. Their accents betrayed them as Americans. It really could be Mary Beth. The two couples continued on down the street toward Knightsbridge, Brian and Kathleen following behind them toward the bus stop. He just knew that Mary Beth was the one in front of him. He wanted more than anything to catch up to her so he could find out for sure. What could she be doing in London? And who was the man she was with? A husband? A lover? It made him crazy to think of either possibility. Short-legged and pregnant, Kathleen struggled to keep up with him as he rushed ahead to catch a glimpse of what he was sure would be the face he remembered so well.

Finally, Kathleen tugged at his elbow and said, "Brian, honey, I've really got to slow down. I'm having trouble catching my breath."

He looked at her as if she had come from Mars. She looked puzzled and hurt by his reaction. But Brian only had eyes for the retreating bare shoulders and curly black hair. He looked ahead and then at Kathleen.

"What's the matter, Brian? Is everything okay?"

The two couples climbed into a taxi. He never did see the woman's face. But he knew that she had to be Mary Beth. He just knew it. He mumbled something to Kathleen about seeing someone he thought he knew and tried to return his attention to his pretty little wife. But try though he might he could not take his mind off those white shoulders and that gleaming hair. Whether or not it had actually been Mary Beth that episode afforded a glimpse into his painful past, turned him away from the elation of the concert and gave rise to a morose and distracted mood.

They climbed onto the bus and sat on the lower level. At first Brian had to stand while Kathleen sat. He peered intently into each passing black taxi as the red double-decker wound its way through the maze of London streets toward Bloomsbury and their bed-and-breakfast. His mood became darker and darker. The longing for Mary Beth seemed to mount each minute as they bumped and jerked along. Finally the woman sitting next to Kathleen got off and Brian was able to sit beside her. In glance after inquiring glance she seemed to say the silent words that he feared he would hear: So, it's the old girlfriend again? When are you going to get over her? Now pay attention to me, you jerk. I'm the one carrying your child. But Kathleen didn't say those words, probably didn't even think them. No reason why she should have. She knew nothing about Mary Beth, except that Brian had dated her several years before. They sat side-by-side while the emotional distance between them grew into a chasm.

Back in their room they got ready for bed with only the occasional word passing between them. For a moment she stood, almost defiant, naked in front of him. It was as if she were daring him to ignore the beauty of her body or the rounded mound on her abdomen, now clearly visible without the covering of clothing. But he ignored her, and she pulled her nightgown over her head. They had managed not to quarrel that night or over the next few days, but the alienation grew. Brian continued to think about Mary Beth. After they were back in their little Cambridge flat they had one of their raging fights that started over something he could no longer remember. But even while they were fighting Brian had had a hard time focusing his attention on Kathleen and kept wondering if it really had been Mary Beth he saw in London.

Sitting there on the train headed into London for another concert at the Royal Albert Hall, he admitted to himself, as he had done at the time, that he likely had not seen his old flame that night. But he also knew that it hadn't mattered whether or not the woman had been his lost love, because the damage had been done to his relationship with Kathleen all the same. The anguish and the terrible fight had resulted from the mere possibility that he might have seen Mary Beth.

Then it occurred to him: this moment in his past served to reveal something important about his sense of Mary Beth. Or, rather, his lack of a sense of her. Her hidden face that night, as on the occasion when he thought he had seen her outside the Round Church and on dozens—hundreds—of other times in various places, was emblematic of what she represented for him: faceless and insubstantial. A remnant of another time and another place. She was hardly a real person at all. But that did not diminish the hold her memory continued to exercise over him.

The Proms program turned out to be the oddest combination of things: a Berlioz overture; the Saint-Saëns, including the rumble of the great organ under the hands and feet of Dame Gillian; and, after the Interval, a selection of Johann Strauss waltz pieces and selected operetta arias. He nearly fell out of his seat on the first of the Strauss pieces when the audience began a thunderous rhythmic clapping as if they had been specially rehearsed. After the concert he and Carol stood outside in front of that great round monument to Victorian ingenuity, looking for a taxi to take them to the rail station. Thoughts of that concert over twenty years before flooded back into his mind. He would have to ask Mary Beth if she had been in London and had attended a performance of the Ninth Symphony at the Albert Hall all those years ago. A taxi stopped for them, and they got in.

"King's Cross, please," Carol said to the driver.

The driver just nodded and started his meter running.

"Have you had any more dreams?" Carol asked as the Cambridge train clacked and swayed.

"That's taken kind of an odd turn, actually. *Another* odd turn." He told her about the Ghost.

Carol became pensive and then seemed to change the subject, "I was talking the other day with one of the priests at my church. Anglican Franciscans, you know. Father Jeremiah's new here. Actually he's an experienced spiritual director and trained psychotherapist. Has a doctorate. I mentioned your dreams to him. I hope you don't mind."

"Of course I don't mind," he said politely. But inside warning alarms began to sound.

"Well, Father Jeremiah became interested, very interested indeed. Said he'd like to talk with you. If you're willing, that is. Said something about those place memories we talked about."

"Yes?" Curiosity got the better of him.

"Just that he knows something about that. Father Jeremiah finds all this sort of thing very intriguing. Would you like to see him?"

"See him?"

"He might be able to help you understand it all."

Brian thought for a moment before saying, "Of course I'm willing."

But he chuckled silently to himself at the idea. Brian Craig going to see a priest. A spiritual doctor? Clergy had always seemed like nice enough people, well meaning for all of that. But see one for something serious going on in his life? What is this, Voodoo in East Anglia? Still, what could it hurt?

"I thought you might say yes," she said, "so I've invited him for Sunday lunch at my house. How would that be for you?"

"You mean I'm actually getting an invitation for a meal at the home of the famous Caramel Apple?"

Carol snorted slightly and pulled down her skirt with both hands in a pretend gesture of annoyance. She looked pointedly out over the train car's interior before turning back and fixing his eye with hers. "It's settled then. You'll come to mass with me at St. Bene't's and home for Sunday lunch afterwards?"

"Church? I think I've been had," Brian said, laughing.

She ignored him. "Father Jeremiah will be filling in for the vicar and taking the service. That way you can see him in action before you decide whether or not to talk with him. He said he would let you bring up your dreams if you wanted. Or not. No pressure."

Right. No pressure. Seeing a priest? Give me a break.

"Do you remember that I have a twin? Jannie. We mostly look pretty identical," Jeannie said. She sounded like she was in the next room.

"You've mentioned her a time or two."

"Well, she called the other day with a problem. It's the same old Jannie stuff: a man and a lack of ready cash. She has very good taste in clothes, cars, furniture—just about everything. That woman can spend! But her discrimination over picking just the right wine doesn't run to men. She falls in love and rushes headlong into a new relationship as if he were the love of her life. A few months later she begins to feel confined or figures out what a jerk the guy is, and she wants out. Well, it's all happened again. Like always, I loan her money. This time I also took her in. She's presently occupying my spare room. Oh, she'll have a job in no time. She always does. Her trust fund will soon catch up with her spending, and the boyfriend will give up and go away. I adore her, you know,. But, well, I now have a semi-permanent houseguest."

"That should complicate your life. How are you doing with the department head?"

"Same old thing. He keeps leering at me—as if he thinks he was about to get lucky that day in the Faculty Club. Dream on, creep."

chapter twelve

The number 11 bus for Bury St. Edmunds left the Drummer Street Station promptly at 8:40. The morning was warm and bright. Leaning back in his seat, Brian felt rather than heard the rumble of the bus's big diesel engine as its driver began to navigate the narrow Cambridge streets. Cars and trucks, bicyclists and pedestrians all going in independent directions at once formed a single undulating sea of people and machines. Brian looked around the spotless half-filled bus. Overhead, open luggage bins ran along each side and held a scattering of packages and about midpoint one small battered suitcase. Brian's laptop sat on the seat beside him. Little by little the driver managed to extract the motorized mammoth from the crowded city streets and pointed this contemporary version of a stagecoach onto the A14.

Brian stared out the window at the passing countryside. Rich fen topsoil covered the clay of former bogs where fields of potatoes, carrots, and celery alternated with freshly plowed earth, dairy farms and hillsides dotted with hogs. Fast moving small clouds raced across the deep blue of the sky. Signs to Exning and Kentfold quickly passed as the bus rolled at its steady sixty-five miles per hour along the wide and fast A14. There was one stop at Newmarket before going on to Bury.

His thoughts drifted to a startling email from Mary Beth. She had been telling him about a recent professional meeting she had attended when suddenly she dropped the bomb, "Now, believe it or not the next conference I 'must' attend is in *London* this fall. I could avoid it. I'm a fill-in for someone else, but it's something I really want to do. It *is* right up my alley: chemical issues in polymorphism and crystallization. Hot fields. Perhaps if you want we could get together. Let me know what you think."

If he wanted? She really didn't get it, did she? If it weren't for what had happened with Jeannie he might be jumping on a plane and going to Buffalo right now. Maybe it was just as well she didn't understand. He had to keep something to himself, retain a bit of dignity. But what could it hurt to see her again after all these years?

The local bus service from Bury St. Edmunds wound south through the villages of Great Green, Cockfield, Stichen-Walling and Lavenham, all wool towns of the late Middle Ages. The route passed through deep sudden cuts and rising low hills in that rolling country on the edge of the Fens. Stichen-Walling looked much like other villages along the twisting road. Except it had a kind of unkempt look. If a town could look depressed, that is what Brian would have said of it. It had a cluster of grimy shops on a steep hill flanking a half-timbered public house called the Flint and Fleece—probably Tudor. Its sign showed a dressed-stone wall and a newly shorn sheep with its wool in a pile at its feet. A butcher, a baker (what no candlestick maker?), a greengrocer and a couple of other stores lined the street of mostly old buildings. Some were of plaster with the intricate curls and geometric designs of artful pargeting. A shop that seemed to cater to farming and gardening had a display of tools and bags of fertilizer and seed on the front walk. A second public house, The Furrowed Field, and another scattering of uninspiring shops stretched out along the other side of the street. Everything clustered around what was clearly the central crossroads in the town. The street widened there into what had probably once been the market square, perhaps with a formal market cross in the middle in centuries past. Now it was only a memory. The Furrowed Field advertised bed and breakfast. Beside it, a small sandwich and cakes shop offered teas and light meals. The village center blended in with the houses along both sides of the main street. Just before a bend in the road stood a large timbered building. Brian already knew from reading the Suffolk guidebook that it was a wool barn from the late Middle Ages through the Tudor era. Across from the Wool House a somber-looking Victorian brick pile housed the village offices, town hall, and justice's court. In the near distance beyond the row of shops, a single stone steeple proclaimed the location of the Established Church. Brian would visit the churchyard in search of Plain Jane and her progeny, though he thought he would have more success with written records than headstones that old. First he would try out the sandwich shop's luncheon fare. The watery pea soup, limp cheese-and-tomato sandwich, piping hot cup of tea and sticky bun got him going again.

If lunch had been ordinary, the church was deeply disappointing. The Gothic steeple sat atop a Victorian building, one unlikely to include the burial places of three seventeenth century women in its churchyard. How odd that a village of this one's antiquity would have a nineteenth century church rather than a medieval one. Had there been a fire? That would likely mean that parish records had been lost. What a discouraging thought. He poked around in the tidy structure, looking at bulletins and posters about parish events, and noted stacks of prayer books and of *Hymns Ancient and Modern*. He felt cheated. Outside, the well-groomed and headstone-littered churchyard fulfilled his misgivings. No grave marker had a date before 1873. Nothing would be learned about Plain Jane or her daughter and granddaughter there. He sat down on a horizontal slab of stone and read that it contained the last resting place of "Farnham, Josiah, his beloved wife, Anne, and their three dear children, 1881," all apparently occupying the same grave.

"Very sad, that," said an elderly female voice.

Startled, Brian stood up.

"Oh I doubt the Farnhams would mind having you sit on their headstone. Lots of us do."

Brian saw a small plump woman, probably in her eighties, dragging a wheeled basket filled with small brown packages.

"1881 must have been a bad year for a whole family to die that way. There were all the others, too." Her arm pointed first to the left and then to the right as she said, "Over there. And there. I've wondered if it was the pox. The Vicar probably knows."

Brian recovered from his surprise and asked, "But the older ones? Where were they buried? You know, the ones before the 1870s."

"That would be in the old churchyard." She pointed beyond a row of trees and bushes around the side of the parish church. "It's pretty neglected these days, I'm afraid. Nobody even uses the church building. Can't remember when somebody did. The village children think it's haunted. They may be right." She smiled innocently.

Brian stepped through the church gate onto the sidewalk. "I'm Brian Craig." He held out his hand.

"I'm pleased to meet you, Mr. Craig," she said, grasping Brian's hand in hers. "I'm Mrs. Burton."

"I've come to Stichen-Walling, Mrs. Burton, to do research about some people who lived here centuries ago. I had hoped to find their graves in the churchyard."

"Centuries ago? Well, then, you'd best look at the Old Church, hadn't you? All its records and books and things would have been moved to the village archives ages ago."

Brian's spirits began to rise from their earlier depths. "Of course: the village archives. Where are they kept?"

"In the town hall, actually. I think they have the parish records from several redundant churches there."

"Yes. I know where that is. Thanks Mrs. Burton. Thanks so much."

"You're welcome, Mr. Craig." She smiled and nodded her head, resuming her walk. Brian turned to follow her directions, a new surge of energy surging through him.

Near the back corner of the Victorian churchyard, he saw an overgrown path and followed it, cautiously suppressing a growing sense of excitement. Almost immediately he stepped backwards in time. This second churchyard was defined by a crumbling chert and mortar wall and filled with headstones, many sitting at odd angles, others fallen over completely. Everything there was softened but made to look more chaotic by knee-high grass and weeds. In the foreground stood a dilapidated lychgate that looked as if a strong wind would bring it down. He imagined Plain Jane's coffin waiting there for the vicar to lead it to its final resting place. The three would have to be in tandem. There was no way that three coffins would fit under that shelter at the same time. He tied to imagine a three-person funeral in this miniature setting. All of the people who would attend something so unusual. It was beyond him. At the end of the yard and surrounded by plane trees and one large oak, sat a squat little church with a round tower, built of the same flinty stone and mortar as the wall around the yard. It was topped by a slate roof. A Suffolk guidebook had described the region's medieval churches as "petrified puddings." It sort of worked. The air around this one stank of dust, rotting vegetation and musty neglect. All in all it looked decrepit and unattended. Brian stepped into the little side porch and tried the door. It opened with a squeak of protest. A stone altar was built into the east wall beyond the chancel arch and step. Some old tools sat keeping a lonely vigil in a room otherwise bare of furnishings: a scythe leaning beside the door, an open cardboard box filled with a junky looking mess of gardener's implements and an old-fashioned long-snouted oil can. A worn lawnmower sat just in front of the door. The interior dampness and musty odor threatened to smother the very breath out of him. Not even the dirty little windows high up on the walls let in enough light to brighten or dry out the soggy feel of the place. Brian found himself nearly shuddering in the cold and gloom; and perhaps with something less physically definable as well. He went back out into the neglected yard, thinking how well the tools inside might be employed there. Clearly he would have his work cut out for him trying to find the three headstones he sought, let alone being able to read them after all the winters and summers that had worked away on the carvings and the lichen that covered what little remained.

Reaching into the computer bag he carried slung over his shoulder, he pulled out a small cardboard box of white chalk, opened it and extracted a stick of chalk. Though he had never had occasion to try the method before, he had heard that he might be able to read some of the old headstones by rubbing the side of the stick over the eroded carvings in the stone. That probably would work well enough inside a building where carvings in floor stones had been worn away by tensof-thousands of feet walking on it. But not outside where orange and gray-colored lichen covered everything but the least porous of stones. For the lichen he had a small bottle of a product called *Bio-Lichen Off*, loaned to him by one of the university archivists; the label identified it as mostly glycerin. He also had a small brush to use with it. He rested the computer bag against a convenient marble headstone and went to work. Taking on a large marble monument first and brushing aside the weeds and tall grass, he ran the flat side of the chalk over worn-away carvings and was encouraged to discover that the technique worked. Almost like magic the name, "Jeremie Downing, Sometime Beadle of this Parishe," appeared. The date was 1751. But the all-pervasive lichen so covered most of the stones that few would ever yield any information without being cleaned. That was a daunting prospect. The chalk was useless on those, and it was impractical to clean an entire churchyard of headstones; nor was he convinced that such a thing would be tolerated by local church officials. There was something undeniably attractive about the lichen-covered stones. How would he ever find graves dating from about 1630?

He picked his way through the monuments, sometimes ripping up tall grass or just shoving it aside so he could get a glimpse at one headstone or another. After scouring the graveyard for an hour, he had seen the names of four women named Jane. None were from anywhere near as early as the one he sought. He was tired and a little grumpy and sat down on an overturned headstone, feeling discouraged and unaccountably jumpy. Something about spending more than an hour alone in an empty old church and its graveyard had gotten to him. Especially when combined with the stillness of the late summer afternoon. But it was more than that. Something malevolent seemed to hang over the place. This particular place. No wonder the village children thought it was haunted and generations of people had steered clear of it. Especially at night, he imagined. Could that be why the Victorians had felt the need to have a new church? They would never have tolerated a building that nobody wanted to go near. Despite their optimism, love of baubles and the fact that they pretty much invented conventional religious sensibilities, the Victorians had a very practical nature. Of course they would build a new church. Brian shuddered at the place and then tried to shake off the dark mood it had generated in him. Suddenly he was anxious to get out of there as quickly as possible. With his recent history there was no telling what might happen if he lingered. He looked at his watch: three o'clock. Maybe he would find more information in the village archives. He left the depressing little church and its collection of askew headstones without looking back. No power on earth would induce him to be in that place after dark. Skirting around the Victorian church again, he soon returned to the High Street and, after a quick stop for a cup of tea, headed for the town hall.

The Stichen-Walling town hall was just like every other old bureaucratic building Brian had ever visited. It breathed officiousness and preoccupied indifference. The standard of cleaning was so low that visions rose up of an elderly broom-pusher absentmindedly making little circular patterns in the middle of the floor with a studied avoidance of corners and edges. Oddly, the air reeked of wax and cleaning solvent. A handyman with an open tray of tools at his feet and a uniformed constable were in light-hearted conversation at the rear of the entrance hall. Behind them an imposing broad staircase of carved mahogany led to the floors above.

"Can I help you, sir?" said the constable.

"I'm looking for the village archives."

"Upstairs. At the top." The constable pointed at the staircase behind him. "Be closing soon, though," he said. "Nearly four now."

"I'd better hurry then," Brian muttered and began to climb the stairs, which, after the initial grandeur of the first course, deteriorated into dull gray institutional concrete.

Three floors above the entrance Brian spotted a steel door with a wire mesh security window. A legend below the window read simply, "RECORDS." He tried the knob and found it locked. He peered through the window. Inside sat a lone elderly man wearing a worn-looking wrinkled white shirt and a slightly-askew striped tie. He was poring over a stack of leather-bound volumes. An independent lock of nearly wave-less white hair fell over his brow. Brian knocked on the glass. No response. He knocked again. This time the man looked up, seemed to register Brian's presence, turned his head away and said something that Brian couldn't hear. Almost immediately a serious looking young woman appeared, smiled, and opened the door.

"Yes?" she said. "Can I help you, sur?" Her accent was as deep and broad as the fens themselves. But in her black skirt and frilly blouse she reflected little of the building's formidable bureaucratic ambiance. Brian looked at her again with appreciation. A rose amidst a bed of institutional thorns?

"I'm wondering," he said. May I see some old parish registers? Seventeenth century. For the Stichen-Walling parish church?" He reached for his wallet and pulled out one of his seldom-used business cards that identified him as Brian A. Craig, Professor of History, Sterling University. He handed it over to the woman, adjusting the computer bag's strap on his shoulder.

"Of course, Professor Craig. It's an honor to have you here." She looked over her shoulder at a wall clock. "But we close at half-past four." That gave him little more than thirty minutes. "Mr. Grimes is working on some of the same registers, though from a later period." She turned to the white-haired man. "Would you mind showing Professor Craig where the Stichen-Walling parish records are shelved? If anybody knows where they are, you're the one." The man looked up from the big volume and laptop computer in front of him and smiled. "Mr. Grimes is recording parish registers of redundant churches for the Public Record Office," she informed the newcomer with a hint of awe in her voice.

Mr. Grimes smiled again. "Let me show you." He turned to the shelves behind him, slid his right hand along the leather bound volumes and stopped at one, raised his eyeglasses so he could look through the bifocals and nodded in satisfaction.

"I'm not at all sure of the dates of the people I'm looking

for, but I think at least one of them died about 1630, perhaps a little later," Brian said.

Mr. Grimes expertly hefted one of the heavy books and placed it lovingly on the table in front of Brian and beside the similar volume he had been working in. He opened the heavy pages "See, here is where you find burials." He pointed to an unlined column. Baptisms and confirmations are generally side-by-side here." He indicated another spot on the tall page. "Marriages have their own location." He turned a few pages. "Here." Then he looked up and flashed his shy grin. "Sometimes you have to be creative and look for the system the particular priest used, but mostly they were done this way."

Brian felt a thrill of excitement as he began to look at the burial records. He searched for a combination of three women—one with the name of Jane—who had all died at about the same time. He felt more like a detective than a historian. What was it about Plain Jane and her progeny that interested him so much? Their draw felt almost familial. Somehow their lives seemed to connect to his life.

"Probably a good idea for you to wear these," Mr. Grimes said suddenly, handing Brian a pair of white cotton gloves like the ones he wore himself.

"Of course. I should have known better," Brian answered. Pulling on the gloves may have broken the spell of the moment, but it didn't alter Brian's enthusiasm for his task. When the attendant reappeared to tell them that the archives would be closing in five minutes, he had found nothing about Plain Jane.

"I know somewhere else that will be opening about now. Like to join me for a pint?" Grimes asked.

"With pleasure," Brian said immediately, glad of the chance to talk with the older man.

"Will you be back tomorrow, gentlemen?" the attendant asked.

"Certainly," Mr. Grimes responded.

This time Brian had to think a little longer. He had brought a small overnight kit in his computer bag for such an eventuality. "Yes, I think I will," he said at last, wondering as he answered if the Furrowed Field would have a room for him.

"Then I see no problem leaving the volumes out. As you know, Mr. Grimes."

Grimes smiled back at her and showed Brian how to mark his page with a clean sheet of white paper. "Low acid," he said, pointing to the paper.

Brian didn't point out that he knew perfectly well about taking such precautions.

The Furrowed Field did have a room, which Brian booked and found at the rear of the building through a warren of hallways and three short partial flights of stairs. Everything about the room came up short of plumb. It was a wonder the door shut at all. The floor slanted toward the outside wall where a parallelogram window looked on the rear courtyard and some small outbuildings.

A glass pitcher of water on the dresser measured the surface's unevenness like a carpenter's level. A ceramic bowl with a stack of fluffy white towels beside it would likely be useful since the bathroom and water closet were both some distance down the hall. At least there was no sign of a chamber pot, Brian noted and smiled.

The bed looked soft and was covered with a fluffy duvet. A worn overstuffed chair sat in a corner beneath a single-bulb ceiling light fixture with a pull string. Old-fashioned flowered wallpaper complimented a new-looking carpet that covered squeaky uneven floorboards. The scent of lavender helped mask the distant odor of food and a hint of stale tobacco smoke. He loved the cheerful room.

After a short stumble around the town—at least that was how Brian experienced his post-libation walk—he went back to his room to clean up. An hour later he ate a tasty traditional dinner at the Furrowed Field.

After another turn around the town, including a look at the outside of the old wool barn and a quick check-in with Jeannie from a public phone, he decided to settle in with a novel he had brought with him.

Finally he drifted off to sleep feeling cozy and contented

with his day, if a bit perplexed about his next step in the search for Plain Jane.

I'm standing at the lychgate entrance to the Old Church. The squat outlines of the slate-roofed stone building gleam in the moonlight in what seems a threatening way. Sounds, probably of tiny rodents, resonate like the crash of gigantic jungle predators and rhinoceroses. I want to turn and run from the place, but am unable to make my legs work that way. Instead, I walk inexorably into the churchyard past the dark shapes of askew and precarious headstones. I trip over one and almost fall. But that only propels me forward even faster as I scramble to regain my equilibrium. A cloud passes over the moon, resulting in an inky darkness. I look up and see that the offending cloud is a small one. I wait until it has scooted quickly on its way. The moon once again bathes the churchyard with its cold light, and I wonder whether that eerie glow is better than total darkness. I think that it must be. But I'm not sure.

Finally I stop and look around, wondering what I'm doing in this place. Will I wake at any moment to find that I'm not here at all? But that's not how I feel. This seems very real. I'm jittery with expectation. Suddenly I hear a crashing sound behind me, and I turn around, defensive, prepared to fight or flee. Whichever seems more fitting. I'm inclined to run. But there is nothing there, at least nothing that I can see. A light breeze passes over the graveyard, and I hear what sounds like the church door scrape slightly and then bang lightly against the jam. I ask myself what I'm doing here. I don't like this place."

Now I stop walking and stand entirely still. I realize I'm waiting for something to happen. I don't know why, but I think it will soon. Sure enough, a dark figure looms up before me. My heart pounds and my legs feel watery. I wonder if I could manage to flee if it comes to that. The figure walks toward me. I don't know what's going to happen. My throat tightens up, and my breathing becomes shallow and rapid. But I know that shape. I recognize my companion from Midsummer Common. *For some reason seeing him is like meeting an old friend; he makes me feel less alone and less scared. He nods at me and I follow him. I wonder why he never speaks.*

He leads me around the church to where the perimeter wall has crumbled away, making an easy exit out of the churchyard; if, that is, one were to step carefully over the rubble. My friend seems to be rescuing me and leading me out of this terrible place. After a few more steps I see that he has something else in mind. Outside the wall is a cluster of small headstones, little more than markers. I count six, and then I see one more. At least seven graves are outside the wall. How odd. All are overgrown with weeds and grass, and covered with lichen—even more abandoned-looking than the ones inside the old churchyard itself. For some reason I know that no one has ever tended these forlorn graves. I look around at what appears to be an open field, and in the distance I can see the lights of houses. Now there is no sign of my elusive companion. He must have brought me here to see this. I can check it out tomorrow.

Right now I want out of this place. Surely I will soon wake up. I feel in my pocket for the outside door and room key for the Furrowed Field and find them. I make a beeline for the small hostelry, out through the lychgate, around the Victorian church and into the town square. Surely this dream will soon end. Everything looks normal on the street, though there is no traffic. Perhaps there never is at this hour. I let myself into the Furrowed Field, and finally I'm back in my room where I'm suddenly very sick.

The next morning Brian ate a full English breakfast of eggs, bacon, sausage, black pudding and fried bread and checked out of the Furrowed Field. Only then did he head back to the Old Church to look at the tumbledown section of wall he had seen the night before. Had that been in a dream? Or as some kind of alert sleepwalker? Either way he needed to check it out. He walked through the lychgate and into the old churchyard. The place looked exactly the same as it had yesterday afternoon. He stepped gingerly over the strewn rocks of the broken wall and looked on the ground for the little cluster of graves and found them. A lone bee, presumably in search of nectar, flitted across the headstones and, in what Brian imagined was disgust, fled the barren spot. Each of the markers stood no higher than a foot, simple identifiers and not monuments to a person's life. Bending over and pulling away the grass and weeds, he looked at the stones, all of which were very old and worn and covered with lichen. With the use of the lichen cleaner, followed up with the chalk, he began to pick out names and dates: "Agnes of Stichen-Walling Common, 1599;" "Arabella Leighton, 1601;" one was indecipherable except for the date of 1642; another hadn't even a legible date. Every identifiable name was female. Finally, Brian found what he was looking for: three graves that had the same date, 1632. Though he could only make out partial names on each all three were identified as being from a place called Thirley Hall, Suffolk. As nearly as he could tell their names seemed to be Jane, Mary and Anne: the graves he sought. He just knew they were. Why else would the Ghost have brought him here? Unaccountably, Brian felt very sad looking at those stones. He would have been hard pressed to explain why. Shaking off those feelings, he looked at his watch: a few minutes before eleven. The archives had been open for two hours. He shouldered his computer bag and retraced his steps through first the one and then the second churchyard, walking briskly back to the High Street and into the town hall.

Brian's task at the Stichen-Walling archives suddenly became simple. He smiled at the attendant and gave a vaguely sheepish nod toward Mr. Graves, his drinking companion of the evening before. Sitting down in front of the same parish register he had been looking at the day before, he resumed his search. Beginning with the year 1600, he looked in the baptismal records for names with a residential location of Thirley Hall and soon came across the record of Mary's baptism. From there he worked his way forward and backward until he had found another baptismal entry, Anne's. Marriage records for all three women—Jane's four, Mary's two, and Anne's one—were easy to find now. Jane's first marriage was to a certain Mr. Athelton of Thirley Hall. He could find nothing about Jane before that marriage date. Perhaps she had come from another parish. None of this collection of husbands survived their wives. All seven of them rested inside the churchyard of the old Stichen-Walling parish church. All of the husbands, except for Jane's last, had been much older than their spouses. Apparently no offspring were left behind, and only one stillborn birth had been recorded for Anne. There was no mention of the deaths of the women in the records or any explanation for their burial places outside the wall. Their passing seemed to have gone unheeded by the Church in any way at all. How very odd. Brian even checked out the other two names he had found on headstones outside the churchyard, Arabella Leighton and Agnes of Stichen-Walling Common. No mention of their deaths had been entered into the parish register either. Nor did Mr. Grimes have more than one small observation to make in explanation.

"I have never noticed those graves outside the wall of the old church. Can't imagine why they would be there. Maybe for some reason they couldn't be buried in consecrated ground. Suicides, particular categories of criminals, witches, that sort of thing. They weren't buried in churchyards, you know. But three of them in the same family? That's curious indeed. I think you have a bit of a mystery here."

Brian wondered what Mr. Grimes would have said about how he had located those graves in the first place. Why were they there? Perhaps Grimes had hit it just right when he suggested witchcraft as one possibility. Women throughout that era were accused of witchcraft and executed for it— sometimes just for being old or ugly: the notorious and infamous witch craze, endemic on both sides of the Atlantic. Witches indeed. What combination of superstition and fear could lead people to behave in such outrageous ways and to treat each other with such cruelty?

chapter thirteen

h i Brian. Hope I didn't wake you. I know it's after ten there," Jeannie's cheery voice returned Brian's suspicious, "Hello?"

"Not at all," he said, trying to shake himself out of his glum mood as he stretched out his legs under the battered desk. He began to play a game of computer solitaire as he talked. "I was afraid it might be Emily. She's being pretty nasty. Wants the house and most everything else. I'm just sitting here unwinding and listening to Mahler on the BBC Proms rebroadcast."

"That's cheerful."

"Right." He chuckled. "Glad you called, though." He noticed that he had missed a couple of obvious solitaire moves and gave it up.

"I tried earlier, but you were out."

He got up and began walking around the room. "Sorry. I didn't get back from that Suffolk village until time for dinner with Jeff. I was thinking about that village, Stichen-Walling, when the phone rang."

"Did you find the graves you were looking for?"

He told her about his night and morning in Stichen-Walling, including the evening stroll in the churchyard.

"You *dreamed* their location? The "Ghost" *showed* it to you? How can that be?"

"I—I don't know exactly. It's all pretty confusing. It also looks as if they were executed for witchcraft. You know: the witch craze. It's the right period. I need the whole thing to settle on me a bit before I try to figure it all out. What's happening with you?" he asked

"Me? You're not just deflecting?"

"No, not really. I just don't know what to make of it. Not yet I don't."

"Well, nothing much is happening with me." There was a pause. "No, that isn't true.

Actually there's been quite a lot. Jannie is still living in my guest room and dominating our lives. Must be making my neighbors crazy, too. At the moment her hair is pretty much the same color as mine. Even about the same length. When she's in one of her less flamboyant moods and dresses down in jeans and shirts the way I do . . ."

"Takes my breath away."

"Right-right-right. Anyhow, then we look as much alike as we did when we were kids and Mom dressed us in our twin suits."

"Twin suits? Makes me think of all those bad old movies about look-a-likes and mistaken identity," Brian laughed.

"Sometimes I feel like I'm living in a B movie. Or maybe Shakespeare."

He could feel her toothy smile coming at him over the phone line. "I don't remember any twins in the Bard."

"And no mistaken identities I suppose." She switched the banter. "I'm still trying to avoid the chair from Hell."

"Cardam? You're sure he isn't just trying to be nice but doesn't know how to do it?"

"I'm sure. Women get pressured like this all the time. You start to feel like tits and ass. It's not just my imagination!" It grew quiet. "Are you there Brian?"

"I'm just savoring the image. Sorry, I couldn't resist." He paused for a breath "Anything I can do?"

"Not really." Her voice's determined edge gave way to breathiness, "I'm looking out at the lake. I wish you were here to go with me on a walk along the shore." She sounded sad.

"I'd love doing that. Walking along the lake with you."

"We've never done that together."

"We ran a few times."

"It's not the same as walking hand in hand."

"We will. I promise. You know, I really miss you."

"Me too, you." She seemed to take a breath. "Yesterday I put on my gray and green-striped tracksuit and went out by myself to run along my usual path. The one we ran together. You remember." She sounded uncharacteristically sentimental. "It was one of those perfect days. Warm sun and blue sky, the late afternoon breeze blowing off the lake. My heartbeat began rising. I had, you know, that sense of exhilaration you get running. It was fantastic. But for some reason—maybe something about the perfection of it all—I missed you more than ever. I felt really . . . lonely."

"I'm sorry." He couldn't think of what else to say.

She carried on in spite of his muted response. "Then I began to think about the complications in my life right now. Francis Cardham is one. Jannie's another. She and I might be twins, but we're ill-suited to live together. She's too self-absorbed to have around fulltime. An adolescent girl is quite enough to cope with, thank-you-very-much." She laughed. "Don't get me wrong, I love Jannie., and you know that I adore Candy. But like all teenagers, she's loaded with emotional needs. Weepy and insecure one minute, determined and opinionated the next. She pushes all the boundaries. Just as she should at her age. She's even started talking obsessively about boys, which brings up the specter of some tattooed head-shaven testosterone factory lounging about the place. That hasn't actually happened . . . yet. Still, between Candy and Jannie, there's more repressed sexual energy in this place than is strictly speaking healthy."

"Only the two of them?" It was his turn to laugh.

"Okay, I'll admit to adding a bit myself. I guess we live in a kind of hormone soup."

"What an image. Sounds dangerous."

"To the likes of you it is!" She giggled.

"Exactly."

She paused a moment, and then shifted subjects again, "Besides missing you, though, running yesterday I had what felt like a real insight. I'd stopped to catch my breath and looked at a cluster of sailboats skimming across the choppy surface of the lake. Each one of them was tacking into the wind or running with it as they headed wherever it was they were going. Suddenly I realized that whoever was in charge of each of those little boats had a destination in mind. Perhaps it was a course into the marina just south of where I was running. Or maybe he was zigzagging out into the lake against the wind. Or it might have been nothing grander than meandering back and forth for the simple joy of it. But one thing was certain, not a single one of those boats would simply stay in place, marking time and space with no purpose or direction whatsoever."

Perhaps it was the tone in her voice, but she got Brian's attention. She might as well have given him notice: I'm about to say something important. He sensed that she was, and he listened with new ears.

"Those sailboats seemed like a metaphor for how my life used to be. I had spent years thinking of myself as Richard's appendage and allowing his ego to define me. I was someone whose own career, even life, didn't really matter all that much. I even had lots of trouble thinking of myself as having a genuine existence of my own. That included making my own decisions and having a professional life entirely independent of Richard. Not any more. Before the divorce it didn't matter that I was only an adjunct at SU. Or so I told myself. Now my career and my second-class academic status do matter. It's about identity. I like having an independent life. In spite of the loneliness and even with the exciting new things that have happened between us, I'm really my own person for the first time in my life. I'm not responsible to anyone for a change. Both Candy and Jannie are dependents—in different ways, of course, but they still both depend on me. With all their needs, I don't have time to feel sorry for myself, and somehow I've gotten the energy to start thinking tough about my own problems and not just whine about them. Take Francis Cardham for example. Suddenly I'm not such an emotional pushover. Now that I know more than ever why my career matters, his sexual pressure is even less acceptable. I'm getting really pissed. I might once have laughed it off. Now I refuse to tolerate it. Or him. I have to figure something out. That jerk had better watch out."

"Oh-oh. Maybe it's a good thing I'm here and you're there. Keeps me from getting wounded in the crossfire." He laughed nervously. "Sorry. I didn't mean that. Actually, I think your head's screwed on real straight."

"Thanks. Sorry to be so intense and for making such a long speech. But it's how I feel, and it's important to me."

"I can tell. To me, too." He paused to think. "It makes

you even more desirable somehow."

"Thanks for saying that, Brian. I love you."

"I love you, too," he answered. "But where did that come from all of a sudden?"

"Oh, I don't know. I just felt like saying it."

"You can tell me that anytime you like."

Brian hadn't been entirely honest with Jeannie about what he was doing when she called. When he had hooked up his laptop a few minutes earlier, three short email messages had been waiting from Buffalo. Mary Beth had written about her upcoming trip to England, and again raised the ante by telling him that she had some real excitement about seeing him again after so many years. What really got his attention, though, was her suggestion that he call her on the phone and gave him her cell number. That invitation had driven out thoughts of everything else. Even Mahler and know-it-all ghosts.

Brian spent Friday in the Library trying to find out something about Thirley Hall and its one-time owners. He even tried checking out the seven men who had been married to the Thirley Hall women—mother, daughter and granddaughter. But his efforts left him frustrated and mostly empty-handed. He had been unable to find more than oblique references to the Hall in the research materials or indexes. The place might as well never have existed. Likewise for the husbands. He ran a search for them by name in online listings of worthies from County Suffolk but found nothing there. He searched through Early English Books Online, known familiarly as EEBO, a resource that held digital copies of every book published in England or in English in that period. There he found that Jane's second husband, one Richard Morris of Brettenham, Suffolk, had written a dull little book on estate management. At least he thought it was the same Richard Morris. That book had been written before the date of the author's marriage to Jane and therefore contained no reference to the management of Thirley Hall or its properties.

Brian pulled out his little pocket notebook and flipped to the page where he had written Mary Beth's phone number the day before, calculated the time in Buffalo as just after three in the afternoon, and picked up the phone. Butterflies flitted about in his stomach as he began to dial the number. He wondered what her voice would sound like after all this time, dreading that she wouldn't sound the same. Or that she would. He feared that he would fall all over himself trying to talk to her. Shrugging, he punched in the first few numbers, stopped and canceled the incomplete sequence. He looked out the window into the night, ran his fingers through his hair, and started again putting in the overseas code only in the end to hang up the receiver entirely. He stalked across the room and back and glared at the phone. Then he went out into the flat's interior hallway, up the four stairs to the bedroom and back down again, muttering in the most unflattering way about women, all of humanity and life in general. Instead of returning to the phone, he grabbed his raincoat, picked up his furled umbrella and walked out of the flat and into the night.

Outside, a gentle rain was falling as it had been all day. He shook open the umbrella. His walking, meant to be aimless, soon assumed a definite destination and a particular purpose: the Eagle and a pint of IPA. He was glad of the place's familiarity. He sat at a small round table near the main entrance. As the door opened to admit a young couple, he looked out across Bene't Street to St. Bene't's Church where he had been maneuvered into joining Carol Heppel for church on Sunday. There he would meet the Anglican Franciscan priest who would also be having Sunday lunch at her house. He tried to imagine what a contemporary Franciscan might look like: a round, pink-cheeked, tonsured, brown-habit-wearing Friar Tuck?

He finished his pint without ever having spoken a single word to another human being except the bartender. Shrugging into his light raincoat, he walked back out into Bene't Street. Glancing up at the little church's outline against the night sky, its squat Saxon tower predominating, he saw a small carefully groomed and headstone-filled churchyard with a decorative iron fence running across the front. In all the times he had been to the Eagle he had never been in St. Bene't's churchyard. But then, Stichen-Walling had left him with more interest than ever before in the collection of stone monuments around a church. Overtaken by a sudden impulse, he stepped through the church's open gate, descended the three steps into the yard and absently followed a path around to the right side of the ancient building, touching first one and then another of the upright headstones. There weren't that many of the tall variety. Mostly they were lower to the ground. He couldn't read the inscriptions in the inadequate light, but that didn't matter. His mind whirled with thoughts of that other ancient church and, in contrast to this one, its neglected graveyard.

He leaned against one of the upright headstones, deep in thought, and wondered about the tumbledown monuments at Stichen-Walling. Why was the whole place so neglected and abandoned in the otherwise ordinary village? What made the old church and its environs feel so malignant? And what about those other graves, the ones outside the wall? Three generations of women in one family dying in the same year was stretching coincidence a bit far. Except in the case of some epidemic. But if they had died from a common disease, then why were the burials excluded from the churchyard and unrecorded in the Parish Register? Witchcraft remained the most logical explanation. But three members of the same family? And why was there no comment in the historical record? Why such secrecy? He grew a little angry as he thought about it. What possible difference could it have made whether they were buried inside or outside of the church's grounds? He remembered that suicides had regularly been denied burial in consecrated ground. Executed murderers' bodies were customarily burned in England during that period and not buried. What was it about the credulity and gullibility of some religious people? As if any kind of god could care where the discarded remains of an immortal spirit, in the event that human beings had such things as spirits, might lie decomposing. Burial location restrictions had to be the meanest sort of discrimination and exercise of social control. The regulations governing them had to have more to do with status and wealth, local conventions, and punishment and retribution in the mortal life than about anything genuinely religious or spiritual. Misbehave and you will be excluded from paradise because your body won't be buried in the right place and in the correct way. Sure.

Without warning (can there be a warning for such a thing?) the tall headstone he was leaning on began to move. At first he thought he was sick and might be about to faint. Could it be the beer? But he had no lightheadedness or queasy feeling in his stomach that might signal either illness or drunkenness. To keep from falling over he grabbed onto the headstone even tighter. But then he realized that the thing itself was moving, rolling and pitching in the most disturbing way. He looked at it hard and immediately pulled his hand away. The movement stopped. Then he saw the still, serene and smiling face of his ghostly companion—as if suspended, hovering above the headstone. The face vanished almost immediately. Had it really been there? But its appearance remained etched deeply in his memory, or possibly his imagination. He couldn't say which.

The whole upsetting moment lasted no more than a few seconds. He expected to slip into one of his waking dreams, almost wishing he would. But it didn't happen. Instead, he stood still and quiet for a moment. Cautiously he reached out to touch the misbehaving headstone. It remained perfectly quiet and still. The stone had a cold slimy feel from the rain, but it stayed put. Brian had no intention whatever of leaning on it again. Instead, he shrugged his shoulders as a shiver passed down his spine, opened his umbrella against the resuming light rainfall and went back onto the street again. He stopped for a moment and glanced back at the stone tower that he knew had stood on that spot for a thousand years. It had been rooted there since before there was an Anglo-Norman monarchy in the kingdom or a university beside the Cam. Cambridge had been just a little market town in those days. What must it have been like to live then? Would headstones have moved in Saxon times? Would that have been a regular event? How would life have been different? Historians' questions formed almost automatically in Brian's mind. But they could not begin to compete with his mental turmoil over what had just happened to him beside that ancient tower.

As he closed the door of his flat, Brian realized—if he had ever forgotten—that the problem of his getting up the courage to call Mary Beth had not gone away. It was as if all that uncertainty now came flooding back, just as if it had lingered in the room for his return. Neither the pint of ale nor his bizarre experience in the St. Bene't's churchyard had done much to stiffen his spine for doing something as threatening as making that simple telephone call. He pulled off his raincoat and hung it on a hook beside the door next to the dripping umbrella. He dropped into the wing chair in the sitting room like a condemned man and tried to face what was troubling him about making the call. There was something about phoning anybody that always made him feel uncomfortable. Perhaps it was the sense that he might be intruding on someone else's privacy and interrupting what they were doing. He always listened in the receiver for a tone or a phrase that affirmed his fears: that his trespass had interrupted something important or had been seriously inconvenient. Why would his phone call not be an interruption? (Did I wake you? No, I was just sitting here hoping someone would call. I never actually sleep at night.) Were people's lives simply on hold waiting for him to call and give them animation? Were they the trees in the forest, making no sound as they fall to the ground? Without, that is, a caller to rescue them from that lonely fate? What if his call were to interrupt an argument that needed resolution, a moment of vital understanding with a child in trouble, or a couple making love on the living room floor? Maybe he would cause the ruin of a special dish in a crucial moment of culinary creation. Or, as had happened so often to him, his phone call would come at the same moment as someone rang the doorbell, the dog started to bark, the baby began to scream and all the demons of Hell were breaking loose over the head of his call's poor recipient.

Calling Mary Beth also had the dread that he associated with her in particular: their history together, the years spent apart, his barely suppressed feelings of longing and resignation over two decades and more, and the hopelessness, the rejection and the anger. It was all there heaped on top of his generic anxiety over causing an intrusive bell to ring in some remote spot. With a sigh and a bow to destiny, he reached for the phone and dialed the cell number she had given him. She answered after the third ring.

"Hello. Is this Brian?" She must have seen on her caller ID that the call originated in the UK.

"It is. The same old Brian. Am I catching you at a bad time?" That felt stupid.

"Oh, no. Not at all. I was just stepping outside to turn off the water on my petunia bed. I can do that just as well talking to you as not."

Mary Beth did ordinary things like raise flowers? And turn on the hose to water them? He looked at his watch. It would be about five o'clock in Buffalo.

"I was hoping you'd call," she continued. "In fact, I've been carrying my phone everywhere. Just in case."

Her candor softened the edge of his fears. Talking to her was easier than he had ever imagined it might be.

She had been waiting for his call!

"You sound much the same," he said. "Oh, maybe the timbre in your voice is a bit huskier. I would recognize it anywhere."

"Your voice seems familiar, too." She laughed lightly.

He imagined her tossing her head in the old familiar way as she let her luxurious black curls fall about her shoulders. He could only think of her as having that same great mane of black hair.

"After all these years all we can find to talk about is the sound of each other's voices? Are you feeling as awkward as I am?" she asked.

He chuckled. "Guilty. You have no idea how long I agonized over making this call."

"But I'm glad you did. Make it that is."

Searching for a neutral subject or at least one that was neutral between the two of them, he asked, "What has happened with your son? Didn't one get into trouble in school?" Something about the kid having pot in a locker.

"Jeremy? The little creep. He's duly enrolled in an Episcopal school. It's quite a good one and has the wonderful advantage of costing his father even more money than the last one." The words were light, but that lightness seemed to cover a bitter edge.

"Still struggling with your ex?"

"I guess I am. I expected you to pick up on my mention of the Episcopal Church. Don't you go any more?"

"No, not really."

"That's too bad. I'm surprised. But I'll bet there's a lot we can find surprising in each other now." She let those words hang in the air for a moment. "As for me, I probably wouldn't feel so bad and be so grumpy about James—my former husband—if I didn't feel like such an idiot where he's concerned."

"Oh come now, that's not the Mary Beth I remember. Since when were you anything but at the top of any list that called for brains?"

"I did okay as a student. And, as you may recall, most everybody hated me as a result. I never could see any reason why I should play dumb just to fulfill people's expectations of how a *girl* was supposed to be. Or to massage fragile egos. Even in graduate school I pushed them hard enough to threaten everybody. But I got the good post-doc, and they didn't."

"Now that's the Mary Beth I remember—taking no prisoners."

"You used to say that to me way back then. I seem to remember that you liked my competitiveness. It was something we shared."

"I did like that about you, and you're right about my being pretty competitive, too." He thought to himself, or at least I used to be.

"Then what happened to our personal lives? Is it the flip side of brainy aggressiveness?"

"'Fraid so."

"Let's swap stupidities," she said with a flippant tone in her voice. "I'll start. My first big dumb thing was letting you slip through my fingers."

"Sure! But it's sweet of you to say so." He scrambled to think of what he would say to her in this intimate confessional.

"I mean it. But even that doesn't match how stupid I feel about my marriage. Marrying my boss."

"Tell me about it." Brian did want to know about her marriage. Wanted to know everything about her. But he also welcomed a momentary escape from his obligation to reciprocate. Especially, he didn't want to confess to her how carrying a torch for her all these years had so dominated his life. It was much better to let her do the talking, and he had a hunch she wanted to do just that.

"It wasn't exactly a Cinderella story," she began, "It also wasn't a case of the secretary marrying the boss and becoming rich, snooty and nasty to all her former friends."

He found that bitterness again, just beneath the light laughing surface.

"Instead, I was the bright promising young scientist on the research staff who caught the CEO's eye. He really had the hots for me. I admit I played him pretty carefully. James was married at the time. I felt bad about that. But those are the rules of the game, aren't they? Our marriage followed his divorce like day following night. I know people accused me of being after his money. But it really wasn't true. I liked him. Loved him even. I never minded that he was fifteen years older than I, or that he was rich." She laughed lightly. "I definitely liked the prestige of being married to him and the positive consequences it had for my career. He was quite a catch. Or at least I thought so at the time. I tried to be a good wife in my way, and I think I do a decent job of being a mother to our three boys."

"Do you still work for his company?"

"Not for several years now. I made a good decision when I accepted the offer to go to work for a German chemical company's US operations. They made me head of research.

R-F (Reinhold-Fenster) gives me about every perk I could have asked for. It's a great job, both demanding and rewarding. I love my work."

"So what happened to the marriage?"

"I guess there's some justice in that. What I could do to one wife another woman could do to me. Or, put another way, James's pattern could be repeated. He found someone else just as he had once found me. Well, not quite the same way he found me. His latest trophy woman, not yet a wife, has her own particular attractions. When I first married James, he described me as 'brilliant and beautiful.'"

"Sounds like he has discerning taste."

"Flatterer."

Brian thought he could read between the lines to conclude that, like him, she had lost herself in work and neglected her spouse. They seemed to have much in common.

"Nobody would describe James's current squeeze as brilliant. If you had to continue the light metaphor, this one's label would need to be dim. Meow."

Brian laughed.

"But she certainly is beautiful. And young. A former Miss Buffalo. She has enough silicone high on her chest to make a billion microchips. I repeat: meow."

"Indeed."

"I can't help being nasty toward the two of them."

"I don't blame you. That sucks."

"He came home one night a couple of years ago, gathered up a few personal items from his room and left. We hadn't shared a bedroom in years, but that's another story. He said I would hear from his lawyers. I can't believe it, but I had been taken entirely by surprise. We never quarreled or fought. Never did much of anything together any more except to care for our three sons. It all felt pretty comfortable. At least it did for me. I suspected him of having affairs, but didn't mind as long as he was discreet. Myself, I remained entirely faithful. Well, I must admit that faithfulness may not be the right description. I never had affairs. But then, I felt pretty relieved to split myself only between work and motherhood. I wouldn't have had any more time or energy for a new romance than I had for James. If, that is, he'd wanted more from me, which he didn't. Casual affairs have never appealed to me."

"No, I imagine not. But it sounds pretty grim. At least the way you tell it."

"I guess so. Anyhow, the divorce dragged on for months, and it included the usual wrangling over the financial settlement and child custody. But I'm pretty much over the humiliation. You know, feeling thrown aside and all. I have refused to let him get me down. I'm not some kind of emotional cripple, after all."

"I'm so sorry about everything you've been through," he said.

"God, but you've been patient to listen to all of that."

"I'm interested."

"I didn't know how much I wanted—no, needed!—to say all that stuff. Especially to you. And right now."

The line fell silent as he considered the implications of those last words. Why did she especially want him to know? Why at this precise moment? Then he thought about her upcoming trip to London.

They went on to talk about their careers and families, and cautiously shared hopes and plans. Brian's self-revelations remained guarded. At one point he almost forgot who he was talking to and accepted the hour-long conversation at face value: as a pleasant talk with an old friend. In the end not even their mutual circumspection kept them from coming around to some careful flirting. Though it was cloaked in references to the past and old times, he knew that the immediate future was the real agenda. For both of them.

Mary Beth said, "There were lots of things we never had a chance to do together as college freshmen." Brian understood her to mean the way they had always stopped short of having sex. "At our age I think we can feel free to be more ourselves, don't you?" Her words formed at once a question and a promise.

Brian felt a wave of excitement pass through his body.

This is Mary Beth! He said, "Yes. When you're in London we can get to know each other all over again." It surprised him that she seemed to share his mounting desire and intent.

After he hung up the phone Brian sat there in his desk chair thinking about Mary Beth. Self-contained, that was the term for her, and that had always described her. It seemed that nothing had changed. He imagined that her three sons gave her most of the emotional input that she needed. He could also understand why she kept to herself, both before and after her husband moved out. Somehow the thought of a mature Mary Beth having affairs and getting laid didn't match with either the girl he had known or the woman she seemed to have become.

Still he wondered why she had contacted him after all these years. That seemed to suggest that perhaps Mary Beth had begun to feel lonely. Why shouldn't she think about him now? What she hadn't said, but what Brian understood intuitively, was the possibility that beneath her controlled outer shell a soft warm heart resided in a woman who just wanted gentle touching and nurturing.

And then maybe not.

As Mary Beth admitted she was used to having plans, and she seemed to have one now. This plan apparently involved Brian, the old boyfriend. The logic ran something like this: he was single; she was single. What could it hurt if they tried to pick up where they had left off in college? It might be fun. What's to lose? But for Brian the prospect of seeing Mary Beth again after all these years was far from simple. Or simply fun.

More than two weeks remained before Mary Beth's arrival in London, and meanwhile his daughter, Bobbie, would soon be there for a visit of her own. The prospect of having his only daughter with him felt safe and secure. Thoughts of being with Mary Beth were scary.

He decided to call it a day and curl up in bed with his current novel. Many things swirled around in his head as he tried to read: women, alive and dead; daughter Bobbie; his work; and his vexing dreams. Perhaps the combination of them all conspired against him, but he slept badly and not enough, dreaming in the ordinary way about capricious god-figures. They played games with him, and he was their unwilling pawn.

Inside, St. Bene't's was a dumpy little place. Brian looked around with a surge of aesthetic disdain as he waited beside Carol Heppel for the morning service to start. The ancient tower had been largely left alone by the Victorian dabblers whose misguided zeal had turned the rest of the church into a jumble of old and new Gothic arches, supports and vaults. The entire interior had been whitewashed. Its surprising congregation of perhaps a hundred souls filled even the side aisles where worshipers had little or no sight lines into the narrow chancel. The tiny place was so packed with people that Brian quietly praised his smiling hostess for having saved a place for him. Personally, he felt a disharmony of jumbled emotions that matched the architectural mishmash around him. His critic's mind rebelled at the place, while lower down, somewhere closer to his breastbone, he felt a little excited. This unhandsome but alive little church made him think of the empty and forlorn old place at Stichen-Walling. By even sharper contrast he thought of those lonely graves banished outside the neglected and disreputable graveyard. The place seemed to scream of miscarriage of justice or some terrible misapplication of Christian zeal, and it stirred an angry response in him. Still, and despite all of these strange notions going through his mind, his final reaction to St. Bene't's that morning was the comfort of spiritual familiarity and a remarkable sense of belonging. This wash of feelings came in a place where he had never been before and where he knew only one other person. As he sat anxiously waiting for the start of the service and for his first glimpse of Father Jeremiah, he realized how much stock he was placing in this day and in this priest.

The organ prelude ended and the church bell began to ring. Brian followed along with everyone else as they stood in place and listened to the play-through of the processional hymn. When the congregation began to sing, he was stunned to find that they did it with gusto, rather than the embarrassed and introverted excuse for singing he had usually found in English parish churches. The liturgical procession had the cross in front as usual, followed by two torchbearers with burning candles. There was no choir. Brian first spotted Father Jeremiah at the end of the line of vested people, walking down the center aisle. The Franciscan seemed to wink and bob his head at every worshiper, fulfilling Brian's image of a latter-day Friar Tuck: a short round, mostly tonsure-bald, monkish priest with a soft gentle face that seemed for all the world like a model for the smiling cherubs that grinned down from the capitals of the jollier sort of medieval piers. But in place of the pink cheeks of a stereotypical English country vicar he had the rich chestnut-ebony skin and facial features of Bombay. Looking at the priest, a person would never identify his birthplace as East London where Carol had said he originated. The priest had a warm resonant voice with the lilting tones of his family's Indian origins, plus the occasional missing "h" of his London upbringing and an unmistakable Oxbridge whine. He was a living composite, both visual and aural, of contemporary Britain with all its vitality and racial diversity. He fascinated Brian from the first.

After the service Carol led them a merry fifteen-minute chase from St. Bene't's to her little house in a quiet neighborhood backed up against the Botanical Gardens. They scooted through the streets, the diminutive priest and Brian both struggling breathlessly to keep up with their hostess. From time to time she would stop, turn around, grin at her trailing companions, and then, head down in determination, take off again down the street like a bloodhound on the scent. Fr. Jeremiah and Brian shared looks of amusement and mock exasperation at her as they scrambled to keep up. Finally they reached a brightly-flowered and carefully-groomed little garden. It led to a brilliant blue door and through it into Carol's front hallway with stairs ascending and a door to the right leading into the parlor. That room suited their hostess perfectly. It had framed family pictures and knickknacks covering every inch of the polished surfaces.

Carol immediately disappeared into the back of the house with the words, "must flip the switch," only to return a few moments later. "Can I get you a glass of sherry? Or," she grinned wickedly, "how about a nice big whiskey?"

"With pleasure. A whiskey would suit with perfection." Father Jeremiah grinned. Again the cherub. "You're a blessing, dear lady."

Brian concurred on both counts and reflected on other Sunday lunches he had had over the years in English homes. Perhaps there is nothing that warms the soul and fills the body as completely as traditional English Sunday lunch. Carol's efforts met all expectations: roast chicken and potatoes, three veg, and a French Chardonnay, topped off with a piece of chocolate cake soaked in fresh cream. Brandy followed cups of rich strong coffee in the front parlor. Brian was satiated, and, he later thought, had had his defenses lowered for Jeremiah's wily ways.

Carol Hepple began the after-dinner conversation's more serious turn, "Father, Brian has talked to me about the peculiar dreams he's been having. You know, I mentioned them to you?"

"Indeed, dear lady." The priest's face instantly changed from affable luncheon guest to serious professional as he drummed his fingers against the bowl of the brandy snifter cradled in his hands. The time had come for him to pay for his Sunday lunch. Carol excused herself to clean up in the kitchen.

Brian sighed, settled back into the embrace of an overstuffed chair and let the moment lull him into telling his story. Except for little cooing sounds Jeremiah made as apparent encouragement, the priest said nothing until Brian had finished. A long silence grew up between them in the wake of the narrative, and after a time Brian began to feel uncomfortable. Carol's return seemed to break the tension.

"And so," Jeremiah said at last, "how do you understand these experiences of yours? Who does your ghost figure seem to be? Why do you think of him as your companion?"

"I wish I knew the answers to those questions." Brian looked at the priest, feeling expectant. It had been okay after all, telling it all to a priest. Clergy believed in weird stuff didn't they?

"And why do you think they are dreams, hmm?" He rubbed his hands together. "Dreams are usually those flights of fantasy that our subconscious comes up with in our sleep, sometimes deeply revealing of our psyches, or—as with Scrooge—of 'a bit of gravy.'" He grinned. Again the cherub. "Your experiences don't seem to fit either of those. Unless, that is, historians have different kinds of dreams than mere mortals." He chuckled, and Brian nervously joined in. "Mostly, you seem always to be perfectly awake and, unlike with ordinary dreams, you remember them in the greatest detail."

Brian felt self-conscious again, possibly even more so than before, "Well, that is . . . you know, it's . . . it's kind of a fantasy of a person . . . somebody, um, let me see, who studies the past, that is—that they might be able to experience it in some way."

"And that's what you think is happening to you, a kind of dream fulfillment of your deepest professional desires?"

"Something like that, I—I guess." Even Brian could hear the lack of conviction in his voice. "No, not really. Ah, I've never done that before." He let his gaze pass to the little china pieces on a shelf beside the mantle. There, along with some sweet little figurines, he spotted the incongruous statuette of a snowman with his arms upraised.

"I suppose a person could concoct a perfectly sound psychological explanation around such a theory." Jeremiah shifted topic abruptly. "And isn't there a fair amount of stress going on in your personal life? A divorce?"

"Yes," Brian said simply.

"So we could conclude safely enough that the dreams come as a result of personal and professional stress. There's always some work-related pressure to rely on when building psychological theories. In your case, getting the book done. Diminished energy for work. That sort of thing. Plus you have a lifetime of desire to experience the past and a predilection toward paranormal experience: your place memories. Just so. Now you have these vivid dreams.

Coming to Cambridge puts you right in the middle, where much of the past you have studied has happened. Potential place memories everywhere. And, voila!" he exclaimed, becoming a living cliché by making little circling motions in the air with an index finger and grinning. "Your subconscious behaves like a good little trooper and gives you everything and more that you ever hoped for or dreamed of." An ironic smile lighted his face. "And it all comes right out of your storehouse of memories and learning."

Jeremiah paused, seemed to think for a moment, perhaps for effect, and then went on, "It's a tidy theory." He paused and looked back and forth between Brian and Carol. "But, there's something more going on here, isn't there?" Neither of his rapt listeners made any comment. "What about those occasions when identifiable historical figures don't appear at all, such as at the Stichen-Walling churchyard or last night at St. Bene't's?"

"That really wasn't one of the dreams—last night. At least I . . . I don't think it was."

"Indeed. Then what was it?" Jeremiah looked hard at him before going on, "And of course there's your central character, the ghostly apparition who carries no historical identity for you at all. What about him? Is all of this dreaming just evidence that you're ready for the lock-up, do you think? Or maybe there's an alternative explanation?"

Brian could only shrug his shoulders and say, "I don't know. I guess. Maybe." He felt expectant.

"Then there's one more piece that I noticed, a sort of shift in the experiences. Know what I mean? Ever since your encounter with Julian of Norwich you've had only one of your historical dreams, and even Julian doesn't exactly fit the pattern of the other historical ones, if I can call them that: portrait known to you; information that you already knew or guessed—that sort of thing. Like you, I've never heard of Julian having a connection to Cambridge, much less to the convent that precedes Jesus College. Though, as you say, there's no reason why she shouldn't have been in Cambridge. There certainly is no portrait of her that I've ever heard of. Not much reliable portraiture at all in England in the fourteenth century, for that matter. That's something that comes with the Renaissance and gives you portraits of all your other dream people. But you're the historian. You know all of this. So something's happened here." The Franciscan sat back in his chair and sipped at his brandy, the pleasure of it painted on his face, his dark eyes intense. "A shift has occurred, hasn't it? Now you have non-personified mystical visions. I think this is the operative word. Visions. Not dreams. It follows that your friend from Midsummer Common is a spiritual companion, not a ghost who is haunting you. The whole thing looks very different when you think of it as your mystical visions and spiritual companion, instead of your dreams and ghost, don't you see? Dreams and ghosts have less to do with each other than visions and spiritual companions do. It's a matter of congruity."

There was that word again. *Vision.* Brian had almost forgotten about Charlie's suggestion that he might not be having dreams at all. He had wanted to forget it. His rational mind could wrap itself around the idea of having vivid dreams, but it had lots of trouble with the concept of his having mystical visions. No North Shore Episcopalian he knew had visions. The idea was laughable.

"What do you know about mystical experience?" Jeremiah asked.

"Not much. What exactly do you mean by mystical?" Brian asked.

The Franciscan answered his question without skipping a beat. "Unmediated experience of the sacred. The kind of thing that Julian encountered and wrote about in her *Showings;* or Elijah with his still small voice; the call of Isaiah, the Transfiguration—any number of gospel stories. What about St. John of the Cross, Teresa of Avila? There are hundreds—thousands of well-known examples."

"Then you think . . .?" Brian thought to himself: but, people weren't mystics anymore, were they?

"I'm just suggesting," Jeremiah went on, "that there may be other ways to describe what's happening to you than having to resort to psycho-babble alone."

Carol stirred in her seat. Brian had almost forgotten that

she was there. He turned to her and said, "What do you think about all of this?"

"I think that what Father says makes perfect sense," she said. She licked her lips before continuing, "After all, I learned a long time ago that not everything that happens in life can be comfortably explained away by logic and physics."

Jeremiah grinned at her. "My experience of God is as a constantly expanding horizon, sort of like the fog lifting at sea. Little by little one can see farther and farther away. But," he looked back and forth between Brian and Carol and grinned, "You still see only the wide expanse of the inscrutable ocean. Just more of it."

"That's pretty obscure of you," Carol said.

"You bet it is," Brian inserted. "My experience of God ..." He hesitated.

"Yes?" said Jeremiah after a time. "You were saying about your experience of God."

"Oh, nothing," Brian said. "Only ... only that there was a time in my life when I thought I had a pretty good handle on God and how He works?"

"There's that old masculine God again," Carol said. "Who is that? The Warrior King of the Hebrew tribes?"

"Something like that," Brian answered absently. "But what seemed to work for me—at least when I was about fifteen or so—was the notion that God really cared about me and about my life. But that was then."

"So what happened?" Jeremiah asked.

Brian began to feel embarrassed. He couldn't really talk about these things. Could he? "Oh, what the hell," he said. "I figured this out years ago. When my mother died—I was just a kid at the time—that same beneficent God seemed to die with her. With the exception of a brief blip here and there, the best I've been able to do since is to keep myself going to services from time to time and receiving the sacrament. I don't even seem to want to do that any more. Today was the first time I've made my communion in—let me see, I think it's been since—since Easter. Or—or was that last year?"

"Why is that?" asked Jeremiah

Brian didn't pause for an instant before he answered, "I

think it was a year ago Easter." He gathered himself, "Because I don't feel obligated to show up and do my duty any more. The way I used to feel."

"So the Sacred Mysteries of blood and flesh are only an obligation for you?"

"That's about it?"

"And what about today?" Carol asked.

"I liked it," he said. "Yes, I liked it very much."

"And what does that tell you?" Jeremiah asked.

"I—I don't know exactly. Except I was glad to be there."

"This is a subject we need to talk more about," Jeremiah said, "I especially want to hear about those—what did you call them? —blips?"

Jeremiah's words sounded to Brian like a shrink ending a session. Maybe there isn't that much difference at the end of the day between psychotherapy and spiritual direction.

"Should we make a regular appointment?" Jeremiah asked.

Despite feeling threatened by this conversation Brian was intrigued enough to take the priest up on his offer. They made a date for right after Bobbie's visit. In the meantime maybe he could borrow a little sanity from his sensible daughter. He excused himself, thanking Carol for lunch and saying he needed to go back to his flat and make a phone call. What he really needed was to get away and be by himself. He ached to sort out the many details of this day. Meeting Jeremiah had offered him more challenges than he had expected.

One final and soft-spoken comment from the priest lingered with him all the way home. "I think that if you can figure out the fierce-looking mounted men who persistently intrude, you will understand all of the rest," he said. "Perhaps *they* are what it's all about."

chapter fourteen

Bobbie Craig's arrival in Cambridge coincided with the coming of early autumn. Reliable sunshine, mild temperatures and the gradually shortening daylight hours put a sparkle in the air. The turning of the leaves into bright reds and golds would come later, but the turn in season put a bounce in people's step and smiles on their faces. Autumn fitted perfectly Brian's sense of his only child. Tall slender and graceful, she always seemed to make the day a little brighter and Brian's senses a bit keener. Bobbie's autumn personality showed in her clothing—burnished wools and jeans, and brown loafers on her feet when she wasn't in tennis shoes. Even in the Chicago winter she preferred a sleeveless down vest to the more usual heavy coat. It was impossible to imagine this tree-hugger wearing anything but clothing made of natural fibers. Polyester had been banished years ago. At twenty-one, her high energy lifestyle always had her doing more and sampling more of what life offered than most of her friends ever did. At once athletic and arty, she was equally at home in front of a canvas with palate and brush or running a marathon: always the participant and rarely the spectator. Her dark blonde hair was cut on the short side and gave her a perky outdoors look. She would be quick to tell you that it took very little fixing.

On his bus ride to meet her at the Cambridge rail station that morning Brian sat with many memories of Bobbie's growing up. Childhood and adolescence blended together into flashbacks of her earliest words, "Daddy" being the very first on record. He remained proud of that feat even now. Her first unstable but determined steps came when she was about a year old amidst squealing excitement as she moved from mom to dad across the living room floor. He still missed the way she would run to him and throw her toddler's arms around his legs. Landmarks of her growing up remained etched in his memory: crayon pictures taped up on the refrigerator door; the discovery of boys ("But, Pops, he only wants to hold my *hand*!"); or fussing with makeup ("Wipe off that lipstick, young lady." "Awe, Pops!"). There were those incessant phone conversations with friends and his teaching her to drive ("Put the brake on now, gently. Gently. Now! Bobbie, stop the car, for God's sake!" "That okay, Pops?" she answered as he peeled himself off the windshield.) She tickled his pride when she mirrored his ways, while echoes of her mother still brought awkward reminders of that first disastrous marriage.

Suddenly and surprisingly he encountered a strange sadness as he thought about Kathleen and their long-ago dreams and hopes. Kathleen: the vivacious and mercurial partner who could always make him laugh. He even felt another of those unexpected waves of fondness for her as he thought about her struggle with relentless depression. For over a decade he had labored to get self-justification over that failed marriage, and in the process had almost forgotten the good things about his former spouse. After all, they did have Bobbie to show for their time together. But now, and for the first time in longer than he could remember, he found himself wondering how things might have come out differently with Kathleen. Old feelings he had thought safely tucked away into the past and stored on the shelf with his old research. But just for this moment he understood afresh how impossible it was to relegate any intimacy to a safe place in one's past. Kathleen with all the joy and pain that memories of her could engender seemed once again very present to him as he anticipated their daughter's arrival. But then he seemed unable to banish even the subjects of his research to a remote and unchanging past. Why should Kathleen be any different?

Brian passed his nearly twenty-minute wait at the station by pacing up and down the long platform. Over and over he passed the same people who also walked back and forth, or sat on benches reading newspapers. Some idled away their time by staring off into space, perhaps dreaming of a better time. Others had looks of excitement on their faces. Still others bore worried expressions with furrowed brows and serious eyes. He admitted to being one of the anxious ones, those who combined excitement with apprehension. Perhaps all divorced parents felt that way: insecure in the presence of their children, unconsciously worrying about competition with the other parent for affection and living with the fear of rejection. Brian had long felt these feelings where Bobbie was concerned. He was always wondering if each visit would be the last one or if their playful relationship would end and never return. Unreasonable fears, he knew, but ones he always felt. As usual, a vague dread of airplane crashes or rail tragedies fleetingly distressed him. But then the 11:23 express from King's Cross pulled in right on time, and Bobbie jumped off with the crowd—long-legged and energetic, the very picture of vigor and health. Planting a kiss on his cheek and enfolding him in one of her bear hugs, Bobbie melted all of his remaining reserve and dignity and brought surprising, but not unprecedented, tears of joy to his eyes. It had only been three months since they had last seen each other; it seemed to Brian like a decade.

"Hi, Pops." She squeezed him again and grinned.

"Don't call me Pops. I'm not some character out of a Disney movie." It was their private joke: she called him Pops; he objected but obviously loved it; she pretended to be reproached. He sobered the mood with, "And hi, yourself. I would have been happy to meet you at the airport."

"I'm good to get here by myself." Bobbie shouldered her backpack.

"Obviously." Brian picked up her canvas bag. It was surprisingly light and gave off an odd rattling sound. He led her out to the taxi rank. "I'm so glad you came. Maybe you can keep your Old Man sane."

"Since when was it a daughter's job to preserve a parent's sanity?" She laughed, flipped her head and shook her rich short mane. Light-brown eyes flashed playfully. Hair and eyes alike were much the same color as Brian's. Bobbie reached her free arm around her father and gave him a sideways squeeze. "It's good to see you, Pops."

He tried to imitate a stern scowl and failed. All he could do at the moment was to ignore another wash of feelings for her and say in feigned neutrality, "What do you want to do while you're here? You've got what, ten days?"

"That's about it. I just want to hang mostly—and annoy you. Keep you from working too much. Oh, I want to do a little drawing with some fresh subjects. Colored pencils mostly."

"No danger of my overworking. I'm not getting much done right now." He glanced down at her large bag at his feet. "Oh, I get it. Why this thing is so light and noisy." He pointed to the suitcase, imagining the portable artist's gear it no doubt held. "How's your painting coming?" Bobbie's devotion to her art major at SU threatened to give her a compulsion for work that matched his own. Or at least his former obsession during productive years.

"Actually, I'm trying a new technique—new to me at least. It's kind of like icon painting in the Orthodox churches. Except that I'm using colored pencils on paper instead of egg tempera and gold leaf on wood panels. I try to create an ethereal stylized effect with a hint of impressionism. There's a set of rules in real icon painting. Light, shading, focus and even prayers to say while you do it."

"How did you get into that?"

"A class. What else? Part of the thing is to have something in the icon that draws the eye to one spot, and then everything else builds upon that, the focus point. Know what I mean?" A question with no answer expected. "The picture itself is built up, layer upon layer. In religious icons, the focal point is usually the eyes of the figure. Like, Christ's or Mary's or maybe some saint's. It's supposed to draw you in. The theory is that it makes a two-way window into and out of heaven. You see into the God mystery and, likewise, you also are seen deep inside. I try to use those techniques with other subjects. It's pretty cool to play with."

"That's interesting."

She flashed him a contentious glance. It was as if to ask for a better response than he had given, perhaps a reverberation of her growing up years when he had been obsessed with his own work.

"No, I really mean it," he said. "I *am* interested. Besides, I haven't seen examples of your work in ages." As usual, she could see right through him. But he *was* interested. At some level there wasn't anything about her that didn't interest him.

"I've been doing all that commercial stuff lately. You know: the internship. I've been lettering signs with computer vinyl for ads and learning magazine layout stuff. I guess I could make a living if I didn't have a Dad to support me."

"Pretty dreary, though?"

"Not dreary exactly, but still I can't wait to do something that really interests me, something experimental. There should be great subjects here."

"We'll find you some. But come on it's our turn for a cab." Brian opened the door to the boxy London-style taxi and followed her inside, dumping the canvas bag of artist's gear on the floor between them. The backpack, presumably filled with her personal items, sat on the seat between them. "Lord's Hostel," he said to the driver.

"Right, Gov."

Bobbie grinned at the driver's back and said under her breath, "He actually called you *Gov*. I can't believe it."

"Damn, but I'm glad to see you," Brian said. He felt the tears well up in his eyes again.

They rode quietly for a few minutes as the taxi driver extricated the cab from the narrow Station Road. Finally she said, "You okay with the Emily thing? Seeing anyone new?"

"Okay. It's funny you should ask. A friend and her daughter came to visit and . . . well, and we found we had more in common that we realized.

Bobbie grinned knowingly. "What's her name?"

"Jeannie Mautner. She's in English at SU. I think you'd like her."

"Better than Emily?"

"You don't like Emily?"

"*Like* Emily? Not particularly. In the future, you really had better let me pick your wives."

Bobbie meant that crack as a joke, but it carried the ring of bitter truth. She probably could do a better job of picking than he had done. What would she think of Jeannie? Of Mary Beth? He didn't even know what he thought about Mary Beth. He had no interest in telling her about the old flame, but delighted in talking about Jeannie. He tried to pay attention to what that decision told him. He knew he should pay attention to it.

The top-heavy cab swerved as it maneuvered its way through traffic. Finally the driver left Hills Road and wove through side streets on a route between rows of connected houses, a usual and effective way to avoid the traffic slow-ups in the crowded little city.

Brian showed Bobbie his favorite Cambridge haunts. They ate in his usual Indian and Thai restaurants and drank pints of ale at the Eagle. A new experience for them to have together. She even seemed to share his enthusiasm for attending Evensongs at Kings. He finally told her about his dreams and his ghostly companion, stopping at St. Bene't's churchyard to show her the animated headstone.

"And there *he* was. My Ghost. Seeming to hover over the top of this very same stone."

"He sounds to me like a saint-figure," she said thoughtfully after awhile.

"What kind of figure?"

"You know, like St. Francis or St. Benedict. One of those medieval guys. Your own personal piece of saintliness in the here and now."

"What would make you think that? You sound like a Catholic—saints and all. I didn't know you went to church. Or anything." He stopped in front of the Corn Exchange, a theater in its present incarnation, and tried to understand what she was saying.

"I'm not any sort of Catholic. There's a lot you don't know about me."

"Sorry." Brian felt chagrined.

"I didn't mean it as a criticism. You're a really good dad, Pops!" She grinned playfully and poked him in the ribs with her elbow as they started walking again. "What I meant was that I have some new interests, and one of them is a meditation group I've joined. It's kind of an interfaith bunch—all from SU. It meets at a local Episcopal church out there in the burbs. We have Buddhists and New Agers. Even a witch who belongs to a Wicca."

"A witch? What the hell's a witch doing in an Episcopal Church in suburban Chicago?" For some unaccountable reason he felt outraged at the very idea. A witch for God's sake! But he soon realized that his knee-jerk reaction covered his greater surprise, to which he gave voice, "I can't believe you're going to church." They stepped around some slower walkers.

"Why does that surprise you? Isn't that what you taught me to do?" she asked. "But I don't buy all those old dogmas. You know, God demanding the death of Jesus for our sins and our needing to believe exactly the right things to be saved. Then there's the idea that God rewards and punishes people for their good and bad deeds: all you have to do is look around you to know that's not true. Some of the worst people I know are rich and beautiful. What did they do to deserve what they have? Or what about people who are born blind, or deaf or with fatal diseases? And it's really stupid to think that Christians have a truth that nobody else has. We just happen to be the lucky ones to be born into the one true faith on the face of the earth. As if God would play favorites that way. All that judgmental junk sucks."

"That junk, as you call it, is Christianity," he snapped. But as soon as he had said it he wondered why he was defending a religion that seemed to make so little sense to him anymore either. He had read somewhere that dogma was the last thing to go when a person lost his faith. Is that what he had come to—defending dogma? But all he could manage to say to her was a hollow, "If that's how you feel, then why go to church at all?" They began to climb the stairs into the back way of the Lion Yard, a small thirty-year-old shopping mall.

"'Cause we talk about really important things," she insisted seriously. "Like, well, understanding the Bible, you know, as something other than literal truth or a roadmap to the details of daily life."

"Like what?"

"Oh, metaphors and symbols. Stories. Like when Jesus says, 'I am the bread of life,' does he really mean that he's bread? Or did Jesus say it at all? What if the group of

Christians who wrote that experienced Jesus as nourishment, and just said it in that memorable earthy way? That's metaphor." She stopped in front of an electronics shop window and looked at a display of portable CD players. "Cool," she said before resuming her narrative. "We talk about insights from other religions and how they can connect with Christianity. Even Wicca." She grinned, acknowledging his discomfort. "Besides, I think the real purpose of religion is not for getting to heaven but for changing the world for the better. I'd like to think that people are something other than selfish little buying machines." She waved her arm in an arc around them at the bustling shopping center.

This surprising wisdom from his little girl silenced Brian for a moment. Finally he replied awkwardly, "But you say that my Ghost, or—or companion." He remembered what Fr. Jeremiah had suggested. "That he might represent one of the saints. I'm not sure I understand what you mean by that."

"I don't pretend to know either. It's just that I'm trying to think outside the box, that's all." She furrowed her brow. "And why not a saint? Or even Christ to you. After all, religion isn't just something that the church hierarchy controls. Why couldn't this be your way of experiencing God?" She paused for a minute. "But what about you? Are you even going to church anymore—all that sin and redemption stuff?"

"Not really. Evensong isn't the same thing. It's all feeling pretty foolish now. Most of my colleagues gave up church attendance years ago. If they ever went. Maybe that's what I should do."

"And not even be connected at all anymore?"

"Why ever should I bother? It's high time I accepted the fact that for me it's been just a museum piece, a vain attempt to keep the past alive long after its actual demise."

Her face adopted a quizzically earnest expression, "I know that church means more to you than that, Dad. Or at least it used to. Besides, there are other options you can choose from. You don't have to have all that old sin and fall stuff. Like . . . oh, where we fit in the scheme of things, for example. Spirituality. "She stopped and looked at him and then around them at the shopping center. "Why ever did we come to this place?" she asked.

"To the Lion Yard? I just wanted to show you something other than old churches."

"I like old churches. This place is just . . . well, crowded and ugly."

"I see what you mean. It is pretty bad. Somehow this feels different than the public market."

She offered no response. They walked on out the front entrance and found themselves on Sidney Street between St. Andrew's Church and Christ's College.

"You know, I'm not sure religion does carry much meaning for me anymore. I don't even know what spirituality is." He was surprised at himself to be saying to Bobbie things he'd hardly been able to admit to himself. Then he remembered that it had always been this way with her. He had always felt free to talk to her.

She tilted her head to the side and continued to look puzzled. Then, as if grasping a renewed equilibrium, she said, "That's a cool church."

"St. Andrew's? It's just a Victorian copy. Not the real thing."

"What *is* the real thing? Does it have to be five hundred years old to be real?"

"Sort of," he said, but recognized as he said it how shallow and predictable the response was.

"Oh, come on, Pops. In Chicago, we'd admire it because it's so *old*." She grinned, looking like she knew that she had caught him in one of his snobbish little historian's judgments. Then she picked up the previous thread. "But if we can't turn to religion to find what's true, then where can we look for the meaning of things?"

"Maybe nowhere," he answered simply, and knew that he probably meant exactly that. Maybe there was no meaning to find.

"Life's a bitch and then you die?"

"Something like that."

"Pops, I really don't think you mean that."

He noticed they were blocking the way and led her across

the street. "Why not? Why believe in something like—like God and the Virgin Birth and Resurrection and all of those legends. It's not exactly logical. There is no good evidence to establish such preposterous claims, is there?" He felt as if the burden of a worn-out belief system had been raised from his shoulders.

"But you've been going to church all your life. Certainly for as long as I can remember. You never used to miss."

"Not true lately, though. I've been asking myself exactly why I kept going at all. Why I bothered."

"Because it matters to you."

Suddenly Brian realized what an odd conversation they were having. It was as if the usual roles of parent and child had been reversed. In this case, the child was the one advocating religion and church, and the parent had become the rebel against everything he had always been taught or believed was true. "Christ's College is open," he said suddenly. "We could go in and look around. You interested?"

"Sure."

He led her through a normal sized door in a set of ancient, weathered and worm eaten double doors big enough to admit a coach and team of horses. They walked past the porter's lodge into the quad. He welcomed the diversion as a break in their intense conversation. Perhaps he would do a bit of research on what theologians were saying these days— find out what had Bobbie so interested in religion. In the meantime, the modest quadrangle where they stood led, he knew, to an even larger one beyond a portico in the opposite corner. They followed around the paved walkway into the inner precincts as he played tour guide and showed her the Great Hall and other features of the college and its grounds. But the words and, behind them the meaning of their conversation, continued to bubble up inside.

The rental car purred contentedly toward Stichen-Walling, navigating busy roads and passing under bright clear autumn skies. Brian's tense excitement grew with each mile. It was all he could do to hold back his mounting eagerness long enough for them to grab a quick pub lunch at the Flint and Fleece. He barely sampled his shepherd's pie. Bobbie downed the bread, cheese and salad of a plowman's as if she had been out in the field all morning. Finally he led her around the Victorian church and through the decrepit lychgate into the medieval church's neglected grounds.

"Well, there it is. Kind of a run-down looking place isn't it?" he said with false lightness. He stood back, appraising the building and its gravestones, remembering his previous visits and again experiencing the discomfort he had felt before.

"Where're the other graves? The ones outside?" Bobbie put down her canvas bag of artist's supplies with a clank and rattle of aluminum tubing and cardboard.

"Over there." Brian pointed toward the tumbledown part of the wall and watched his daughter in wonder as she walked around, professionally sizing up the scene before her. Her long-legged gait quickly covered the distance to the break in the wall where she quietly surveyed the area outside and turned to appraise the layout inside with a serious practiced eye. How had his little girl turned into this competent young artist with a manner so experienced and professional?

He looked down at the headstones of the banished graves and felt mildly embarrassed by the places on the stone where he had removed the lichen. Those spots looked like nasty gashes in the natural growth of the orange and gray plants.

"This is terrific," she said. "It's a great subject. Thanks for showing it to me." She returned to where she had left her bag. In a moment she had selected her spot and set up a canvas-seated stool and matching low side table, both made of aluminum tubing she had taken from her bag. She laid out a box of carefully arranged colored pencils on the table, sat down with a large sketch pad in her lap and studied the scene.

He stood behind her and looked out across the litter of headstones and the unkempt grounds, trying to see it all through her eyes and to find out through her chosen perspective why the place had pleased her so much. On the near left stood the round-towered little petrified pudding with its sagging roof and aura of neglect. In the foreground a jumble of stone monuments were all tangled with tall grass and weeds as they pointed skyward at contrary angles and postures. The opening in the wall, its stones splayed inward into the churchyard, gave a kind of eerie—or so it seemed to him—focal point of her selected line of sight. Outside the wall, and clearly visible from this angle, one of the excluded headstones shined as it caught the early afternoon sun. Brian already knew that this very headstone marked the grave of his Plain Jane, though he no longer had to think of her as *plain*. He now knew her real identity as Jane of Thirley Hall in the county of Suffolk, a woman with a lengthy string of surnames. Thus far Brian had not been able to turn up details about a place called Thirley Hall, and that had been discouraging. Today he meant to go back to the town archives to do some more checking in land records while Bobbie worked on her drawings.

The collection of deeds, letters, wills and land transfers in the archives were still mostly in a jumble and needing the hand of some patient soul to index and analyze them. Nevertheless, by using a combination of instinct and patient searching Brian found a number of unmistakable references to the site of the late medieval manor in an area generally defined as Thirley Green. It lay in the countryside some three miles outside Stichen-Walling. He thrilled especially to discover a will dated 1528 that gave an inventory of the small but prosperous country house and much detailed information, including lists of furniture and bedding, outbuildings, livestock and even the contents of the larder. Thirley Hall had been well established at least two centuries before Jane was born and had been owned in its earlier years by at least two prominent local families, each of which had tiny villages named after them—the Sackwells and, before them, the Belchamps. An Alfred Sackwell had married a woman named Jane, which Brian had already confirmed from the marriage records. After Alfred's death, Jane retained possession of the property on behalf of her daughter, Mary, their only child. He could find no more new information about Jane or her daughter. Nor was there anything about the fate of Thirley Hall. Surely there would be a record somewhere of what had happened to it and to its owners. Somebody inherited from Jane and her progeny, and that family's papers could very well be extant. The question was where.

He sat at one of the tables in the archive room feeling a combination of elation at having a pretty good idea where the Hall probably had been, and frustration that he still lacked details of its demolition. If the Hall had been destroyed by fire, as was likely, there ought at least to be some record of that. But he found no such details. Finally, he checked with the woman who oversaw the archives. "Do you know where I might find this place?" He showed her the description of the Hall, including the name, "Thirley Green."

"Oh, yes. I think I know where that would be," she said. "Just a minute." She began to rummage in a stack of rolled up papers and found what she was looking for. "Here's the area's Ordinance Survey Map," she said as she unrolled it and spread it out over the counter that separated her work area from the public portion of the room. She began to trace the map's representation of contours, roads and streams with an index finger. "Here," she said at last, pointing to a spot on the map.

Brian looked at the place where her finger rested. "Yes, I see what you mean. Thirley Green all right." He gauged the distance from Stichen-Walling and began to write down on his pad of notepaper the road directions for getting there from the town.

"Actually, I think the location you're looking for would be just here." She pointed to a wide low hill beside the Green. "My guess is that this is where the old manor house would have been built."

"Overlooking the Green?"

"Yes. There was less need in this part of the country to seek protected places against winter storms than in coastal or even mountainous area. Many of the old manors around here were on hilltops for defense and for the prospect such sites gave them."

"I see what you mean." Brian finished writing out the directions he would need to get to the place. With mounting excitement, he thanked her and headed back to the old churchyard to see how Bobbie was doing. Then they could go find the site of Thirley Hall. He could barely wait.

Brian stepped out of his own excitement and anticipation of seeing the site of Thirley Hall long enough to look hard at Bobbie's striking series of three nearly completed drawings of the church and yard. Once again he marveled at her skill, now displayed before him, but he had to admit that there was something about the drawings that made him uncomfortable. He shrugged off that eerie feeling.

"I'm sorry to drag you away, but I'd like to go and find where that Thirley Hall place used to be."

"No problem. I can finish these up later. Back at your place." She quickly closed the big book of drawing paper, packed up her gear and put it all in the car.

They followed Brian's scribbled directions and took the A134, leading from Stichen-Walling to Bury St. Edmunds, Brian not bothering to say goodbye to the ugly village. He drove with mounting enthusiasm as Bobbie studied his notes and the road map, a version of the ordinance survey for the area. Finally, she looked up and said, "I think this is it— coming up on the left. The road where we need to turn. Yes, I'm sure it is."

Brian downshifted and maneuvered the snappy little English Ford onto a narrow road.

"Now, according to your directions there's another turn very soon—to the right, but then it veers to the left, a really tiny road. Smaller than this one, if that's possible."

Brian swerved to avoid an on-coming car that had come hurtling around a sharp bend in the road. "That must be it there."

"Could be. Yes, I think it is."

Brian turned the car onto an even narrower track, one that looked ribbon-like and meandered through the countryside. Had it begun its existence as a cowpath? The way became so narrow that any vehicle approaching from the opposite direction had no chance whatever of getting past except at one of the slightly wider spots, or way-byes, in the road. Hedgerows that formed fences for the pastureland beyond lined both sides of the narrow path. Occasionally he could feel tall grass and weeds brushing against both sides of the car as if they were in an automatic car wash.

"Now, we're looking for a gate on our left that makes a break in the hedgerow," she said.

Almost immediately an opening appeared. He pulled the car in against the aluminum gate and looked through it at a long slow rise to a crest at the top of a low hill, one that commanded the highest point around. "That's exactly as the archivist described it," he said. "What a stroke of luck to have talked to someone who knows the area so well."

"Must have been meant to be." Bobbie grinned with enthusiasm. "Let's go, then." She opened the passenger's door and jumping out onto the ground.

Brian followed her as she squeezed through a narrow opening beside the gate. He finally caught up with her, his strides just matching hers, as they got to the top of the long rise. They stood looking out over a 360° panorama.

"What a pretty spot. It makes a person understand why English painters have been so into landscapes," she said.

"Right," he said abstractedly. He surveyed the fields and walked across the broad open area at the top of the hill, studying the near-at-hand topography. "See these mounds." He pointed to the left and then to the right at incongruous features of the grass-covered soil "They don't seem to fit with the lay of the land."

"Yes. I see what you mean."

"That's likely where buildings once stood. If you were to dig down there, archeologist style, you would probably find remnants of buildings, probably artifacts: bits of pottery, tools, that kind of thing. Bones." He chuckled.

Bobbie was silent for a moment as she glanced around. Finally she said, almost inaudibly, "It is pretty here, but . . . but—I don't know—there's something kind of creepy about it. And I don't mean your crack about bones." She flashed him a semi glare.

"I know what you mean. I feel it too." And he did. How curious that Bobbie might respond much as he did to the place. He decided to test out this apparently shared sixth sense. "What about the old church at Stichen-Walling? What did you think about it?"

"Oh, I liked it. I liked it very much. What a great setting."

"You didn't find it creepy too?"

"No, I'd say more sad than creepy."

He shivered as they stood silently looking around. "Well, let's get out of this place. It definitely falls into the creepy category. It's—it's so . . . lonely. Besides, I'm already starting to get hungry." He gave the site one last appraising glance. He was glad to have found it, but gladder still to be leaving it behind.

"I'm not sure which one I prefer," Brian said as he looked at one then another and finally the third of the drawings Bobbie had made at Stichen-Walling. As she had been finishing them up the next day, she asked if he would like one to hang in his flat. Finally, he made a decision and pointed to one of the colored pencil renderings. "This one," he said.

"Good choice," she said. "I think I like that one best, too. I feel better about the shading there at the side of the church building. It kind of focuses on the opening in the wall more than the others do."

"That's probably what I like about it. It captures the mystery of the place—at least the mystery for me." She had used the icon technique she had told him about, and the churchyard seemed to shimmer and dance before his eyes. Her use of perspective even seemed to give the picture a kind of three-dimensional depth. Later in the day he proudly took the drawing out to have it framed under protective glass. Despite his pride in her and these examples of her talent, he had to admit that looking at the pictures had given him an uneasy feeling: perhaps one measure of her success. The old church at Stichen-Walling remained a troubled place for him, and seeing it this way reinforced his uneasiness. He intuited something in the drawing, something uncomfortable that not even association with his adored daughter could quash.

As he was walking back to the flat at Lo-Host from the framing shop he got to thinking about Bobbie's instinctive sense that something at the Thirley Hall site was not quite okay and that the Stichen-Walling church seemed "sad." He remembered times in her growing up when she had displayed a kind of ESP. On any number of occasions when the phone rang, she correctly identified the caller. Caller ID was unnecessary in any household that had Bobbie in it. Family jokes contended that if some object came up missing she could sit down and think about it for a little while and shortly put her finger on the item. That often proved to be true. At the time of her grandfather's death, something even eerier happened to show the depths of her sensitivity to the non-material.

Shortly after they got back from the funeral in Peoria she had come to Brian and asked if she could talk to him about "something weird" that had happened to her. Since he had been looking for an opportunity to improve what felt like a strained relationship between them at the time and to forge a new bond, he had set aside some work and listened. She had told him about how her grandfather, who had doted on her as his only grandchild, had appeared to her in a dream. At least she thought of it as a dream.

"He talked to me," she had said, "and I spoke to him. It was so real, so weird. Not like a regular dream. The room became all bright and light. He told me that he loved me and that I shouldn't worry about him, because he was very happy. Have you ever had anything like that happen to you?"

"No, I haven't, sweetheart," he had said and passed off a subject that felt uncomfortable at the time. Actually, he did remember something similar that had happened to him. Even now, he couldn't explain why he hadn't mentioned it to her.

As he continued walking through the streets of Cambridge, his thoughts turned to his own adolescent encounter with the recently dead. He had been a little younger than Bobbie had been at the time of Hiram Craig's death: shortly after his fifteenth birthday and less than a month after his mother's death from cancer. He had been alone in his bedroom when he felt his mother's presence, sitting as she had so often done in a straight-backed wooden chair in the corner of the bookish room. He remembered that at first he had been frightened, but soon felt reassured in the moment. He had only seen a faint glimpse of her. No words had been spoken, and he took no substance, advice, or anything specific away from the spooky occasion. Afterwards he had turned the corner on his fear and loneliness. His grieving became less abject, and he had seemed better able to cope with her death. Even more importantly he had recaptured an interior confidence that he had lost during the time of her illness and dying. He now realized that it had been this affirmative metaphysical encounter that had nurtured a tiny spiritual flame in him and kept him going to church all those years. A kind of vague belief system remained long after his academic cynicism had robbed him of much of the rest of his faith.

He went on to consider that adolescent encounter with his mother's spirit in light of what had been happening to him in Cambridge and in Stichen-Walling. He didn't have any answers, but he couldn't help but think that it contributed to his taking his dreams seriously and not being freaked out by them. That earlier brush with a truth he could neither see nor touch may very well have helped him to accept the possibility that his dreams were more than mere dreams—or the ravings of a sick mind.

The night before Bobbie returned home for the start of the fall semester, Brian hosted a dinner party in her honor at Brown's, an eatery on Trumpington Street. He was glad of the occasion to show her off to his new friends. The evening also brought Carol Heppel and Jeff and Charlie together for the first time. Noisy and casual, the restaurant and its tasty plain food contributed to what became a terrific evening. Charlie gave Bobbie lots of attention, and Carol was the life of the party. Jeff was almost courtly. They ended the evening as a kind of small community gathered around Brian, and he badly needed to feel that sense of belonging. Only Jeannie's presence would have filled out the party for him and made it complete. It never occurred to him that Mary Beth might have fitted in.

Brian said goodbye to Bobbie at Heathrow Airport the next day. His insistence that he drive her had prevailed over her determined self-sufficiency. But the occasion replayed their many leave-takings over the years. "It's the familiar sorrow of parents who don't live with their children," he said to her to explain his teary eyes. She just hugged him and wiped some tears from her own cheeks.

"Pops, I want you to talk to that priest friend of Carol's. Father Jeremiah was it?"

"Yes, Father Jeremiah."

"I really do want you to talk to him. You keep that appointment you made. No canceling, okay?"

"Okay."

As he watched her walk away and disappear into the secure area of Heathrow Airport he couldn't help thinking how right she probably was. Premonition was probably too strong a word for what he felt, but he did have a sense that knowing the priest was going to be important to him. He would keep his promise to her.

chapter fifteen

'm standing on a low hill. *Everything seems normal enough, but I don't remember getting to this place, so it has to be a dream. The quiet here is absolute. I look around at the undulating topography with its mixture of green fields and pasture land. Small clusters of trees dot the landscape. There isn't a single building in sight, nor a road or even a path. Except that fields are in one stage or another of cultivation I might be thousands of miles away from any human beings. With, that is, the one exception of my ghostly companion. His square jaw is set and serious. He sits on a large rock about twenty-five feet away and seems to be keeping watch over me. It's odd, but I am both comforted and spooked by his presence.*

Now I recognize this as the place where Thirley Hall once stood. Fully four centuries ago now. I don't know how, but I can feel the house. Even though I don't see anything of it. I step to the highest point on this uncultivated patch and look out across the fields. Suddenly I feel rather than see or hear, a great disturbance, a sensation that's typical of one of my place memories. Above the fields I see an October sky that is as clear and the air as warm as a person could wish. I even catch the occasional scent of freshly turned soil and the faint but pungent odor of manure. But I sense the searing pain of fire, the explosion and clash of weapons, the misery of the wounded and dying. I imagine captives being dragged away screaming and pleading. The reek of violence breaches the apparent peace of the scene. I see and hear nothing. But I experience the impact of it, and it frightens me. Only my companion seems to hold out the promise of something else. The firm line of his jaw softens. A smile that combines compassion and understanding warms his face. Just for a moment. His eyes become dewy and doe-like.

Now my gut wrenches and my eyes fill with tears, almost as if I'm having a bad allergic reaction to pollen or mold. My muscles ache. The scene is fading before me.

Brian was in his sitting room. Every bone in his body felt as if it had been rattled. He shook his head to clear it. Then it occurred to him: what he had just experienced combined his recent dream world and his place memories. Everything seemed to blur together now. Nothing made sense anymore.

"There's something strange and compelling about my daughter's picture of the old Church in Stichen-Walling." Brian sat with Father Jeremiah near the entrance door of St. Bene't's church in a cozy cluster of chairs arranged around a low table. A wooden rack on the wall held an orderly collection of pamphlets about the parish, its history and its work. Untidy stacks of hymnals, *Common Worship* books and some leaflets left over from Sunday's services covered a wooden table beside the door. It didn't seem like a very private place for talking about something as personal as someone's spiritual life. But Brian soon forgot about that in the quiet and undeniably nurturing atmosphere of the plain old church. It was his first scheduled appointment for spiritual direction. Their quiet exchange about Brian's life and his dreams, what Jeremiah continued to call visions, seemed less and less threatening to him the longer he spent with the Franciscan.

Jeremiah's expression became intent, his round dark face serious with expectation.

"Bobbie said she'd been studying the art of icon painting," Brian continued. "You know, Eastern Orthodox-style. I don't see anything especially icon-like about it. There are no penetrating eyes or stylized figures or Madonna and child, that sort of thing. Still, I feel myself sort of pulled into the drawing. It's the strangest sensation. I had thought at first that it was just my parental pride. But, I don't know . . ." Brian looked up from studying his hands. "I told you about the two Stichen-Walling churches."

Father Jeremiah nodded and his face warmed with what Brian was beginning to recognize as his enigmatic smile.

"When I stand there and look at the picture it becomes positively hypnotic—as if it's trying to pull me in."

"And what about your spiritual friend, the one you saw first on Midsummer Common? Do you sense him in your daughter's picture the way you saw him at Stichen-Walling or in the fields of Thirley Green?"

"No he's not part of Bobbie's drawing. She's never seen him, after all."

"But her unfamiliarity with your spiritual companion or the fact that she didn't put him in the picture wouldn't keep you from seeing him in it. Isn't that right?" The priest glanced up from studying the coffee table in front of them and looked penetratingly at Brian.

"I guess not. What is this, some version of Harvey the six-foot-tall rabbit?" Brian's laugh felt awkward and uncomfortable, much the way he was beginning to feel about the direction the conversation was taking. His dreams were one thing, but it was quite another to think that his subconscious was dragging Bobbie's work into his murky world. He began to feel slightly annoyed with Jeremiah; then he realized that that attitude had nothing whatever to do with the priest, but with his own growing frustration over everything. It was all so illogical, so medieval. He changed the subject abruptly, "There's something else I wanted to talk with you about, something that has me pretty agitated at the moment."

"Yes?" Jeremiah said, a simple response, but enough to encourage Brian.

He opened up a deluge of words about Mary Beth, outlining his long emotional connection to her. He talked about his mixture of anxiety and excitement at seeing her again after all these years and about his sense that in doing so he would somehow betray Jeannie. "Why should I feel so guilty about her? I don't get it. Jeannie and I've made no promises to each other. We've only just begun an intimate relationship."

"You seem to be bonded to this Jeannie, whether or not you have actually spoken words of commitment. Regardless of how long you've been intimate with each other." Jeremiah paused seemingly deep in thought. Finally he said, "How do you think these living and breathing women relate to the dead-and-buried ones at Stichen-Walling, hmm? Or to your visions?"

Father Jeremiah seemed to Brian to be ignoring the heart of his predicament. "That's a funny question," he said. "Relate? I don't see that they do relate. Or that Jane of Thirley Hall connects to the so-called visions." But he had to admit to himself that clusters of women did figure prominently in his life at the moment.

"Of course Stichen-Walling and Thirley Hall relate to your visions. Your spiritual companion links them all together. Right?"

"I hadn't thought of that. I—I suppose so."

"Besides, I learned a long time ago that in matters of the mind and of the spirit there are no discrete disconnected pieces. No clear boundaries. Every part plays its role in the larger drama of living."

Brian was left without words. He just sat there, staring at the priest and feeling confused.

By the end of the spiritual direction hour he had come to two decisions: that seeing Mary Beth again was probably okay; and that he had to tell Jeannie about it. He felt no reciprocal obligation to Mary Beth to tell her about Jeannie. He had a hunch that that wouldn't matter to her anyhow. Did he do her an injustice thinking that? Probably so, but that was how he felt. Despite all these insights, he felt no wiser about his dreams—or mystical visions—than before. Except the sense that it all did fit into a larger picture. But he had the comfortable sense that Father Jeremiah, with his smiling dark face and blunt observations, had somehow drawn him into his own personal spiritual orbit. That felt encouraging and safe.

"I have a group here in the church this evening," Jeremiah said as Brian was leaving. "Actually, we're going to do an icon meditation tonight. Maybe you'd like to come and see what it's like? Might be interesting for you. Especially considering your daughter's work."

Brian hated to commit himself to things he didn't understand, or to try out something new and, in this case, potentially weird. But he remembered that Bobbie had spoken about this kind of meditation. Maybe it would be okay. He agreed to return to St. Bene't's later. As he walked away from the church building and turned onto King's Parade, a sense of anticipation about the evening replaced the ho-hum he so often felt about church obligations. As if anything that involved Father Jeremiah promised to be considerably more than just a dull meeting or a lifeless service.

Brian looked down at his watch: almost five o'clock. The meditation group met at seven. That gave him just enough time to walk back to his flat, make a couple of quick phone calls, eat a light supper and get back to St. Bene't's for the meditation. He picked up his pace, even overtaking the characteristically brisk English walkers.

First he called Bobbie, just seeing if she had gotten back home okay. He also wanted to talk to her, wanted the connection. She answered on the second ring.

"Hi, this is Bobbie Craig."

"Hello, Sweetheart. You have a cheery way of answering the phone. Kind of makes my day."

"Oh, hi Pops," she acknowledged him lightly.

"Jet lag not too bad I hope. School getting started okay?"

"Sure. Everything's great," she said. "Guess what, I had one of those small-world experiences today. I've been bursting to tell you. I was over in the English Department trying to change a class, and I ran into your redhead."

"You saw Jeannie?"

"Yeah, I was pacing up and down waiting for this Prof to show up. I needed him to sign a drop slip. I was, you know, reading doors."

"Reading what?"

"Doors. You know the junk people put up on their office doors. It's a kick. If you've never done it, you don't know what you're missing. All those clipped comics and inflammatory political diatribes, ancient movie posters, arcane announcements of conferences and seminars. That kind of stuff."

"You mean to tell me that people actually read all that crap?"

"I do. It's so silly. Lists of course grades are always hilarious, sometimes with the funniest scrawled comments written all over them, especially the 'f' word. One I saw was for a class from years ago that had so many comments that you really couldn't read the original print anymore. But this time I probably saw the all-time prizewinner in that category, the envelope pl-*ease*. No fewer than twelve. I counted them. Class grade lists for the same course stacked on top of each other like archeological layers. I can't imagine why that professor would want to save them up that way." She giggled, almost childlike.

His heart melted.

"I also love checking out the taped-up photographs. There're usually lots of those. I make up stories about how the guy in the office knows the people in them and who they are: love children they are forbidden to see, students they've killed with final exams. That kind of stuff. I love reading doors."

"You're too much."

"You taught me to do it."

"I did?"

She giggled again. "Waiting for you to show up."

"For me?"

"Sure. What do think I did all those times I waited for you to finish with a meeting or something?"

"Sorry about that."

"No biggie. Anyhow, as I was waiting for that guy and reading doors, this gorgeous redhead comes bursting out of an office. She nearly runs me down. 'I'm really sorry,' she says. 'That's okay,' I say. Then I have an idea. 'You aren't Jeannie are you? I'm Bobbie Craig,' I say. 'Yes, I am,' she says. 'Hi Bobbie, your father has told me a lot about you. You're an artist.' She looks a bit uncomfortable, so I say, 'He's also told me about you—barely doing you justice.' At that I get a big grin out of her. She has a great smile. She's really pretty. Nice, too. I got her to promise to sit for me sometime. Then I asked her what she was teaching. She told me about a class that really excites her. On the war poets."

"That's her specialty."

"Exactly. I asked what day and time it was. Guess what? It works for me. So I got her to sign an add slip. I'm taking her class."

"My goodness." Brian didn't know whether to be excited or intimidated by having these two important females in his life spending lots of time together. In a class.

After they hung up he stood, stepped across his sitting room and, thinking about her, felt himself drawn to the colored pencil drawing of the old church at Stichen-Walling. Once again he experienced the same strange feeling he had described to Father Jeremiah. The picture seemed to beckon him, almost as if it were seeking to draw him into another world inside itself, or even somewhere beyond it. The drawing appeared almost to throb and surge. He began to feel a light-headedness akin to what he sometimes felt as his dreams ended. But it went no further, and the sensation soon passed. After a time, he shook his head, both to clear it and in disbelief of what had just happened. Whatever had become of the rational, pragmatic, tough-minded scholar? He tried Jeannie's numbers but didn't reach her. Turning toward the door, he stuffed the final bite of the sandwich into his mouth and began the ten-minute walk back to St. Bene't's.

Inside the little church Brian found the dimly lit sanctuary illuminated only by a pathway of burning candles. He felt the familiar chill in the air, one born of stonewalls, damp and darkness. A small group of about a dozen people sat clustered on the front pews. Brian carefully followed the candles to the back of the group, tripping and almost falling as he stepped up onto the two-inch high raised wooden platform under the pews. Father Jeremiah sat like a brown Buddha in his habit. A pool of light came from a cluster of burning candles on the table at his side. Brian felt vaguely uncomfortable sitting there in the silence. None of the gathered people, including the priest, seemed to move at all. They weren't even talking or whispering among themselves. But it was a companionable silence. Not awkward or tense. Brian's elevated respiration from the walk gradually returned to normal as he picked up and absorbed the peace in the room. The sweet smell of incense filled the air. He noticed a faint wisp of smoke rising from a low bowl beside the candles on Jeremiah's table. One more person arrived. He settled into a pew across the aisle and directly opposite from where Brian sat. No one seemed even to stir.

The Franciscan cleared his throat. Then, without standing, he began to speak. His voice was soft and low. He explained first about the structure of the evening and how he would be ending it with a short celebration of the Mass to which all were invited. Coffee and conversation would follow. Then he talked about the art of icon painting and the way in which the icons could become, as he put it, windows of the soul. Brian thought about Bobbie and what she had told him about painting icons and how excited she had become about the technique. He found Jeremiah's singsong voice hypnotic. Could this be an intentional part of the experience?

"*The Savior* is a fifteenth century Russian Christ," he said. "It's by the best-known iconographer of the time, one Adrei Rublev." Solves several little problems in this paragraph.

Brian looked up to see the outline of a large white screen in the front of the chancel and the shape of a slide projector on a low table in the center aisle near where he sat. He privately chuckled, silent and cynical: visual aids. They were going to have a slide show? He missed the rest of what the priest had to say.

Then Father Jeremiah turned on the projector, and what Brian saw on the screen drove away all of his contemptuous thoughts. Projected in an image five feet high and nearly as wide, the penetrating eyes and coarsely serene face of a Christ painted nearly six hundred years ago loomed up before him. He barely noticed as Jeremiah returned to his seat. The icon had apparently suffered damage over its long life. Its paint had worn away with abuse and neglect, and it wasn't nearly as brilliant as no doubt it would have been when it was first painted. All along the edges the finish had completely worn away. In some places, portions of the image of Christ itself were gone. But despite the damage and wear, the icon carried such power that Brian found it impossible at first to look away from the hypnotic figure. The eyes drew him and compelled him into a fixed gaze on them and on the surrounding face. He remembered how Bobbie had said that the eyes were often an icon's focus. That was certainly true for this one. He heard the Franciscan, as if from a great distance offer a prayer for openness and an invitation for them to find the sacred this evening. The quiet returned. Broken only by the soft hum of the slide projector's cooling fan.

Once the initial impact of the face had passed Brian's stare became vacant, indifferent to the icon's initial appeal. Soon he occupied himself glancing around the room at his fellow sufferers. The now-awkward situation felt very like a sort of suffering: sitting in the dark and silence and staring at a slide. Then with a mental shrug he concentrated on the icon alone, looking at it for what seemed like a very long time. Nothing happened. He wasn't exactly sure what was supposed to happen, but he thought it had to be more than this. Initially, he had felt a kind of calm and quiet relaxation, but that had given way to this impatience and restlessness. Boredom. Brian hated to be bored worse than anything. He looked at his watch, moving the band about on his wrist and adjusting it in the dim candle and slide projector light. Twenty minutes had passed already. No wonder he felt so restless. His legs began to feel jittery the way they did sometimes when his body wanted to fall asleep but his mind insisted on staying awake. He shifted sideways and looked around the room. He drilled holes with his eyes into the backs of other people sitting in front of him and wondered if they felt as unsettled as he did. Some nervous shifting around suggested as much. A feeling of warmth crept over him for those dark objects sharing his misery there in the confines of the murky church. He examined the whitewashed shadowy outlines of the building's too-large Gothic arches and tried to see beyond the edges of the projected icon to the altar in the chancel behind it, but he could only see its legs beneath the screen. He tried mentally to drive away the gloom so he could see inside the chamber where the organist sat to play the Sunday service, anything to keep from looking at the image on the screen. Finally he came back to the icon for lack of anywhere else to look. Nothing had changed. What a bore. His eyelids began to feel heavy, and he let himself drift off toward a doze. Lower and lower went his eyelids. The image on the screen began to blur.

As he looked at the eyes of the Christ figure through his own narrowed eyelids, he saw the face of the icon begin to change. Did he imagine it? Instead of seeing the Christ figure as it had been painted by Rublev, he saw other likenesses begin to appear: shadowy, unsteady ones to be sure, but changing reflections flashing before his squinting eyes, settling finally on the face of his very own ghostly companion. That got his attention. What was the Ghost doing up there? Brian sat up straight in the pew, his eyes wide open then, and stared, incredulous, at the icon that once more looked exactly as Rublev had painted it and the centuries had weathered it. He stared for what felt like a long time, his restlessness gone now. But nothing happened. Once more, he began to feel sleepy and his eyes began to close. Suddenly the face of his companion seemed to leap out of the icon. Brian opened his eyes wide, and the square-jawed image vanished as Rublev's Christ resumed its ascendancy. This time he squinted his eyes with intent, and again the ghostly face reappeared: the familiar set to his jaw and pockmarked skin, the same shaggy hair and patchy beard, and, like the painted icon itself, the now-familiar penetrating dark eyes. He felt confused but mesmerized.

Sitting there with his own eyes only slits in his face and focused immobile on the screen image, Brian tried to sense the room around him. Nothing had changed. He recognized the same shadowed outlines of the people in front of him, the faint light coming through the tall Gothic windows, the empty pews and the raised wooden floor beneath his feet. Nothing had changed from the time he had entered the church half-an-hour before. Everything had changed. This was not one of his dreams, and yet the ghost figure looked at him from the face of the icon. Soon he realized that he could manipulate what he saw by opening his eyes little by little, and then, by squinting them again, going from the Savior of the icon to the ghost of his dreams. Going back and forth became a kind of game for him. It gave him a sense of control over the strange things he saw. This was something new in his recent experience. He felt giddy, almost child-like.

Just as he had adjusted to seeing his ghostly companion Brian saw a procession of faces begin to appear in the icon as they had done before. Only more rapidly now. His eyes were startled wide open, and Rublev's painted image reappeared before him again. Cautiously this time, he closed his eyelids back into the narrow squint and once more saw the face of his familiar companion looking directly at him, finally giving way to the procession of faces. They mesmerized him: males, females, ancient hags, wizened old men, young faces, skeletons with no flesh left on their bones. All of these faces flashed before his eyes in a rolling succession. It was as if, unannounced, Jeremiah had begun to change slides faster than any projector could advance them. He opened his eyes wide only to see the Rublev face again. Resuming the squint, he saw the progression of faces continue to flash before him, none of them ever staying long enough to see clearly or to study. Who could all these faces be? Perhaps the saints?

Of course: the saints. He saw the great men and women, the martyrs, the monastics, poets and philosophers, scholars and simple peasants. They were ordinary and extraordinary people, ones whose lives had somehow been touched by the Holy in some special and uncommon way. What an extraordinary idea. He was stunned by the gift he was receiving, captivated by it. He wondered why he felt no fear or even disbelief. If someone had told him back in Chicago that this would happen to him, he would have laughed in their face.

The succession of visages faded. In their place he saw, as if from a great distance and through some kind of tunnel or enclosure, a pastoral scene colored in soft delicate greens and bathed in dappled light. That place invited him, beckoned him to draw closer, which he seemed to do without any effort of his own. It was as if he were riding on a seamless railroad track, silent and smooth, one that gave off no sense of movement. Little by little he came closer each second to the spring-like green fields and forest grove that drew him. Was this heaven? Was it one of those out-of-body experiences he had read about? Was he dying? Brian sat up straight on his pew and forced his eyes to look away from the icon and focus once again on the surroundings of the room. Everything remained as before: Jeremiah turned toward the projected icon; Brian's unknown companions staring in that same direction; the mismatched structure of white walls and small alcoves outlining the room; opaque high windows framed by soaring Gothic arches straining in their symbolic reach toward heaven; wooden pews filling the room; the faint lingering odor of incense; and the projected image of the Rublev icon staring down at them all. He knew it was all real because his butt hurt from sitting on the hard wood, and his eyes burned from the strain of squinting at the icon. But he didn't have nausea or disorientation, common feelings when ending one of his dream/visions. This was no dream. This was something else entirely.

He looked back at the icon and squinted again. The progression of faces resumed. Then a familiar scene flashed before his eyes: the old church at Stichen-Walling with its tumble-down roof and its neglected graveyard and broken wall. Even more important than what he saw was what he felt. The presence of evil seemed to flow from the scene and with it a profound discontent rose deep within him, restlessness greater than that he had experienced earlier in the evening or perhaps ever before in his life. How long ago had it been since the meditation began? How much time had passed since he had begun to encounter first the face of his companion and then the procession of saints? He tried opening his eyes wide and then squinting them again. The picture of the old church at Stichen-Walling vanished, and in its place appeared the face of his companion soberly staring directly at him and what felt like deeply into his soul. The procession of faces resumed, slower than before, but still vanishing too quickly for him to study any individual. Longer blurry periods came between the images. It was almost as if his mental receiver had begun to have trouble giving resolution to the images coming into his brain. They faded in and out like a weak television signal. After a time he gave up looking at the icon, except in occasional flashing glances, and tried instead to sort out his feelings. What on earth had all of this been about? What was happening to him now? He kept coming back to the sense of evil that had crept up in him as he looked at the Stichen-Walling scene. Jeremiah's promise to celebrate a mass as soon as the meditation ended kept coming back to him. For some inexplicable reason, Brian wanted nothing so much as that. For the first time in his life, he felt a profound hunger to taste the bread and the sweet strong wine of the Eucharist. The restlessness swept over him again.

Finally, Jeremiah cleared his throat. Brian looked up and saw him reach out onto the table beside him and ring a tiny bell. As if a spell had been broken, the people in the forward pews began to stretch and move. One rubbed his neck. Another ran her fingers through her hair and shook it out. One youngish man stood in the aisle and bent down and then twisted from side to side to stretch his back muscles. The room had suddenly become filled with animation. The Franciscan stood and walked across the front of the church and disappeared behind an ancient wooden door. First one thin beam of light then others came on in the chancel as a man turned off the projector and folded and removed the screen. Brian could now see the altar, bathed in the soft narrow beams of electric light piercing the dark from the distant ceiling. It had already been set for Mass. A brilliant jeweled silver chalice with a crisply pressed purificator draped over it sat at the center of the altar as the focus. Two short, stubby candles stood unlit at either side of the nearly square table. Presently Father Jeremiah, now clothed in simple white cassock-alb and stole, came through a nearly invisible side door into the chancel with a lighted taper in his hand. He went around to the front of the freestanding altar, genuflected, and lighted the altar candles. Then he turned, smiled in his gentle manner and invited the others with simple sweeping arm gestures to join him in the chancel. He went back around to the other side of the altar to face the half-circle of people standing before him.

The bare-bones Eucharistic liturgy moved Brian deeply. The priest said the familiar and time-honored formula in spare contemporary English, read a passage from John's Gospel, led a brief set of intercessory prayers, punctuated by moments of silence, and invited everyone to share the Peace of Christ, which they all did with warm embraces. They felt like family.

Finally the priest said a simple unadorned prayer of consecration with words both new to Brian and familiar in their content. Jeremiah pressed a soft piece of fresh whole wheat bread into the cupped hands of each member of the awe-struck congregation. He came around the semicircle a second time with the gleaming silver chalice, wiping the rim after each person had taken a taste of the consecrated wine, saying with each one of them, "The Blood of Christ keep you in everlasting life."

Brian's rush of feelings nearly swamped him. In the end he acknowledged to himself a simple gratitude. Even more, he felt another wave of compassion for each of the people in the semicircle beside him—none of whom he had ever spoken to or perhaps even seen before that evening. Still, he loved them. Where had all of these feelings come from? That had never happened to him before. Oh, he often had a wash of emotion when he thought of Bobbie or another intimate person in his life, including sometimes his changing sequence of temporary partners. Now this. That he might feel such loving feelings, such connection with people he didn't know, might never see again stunned him and gave him a sense of awe.

He felt energized and suddenly knew what the Biblical phrase, "filled with the Holy Spirit," might mean. He had always thought of such a concept as disingenuous or sentimental, something that evangelicals experienced. This was none of those. He wanted to sing, to shout, to share what he had just experienced and to keep hold of these feelings forever. The Eucharist would never again be the same for him, of that he was certain.

Jeremiah concluded the liturgy with a reiterated invitation to stay afterwards for coffee and conversation, gesturing toward the rear corner of the church where Brian had had his spiritual direction session that afternoon.

Ten minutes later they all sat in a compact little circle, twelve of them, knees all but touching. Cups of steaming instant coffee held in their hands. Deep in conversation unpacking the icon meditation.

"I saw ugly faces in the icon. You know, skeletons and things like that," said one woman in jeans and a blue sweater.

Brian glanced toward her, stunned by the similarity of what they both had seen. She was pretty in a scrubbed natural way. He listened to what she was saying. Really listened. They had definitely shared a common experience, even though what she had seen differed from his encounter with the icon in a number of respects. This had been no case of a film rolling on a single sequence. He looked at his watch. Nearly two hours had passed since he had first walked through the church door. Where had all the time gone?

A middle aged woman said, "I saw the lips of the icon move as if it were speaking to me."

"Yes, I saw that, too," injected a slender man in his thirties.

"I strained to hear the words," she continued, "but I couldn't hear anything whatsoever."

"I couldn't either," said the man.

Father Jeremiah nodded and made his usual little cooing sounds.

"Well, I didn't see anything," said one man.

"Nor did I," said a woman.

Brian found himself speaking, "I had the feeling of something evil in the midst of a succession of faces." He hadn't meant to say anything.

"Yes, I saw faces, too," said a young woman in her twenties.

"What about the evil?" Jeremiah asked, focusing on Brian.

"I saw an old church in a little Suffolk town," Brian said. "A place I've been doing historical research on. It's become a kind of mystery for me. There it was in this meditation. I had already sensed that there was something not quite right about the place. But actually to feel something *evil* in it—here and in this way . . ." He let his words trail off and then added, "Now I . . . I'm really driven to find out about it." He felt vulnerable and exposed. Why had he said those things to a group of strangers? He looked at the priest and got a knowing glance back from him.

"That must have been very upsetting," a young man said.

"Yes, it was," Brian answered.

"How about the experience of the Eucharist?" Father Jeremiah asked. Brian felt like he had been rescued.

"It really moved me," said the woman in the blue sweater.

"Yes, I felt that way, too," said the young man.

"I really liked receiving Communion," Brian said. For some reason he couldn't keep his mouth shut. "But I felt even more than that—an urgency for it. It was as if I couldn't taste the bread and wine soon enough. I almost felt a little panicky."

"My goodness," said an elderly woman.

"Indeed," said Jeremiah.

While other people continued sharing their experiences, Brian's mind worked at processing the whole evening. Suddenly he began to understand why Jeremiah, Bobbie and even Charlie Huff had described what he had been experiencing as visions. This had been no dream. He felt humbled and awed. He thought about everything that had been happening to him. What about the identity of his spiritual companion? Bobbie thought the Ghost was a saint— or at least Brian's version of one. But what did Brian himself think? Somehow the word saint didn't feel quite right. Friend. Companion. Guide. Mentor. All of those labels came to mind, but none of them seemed right. Second only to that identity puzzle came the enigmatic feeling of evil he had experienced when looking at the image of the Old Church at Stichen-Walling and its yard and graves. He weighed his sense that he encountered evil there. What on earth did he mean by evil? What was evil, anyhow? Surely he didn't mean little devils with pointy ears and tails. Rather, the evil he encountered in the meditation, as in the strong feelings he got from looking at Bobbie's picture, now seemed to emanate from the broken spot in the wall—from those exiled graves. Had they been wicked? Terrible women? Actual witches? He had no answer to those questions. Still, his instinct told him that something iniquitous lingered there.

Brian walked out into the night. Originally he had thought about stopping across the street at the Eagle for a pint, but instead he turned the other direction, wending his way out of the busy little streets and struck off across Coe Fen in search of the black swan. For some vague reason he very much wanted to see that bird. He scoured the whole area along the river without finding any of the swans, let alone the black one. Not willing to give up, he retraced his steps and walked across the Backs to the Garret Hostel Bridge. Still no black swan. He stood looking at the river, watching the ripples shine on the water in the glow of the bright almost-full moon overhead. Suddenly, as if in an extension of the icon meditation, Brian saw the face of the Ghost momentarily reflected in the water. After the initial shock had passed it left him with a feeling of well-being that made him almost giddy. A profound sense of gratitude stole over him, leaving him aching to thank . . . somebody . . . anybody . . . for what he had received tonight. God? "Thank you, God?" Was that what he meant? But that felt trite, insincere. Then he thought about an exercise he had learned a few years ago on a retreat. He had been trying to get over his fizzled affair with his graduate student, Alison, and the lingering pain and humiliation of his first divorce. The Episcopal priest retreat leader had invited them all to pray the "Jesus Prayer," using the name of Jesus as a kind of mantra or prayer word. The simple repetition over and over of the two-syllable name of Jesus had been so focusing and, at once, a supplication and an expression of gratitude that it had helped carry him through a period of serious depression and self-doubt. As he recovered from the failed relationships, he gradually let go of the prayer. Now he thought of the Jesus Prayer with great fondness, and, centering himself as he turned to begin the walk across the Backs, he started to repeat the name of Jesus over and over in his mind. By the time he got to his flat at Lo-Host, the odd and exaggerated disappointment at not seeing the black swan had passed. Instead, his hopeful and puzzled mood from the icon meditation had solidified. He seemed truly to have offered thanks. It felt very good to have renewed his long-abandoned personal prayer. It was like the return of an old friend after a long absence.

chapter sixteen

Brian sat reading, thinking and savoring the still-warm night air coming through his sitting room window. He was in no great rush to get to sleep. After everything that had happened that evening sleep probably wouldn't come quickly anyway. He felt a lightness of heart that he'd rarely known—an urge to dance or to sing or simply to share what had happened to him with someone who was important to him. He got up and went over to the phone and tried Jeannie again, but she didn't answer any of her numbers. Neither did Bobbie answer hers. He thought about calling Mary Beth and talking to her, but that idea made him feel like laughing. Laughing? It was certainly of a piece with the giddiness he felt. Still, what an odd reaction. Sharing something as personal as his spiritual life with Mary Beth seemed ridiculous. So he gave in and laughed, a full-bodied eye-watering laugh.

Thoughts of Mary Beth lingered. He sat at his laptop and called up the digital photo she had sent of herself. She didn't look just as she had in college. Her still-dark hair was short and perky. Her eyes were still the startling blue he remembered. But when he closed his own eyes she reverted to her nineteen-year-old self. The prospect of seeing her again tantalized him. What did he feel for Mary Beth? That was the real question. Was it just a sexual thing? He certainly felt sexual desire for her, or at least for the girl she had once been. He looked again at the photo on the computer screen. No question about it, she remained an attractive woman. The same small high breasts, slim waist and lovely photogenic face he remembered from all those years ago. Only now she was more mature, more adult. He edited the picture to increase its size, centering in on her face. Her eyes were even more stunning than he remembered. He felt a stirring of the old devotion.

Or again, was this sexual desire alone? But what about sexual desire? He tried to be analytical. Surely it must be mostly a product of the imagination: a pair of mounds under a blouse translated by the mind into the contours and softness of two breasts. The projecting points of two nipples looked different and erotic when they were attached to a female body than they were on his chest. The rise of hips suggests depths of moist softness and warmth between them that can only be female. How do these prurient thoughts differ from the larger obsession of full-scale romantic love? Surely love must be one part sexual, one part self-projection and one part a yearning for intimacy. Perhaps it's all simple delusion. Do we fall in love because the beloved is more admirable than anyone else? Or maybe we love because the object of our love is dependent upon us. Or perhaps it is just biology: hormones. Why do we connect with one person more than with some other person? He remembered a line from a song he had heard one night in a New York cabaret, "I live for the you that lives in my mind." Is that all there is? Is there nothing but projection? He wondered if he would feel about Jeannie's twin the way he felt about Jeannie herself simply because they look so much alike—interchangeable pieces in a primal puzzle. Then comes his emotional obsession with Mary Beth over the years. Why does she have the power to turn him back into a stammering adolescent just by her existence? Just the thought of her existence? And Jeannie? Thinking about her gave him an empty pain in his chest.

It occurred to him that he was not the first male to feel these feelings, think these thoughts or ask these questions. Far from it. Did that make him feel any better? Not really. How about women then? Were their thoughts and feelings similar, or were they actually from Venus?

Brian waited until nearly midnight before he decided to try Jeannie in Chicago one last time. Candy picked up.

"This is Brian. How are you?"

"Oh, hi Brian. I'm okay. At least for a girl with a crazy person as a mother."

"Crazy person? What's going on?"

"She's sitting on the living room floor with Aunt Jannie.

They're all dressed up in twin clothes and giggling like little kids."

"Twin clothes? What on earth are twin clothes?"

"Oh you know. Just alike.

"Yes, I remember."

"I guessed which one was which when they tested me."

"What on earth are they up to? And do they look *that* much alike?"

"You got that right. They want to play a trick on someone."

"Well, I guess you'd better let me talk to her and find out what's going on."

"Mom," Candy yelled away from the phone, "It's Brian." She continued in a softer voice, "Say hello to the moorhens for me. They're still there on the river, aren't they? And the black swan?"

"Of course they are. They all are. I'll do it," he said, thinking about the swan and wondering where he had been tonight. Then Jeannie was on the phone. "So what's this about you and your sister dressing alike?"

Jeannie laughed. "Remember the hassle I've been having with Francis Cardham?"

"The department head? Of course."

"Well, it's still going on. I knew it was a mistake, but I agreed again to have drinks with him—the Toad. That's my new name for him. For a moment he almost had me convinced that he was just doing his job. He asked me to submit a Vita, a couple of my papers and the names of some outside referees. Seems he's planning to bring me and James Delgado up before the promotion and tenure committee for tenure track consideration. I almost fell off my chair."

"That's great. Sounds really positive. But I gather there's more to it than that."

"He showed his real colors—bright green. The Toad! He imposed an implied condition: that I have dinner with him. It wasn't so much *what* he said as the expression on his face when he said it that gave him away. The jerk! How dare he? I stalled and kept my mouth shut. Put him off with some vague promises about the future, maybe next week. But now I feel that I'm back to square one. I hate this. Damn the man! He really pisses me off. At least I know I wasn't imagining things. Now I'm trying to figure out what to do about him?

"And that's why you and your sister are dressing up in, as Candy put it, twin clothes?"

"That's the reason. I decided that it might be fun to have two of us—two of me, in a manner of speaking. We've dreamed up all kinds of scenarios. Not that we're actually going to try to fool him. But we had fun going out and buying matching shirts and shoes and stuff. We hadn't gone shopping together in years. But I *do* need to do *something* about him."

"Other than behaving like you're in a Restoration farce?" He laughed, and then changed the subject. "I've got a couple of things to tell you," he said.

"Sorry for being so self-focused."

"I'm the one who's self-focused. But I do need to talk about what happened to me tonight. I went to this meditation."

"That's what you said on the message you left."

"Well," he drawled, "it was amazing." He told her about his visualizations and the emotions he felt. "And I'm still so alive and energized."

"That's pretty weird. Cool, but weird—about the icon. I remember a couple of years ago when everything was getting pretty tough with Richard. Not long before you and I met, actually. I joined a prayer group at St. Michael's for a few weeks. One night we were doing something that Mother Lilly called Ignatian exercises—you know, from Ignatius of Loyola."

"The founder of the Jesuits?" How odd, he thought, the way things change. Walsingham, the Elizabethan spymaster, must be rolling over in his grave at the thought of Anglican churches using Jesuit techniques and thinking nothing of it. He would have had them drawn and quartered. The idea brought those two widely separated centuries together and gave Brian a sudden sense that very little separated them. At least in his mind.

"Yes, the same," she said as he shook off his thoughts.

"Anyhow, she invited us to close our eyes and 'enter into the scene,' as she put it. First we had a breathing exercise. To get centered. Then she instructed us to use our senses as she read the story about Jesus leaving Jericho and running into Bartimeaus, the blind beggar. All of a sudden I found myself right there. This wasn't a vision or a waking dream like what's been happening to you. It's more like your icon meditation, and when I opened my eyes it all went away. But I swear I could smell the animal dung and sweaty human bodies, and I could even taste the dust on my tongue. I imagined I was walking along with the crowd and hearing the whole thing: the beggar approaching Jesus, the disciples trying to send him away, and Jesus asking what he could do for him. The blind man asked to get his sight back, and Jesus cured him. I saw it all. I still get chills when I think about it."

"How come you never told me about this before?"

"Oh, it never came up, I guess. You don't launch right into your spiritual life until you get to know somebody really well."

"It's funny that you should mention that passage about the blind man," he said. "Years ago when I attended a retreat, we learned a prayer that comes from that same passage."

"The Jesus Prayer?"

"Yes. Do you know it?"

"I know about it. I can't say that it's ever been particularly important to me, though."

"Well, it was for me. I started doing it again tonight."

They were quiet for a few seconds. Then she took the lead, "Tonight—the icon and all—kind of comes together with the dreams, though, doesn't it?"

"You think?"

"Don't you? You're the one whose insight is important here. But tonight must have been a positive experience. You don't seem as troubled as you were."

"Have I seemed troubled? Of course I have." He paused to think, "Partly I don't believe I'm going nuts. That's a big relief." He chuckled.

"What do you think *is* going on?"

Overcoming his reluctance to say out loud the words he

had been thinking, he finally managed to say, "I feel there may be some kind of purpose in all of it. I hate to admit it, but I think the dreams may be something like . . . well, like mystical visions. Whatever that means. Here's another odd piece: I have found indications that one part of the Thirley Hall estate had been former monastic property. You know: the real subject of my research project. I have to check a little further to be sure." He collected his thoughts before going on, finally continuing with a tentative tone in his voice, "It's . . . it's all coming together—as if I'm being led somewhere, maybe even supposed to *do* something."

"Wow! And what is it you think you're meant to do?"

"I'm not sure, but the obvious choice seems to be the old church at Stichen-Walling and those three dead women."

"How can that be?" she asked.

"I wish I knew."

The line grew still. Finally she said, "That's a lot to think about."

"I hardly ever think about anything else—except you."

"You're sweet. But wasn't there something else you wanted to tell me? You said there were a couple of things."

This didn't seem like the right moment to tell her about Mary Beth. Was there going to be anything to tell? He wasn't so sure he really wanted to continue dredging up all those old feelings. Anymore than he had already done. "No, not really," he said at last. "I think that's about enough, don't you?"

She laughed. "Yes, I suppose it is." Then she sighed. "I wish I were there right now. With you on that narrow little bed in your living room. The way we were."

"Just thinking about it gets me a bad case of watery legs." That achy yearning in his chest returned: the one he had been feeling ever since she left.

She laughed and then sighed. "You know, I really liked making love with you."

"I wish I had you here right now." He chuckled. "All sorts of ideas are running through my head. Funny the way my spiritual evening has taken a very different turn."

"You mean to the erotic?"

"I was thinking about that . . . and you, that way . . .

earlier. Isn't that pretty inconsistent of me?"

"Aren't the spiritual and the erotic just two parts of the same energy?"

"You think?"

"Women know about these things." She laughed. "There's a dark side to sexuality precisely because it's the flip side of the spiritual. Explains all the strong feelings. When it's right, well, it's sooo right."

"And when it's wrong . . . I get it. I still can't believe how long we denied what we were feeling, he said"

"I have no regrets. Somehow the long slow preparation made it all the sweeter when it happened. Once you had become free."

"You sound like a Jane Austen heroine."

"Not Elizabeth Bennett, I hope. But now, after everything that's happened, I—I miss you more than ever." Her voice had lost its bantering timbre and became very small.

"It makes me sad to think about it."

"Me too.

Brian stepped into his sitting room to be greeted by an early morning ray of autumn sun spilling through the window and brilliantly illuminating Bobbie's colored pencil drawing of the Stichen-Walling churchyard. The combination of the drawing and the sun seemed to beckon to him. Rather than avoiding the picture as he had done before when its attraction had felt this strong he stood in front if it, cradling his teacup in both hands and allowing the likeness to draw him in. Its effect differed from that of the icon because no succession of faces appeared to mesmerize him. But the moment felt analogous. A kind of magnetic throbbing seemed to arise from deep inside the drawing as its pastel colors and dark shading together gave him the sensation of actually entering the world of the picture. In no way did he leave the room where he stood, nor did he feel himself actually or even symbolically standing inside the Stichen-Walling churchyard, and yet his senses were alive and alert, each nerve ending reaching out in the expectation of sensation. Is this what it was like to be under hypnosis:

absent though present, passionate but insensate, vigilant but
anesthetized? Even though his body remained at attention in
his flat's sitting room, his energy somehow became united
with the drawing, not at first so much the Stichen-Walling
churchyard as the picture itself.

Little by little that changed and he felt as if he were
passing through the drawing in its undulating two
dimensions, which somehow had become three, into another
world or reality. Like the Stichen-Walling churchyard, the
world of the drawing was quiet, but every object he sensed in
it radiated a kind of emotional power that he could not avoid
feeling. Trees seemed silently to cry for their leaves as they
drifted toward the ground in the annual autumn abdication
to the cycle of life. Late flowers in fading hues of red, yellow,
blue, orange and magenta in beds of fallen leaves formed a
silent but plaintive and mournful chorus emitting soundless
rhythms and counterpoints. Stones emanated chilled
vibrations. Blades of grass quietly curled in upon themselves
in sad resignation at the coming of winter. It was a still world
of emotional animation. It held Brian captive. Beyond the
broken wall, he sensed, though he did not exactly see, a
presence, an energy, a being or beings, inviting him to share
something painful, a sorrow as real as the life captured on the
face of the picture. Is this the Thirley Hall women? He didn't
share their pain, couldn't know it, felt kept from knowing it,
restrained by some power or force from perceiving this
knowledge that suddenly felt so precious to him. At that
moment his hunger to understand seemed more important
than anything else in the world. It rose up stronger than
anything he had ever desired in his life.

Gradually Brian became aware of the teacup in his hands.
It had become icy cold, much colder it seemed than the air in
the room. The bone-chilling frigidity crept from that icy tea
to his very core. He began to shiver and dropped the cup to
shatter on the floor. A tea stain spread in the carpet. He
found himself resuming the prayer of Jesus.

Still shaken by his experience with Bobbie's drawing
Brian sat fretting in the manuscript reading room at the

university library. The tables of blonde wood were piled with stacks of cartons and papers. The air smelled of dust, old paper and parchment and vibrated with the busy click of laptop computers. It all went largely unnoticed as Brian sat trying to reason out some logical way to understand what he had been experiencing since he had been in Cambridge—trying to fit it all together. Even if he admitted his sensitivity toward events that had happened in the past—place memories and that sort of thing—still the sheer quantity of it all was more than a bit much. Suddenly he stood up and dropped the handful of papers he held in his hand back into the carton in front of him. "This is getting me nowhere," he muttered quietly to himself as he closed the lid on his laptop and went out to look for Jeff.

He checked the main reading room and walked through an area in the stacks where Jeff said he often hung out. No sign of that lanky frame in either place. He looked out at the smoking patio and in the teashop. No Jeff. His friend was nowhere in sight. He gave it up. A check at his watch showed it was almost noon. He began to think about the Eagle, longing for a mound of shepherd's pie and a pint of Greene King. He turned on his heel and left the tearoom. He had reached the main staircase and had taken two steps down it when he stopped, reconsidered what he was doing and went back for his laptop. He really didn't want to come back and try to work this afternoon.

He exited the library and made a beeline for Lo-Host. After dropping off the computer, he would go on to the Eagle.

The Eagle's main dining room was full. Brian toyed with his shepherd's pie, more interested in his thoughts than in eating. Around him people were ordering their pub lunches at the bar while others were eating theirs. Sounds of laughter and snatches of conversation made friendly if impersonal companions. Looking around the room, he picked up on the World War II memorabilia, the photos and framed newspaper clippings on the wall and, of course, the tin ceiling above. The inscriptions stirred his imagination as usual. He thought about the pressure on those RAF and US Air Force pilots and crews who had made them. The certain knowledge those men had lived with: even if one's own number weren't up on the next bombing run, certainly someone's you knew would be. How appalling that must have been. He thought about the demands in his own life, pretty pale in comparison. Especially he considered the prospect of Mary Beth's arrival in England next week. Last night as he was talking with Jeannie he had temporarily let go of the whole idea of seeing Mary Beth again and of exploring that old relationship at all. But today, well, today was another day. He did want to see her. More accurately put, he needed to see her. That realization brought back the same old problem that he had avoided yesterday by ducking the issue of telling Jeannie about Mary Beth. But seeing her didn't necessarily imply that sex must be the outcome. Maybe it could simply be a meeting of old friends, one that would purge him of his unhealthy lingering obsession. Maybe it wouldn't be so difficult to talk with Jeannie after all.

He drained his pint glass and got up, leaving his half-eaten plate of food on the table, and wrapped a slice of bread in his paper napkin. He would go look for the black swan and feed him a few crumbs. Some fresh air would probably feel good and help clear his head. Besides, the day couldn't have been better for walking—warm golden sun and clear blue sky with a few puffy white clouds laterally chasing each other across it. He went to the Cam and walked along it, keeping his eye peeled for the bird. Just as he was about to give up and turn around, he spotted the familiar elegant figure skimming effortlessly across the surface of the water. He was alone as always, no sign of the family of white swans. Brian stepped over to the bank and tore off a piece of bread and tossed it into the water. The bird moved instantly to scoop up the scrap from the river's surface with his bill. Brian stood like that, tearing off pieces of bread and tossing them toward the swan until the slice was gone. He pocketed the napkin.

"Well, old boy. That's all there is."

The swan seemed to understand. He turned slowly and returned to his previous post in the center of the stream almost as if he were keeping watch for something.

"I wonder what you're up to," Brian said softly to the swan. "What do you think about everything that goes on around you? How do you cope with your lonely life? Or do you think about such things at all? How wonderful to be a swan swimming on the river."

Just then the big black bird twisted his head on his long neck and looked at Brian as if he understood not only the human words but their underlying meaning as well.

Startled, Brian could have sworn the swan was about to say something to him, perhaps to offer a retort of some kind. But nothing of the sort came. Swans are swans after all. All the same it felt eerie. Brian turned and walked across a footbridge over the Cam, wondering if he had grown so used to a life filled with improbable things that now he was anthropomorphizing water foul.

Brian and Jeannie had been talking for about ten minutes when he realized he really couldn't put off any longer telling her about Mary Beth. "There's something I need to say to you," he said.

Perhaps she sensed his tension and discomfort. In any case, she seemed to breathe deeply and an edge developed in the tone of her voice. "Yes? What is it?"

Brian paused and took a deep breath of his own. "I don't think I ever mentioned this to you before. There was no reason to. But back in college I had a relationship, a very important one. It never really went anywhere and ended very badly for me. Her name was Mary Beth. In some odd way I've never entirely gotten over her. Now I've had a letter from her. Right out of the blue."

"She's been in touch with you?"

"Yes. She's going to be in England. This weekend." He realized he wasn't telling her the entire truth. But maybe that didn't matter.

"This weekend?"

"Yes."

"What are you going to do?"

"I'm going to see her. I think I have to. Part of me wants to. But part of me is scared. I was really badly hurt by our break-up back in college." Surely she would understand why he had to do this.

"Are you going to sleep with her?" Her voice was flat.

There was a long tense pause before Brian said, "I don't know." Was that true? Did he really think he and Mary Beth would merely have a rerun of their college days when they had played around a bit but never had sex? Besides, the tone in Jeannie's voice lacked the understanding he had expected to find. What was going on here?

"What do you mean you don't know?" A kind of icy calm seemed to creep into her voice. She had become almost matter-of-fact.

"I never have."

"And what's that supposed to mean?"

"I mean that one of the ways she always manipulated me was by holding back sexually." As he said those words he knew afresh the truth of them. That was what Mary Beth had done. No matter what she said now about not having wanted their relationship to go too far or too fast, that it had scared her, the real reason that she had held him off was to keep him where she wanted him: dangling in the air like some kind of puppet, perpetually insecure and miserable; or heeling tamely behind her like her own little doggy on a leash. But the issue here wasn't Mary Beth, it was Jeannie and her reaction to what had to be very sudden news. He realized that the silence had lengthened. Something about that silence felt ominous.

"I won't pretend that I'm happy about this little adventure of yours," she said at last.

"I understand."

"Maybe you do. Then again maybe you don't. But I have no claim on you." She was beginning to sound quite angry. "Just how much communication have you been having with this Mary Beth?"

"There have been some email and a couple of phone calls."

"Email and phone calls?"

"Yes.

"You've been communicating with her. Without saying a

word to me about it?"

"Yes."

"Even when I was there? Did you have email from her then?"

"Yes.

"What a jerk."

"I'm sorry, but I feel this is something important. Something I've got to do. It's like unfinished business I have to attend to. I've—I've begun to think that the ghost of her hanging over my head has ruined all of my relationships. Now it's raised a barrier between *us*."

"*Really?* Come *on*, Brian. Get real! You're just loaded with ghosts these days, aren't you?"

"Try to understand.

Well, spare me the instant replay."

"Jeannie, honey . . ."

"Oh, fuck you!" She hung up.

He sat there, all of his earlier contentment gone. Why couldn't she be more understanding? She'd get over it—especially if nothing happened with Mary Beth. He didn't want to lose Jeannie. He suddenly realized the truth of that with surprising force. Still, what could he do? Mary Beth would be in England in less than five days. He did have to follow this through, didn't he? What else could he do?

CHAPTER
SEVENTEEN

Brian stood at the counter of Cambridge Carriage Hire, a locally-owned car rental company hidden away in an industrial area beside the railroad tracks. Just then he was feeling skeptical about the car he was about to rent. It must have showed.

"But it's not a new car, now, is it?" The middle aged female clerk acknowledged Brian's misgivings with a smile. "If you like I'll include a mobile at no extra charge."

He thought for a moment. A cell phone might come in handy while Mary Beth was in London.

"And it's a good car," said the grinning tousle-headed twenty-year-old yardman standing beside the clerk. "I drive it home myself whenever I can, don't I? It has a lovely radio."

Brian looked again at the elderly brown Rover saloon car waiting outside the front door. It was admittedly larger, heavier and more luxurious than the English Fords, Renaults and Volkswagens on the lot. It was so English—stodgy right down to its rusty undercarriage. Cambridge Carriage Hire's entire inventory had lived long lives, a decade or more each. They had scratches, dents or rusty spots on their bodies and worn places on their interiors. But they were without exception spotlessly clean inside and out.

"You'll like it. Everybody does," the clerk said.

"Well, okay then. I guess you talked me into it." Brian flashed his most winning smile. He remained doubtful about the ancient bus painted the muted brown of a faded UPS truck. But he dutifully signed his name to the contract and damage description. Inside, his heart sunk at the prospect of picking up Mary Beth in a vehicle that might be better off rusting away in a parts yard than negotiating the streets of London. He tried to imagine how this inelegant antique might be at maneuvering the narrow roads and byways of rural England. Probably like a farm vehicle: slow, awkward and cumbersome. Oh well, he would try it for a few days and if it didn't work out he could always try to get something from Hertz or Avis on the weekend. Meanwhile, the price was right, especially for a long rental, and there was something likable about the old sedan.

"Come, and I'll show you how to find everything," said the yardman.

Brian nodded and followed him to the waiting car, stuffing the contract into his jacket pocket as he went. The young man went through a practiced routine as he pointed out the levers, switches and pedals where Brian would find what he needed to operate the car. Finally, he nestled into a comfortable seat that was covered in well-worn soft dark-brown leather. Everything lay readily at hand: gearshift, pedals, steering wheel and the knobs for the vaunted radio. A veneer of oiled light wood covered a narrow strip of the dashboard and continued around the interior of the car's four doors. Suddenly he knew what they had meant about this car. It was old and unlovely, and he felt sure it would have some peculiarities. But it had a dignity about it that suited him and his hopes and dreams for the two weeks he would have it. What was it that he had read? Something about cars and transportation standing in dream analysis for a person's life. He chuckled inside. Something in the awkward but serviceable look of the Rover matched his sense of how he wanted to think of himself just then: solid, reliable and serious. So what if it wasn't romantic? He wasn't trying to sweep anybody off their feet. Indeed, he was decidedly uncomfortable with the whole idea of romance. Especially with Mary Beth. Perhaps the car would, in a manner of speaking, help him keep his feet on the ground. He chuckled to himself.

Brian returned his focus to the Rover and started it up, pressed down the clutch pedal and put the gear lever into first. As he engaged the clutch the car lurched and died.

"You'll probably need to pull out the choke for a little while, won't you? Just until she's warmed up?" The lot attendant grinned.

Brian swallowed his embarrassment, determined not to

repeat his mistake. He pulled out the choke, started the motor again and slowly eased out the clutch pedal. This time the Rover moved forward with surprising smoothness. He beamed at the attendant, and, negotiating the potholes in the lot, rotated the ivory-white steering wheel into the traffic flow back toward Regent Street. The car handled very well, just as they had promised it would. Maybe it would be okay after all.

Lumbering Lorries with their sides of lashed plastic leaned as they negotiated turns on the road or changed lanes. Bicyclists pumped their bikes silently along the shoulder, sometimes overtaking and outdistancing the stop-and-go motorized traffic. Farm vehicles inched their way along the highway dragging long tails of Cortinas, Golfs and Minis behind them. Above, small clouds danced with each other across sapphire skies. Thin wisps of smoke from farmers' autumn fires rose straight up until, caught by the winds aloft, they were deflected and scattered. Field after field showed the black of freshly turned soil. The morning crispness had begun to appear alongside October's thinner light and waning intensity of color as the landscape made the gradual transition from green to brown. Soon there would be frosty patches and the inevitable appearance of dense banks of gray clouds bringing the long winter of drizzling rain. Brian shivered at the prospect of the damp and the gloom—still only hinted at. For now, the air was soft and dry, the breezes light, and they carried the mingled scents of turned soil and manure. It was a perfect day for doing whatever a body had a mind to do.

The trouble was that Brian had nothing specific in mind at all. His restlessness had driven him to point the car toward Stichen-Walling because he could think of nowhere else he wanted to go. He was in no hurry, because he had no schedule to keep and no plan to follow. In a larger sense he was like a tightly-wound spring, holding in check the tension of a repressed impatience that would only be released when he had solved the mystery of Thirley Hall. Or when he and Mary Beth met in the flesh.

He had high expectations and great fears for what the next two weeks might be like. He imagined candlelight dinners and gentle country walks. He pictured himself curled up with her before the fireplace of a deluxe Bed and Breakfast in the Peak District he had once visited, living out his two-and-a-half decade's old and admittedly naive desire. But there he reached the limits of his imagination. He had no picture of the future beyond the next few days, no tomorrows filled with bright mornings and tender nights, no growing old together. He couldn't even move the flesh and blood Mary Beth in his mind past their first year of college into the present. He knew he was yearning for a past that would not return. That was a Mary Beth who no longer existed—except in the same way that his teenage self still lived inside him. He even failed in his attempts to fantasize about making love with her. For some reason clear images simply wouldn't come. How could his imagination conjure up people who had been dead for four hundred years, provide him with a ghostlike companion who dogged his every step, and generally jerk him around emotionally in a dozen different ways, and yet fail him in this? Why didn't his otherwise overactive imagination play out for him a vivid scenario—any kind of scenario—of the simple act of coupling with a woman he had desired either consciously or unconsciously for his entire adult life? Was he too fearful about seeing her? Or had Mary Beth represented the unattainable for so long that he couldn't imagine a new intimacy with her until it actually happened? If it happened. Whatever the source of this block, it left him with vague unclear hopes and a gnawing anxiety for the time they would spend together.

Time together. That was what he ached to have—a bridge across the years to recapture those long-ago days. On the fringe of his consciousness lingered images of Jeannie and her anger and the rift Mary Beth's reappearance and his obsession with her had brought into their lives, into their fresh new relationship. He avoided asking himself the obvious and crucial question: was being with Mary Beth worth ending his relationship with Jeannie? But he didn't ask it. Perhaps he couldn't ask it.

In the meantime Stichen-Walling made as good a destination as any, or so he told himself. He hated to admit his obsession with the dingy town, its churchyard and its gravestones for fear that by acknowledging that fixation he would lose all grip on the rational old Brian. Somehow estimating the number of grains of rice in a cup didn't do it for him anymore. He had much bigger fish to fry. So, he pointed the Rover toward Stichen-Walling, even though he had no idea of what he might do in the village when he got there. Besides, that is, paying a visit to those banished graves. So far as he knew he had already exhausted the research possibilities in the town archives. At this moment he lacked even a glimmer of a lead.

Pulling off the A-134 onto a smaller B road and checking his map, he decided to continue in a meandering way on the smaller roads toward Stichen-Walling, pleased with the way the old Rover negotiated the turns and liking the sound of its motor as it moved through the gears. The rather homely somewhat cranky old car with its bulky square body and inelegant style was transformed in that moment into a powerful well-tuned sports car speeding along the twisting roads of rural Suffolk. Downshifting around curves and then accelerating again through the gears, he became entirely preoccupied with the simple pleasure of driving. Thoughts and obsessions were left behind in the hypnotic absorption of maneuvers and turns on the winding macadam.

He had just overtaken a slow-moving tractor dragging a loaded manure wagon and had followed a looping curve in the road when the route suddenly felt familiar. Directly ahead the unmistakable landmark of a big decaying oak tree loomed. He remembered it as marking the turnoff to the site of the former Thirley Hall. On a sudden impulse, he down shifted the Rover and made the shallow left-hand turn almost without slowing. The old car bounced over the verge and put him on that same narrow lane that he had followed with Bobbie. Tall dry weeds spilled out across the lane. Sometimes in especially narrow places he could feel the dry roadside grasses simultaneously brush against both sides of the car, an identical experience to the other time he had come this way. As before no oncoming traffic forced him to use one of the occasional lay-byes. He twisted through the pastoral countryside on the tiny road. Finally he saw in the distance the unmistakable rise of the hill and open meadow where the medieval manor house had once stood. "That *was* a good place for a country house," he muttered aloud. Why had nobody rebuilt on the site? Judging from the absence of contemporary comment, the one and only Thirley Hall must have been undistinguished either by its architecture or by its various inhabitants. Still, the site was undeniably striking, and thoughts of the place fascinated him as much as if it had been Hampton Court Palace.

He pulled the car over in front of the aluminum gate in the hedgerow, turned it around to face the direction he had come and edged the passenger side of the Rover against the gate. Making his way through the dense row of shrubs by the same tight staggered passageway as before, he climbed the gentle slope some two hundred yards to the spot where the Hall had stood four hundred years earlier. Seeing the grassy mounds gave him a little thrill. For a moment he even wished he had a shovel to dig for artifacts.

Spotting a single rock sticking out of the autumn-brown grass, he walked to it and sat down. From there he could look out over the small groves of trees and broad fields stretching to the east, north and south and behind him to the gate and the lane. More of the fields had been plowed over than when he had last been there with Bobbie three weeks before. Then he thought about his dream/vision set in this place and the sensation of violence and death he had felt during it. None of those feelings lingered on this quiet October morning.

Or did they?

Brian sat very still and listened, half expecting to hear the sounds of battle, to smell the stench of fresh blood, human feces and piss and to feel the searing heat of flames destroying an ancient manor house. But he heard and saw nothing out of the ordinary. Still, an indefinable legacy of pain lingered here. Was this feeling merely the product of an overactive imagination? More than that? Nothing would dissuade him from the conviction that Thirley Hall had been destroyed in some violent altercation accompanied by pain and bloodshed. Perhaps it was in the Civil War of the seventeenth century. But he lacked a single piece of data to support that or any other conclusion.

Then he remembered that his dream set in this place had his ghostly companion sitting on the very rock where he now sat. He jumped up and leaped back, almost tripping over his own feet and only just restrained himself from fleeing back to the Rover. His heart was pounding. Why had that memory startled him so? Asking that question helped to settle him. Rather than running, he turned around and looked again over the panorama of fields and pasture, gradually calming down inside. Still, he did not return to sitting on the rock. Broad cultivation stretched as far as the eye could see; many fields were plowed and dark, others still golden with stubble. Pastureland often divided from the fields by hedgerows and punctuated by little groves of trees. A movement in the distance caught his eye, and he focused on a small but dense grove in the pasture two hundred yards northeast from where he stood. At first he imagined it might be a mounted rider. But it was only a brown and white cow, her udder swinging as she walked, grazing contentedly as she moved away from the trees into open pasture. He smiled at himself and then returned his gaze to the rock, wondering at its vivid role in his dream. Why had his mind held onto that insignificant detail to put it in his dream?

An uncomfortable feeling crept over him. Perhaps the emptiness of the site had gotten to him. He shivered and said aloud, "This place *is* creepy."

Again he felt as much as he saw movement coming from around the side of the same grove of trees that had emitted the cow. He looked directly at the spot, expecting to see another bovine join the first one. But the original cow had slowly grazed in her meandering way perhaps fifty yards from the grove, and no companion came lumbering through the grass toward her. Instead, this new movement, which he saw indistinctly, was more than one animal. A shiver ran up his spine. "My God," he said aloud as he recognized the familiar band of horsemen, gradually becoming more distinct and recognizable as their bodies gathered substance. Had he slipped into a dream unawares? It didn't seem like it. Why were they growing more solid looking?

As usual the band of about a dozen mounted men was riding hard. What were they doing here? Suddenly he felt no surprise seeing them in this place. It made perfect sense for them to be here. They seemed to belong. As he stared at the horsemen, they continued to become more substantial, more real, and, unlike on previous occasions, he could hear on the faint breeze the sounds of the horses' livery jingling, the slap of leather on flesh, and even the blowing sounds of the horses' rough breathing. As always they were too far away for him to be certain, but the riders looked resolute and coarse, grim and determined. They carried their usual antique firearms and had swords at their sides. The leader of the pack, brandishing a sword in a hand held high over his head, seemed to be calling his men to greater speed, urging them on to greater effort. Just like always. There was something clearly maniacal about him.

But no matter how hard they rode—and they were riding very hard, indeed—they got no closer to Brian.

He stood fascinated, watching the horsemen, elbows and arms flailing and gesticulating. Gradually they lost their transparent look so he could no longer see right through them. Shifting his gaze back to the leader, he felt a stab of fear go through him. The man's fiercely-determined face was as clear as if he had put a pair of binoculars to his eyes.

Brian looked around for signs of life, as if to confirm that he was actually here and not having a dream. Seagulls were swooping over a new-plowed field. Insects buzzed. A lone hawk sailed past him, gliding on the wind. The same cow he had seen before grazed without alarm, paying no attention whatsoever to the riders.

What riders?

Both men and horses had vanished so completely that he couldn't swear they had ever been there. He stared until his eyes began to smart and his head to ache. This had not been one of his dreams. He really was here. In every respect ordinary life went on around him. A place memory then? He sat down on the rock, less spooked about sitting there than he had been before. Long minutes passed while he waited for something else to happen, but he only saw the cow grazing, the birds flying and a tractor and driver working a far-distant field. The quiet enveloped and seduced him.

Just when he had begun to appreciate and think consciously about the peace and stillness of the place and how much he now liked being alone in it, a sudden thought struck him. At first it came in the form of a question, and then, finally, in the shape of a plan. The question was simple and obvious: who presently owned these fields and this hill? The plan followed naturally from that question: find out the owner of this place before the present one and then the one before that, moving backwards through the centuries to Jane and her family. If he couldn't learn anything about the destruction of Thirley Hall by going at it directly maybe he could get there by starting in the present and working through ownership records, family papers and local legends to the time the building had been destroyed. Perhaps even to when it had been transferred from Jane to its subsequent run of owners. Or did the destruction of the place and its transfer from Jane come at the same time? Was Thirley Hall's destruction, as seemed entirely possible, connected to whatever had happened to Jane and her family? Working backwards to find answers to these questions would be like charting an underground stream by following it from where it appears aboveground back into the dark recesses of its subterranean course.

"Yes, that's it," he said aloud, standing abruptly and, turning on his heel and walking back to the Rover. He was glad to have a sense of purpose again.

Brian sped along the narrow lane back toward the Stichen-Walling road, anxious to implement his new plan. The warm air bathed his face as it poured in through the open window.

"What the . . .?"

He still had perhaps a quarter of a mile to go before rejoining the B road. And now this. Stationary in the middle of the roadway stood a mounted rider astride a big roan. This was no ordinary mounted rider. It was the leader of the band he had just seen riding on its treadmill. Both the speckled brown-red-and-white animal and its rider stood perfectly still, expressionless, looking directly toward the car. Toward Brian. The man, his neck craned pointedly, was dressed in plain brown trousers and leather jersey as always. He held a drawn sword in his hand. His expression suggested that he would give no quarter to any adversary. Brian had never been this close to the mounted leader before and, like the sighting a few minutes earlier, this was not an opaque image. Horse and rider seemed entirely real.

Without stopping to think—there wasn't time for that—Brian simultaneously hit the brakes on the Rover and swerved the car into the hedgerow. The sickening snapping and tearing sound the car made going through the centuries-old stalks and branches came to an abrupt end as the car's front wheels sank into the mud of a low and very damp spot of pasture. Two black-and-white cows looked placidly at him while a calf bounded away from the car's sudden intrusion. Brian glanced back over his shoulder to where the horse and rider had stood only seconds before. A feeling of terror immobilized him.

Nothing.

He scrambled out of the car and, stepping gingerly over the sodden soil, made a quick survey of the ground. He was entirely alone except for the cows. The car, with some new scratches to be sure, seemed unhurt. But the heavy Rover had sunk into the mud so completely that it might as well have taken root. He got back into the car and tried to back it out, but without success. It would have to be hauled out by force.

It took Brian the rest of the morning to extricate the hapless car: to check his rental papers for the right phone number; to figure out how to make a call on his new mobile phone; and to reach the Automobile Association. By the time the AA truck had dragged the Rover out of the mud and Brian finally managed to get to Stichen-Walling in it, he was tired, hungry and grumpy. He wanted to be in a quiet pub with a pint of bitter and some food. Mostly he needed to sit by himself and recover from the disturbing and frustrating turn the day had taken. The gloomy interior of the Furrowed Fen, whose garrulous proprietor Brian had come to know on previous visits, fit the bill perfectly.

The landlord soon sensed Brian's mood and quickly drew the pint and found a wrapped ham and cheese sandwich left over from the lunch crowd. "Bag a crisps with it?" he asked.

Brian mumbled an affirmative response.

"Salt and vinegar all right, then?"

Brian said, "That'll be fine," and took a long pull from the pint glass. He managed a smile for the landlord and put a ten-pound note on the bar. His change soon materialized. Gathering up his money, the sandwich, potato chips and beer, he made his way to a remote table.

There he sat amidst the odors of spilled beer and stale tobacco smoke thinking about his day so far. All things being equal, he would rather have the Ghost and all the rest—the visions and dreams, the dead women and the mounted warriors—just go away and leave him alone. He pulled out his current paperback novel from a jacket pocket, opened the book and stuffed a bite of sandwich into his mouth. Escape was almost immediate as his conscious mind disappeared into nineteen-thirties Oxford instead of twenty-first (or seventeenth) century Stichen-Walling. For the moment his companions were Harriet Vane and her aristocratic sleuth associate, Lord Peter Wimsey. The food, drink and flight into the world of Dorothy Sayers soon restored Brian to a less agitated state of mind. The black mood passed along with the hunger. By and by he remembered the first step of his new plan, which was to find out who currently owned the Thirley Hall property.

Looking at his wristwatch he saw that the offices at the town hall would close before long. Maybe he had just enough time to locate the name of the owner. A surge of purpose and resolve coursed through him. He closed the book cover on Harriet and Lord Peter and stuffed it into his pocket. Downing the last ounce of liquid in his glass, he slid a battered wooden chair out of his way and waved goodbye to the landlord as he went through the door into the warm dry afternoon air. Now brimming over with energy and purpose, Brian had become more himself again.

The door to the first floor office announced "Real Property" in two-inch high black lettering. Brian could see shelves of heavy bound volumes that probably would hold what he was looking for. The place smelled of dust and bureaucracy. The man behind the counter looked about sixty, perhaps a little older. Straight wispy unruly white hair sat atop a face of smooth soft-looking skin and a small wiry body. His eyes were a clear gray. Brian guessed his weight at not an ounce above 120 pounds. Or seven stone as the Brits would put it. "Can I have a look at the plat books?" he asked. "I want to identify the current owner of an estate."

"Oh, those records are all on the screen now," the clerk said, tapping a bony hand on the top of a computer monitor and beaming at Brian.

They soon identified the property, made easy because Thirley Hall's site formed one small part of a large tract of land held by a single owner. The clerk soon found the record and gave Brian the name of James D. Arnold and the address in Bury St. Edmunds where tax notices went. It had taken at most ten minutes from the moment he entered the building. His next step would be to ask who the previous owners might have been, something he hoped to get from James D. Arnold. Otherwise, he would have to scour those old plat books after all. This one piece of business finished, Brian felt as if the day had not been a total loss. Far from it. He could now let himself be drawn, as if by a magnet, to the dilapidated old church.

The sun was beginning to set as he walked around the tall Victorian building and entered the medieval churchyard through its ramshackle lychgate. Presumably someone occasionally used the lawn and garden tools that he knew were stored inside the church building. But no such thing had happened since his last visit. The tall grass had browned and withered without attention, and leaning headstones were as crusted over with moss and lichen as on his first visit. The broken wall's loose stones still spilled into the churchyard. The family graves inside the wall had received no apparent attention from descendants, perhaps in a century—and certainly not since Brian had last been there. The lonely church and its sagging roof needed attention as much as ever. There remained little of beauty in this neglected place. No residue of holiness clung to it from the centuries of prayers said there. It looked forlorn and decrepit. Judging from the overgrown public paths, nobody ever visited it at all. It looked and felt so lonely and unhappy that it made Brian sad just to look at it.

He stood surveying the hole in the broken wall and speculated at the cause of such abandonment and neglect. His attention shifted to movement he saw in the corner of his eye. Now what, he wondered. He swung his body toward the little church where he had seen or sensed the motion, expecting to see some horrible new apparition or maybe his ghostly companion. He saw neither. He did see a gray tabby cat stalking something, perhaps a bird or a mouse or some other little animal. But she was behaving very peculiarly. As the cat stalked, she kept looking around and glancing over her shoulder as if fearing some predator. Perhaps she was afraid an owl might be hunting at dusk and would make a tasty morsel of her. But her suspicious glances were not up into the sky on the lookout for a winged enemy. He couldn't identify anything that might possibly be worrying her, except perhaps himself. But the cat didn't look in his direction either. Instead, her repeated glances seemed to be toward the open place in the wall. Perhaps she feared that a dog or some other feline enemy would come into the churchyard from that unprotected direction.

Without warning, the cat suddenly freaked, or so it seemed to Brian. She jumped straight into the air. The hair on her back stood up, and she let out an eerie scream that sounded as if she were in very great pain. Or had become terrified. The tabby fled around the side of the church and out of Brian's sight. He stepped briskly to the corner of the little building for a look but could see nothing more of the cat. He scanned back in the direction of the broken wall. He couldn't see anything there either.

"Must've seen a ghost," Brian said out loud, chuckling to himself. Then he remembered where he was and asked who he was to ridicule the poor cat? With his recent history, he had nothing whatever to laugh about.

He stepped toward the hole in the wall, suddenly feeling apprehensive. Once he got there, he stood looking at the excluded graves, wondering about those lonely exiles banished from the churchyard. He wondered if he were about to see some kind of ghost. But nothing appeared. He laughed again at the thought. But still he lingered, entranced, growing more and more nervous.

Dusk was rapidly turning into dark, and Brian remembered from his earlier visits to the Stichen-Walling churchyard that he really didn't like hanging out there after dark. He looked around one last time, almost hoping he would see something unusual. He saw nothing. Instead, he walked back to the other churchyard, strolled around the Victorian church and returned to the main street where he had left the muddy Rover. The poor thing. He really should get it washed.

The busy Indian restaurant, dark with red-flocked wallpaper, thick carpet and Indian artifacts and decorations, had an atmosphere rich in the smells of the East: spicy curries, searing chicken and baking Naan bread. The waiter spread heavy maroon napkins in their laps, brought a plate of pappadums with a selection of chutneys, poured tall amber glasses of Taj Mahal lager and took their dinner order. Only then did Brian and Carol Heppell talk about the icon meditation, the ostensible reason they were having dinner. To Brian's astonishment, Carol showed no surprise about what had happened to him.

"When I did that a few years ago," she said, "I saw some of those fast-changing faces—both men and women, lovely and horrible. It's all pretty startling, isn't it?"

He nodded.

"But I'll pose the same question to you that our

meditation leader asked me: what are you going to do with this grace? And, in your case, how do you plan to deal with that sense of evil you felt?"

Her questions jolted him. What, indeed, did he intend doing about it? He couldn't even figure out what to do with living women. What might he do with dead ones, even if, as he had come to believe, this entire puzzle centered on the three women of Thirley Hall?

Suddenly he thought about the eerie moment he had had the day before in front of Bobbie's picture of the old church at Stichen-Walling. He told Carol about it, concluding with, "And the picture seemed determined to draw me in—physically."

"That does sort of complete the call for you, then, doesn't it?"

"The call? Did you say *call*?"

"I know it's kind of a churchy word. But you seem to be—well, called. Called maybe to take some action in that village. I don't know what else to say. It's as if the little medieval church is reaching out to you. Maybe you just need to go there and use those tools you told me about to do some gardening." She grinned. "I don't know what you're called to do. But it seems pretty clear that you're meant to *do* something. How do your particular skills and experience fit into this situation? Why you?"

"Why me, indeed? If there *is* something I'm meant to do, it probably has to be related to unraveling things about the past, since that's what I do. Maybe finding out about those women—learning what happened to them—is my *call*, as you put it."

If he thought about it Brian had to admit that he had a penchant for unraveling puzzles. He was an inveterate worker of crosswords. His most successful book, though he would be quick to contend not his most important one, had been the resolution of the murder of a London merchant tailor in the Tower of London early in the reign of Henry VIII. Brian always thought of himself as a practical man. He liked theories and knowledge. Indeed, he thrived on them. But he also had a need to translate the stuff that went on inside his head into something solid. He would always write a book or an article or give a lecture on something that interested him. Other than writing a paper about it, and he was nervous about doing that because it was all so unlikely, he couldn't see how he might make something solid out of Stichen-Walling. What possible good for anyone could come of that?

Back on Sidgwick Street, the Rover settled into the car park at Lo-Host, Brian had no greater ambition than to get a good night's sleep. But Carol's parting words kept echoing in his mind: "I think that in some way neither of us understands, you have been led to this place and to this moment. Put another way, who you are fits into something waiting to be done. Anyway, you seem absolutely poised to take some action. Stichen-Walling seems to be where you're meant to do it."

Meant? What was that supposed to suggest?

chapter eighteen

Brian lounged in his sitting room, reading in his London guidebook about Mary Beth's hotel: "a late Victorian purpose-built hostelry of red-brown terra cotta and imperial pretensions." It was Friday afternoon. Mary Beth should be arriving at the hotel at any moment. Perhaps she already had. He cast his eyes back to the type on the page, reading on, almost without thinking about the words. "Houses less gaudy, earlier and nobler for the most part, surround Russell Square in graceful Georgian symmetry." He liked that area, especially the feel of the University of London and its echoes of John Maynard Keynes and Lytton Strachey. University College, the Slade, Montague Street's row of converted bed-and-breakfast hotels, Great Russell Street and the pillared front of the British Museum. Bloomsbury was a splendid choice for the annual meeting of the Anglo-American Association of Chemical Engineers. He imagined its technical and scientific presentations, busy networking and gossip. No doubt this was much like a history conference, at least in the particulars. The location and timing certainly suited Brian for his reunion with Mary Beth after so many years. The jangling sound of the phone interrupted his musings.

"Hello, Brian," he heard over the receiver. Mary Beth must have called as soon as she got in. That felt like a promising sign. "I'm here in London. Glad I caught you in."

"It's good to hear your voice . . . on this side of the Atlantic. Being here, I mean." He felt flustered and awkward.

"I'm pretty travel worn," she said.

"No doubt." He remembered his own crossing of the Atlantic in June. But she's so much younger than he, isn't she? No, that's not true. Of course not. She's his same age and not nineteen anymore. He shook his head, trying to make sense of this present conversation and reality. "Is your room okay?" he asked, still ill at ease.

"Yes. It's a bit small, but it's fine. You were right about

the area. It's terrific." She sighed softly.

"Why the sigh?"

"Oh nothing. I picked up the last-minute details about the conference. My session is late tomorrow. Saturday afternoon. Right?"

"Right."

"Then I have Sunday morning and afternoon free. One final obligation Sunday night that takes up the whole evening, I'm afraid, and then the conference will be over."

"Shall I come and hear your presentation?"

The line seemed to go dead. She continued, "That's sweet, but do you really want to hear about ways of discovering the thermodynamics of polymorphism. Besides, I really do need to concentrate, and having you there would distract me. There really wouldn't be a lot of time to talk with an old friend."

He imagined her smiling as she called him her *old friend*, and chuckled lightly to himself. No doubt she was right. "The thermodynamics of what? Why don't I pick you up on Sunday morning, then? We can go somewhere outside London that's nice, get a leisurely lunch, and then I'll have you back in time for your evening commitment."

"The closing banquet. Hmm, lunch on Sunday? Would it be too far to go to Oxford? I love that city, and it's been years since I've been there."

"No, not too far." He felt more confident now. "Sure. Sunday traffic will probably be pretty daunting, especially later in the day, but we can brave it. I even know a good place in Oxford to get a pub lunch. If, that is, you're into literary gastronomy."

"That's a mouthful." She laughed.

He grinned and felt more like himself, thinking about the gathering places of Oxford's famous writers and intellectuals of the 1930s. Then he realized gratefully that he and Mary Beth were becoming lighter and easier with each other. Maybe like him, she was holding back a contained excitement about being together. "Pick you up about ten?" he asked. "I'll call as I'm getting close."

A serious tone crept back into her voice, "I'm so glad

we've been in touch again. It will be—ah, fun to see you after all this time."

After he hung up the phone, Brian was left coping with the lump in his throat and alternating waves of excitement, anxiety and guilt. Now he only had to occupy himself somehow until Sunday morning. He sat back, guidebook in lap, and let his eyes drift unseeing across the pages as his mind wandered off into a different time and space. Awake or asleep he couldn't say.

I'm standing at the back of the old church at Stichen-Walling. Somehow I know it's that church. Only I've never seen the place look this way—cheerful and friendly. Colorful tapestries soften the hard stone of the walls; an array of candles gives off a warm glow; the high spirits of the laughing crowd inside spills over even to the building itself. An explosion of color and the smell of abundance come from a large spray of fresh flowers in front of the pulpit. It's a happy church in what appears to be a prosperous village—a marked contrast to the church I've come to know. Most of the people are dressed in simple drab clothing with loose over-garments, a style that could have been worn in a rural English village anytime from the late middle ages until the mid-nineteenth century. None of the clothing is decorated, but it probably represents the villagers' Sunday best. A small grouping is distinguished from the crowd by its brightly-colored and flamboyant costume. These would be local gentry. Even among that group two couples stand out—both by their elegance and by their being the obvious focus of attention. Their style fits the royalist Cavaliers at the outbreak of the English Civil War. The men carry thin dress swords. Both of the women wear their hair well back from their foreheads in softly falling ringlets and have tiny squares of lace perched on top of their luxurious curls. They are both beautiful, but the older one—surely she is Jane of Thirley Hall—has a mature loveliness that rivets my attention. She has delicate features, tiny ears and exquisite green eyes with a wary knowing expression in them. A black beauty mark stands out on the left side of her pointed little chin. Both couples stand with their backs to a clergyman wearing a flowing white surplice and brocade stole. He also faces the congregation from the chancel step.

Despite their dress style and what that tells me about the period, this does not feel like a countryside torn by conflict. There are no signs of weapons, sentries standing guard or the tension of a people faced daily by unpredictable violence. More likely, this little scene reflects a time before the outbreak of the Civil War. The time of Jane and her daughter and granddaughter. It all works.

I stand watching as they retreat down the aisle. Everyone turns to follow amidst a buzz of happy conversation. The whole affair carries a heady atmosphere of celebration and good fun. It feels like a wedding party. Certainly, it must be a wedding party. The parish register had Jane and her daughter with identical marriage dates, Jane's fourth and Mary's second. Surely I am seeing that very occasion. At what other seventeenth century wedding might I find myself an uninvited and unintentional guest?

I watch as the crowd spills out into the churchyard, and I follow, apparently unobserved. Outside, the old church looks much like my own twenty-first century version, though without all the deterioration and neglect. The roof is strong and solid. The wall around the yard looks new, and the stones have been carefully pointed. Most of the headstones stand straight. Other familiar monuments have yet to be placed. Trees are where I expect them to be, but they don't always appear to be the same species; they seem smaller. Even the grass is carefully tended. I smile as I see the gardeners at work: a pair of sheep grazing in a distant corner. The tiny church feels like a lively center of village life rather than the neglected and lonely spot I have come to know. I find that difference intriguing and slightly unnerving.

The company flows in the direction of the village center, crossing the place where one day the Victorian church will be built, and scattering a flock of chickens and geese around a cluster of cottages. As I follow the crowd I begin to pick up the strains of lively rhythmic music: plucked and bowed stringed instruments, wooden flutes and drums. Male and female voices sing with the instruments, but at first I can't make out the words. Gradually I distinguish the text of a song, an earthy number sung by a young woman who keeps repeating the refrain, "My thing is my own and I'll use it as I wish." I laugh out loud at the bawdiness of it. Other wedding guests are dancing and laughing and raising dust on the unpaved road. The two couples are seated in the midst of it all—the center of attention.

I look around and recognize the Stichen-Walling town square. An ancient wooden market cross sits in the middle of the intersection. It has small stalls on all sides for merchandise. Behind the cross is what I know as the Furrowed Fen public house and hotel. The familiar building is painted a pale blue instead of the white I'm accustomed to seeing, and has small attached outbuildings instead of other adjacent full-sized storefronts. But its outlines are the same. The hanging sign in front is entirely different, though. It has the picture of a disheveled man in a huge floppy hat. The name of the place, an apparent coaching inn, seems to have changed over the centuries. There are no explanatory words or names on the sign or on the gated courtyard beside it. Perhaps it is named for some local rogue whose picture is known.

I enjoy wandering unnoticed among trestle tables loaded with beakers of ale and lots of food. I'm tempted to sample it, but I can't do that. And for the simple reason that I'm not really here. Wherever here is. Dancers whirl to the sounds of the music. I see one old man pat the rump of a young woman only to have her turn on him with a glare on her face that would have frozen a bowl of steaming porridge. The scowl soon melts and is replaced by a flirting grin. I'm having the historian-voyeur's time of his life.

Now the oddest thing is happening. Both of the upper class women—Jane and Mary of Thirley Hall, each of whom is a new bride this day—are gazing at me with startling intensity. It stuns me. I am not mistaken. It makes me feel very uncomfortable to be seen in this way by these particular women. The intense expressions on their faces

have what look like unspoken questions painted on them.
They seem to be asking something of me. No, it's stronger
than a request, more like a demand.

Suddenly a throbbing headache and nausea nearly
knock me off my feet, and I know that the dream/vision is
ending. I don't want to leave the wedding feast. Despite the
silent and unspoken demand I feel coming from the two
women: I want to stay. I'm enjoying the occasion, one that
seems to hold the promise of answering so many of my
questions.

Brian sat with Father Jeremiah as before in a quiet
corner beside the side entry to St. Bene't's Church.
Occasionally someone came in from the street, looked
around, picked up a piece of literature about the little
building and its work, perhaps wandered about for a moment
and then left. Such minor intrusions as these troubled Brian
and Jeremiah very little.

"Say that again, I want to be certain I heard you,"
Jeremiah said.

"I think you heard me," Brian answered, a little testy.
"But you just don't believe what you heard."

"I do believe you—and my own ears for that matter. I just
want to be certain that I get it right."

Brian rehearsed the story again. "Stranger than the
dream," he concluded, "was what happened later in my flat. I
was looking at Bobbie's picture of the old Stichen-Walling
church. It's not that the picture has changed, because it
hasn't. But its effect on me is entirely different than before.
The roof is still sagging, and the wall remains broken as
always. The grass needs clipping. If I stand and stare at it for
a moment, I still feel drawn into it, almost as if the picture is
undulating in its urgency to drag me in. But I no longer feel
frightened by it. Now it attracts me, makes me oddly yearn
for it. It seems to promise me something, kind of like an
invitation. Before, it felt negative—maybe as if there were
something evil in it. That no longer seems to be true. After
this last dream," he looked up at Father Jeremiah and
corrected himself, "mystical vision? It—it feels like

somewhere I want to be, *need* to be."

"What do you suppose this new attraction to the church means? Sometimes God really *is* found in the details." He paused and became pensive. "And what about your old love, the woman Mary Beth? How do you see her relating to the rest of what's happening to you?"

"You asked me about Mary Beth once before. I still don't get the question." Brian tried to keep the irritation out of his voice. "How could Mary Beth and my, ah, mystical life have anything to do with each other?"

Jeremiah sucked on the tip of one index finger for a moment before going on. "The puzzle of your life just now seems to have two sources: the accumulation of experiences and stresses in work and all; and something genuinely metaphysical. I've never known someone to have such intense and frequent mystical experiences without having the rest of their lives connected in some way.

"What about the people I've dreamed about? Why them?"

"Let's look at that. Queen Elizabeth—the first one, that is—sets the stage. For you she has a premier place. Julian is the mystic/theologian. Erasmus presages social upheaval—through new theological and cultural thinking: Renaissance humanism and all that. Then you have a cluster of politicians and statesmen. What do they stand for?"

"I've thought about that. They seem to represent the factions in the kingdom in Elizabeth's time. The Duke of Norfolk and the Howards are great aristocracy. Many of them were Recusants—Catholics who refused to conform to the state religion. They headed one faction. Lord Burghley was the great bureaucrat and administrator, firm supporter of the established church and Elizabeth's religious settlement. Walsingham was a powerful Puritan leader. Each of these heads separate factions."

"What about George Herbert?"

"Alone among the others, he was an exact contemporary of Jane and her immediate family. But he wasn't especially political. Neither was he a theologian as such. So he doesn't fit with either group—theologians and politicians."

"Let's see, Herbert *is* a representative of the established church in an age of social and religious upheaval. You did dream about a poem of his on the English church, didn't you? But, leaving him otherwise aside, when you put the others together what do you come up with?" Jeremiah wrinkled his brow.

"A cross section of Elizabethan and early Jacobean parties," Brian said simply and looked at his hands.

"And they are all people connected to Cambridge, aren't they? Forming an extension of your old place memories?"

"But where does the Thirley Hall/Stichen-Walling business fit into it all?"

"That's the question isn't it? Do you suppose that this village got caught up somehow in the political and religious controversies of the age?"

"I suppose that's possible. Everywhere did at one time or another. But the timing's not quite right for that. The Civil War doesn't come until the 1640s—when the three women were long since dead and buried. Still, it is possible. The wedding party had a decidedly established-church feel about it, not a Puritan or Catholic event. Too much celebration, drink and high spirits for the Puritans. Too public for the Catholics. Perhaps the straight-laced types had their ire raised by the wedding itself and the general lifestyle of these women. That seems to have been pretty earthy."

"You're the historian. Does all this analysis seem viable to you? And remember it only has to make sense in your particular brain, not in some classic textbook kind of way. It's your psyche we're talking about here." Jeremiah sat back in his chair and examined Brian over the top of the rimless round glasses he always wore.

"I suppose so. But what about Bobbie's picture?" Brian asked.

"Yes, Bobbie's picture. It's the link that binds it all together, isn't it? Your personal life and the Stichen-Walling puzzle come together in the work of your daughter like a bridge linking your former life—controlled and predictable—to your present, highly susceptible and unpredictable one."

"A bridge over troubled waters?"

"Exactly." Jeremiah grinned enigmatically.

"But why is all of this happening?"

"I can't answer that question for you. But perhaps you can do it for yourself. Think of it this way. The world's great mystics often encountered the mystery we call God and felt their own special call under severe physical, emotional or spiritual stress—illness often. Julian of Norwich's fever and near death; Francis of Assisi's despair; John of the Cross's Dark Night of the Soul; Ignatius of Loyola's severe battle wounds: it's as if these stresses made them available to experience another dimension, one that transcended the physical world. Their senses were alerted and their awareness had become more acute, and so they heard voices and saw visions. It's like when you have a fever. You know, when your entire body is weakened and yet your mind is alert. It's as if you've become dulled to your usual feelings and sensitive to unfamiliar ones you seldom have. Fevers are particularly conducive to visions.

"Hallucinations?"

"At the extreme, yes. But I'm talking about this side of raving madness. On the way—in the doorway, as it were— into craziness we can sometimes pass through a time of acute lucidity."

"And this is what you think is happening to me?"

"Something like that."

"But I'm hardly St. Francis. I'm certainly not setting out to change the world."

"No, probably not. But even if the scope of the new life you are being called into is smaller than theirs, that doesn't alter the process."

"But I still don't get it. What am I supposed to *do*?"

"I don't know, but I'm sure you'll find out. Perhaps nothing more than unraveling the mystery of those women and their deaths. By connecting the dots perhaps you can discover in what direction God is calling you. Where your redemption in particular is found."

"Redemption? God? And there's that word *call* again. This all makes me very uncomfortable. Why does this have to be about God and all that?"

"These are the conventional words for the mystery of the universe. God, redemption and call—the language of unseen truths that we all sense is there around us. What do you think redemption is meant to refer to? The Happy Hunting Ground? A place where you float around on puffy white clouds strumming a harp? Pie in the sky by and by? No, redemption is something we are all engaged in all of the time. It's the making-right of the mishaps of living. Putting the broken pieces back together again. Becoming new people out of the ruins of the old. We are all God's coconspirators, in a manner of speaking, in this on-going process. Perhaps one of your particular tasks at this moment—I won't use the word call since that seems to upset you—is to get to the bottom of an old mystery. Perhaps even set the record straight on some things that are broken. At least in the lives of three seventeenth-century women. Satisfy your own historical curiosity." He paused to take a breath. "There are puzzling pieces to this thing we call life. Sometimes there is no rational explanation for all of those pieces. The conclusion you're headed for—and believe me, you are headed somewhere—may never seem entirely logical. But I believe that it will eventually make some very good sense." Jeremiah fixed his gaze on Brian. "I think that you're being led somewhere and that your spiritual companion from Midsummer Common is a kind of guide. In time, we'll know more about the destination and the path—or paths—leading there." He cleared his throat. "Now with that, I must be off. You're welcome to sit here for awhile if you like."

"Thanks. I think I will."

Brian moved over to his regular pew and sat there gazing at the altar deep within the small chancel. He had a lot to think about.

chapter nineteen

The old Rover purred along the A14 like a contented cat soaking up a beam of sunlight on a windowsill. Brian drove. Jeff sat beside him, and Charlie rode in the back seat with a guidebook in her lap. They talked about their destination, Bury St. Edmunds.

"The book says the abbey gardens are interesting," Charlie said.

"Yes, they're pretty spectacular," Brian said. "It's a bit late in the season and the flowers may be a bit tattered. The grounds will still be interesting. With the use of a little imagination, you can really see how the place was laid out. It was huge."

"And the old houses. There's supposed to be a lot of 'em," Charlie continued.

"I'm afraid I don't know much about the houses," Brian said.

They drove quietly for a couple of miles when Charlie observed suddenly, "Today's Saturday. It's market day." She dropped the guidebook back into her lap. "In Bury St. Edmunds, I mean."

"Yes?" Brian muttered. "That will make it harder to park. I should have known that. We'll figure out something."

Quiet settled on the car again as it passed other traffic on the road, little steel and plastic worlds that, like the Rover, hurtled along that strip of concrete and asphalt under the thin October sun. They passed farms, turn-offs to fen villages, road signs identifying local country houses in the National Trust and quiet meadows.

"Don't you have some sort of date tomorrow with somebody out of your past?" Charlie asked.

"I told her about your old girlfriend," Jeff said. "Hope that's okay."

"Of course it's okay," Brian answered. "She was my girlfriend back in college. My first love, I guess you'd say."

"So what are your plans?" she asked.

"To get laid," Jeff inserted.

Brian laughed. "Not necessarily," he said—perhaps a bit too quickly to be convincing.

Jeff guffawed, always the cynic.

Soon the Rover and its three occupants reached the outskirts of Bury St. Edmunds. Brian negotiated the twisting route through commercial streets and homes, past a large builders supply lot, small public houses and tea shops. Rectangular blue signs with the white letter "P" directed him to a car park where he soon found a space.

"Well, that was easier than I thought it'd be," he said as he attached the machine-dispensed parking fee receipt to the inside of the windshield.

They walked through a covered passage between buildings into the town square where the weekly market was underway. Busy stalls offered vegetables, fruits and berries, fresh bread and meat, and clothing on racks and in stacks. Sellers of used books had spread out boxes full, spines up, on tables. Cheeses, a vast collection of sun catchers, trinkets and other wares by potters, wood carvers, leather workers and glass blowers. Cheap manufactured goods lay right beside all the rest. The air carried the scent of grilling meat. People shouted and laughed, pushed and jostled. Brian half expected to find pickpockets working the crowd and shouts of "stop thief" ringing out amidst the bawling and clucking of livestock. But no such alarms issued and no live animals, save the occasional dog, added to the feeling of timeless enterprise. Otherwise this market day was probably much like ones that had been occurring here for centuries. Overhead, the October sunlight was giving way to a rapid build-up of clouds that threatened rain within minutes.

"You'd better be getting a look at the abbey grounds pretty fast," Brian said, looking upward. Charlie and Jeff followed his gaze. "Here, let me show you where I'm going to be." He reached for Jeff's street map. Pausing a moment to orient himself, he pointed to an intersection. "Right there," he said. "If the weather gets as nasty as I fear it might, you may want to be inside the cathedral or at one of the museum exhibits. If you need me, I'll be here," he pointed to the map again, "at number thirty-seven Lamb's Court."

"Number thirty-seven. Right. Otherwise, we meet at 12:30 for lunch at the little restaurant overlooking the abbey gate," Jeff said.

"Or, if I get done real fast, as I think I might, I'll come looking for you."

Number thirty-seven Lamb's Court sat halfway round a gently curving cul-de-sac of uniformly plastered houses painted shades of off-white. Number thirty-seven's bright green trim made it stand out from its neighbors. Generous flowerpots still overflowed with tired-looking pansies, geraniums and alyssum, making up, it seemed, for the absence of front gardens. The indeterminate ages and differing sizes of the multistory houses of varying heights and designs set Brian to wondering about their occupants and owners. They were probably people of some substance as befit, in the case of number thirty-seven, a significant county landowner.

Brian twisted the bell in the heavy front door and heard its sharp crisp ring. Something about the place felt familiar, and that gave him a moment's pause to wonder if some kind of spooky thing were about to happen. He knew he had never before stood in front of this door, or rung that bell. Still, both door and bell felt familiar. He just shook his head and accepted the familiarity. After a moment's wait the door opened to the smiling face of a young man all dressed up in blazer and striped school tie. His unmistakable upper class manner suited the cul-de-sac and house perfectly.

"Hello," he said. "You must be Professor Craig. I'm James Harris. The grandson, you know. We talked on the phone. I'm just back from a meeting in town. Afraid I wouldn't get back in time."

"You're named James for your grandfather?"

"That's right."

"Thanks for seeing me. How's Mister Arnold this morning?" He was thinking of their phone conversation. Young James—not a day over twenty-five, Brian guessed—

had shared the old man's tendency to become rather vague at times, especially later in the day.

"Grandfather is having a very nice morning, thank you." He grinned, showing he understood Brian's purpose in asking. "He's looking forward to meeting you. Not many visitors come these days. Here, let me take your coat and umbrella." He quickly hung both on a coat tree beside the door and led Brian from the polished-wood entrance hall to a narrow flight of stairs and into an upstairs sitting room.

The interior of number thirty-seven Lamb's Court had all the signs of antiquity and taste. It had uneven floors, slightly skewed door and window frames, ten-foot-high ceilings, and an astonishing jumble of furniture that would be an antique collector's delight. It smelled of beeswax and wealth. Floors covered with expensive rugs made crinkling sounds as Brian followed young James across them.

More creaks and squeaks came from the stairs as they climbed to the upper floor. Wood trim several centuries old was either painted glossy white or had been, as in the entrance hall and on the stairs, finished naturally with a dark stain and then treated to innumerable coats of wax. Gilt-framed paintings hung everywhere.

Brian had come into what he would bet had been this family's town home for many generations, and that knowledge gave him a mounting sense of excitement. The odds of discovering something of what he came here to learn seemed much better than if this were a family new to wealth and position.

James D. Arnold was a frail-looking elderly man with a tonsure of white hair outlining a shining pate. Watery blue eyes and very large ears were his most prominent features. He sat there like a skinny Buddha in front of the lace curtain-covered bay windows. An overly warm electric fire glowed at his feet. He had on a loose open-collared crisply-pressed white shirt, dark green cardigan and baggy black trousers. All of his clothing looked left over from an earlier day when he weighed more.

"Grandfather, this is Professor Craig," said young James. "Professor Craig, my grandfather."

"It's good that you could come," the old man said without rising. He peered through round, thin-rimmed glasses at Brian and extended his right hand. "Jimmy, please ask Mrs. Kenny to bring the coffee. There's a good boy."

James Harris flashed Brian an indulgent smile. "Right, Grandfather."

A silver tray soon materialized with stacked cups and saucers, a matching bowl of cubed sugar and milk pitcher, and a steaming silver pot of fragrant coffee.

"I think you have some questions for me about some of my family's county holdings, don't you?" Mr. Arnold asked after a time.

"Yes, and thank you for the coffee." Brian paused, trying to decide just how much he needed to tell his host. Not very much. "I'm doing some historical research on Stichen-Walling and the surrounding countryside in the late sixteenth and early seventeenth centuries, and I've come across some puzzles that I'd like to solve. One of them has to do with a former manor house, now long gone, on a piece of your property. Thirley Hall was its name. Does that ring any bells for you?"

"Well, now." Brian's host rubbed his chin and then his bald head. "I may be a bit fuzzy about what happened yesterday, but I'm still pretty clear about events from years ago. Long-term memory it's called." He chuckled and shook his head. "But I don't remember a blessed thing about a Thirley Hall. I know that several locations on the property once had cottages, or perhaps as in this case, a manor house or two. But I don't remember any of their names—if I ever knew them. I've never known where any of them were supposed to have been. I seem to recall that there is a Thirley Green, isn't there?"

Brian nodded.

Arnold looked at him, "Not a very keen historical mind, I'm afraid." A twinkle appeared in his eye. "Except that now I've become a bit of an artifact myself, haven't I?"

Brian laughed, but inside he felt a sinking sensation. Had he come to a dead end? Would this trip to Bury prove to be a waste of time after all? Then he remembered. "One other thing," he said. "How long has the property been in your family?"

"Oh, a very long time, I think. We came to have most of those county estates by a purchase from the Crown. That was during Stuart times, you know. We don't actually work the land ourselves."

Brian nodded. Rents were a traditional source of landed income. Since Stuart times was it? The very century Brian was interested in.

"But, of course you can check that all out for yourself up there, can't you?" James Arnold pointed to the ceiling.

"I'm sorry?"

"All the family records are up there." He pointed upward again. "In the attic. Lucy Ellen had that as one of her projects when we came back here to live."

"Lucy Ellen?" Brian covered his returning excitement with a simple question.

"My wife. Dead now for . . . for a very long time, I'm afraid." He managed to avoid looking wistful.

They sat silently for a time. When Brian decided that the awkwardness had passed, he asked, "And you will let me look at the family records?"

"Why ever not?" James Arnold glanced toward the doorway and raised his voice above the near whisper of his conversational tone, "Jimmy, are you there, lad?"

"Yes, Grandfather," he called from somewhere near by.

"Can you come here, then?"

The grandson soon appeared at the door. "You wanted something, Grandfather?"

"Yes, thank you, Jimmy. Please take Professor Craig up and show him the family archives in the attic."

"Right, Grandfather," he said. "I had thought of that myself." To Brian he said, "This way."

Brian put down his empty cup and saucer, noticing that his hand shook as he did. He stood up and followed the grandson to a narrow staircase that ascended from the rear of the house past two upper floors to the attic, an unfinished cavern of pitched ceilings, dormer windows, bare unfinished walls and the mingled odors of dust and mouse droppings.

Various objects stood around: boxes of unidentified treasures, an old baby carriage and a lot of stacked-up old furniture. Brian also found three black four-drawer and double-thick fireproof file cabinets pushed up against one wall. An old wooden table and a single chair stood to one side. His astonishment and excitement mounted as Jimmy reached up, switched on a bare overhead light and opened one of the file cabinet drawers.

"There you go," he said. "I'm told they're all very well organized. My grandmother's a kind of family legend. I never met her, you know. But it seems she worked as an archivist when she was young. At the Public Record Office in London. I think that was on Chancery Lane."

"That's the street."

"Right. Well, I'll leave you to it then."

"Thanks for everything."

Brian was delighted with the condition and order of the records and stunned by his good fortune. The archive held documents spanning several centuries, the earliest dating from the late fifteenth century. File drawers had been stuffed with carefully organized papers, all in folders. Even more amazing than that, he found a bound and hand-written cross reference that divided the records into several categories: wills, deeds, family letters and personal papers, diaries, property records, household accounts and various business interests and investments. One cabinet held all of the material dating from before the accession of Queen Victoria. The second drawer from the bottom held a group of file folders labeled, like all the others in bold black felt-tip printing, as "Suffolk County Holdings." Those folders contained papers that were chronologically organized beginning in the late sixteenth century. Included there Brian found documents relating to the acquisition of the "Thirley Green Property" in 1646—only a decade and a half after the death of Jane and her daughter and granddaughter in 1632. He felt a small wave of disappointment pass over him. He would likely not find any quick and definitive answers there about how the three women died, but he expected there would be a world of other information.

He got right down to work, looking first at one document, then at another in the Thirley Green folder, glancing from time to time at some cross-referenced material, furiously jotting notes and copying out important texts in his small pocket notebook.

"Yes. That's it," he muttered aloud, and at another point, "I thought so. Even as early as that." His excitement mounted with each new document he examined. In short order he saw everything these archives contained about Thirley Green during the first few years the family had it, finishing well before time to meet Jeff and Charlie for lunch. There was much in the family archive he could deduce about the women's lives. But he found very little that was definitive about exactly what had happened to them or to Thirley Hall itself. Most importantly for this quest he had another name, Sir Anstel Sanderson, the person who had owned the property immediately before Mr. Arnold's family. There was even a short marginal note in the same orderly hand as the file folder labels that said Sir Anstel's papers could be seen in a family collection at the British Library in London. He scanned later entries in the files in the hope that some reference to the house's destruction might be found. He saw nothing.

Having completed his work, Brian spent a few minutes perusing the other drawers in the cabinets just to get a sense of the full range of archived materials. What a goldmine he had found, and it set him to thinking. As he was leaving number thirty-seven Lamb's Court and after he had thanked Jimmy Harris and gotten his promise to convey his gratitude to the dozing James Arnold, he asked, "Do you know much about your family's history?"

"Not really," he said.

"You know there's a world of research material up there." He pointed back up the stairs. "Describing all those resources, beginning to clarify some of the outlines and drawing some tentative conclusions about the family's history would make a great project for a doctoral candidate. Do you think your grandfather would permit one of my graduate students to do some work here?"

"No problem. He'd love to have someone rummaging around in those old papers. Would give him someone to tell his stories to. You really think that old stuff would interest somebody?"

"Oh, it would interest somebody all right. By the way, your grandmother was a superior archivist."

Jimmy nodded, ever the polite host.

"Thanks again."

"I'll look forward to hearing from your student."

They shook hands, and Brian had all he could do to keep from shaking his head as well in amazement at the experience he had just had. Returning the way he had come through the twisting streets of central Bury St. Edmunds, he thought about his students. Which lucky one should he bestow this gift on? He was bursting to share everything he had found with Jeff and Charlie.

Brian watched his friends as they came through the front door of the Cottage Cupboard, shaking the rainwater off their umbrellas and looking around, presumably for him. They were on time. Brian stood up to help them spot him there at the back of the open dining room. The restaurant had been decorated with pale yellow paint and coordinated wallpaper with tiny blue cups and saucers. Frilly white tablecloths gave an added homey touch. It was as cheerful and cozy as Brian remembered. Not even the stern-faced buxom middle-aged waitress who had slapped down menus on the table when he arrived had detracted from the homey feel. He waved. They made their way to the table through mostly filled chairs and bustling wait staff.

"The intrepid tourists," Brian said with a big smile on his face.

"Sherlock, I presume. Where's your deerstalker?" Jeff grinned back.

"And your trusty briar?" Charlie chipped in.

"From the looks of things, I'd guess you two had a good time."

"Smashing, as they say," Jeff replied. "And what about you? You're beaming."

"Yes. Our adventures were pretty tame and will keep. What happened?" Charlie looked genuinely interested.

"Well, I zipped through their family archives in no time," he said. "Incredible. I don't think I've ever heard of family records so well organized, so complete."

"Yes?"

"This same family acquired the place in a deal made in 1646 with Oliver Cromwell and his Parliamentary friends. They got a bargain price, too. Former owners—Jane and her daughter and granddaughter, I imagine, though I found no mention of their actual names—had been accused of witchcraft and murder 'by necromancy.' Incredible! According to these second- or third-hand accounts, all three of the women's husbands had died during the same month. Since no signs of foul play could be discovered nor were there any outbreaks of widespread diseases in the area, the locals seem to have concluded that it must be witchcraft."

"A natural conclusion," Jeff offered in sardonic quip.

Brian nodded. "The Crown confiscated the estate and gave it to a favorite of the dead King, James I. Charles I was king by then. I have the name actually, a Sir Anstel something. I don't know exactly what happened to him, but he lost the property when Crown officials seized it again in the 1640s—I'm not quite sure of the date. Then the current family got it from Oliver Cromwell a few years later, and they have passed the gathered estates on down through the generations ever since. The present owner is this James Arnold whom I met today."

"So what happened to the three women?" Jeff asked.

"I'm not sure, but I imagine they were tried and executed. Or some such thing."

"And the house?"

"There's no record about what happened to it."

"So that's it then? You've solved your mystery?" Charlie said.

"Well, sort of. There's still a lot of stuff I can't explain, like exactly what happened to the house and to the women. Maybe I can fill in some of those blanks with a further lead I found in the files. Sir Anstel's papers."

"But that's great," Jeff said.

"Yes, congratulations. No doubt the rest of the pieces will come together," Charlie said.

"Thanks. I'll just gather some more details, and then maybe I'll have it *all* figured out." Including how it fits together and why I've been dragged into it, he thought to himself.

chapter twenty

Brian dreamed about Mary Beth. Not today's Mary Beth, but the nineteen-year-old girl she had been. She had taunted and teased him as she always did in those recurring dreams. It took a few minutes to shake off the effects. Finally he pulled himself together, dressed, drank some coffee and stuffed in some dry pastry as breakfast. It was ten minutes before eight. Still time enough to get to St. Bene't's for the early morning Mass. If he hurried.

Perhaps it was the rush of emotions he was feeling, anticipation over seeing Mary Beth again and everything that meant. Or he was driven by a spiritual hunger unrelated to her. Whatever the source he felt a gnawing urgency to be in that little church this morning. More than the mere habit which had taken him weekly to the Eucharist back in Chicago for years, this was a new and focused desire: to be in that simple place; to experience the peace which its centuries offered; and to participate in the celebration of the ancient and primal sacramental mysteries of blood and flesh. He was surprised at himself. But it was how he felt. Grabbing his raincoat and umbrella from the hook beside the door and pulling it shut behind him, he bounded down the stairs toward the waiting Rover.

Ten minutes later he walked into the dim and rather chilly little church and slipped into a pew just as the priest began the service. His disappointment that Father Jeremiah wasn't presiding soon passed. He stood as the opening words of the liturgy were said and sat with the rest of the sparse congregation for the reading of the scripture lessons.

His engagement with the Mass was at once absent minded and immediate. He heard the lector read a passage from one of the Hebrew prophets, but he didn't so much listen actively to it as he sat in its presence. A very different thing from either letting his mind wander onto other subjects or actually focusing on the text. He felt very calm and centered. No visions or dreams interrupted his composure. No obsessions intruded upon the stillness of either his body or his mind. He picked up the worship book, following the instructions to turn to Psalm Eight-Four, and participated in the responsive recitation. The specific words passed through him—again without sticking. The lector went on to a reading from one of the Pauline Epistles. Brian's awareness of the text remained in that same middle place as before. Not even the priest's semi-chanted intoning of the Gospel passage fully penetrated Brian's conscious mind. He stood in the time-tested way of honoring the proclamation and let it resonate inside him to create a context for his quietude. Instead of a sermon, the priest invited the handful of worshipers to a period of silent reflection. That suited Brian perfectly as he went deeper and deeper into an interior space of his own; one that a few weeks ago he had not even remembered was there. The Mass enfolded him. He knelt to receive the host and the cup.

On his way out of the church, he paused, letting his hand play across the old wood of the last pew. He looked around at the inside of the Saxon tower with its bell rope hanging limp, and then rested his glance at the corner where the icon group had sat and where he and Fr. Jeremiah had talked. He acknowledged to himself how very different being in church this morning had been than ever before. Today's liturgy had somehow transfixed and renewed him, and without his even having to think about it. Especially because he hadn't thought about it.

Brian suddenly remembered the Ghost. Where did he fit into everything? Just what was this apparition? Bobbie had suggested one of the saints, but that still didn't feel quite right. A new phrase came to him: the embodiment of the sacred. But how is the sacred embodied? And what does it mean for the holy to inhabit the world of the profane? He thought about the Incarnation, images of Christ and the like. "I don't want to go there," he muttered to himself. Wasn't there something else that Bobbie had suggested? He couldn't remember.

Then he thought about the liturgy he had just

experienced. He imagined that he still tasted the sweet wine of the Eucharist on his tongue. Or was it more than imagination? Suddenly he felt humbled. How many hundred times had he received those consecrated elements? And how many times had he missed—really missed—any sense of its meaning? He let his hand run across the back of the pew again. In that moment of tactile contact and mental reflection all of the disparate pieces of his life seemed to flow together like merging small streams conjoined to form a great river. Dream figures, failed marriages, complex and threatening personal relationships, unorthodox burials, ghostly apparitions—they all merged. His confusion was lost in that flowing surge.

A feeling of tenderness passed over him for the priest who had just said the Mass. Then what had begun as a small emotional ripple became a tidal wave of feelings that included a deep tenderness for Bobbie, for her mother, Kathleen, for his one-time girlfriend, Alison, for Emily, for Jeannie—and, for some odd reason, for any number of other people, too. That swamping of affection included Jeff and Charlie and Carol Heppel, his parents, and even some childhood friends he hadn't remembered in years. Then he thought about Father Jeremiah and loved that little man who saw so deeply into what went on inside of others. Inside of him. He found himself for just a moment connected to dozens of human beings in a compassionate intimacy that astonished him. Images of his fifth grade school teacher and of his doctoral adviser floated briefly across his conscious mind. In a sense they were all resurrected in his affections.

And then the intensity passed. But its effects remained. Armed with a new confidence, Brian found himself looking forward with a renewed eagerness toward whatever might happen during the day ahead. He removed his hand from the back of the pew, and, turning toward the door, began to walk out into the brightening light of the October morning. A far more hopeful and less anxious Brian left Cambridge that morning than had crawled out of bed a couple of hours earlier.

Brian aimed the Rover south on the M11 and entered metropolitan London on the A10, following the map into Bloomsbury. He picked up his cell phone from the seat beside him and punched the single digit that he had programmed to dial Mary Beth's hotel. When the double-burrs finally stopped and a voice announced that he had, indeed, reached reception, he asked for the room of Dr. Mary Elizabeth Schumann.

Quicker than he could negotiate a single turn on the one-way system and begin to find his way toward Russell Square Mary Beth's voice came into his ear.

"There you are," she said. "I'm ready to go."

"See you in five minutes," he said.

"Five minutes it is. I'll be out front."

It all seemed so normal. But it wasn't normal. His heart felt as if it had suddenly taken leave from his chest to become lodged in his throat. With a forced determination, he closed the phone and pointed the Rover inexorably toward Russell Square.

Although he knew he was being stupid, Brian couldn't keep himself from looking for a slender nineteen-year-old girl with a mass of curly black hair and a denim backpack slung across her left shoulder. He knew Mary Beth no longer looked that way. But his heart didn't feel what his mind knew, and his eyes sought what his heart wanted them to seek. Not what his mind knew they would find. He tried to force today's image of Mary Beth, the well turned-out middle aged woman, to dance out of the photograph into his disobedient eyes, but the slender teenager kept popping up in his imagination, demanding his allegiance. He didn't think of the earlier Mary Beth as a teenager, at least not like the teenagers he knew back at SU. They all seemed like children compared to the Mary Beth of his myth: a timeless being, young but mature, beautiful and unattainable, a goddess. His Isolde. He was both terrified and excited to see her.

He pulled the Rover up in front of the hotel's elaborate facade and stopped. Neither a middle aged woman nor a skinny child-goddess with lots of hair stood waiting for him. In fact only an elderly man holding the lead of a small dog in one hand and a cane in the other strolled haltingly down the sidewalk. The dog did his duty with everything that stood upright. The old man was patient with him. Just as Brian began to feel restless and worried about parking there, he heard a tapping on the passenger's window, the side of the car away from the hotel and toward the street. He shifted his gaze from watching the old man and the dog to see an attractive stranger in a light green dress and an open white cardigan with a raincoat draped over her arm. She peered at him from behind a pair of sunglasses and below carefully groomed short dark hair. He finally recognized and slowly accepted this Mary Beth, the one with a smile of recognition on her face. He reached over, pulled the handle and pushed open the passenger door.

"Dr. Schumann, I presume."

"Dr. Craig.

They both grinned like the teenagers he had only moments before imagined her still to be.

"Your chariot. . ."

She slid into the seat and then offered her cheek to him to be kissed. He obeyed. She smelled faintly of soap and a light sweet perfume.

"Damn, it's good to see you—ah, after all this time," he said.

"You, too," she answered.

He noticed that she had shed the confident air that had cloaked her when she first knocked on his window. He, too, felt self-conscious and ill-at-ease. "To Oxford, then. Do you mind navigating?" He broke the tension by handing her the spiral-bound road atlas he had taken from the passenger seat. "After we get out of London, the maps we need are on pages forty-two, forty-three and forty-four, but in reverse order, starting with page forty-four." Characteristic of him, he had it all worked out.

"I can do that," she said.

They both laughed, as if to say, "What me nervous?

Brian pulled the Rover away from the curb, moving the car's cranky transmission through the gears. Still, something about driving that car gave him a sense of being in charge, never mind its eccentricities and its leap through a hedgerow into a field of startled cows a few days before. Being at the wheel meant for Brian that Mary Beth did not call the shots— he did. It also gave him something to do with his hands and to occupy his mind. No need to try to avoid staring at her. He drove, and they talked haltingly about people they both had known in college.

After a time she said, "Remember how competitive we were with each other in freshman writing?"

"It seemed like you always got one point higher than I did on the essays."

"No. You were the one who always edged me out."

"That's not how I remember it. It was kind of fun, though, wasn't it?"

"It was," she admitted. "I guess I've always been pretty competitive. At one time I would have thought that my work was the only thing that really mattered in my life. But I've surprised myself by how much I like raising my boys."

"I'm afraid learning that lesson come too late for me to do much about it. My daughter's all grown up—probably more of an adult than her father is." He turned and grinned at her.

The conversation lagged. From time to time it was rescued in that singular way that driving in a car can help smooth out conversational clumsiness. By offering a field or a distant steeple to look at and comment on. "Over there are the two towns of Great and Little Milton. "He pointed across the right front quarter of the car. "Cool places."

"What's so cool about them?" Was she mocking his earnestness?

He decided not, "Well, Great Milton has a fine old church. Fourteenth century as I recall. But Little Milton is even better. It's a well-preserved stone village. It's been years since I've been to either of them."

"Maybe we could visit them later?" she asked.

"Sure. Later."

Even this brief excursion into the future had become a conversation stopper. Minutes passed.

The miles and the minutes advanced.

"How did your paper presentation go?"

"Oh it was fine. They invited me to give another one next year. Back here in London."

"That's great."

The common ground between them was pretty thin. Awkward silences grew. Neither of them seemed to want to talk about their personal future or their own short relationship many years before. Brian thought of little else during the silent minutes. He wondered what she might be thinking, but lacked the nerve to ask.

They drove into Oxford across the Magdalene Bridge, passed walls hiding college buildings and quadrangles, up the High Street by the Old Miter to Carfax. Gothic facades, crenellated shop fronts and busy streets and sidewalks lined the road.

"I'd forgotten how charming it is here," Mary Beth said. "And it's such a gorgeous day." Above, fluffy cumulus clouds skittered across blue skies and cast fleeting shadows over spires and pinnacles, climbing up and down storefronts, casting them in shadow and then opening them up again to the late October sun. There was a fresh autumn scent of burning leaves in the air.

Brian turned right onto the one-way system around Corn Market and pointed the Rover toward the Eagle and Child public house, the place he had in mind for lunch. "Are you hungry?" Traffic seemed to converge from all directions at once, each intersection jammed with cars and swarming with pedestrians.

"Yes, I really am," she said.

Brian maneuvered the car through the traffic, looking to the left and then to the right with growing desperation. "This is when having a car becomes a serious problem in this country," he said.

"Parking?"

He nodded. "I think I'll try down here," and made a sharp left turn only to find, like on every other side street, two solid lines of identical houses fronted by similar rows of parked cars on either verge. Barely enough passage was left to drive between them. No vacant spots suddenly appeared. "I'll bet C. S. Lewis didn't have this problem when he lived here." He laughed.

"Excuse me, the name is familiar. Didn't he write that movie? Something like . . . Oh, I've got it. *The Lion, the Witch and the Wardrobe?*"

"Yes, that's him: Oxford scholar turned Anglican apologist and fantasy writer. The Inklings—the group he belonged to—included Tolkein, Charles Williams and a bunch of their friends like Dorothy Sayers and Owen Barfield. Writers from the thirties. The Eagle and Child was their favorite lunch place. It's not a bad spot for a pub lunch even today. Or at least it was the last time I was here. Their Sunday lunch is supposed to be especially good. As far as pubs go, that is. The Inklings passed hours there talking about works in progress and the appalling state of world affairs."

Mary Beth seemed unimpressed. "I guess we could continue that tradition."

Brian remembered how much agitation her conservative politics had created in him back in college. He decided to avoid the whole subject. Three more passes in front of the pub and jaunts around residential corners, and Brian gave up.

"I noticed that we passed the Covered Market back on the High Street," she said. "I recall that it's filled with little stores and food shops."

"Yes, but we'll have the same parking problem there."

"What if you stop in front and drop me off. Then drive around while I run in and pick us up a picnic lunch?"

"You're sure? You don't mind?"

"Of course I don't mind. You really have forgotten a lot about me, haven't you?"

"I guess I have."

Brian remembered. The teenage Mary Beth had always been resourceful; no ordinary obstacle had ever seemed to defeat her. Sometimes her self-reliance had frustrated his need to be in control of their relationship. Or even to be an equal partner. It was one of their issues.

"That's a great idea," he said.

"Any food preferences or allergies?" she asked.

"None in either category. I promise to be happy with whatever you bring." He grinned at her and stopped at the curb in front of one of the twin entrances to the Covered Market. She got out, waved and smiled, and then disappeared inside.

Snatches of memory came. Ways she had always done little things for him, presumably to make him feel special and cared for. Lighting his cigarette—in those days when he smoked. Making sure his wine glass was always filled. Times like right now. More often than not he started out being flattered and ended up feeling helpless and patronized. As he drove once more by himself he thought about this new Mary Beth. At least she looked like a different person. Certainly not the Mary Beth he remembered. Not the one he had obsessed over for all those years. Perhaps he should call her Dr. Schumann. Or Elizabeth? She seemed like a perfectly nice woman—attractive and bright. Even though her education and interests had taken her into different places than his had taken him. She didn't know C. S. Lewis and the Inklings! But should she? What did he know about morphology after all? Whatever that was.

But he really didn't know this Mary Beth.

Brian thought about the Market as it had been the last time he had been in Oxford. He saw no evidence from the outside that any great changes had occurred. No doubt, inside she would find the same warren of walkways between small permanent shops, miniature breakfast and lunch restaurants, clothing and gift stores and food stands offering cheese, sausages and meats, fruits and vegetables, breads and bakery goods. It was a kind of mall prototype with the feel of Victoriana on it. Mary Beth was actually walking around in there, selecting things for them both to eat. How did he feel about that? He had to admit that he felt very little.

He drove back across the Magdalene Bridge to a roundabout and returned up the High Street past the twin entrances to the Covered Market. No Mary Beth. He pointed the car beyond Carfax, going down the hill, negotiated a U-turn, and came back along the same route. On this pass Mary Beth stood out front with several small brown paper bags clutched in her hands.

Mary Beth? Is this really Mary Beth? He shook his head slightly, trying to come to grips with everything that was happening. What had brought him to Oxford, to this very moment, and with this stranger? That's exactly what she was, a stranger. How did he reconcile this woman with the memory that had haunted his thoughts and his life for a quarter century?

"I thought of a place for us to eat," he said as she got in. "Remember when we crossed the bridge just before we came into the town center? Beside Magdalene College?"

"Not really."

"There's a spit of land there that divides branches of the Cherwell. Anyhow, that's the botanical gardens, roses mostly, and it has public walkways, shady areas with benches and lots of grass."

"I'd pick a bright sunny spot over a shady one." She seemed to shiver slightly.

He quickly converted the Celsius 17 degrees he had seen on a sign outside a business on the High Street into the Fahrenheit 63° that made more sense to him. Yes, a sunny spot would be better. Brian had no trouble finding a parking place outside the city center. They soon walked to the place he promised, found an unoccupied iron-framed wooden bench in full sunlight and sat on it. Mary Beth spread the contents of the bags between them. A restless breeze rustled the paper and napkins, but she efficiently weighted them down with cheese and tomato sandwiches, a small bag of crisps and cans of Woodpecker Cider. She had also found some small cakes for dessert. They said little while they ate.

"I guess I was hungry," he said, a bit self-conscious.

"I was, too."

Brian began to feel as restless and unsettled as the air, flighty but without clear direction. Inside he was reliving a distant past while he doubted what his own eyes told him in the present.

Mary Beth completed her self-assigned tasks by

gathering up the remains of the lunch and throwing it all away in a convenient bin. "Are you up for a little walk?" she asked, still standing in front of him, hands on hips. "I'd really like to wander through the city and past the colleges, off the High Street this time, just poke around. Maybe relive some old memories."

As he stood up she took the two steps that brought her close to him and took off her sunglasses. Her eyes, obscured until that moment by the dark lenses, were still the startling blue that Brian remembered—and held the intensity that had haunted him. Those same eyes now looked at him with invitation. Finally something inside him began to stir. She reached out her hand and touched his arm. Her lips parted and she tilted her head up to him. He leaned toward her. The kiss that followed felt tentative and unsure, like an act performed by strangers, lips soft—perhaps too soft—and yielding, but unfamiliar. It was neither a moment of great passion nor a long-awaited reconciliation. They kissed for a second time. No bells. No fireworks.

Only those eyes had touched something deep inside of him.

When Brian had time later in the day to think about this lunch and those first tentative approaches to intimacy it occurred to him that he had just taken the normal steps in beginning a new relationship with an attractive woman he didn't know. But Brian did not think those thoughts even as they left the rose garden. Instead, he kept telling himself that this was Mary Beth, *the* Mary Beth, *his* Mary Beth. Mostly he felt confusion.

"See that building, the one with the white facade?" she said.

"The Holywell Music Room?"

"Yes. I went to the most amazing concert there when I was here before."

They walked a little farther.

"I don't normally care that much for chamber music," she continued at length. "But in that place, with all the seats so close to the performers that you can hear them breathe . . .

well, it was riveting."

They walked on in silence.

"I came to Oxford that time with James, my ex. To attend one of the Gordon Research Conferences when I was just the young employee he was sleeping with. His divorce had become final right before we left on the trip. That night after the Holywell concert we went to a little café, and he proposed to me right there. I can't seem to remember its name or where it was. I accepted. I remember how giddy I felt."

"Is it very hard for you to be here, then?"

"Oh, I suppose I'm a little misty-eyed." She took his arm and drew herself companionably against him. "It doesn't seem to matter that I stopped loving James years ago. When we were together the last few years I spent most of my time being critical of him, finding fault and either commenting on his shortcomings . . . or just thinking about them. Still, I felt so humiliated and discarded when he walked out."

As she talked, Brian felt that old reservoir of anger leaving him. Why had it stayed with him so long? Now, he found that he rather liked her. Perhaps the basis of a new friendship between them existed. Even though they had gone in such different ways and their lives seemed to have so little in common professionally. Today's Mary Beth seemed less confident and more vulnerable than the college girl he remembered. But memories of that teenage Isolde lingered, outside and separate from the flesh and blood of this very real woman who bore her name.

Brian guided the Rover through the darkened streets of Bloomsbury and into an empty parking space on Russell Square. It was just five o'clock, and it was dark. The facade of the hotel glowed brokenly through the trees, its indirect lighting giving the place a fairytale look. He wasn't sure which dream predominated: of Camelot or of Disney. He and Mary Beth got out of the car and walked arm in arm slowly across the grass of the park, feet crunching on a carpet of dry leaves fallen from the trees overhead. It made a companionable moment. Brian was reluctant to let go of the day. They slowed their footsteps and finally stopped in the midst of the common. Their bodies were held in an embrace and their lips touched with what felt to Brian like surprising tenderness on both their parts. The air smelled of dry leaves and auto exhaust. From above they were framed and marked by spidery shadows as the illumination of streetlights fell across the bare arms of plain trees.

"I've loved today," she said.

"I have, too. Very much," Brian echoed, realizing as he said it that the words were true. The day felt to him like a respite from the loneliness of his solitary life in Cambridge, days and nights often spent with no other companion than the unsettling ones of his dreams. Despite the awkward moments, he had not felt lonely all day.

Their stop beneath the bare trees of Russell Square for that lingering kiss, one that seemed to promise that there would be more to come, evoked for Brian a tenderness for this woman akin to the wash of feelings he had felt that morning for so many of the other people in his life. Now Mary Beth, the Mary Beth of today, had joined those others and had claimed a fresh new spot in his heart. He wondered where the two of them would go from here.

"I wish I could invite you up, Brian. I really do. But I must hurry and get to that dinner meeting and finish up my obligations." She touched his lips lightly with one index finger and then kissed him with the same tenderness that the touch had promised. "It won't be the way it was in college. When we're together tomorrow." She rested her head on his shoulder.

For the first time that day, he felt the stirring of excitement. Whether those feelings meant the rekindling of an old passion or the beginnings of a fresh new relationship, he couldn't really say.

They resumed their walk to the front entrance of the hotel and kissed lightly one last time before she hurried inside to change and he to drive back to Cambridge. He had considered staying in London for the night but had decided to sleep in his own bed. That would give him some time—and distance—to think. He had thought that he might need that.

"Until tomorrow . . . For lunch, then," he called after her

as she went up the stairs.

"Yes, lunch," she flung back over her shoulder.

As Brian drove back to Cambridge he thought about the future and pushed himself to see past the present moment. He tried to imagine a scenario that included Mary Beth, but failed at it. He tried to conjure up his youthful passion for her, but that also eluded him. He liked today's Mary Beth well enough. It had been a nice day, a very nice day, and he found that he cared about her and the pain she had endured from her divorce. As he thought about tomorrow, the very real and immediate tomorrow facing him, he had to accept that he could neither imagine it nor control what it would be like. It would be what it would be. He was obliged to accept whatever came and then go on from there. A warm contentment kept him company as he settled into his flat for the evening.

The night is bright from the moon's silvery light shower. Fields shimmer and dance in the pale brilliance; small stands of trees lie deep in shadow as they flank the horsemen on either side. Once more I watch these same rough-looking mounted men. Their music comes faintly on the breeze—the squeak of leather, the jingle of bridle and spur, the pounding of hoofs on hard soil—sounds I've only recently come to hear from them. This time I also hear shouts from their horrible leader as he urges on his men. I notice that I'm once again watching them from the hill where Thirley Hall once stood. These horsemen who never go anywhere, a dozen strong like always, ride hard across the field. The cows are quick to move out of their path. This is unlike their normal lumbering movements. I pay sharp attention and feel a stab of fear. I've never seen other inhabitants of my dream world, even the bovine ones acknowledge any sense of the mounted riders. I alone seemed to have been aware of them. Now the cattle flee from their path.

I look again at the riders. Is it my imagination, or are they getting closer? I begin to suppose that I smell the horses' sweat as it mingles on the breeze with the sweet fragrance of manure and the dusty dry scent of cut hay. I look around and see that I'm no longer standing on a bare hill, but in the courtyard of a modest country house. Thirley Hall? It could be none other. From its thatched roof on down, the squat building is not handsome, more utilitarian than elegant, sprawling rather than planned. Smaller and even less impressive utilitarian outbuildings like barns, sheds and so forth, ring the house. The courtyard is filled with chickens, geese, some lambs, a couple of dogs and a pen of goats. I hear the grunts of a pig. A low wall, perhaps four feet high encloses it all. There is an open gate. The riders pour through the gate. Chickens and geese scramble to escape the horses' hoofs. One of the mounted men moves through the mud and muck to the house's undecorated front door

"Awake, the Hall!" he shouts as he bangs against the heavy wood with the butt of his musket. "Awake, I say."

Two other horsemen dismount and begin to kick against the sturdy door and to batter it with their shoulders. The leader remains mounted, apparently unmoved by everything that is going on.

One of his men shouts, "Where are the murdering whores, then?"

"I say, bring out the whore-witches," says another.

I notice that yet one more of the riders has dismounted and is trying to strike fire to what looks like a bundle of straw. A mounted horseman hurls something into a window in the bottom floor of the Hall, bringing the sound of shattering glass to cut through the other noises filling the night air. The two men continue to bang on the stout front door amidst shouted curses and threats. The man with the bundle of straw now has a good flame burning.

Suddenly my eye is drawn to movement in the near distance. A track there leads into the Thirley Hall courtyard from the south, a different route than the easterly one used by the horsemen. I see the dancing lights of many torches and the shadowed glow of the people carrying them. The bumping and rumbling sounds of carts and wagons reaches me.

I realize with horror that I'm witnessing what will likely be the destruction of Thirley Hall and probably the deaths of its three mistresses. Probably others will die as well. I want to do something. I yell out, "No! Stop!"

Is this what I'm here for? Am I meant to intervene and divert a ghastly slaughter? Only the leader of the mounted troops seems to hear my voice. The piercing stare he flashes in my direction sends a fresh shiver down my spine. But my voice has otherwise gone unheard. I am unseen. I feel desperate in my helplessness. This makes no sense. None of it makes any sense.

The dismounted rider with the torch holds his flame aloft, but it gives little illumination in the already bright moonlight. Then he does a horrible thing. Stepping up to the broken window, he shoves the burning torch into the darkened house.

I see and hear everything. I even imagine that I feel the heat inside the house as the flames begin to flicker and dart. At first they are only tiny dancers, and then angry devils pirouetting in the furnaces of hell. I want to act, to stop it, but I cannot. I wade into the horsemen's midst, but not even the leader pays any attention to me now. I reach out a hand to touch one of the horses on the flank, but my hand encounters nothing but air. The horse has all the properties of a living creature—lathered neck, excited eyes and the strong smell of heated horseflesh—but it has no material substance. At least for me it doesn't.

Now the mob has arrived. They don't seem to see me either. Two of the men step up and fling their torches on top of the roof and look back grinning toward their companions. I watch the fire spread across from one side to the other and jump onto a lower addition with a falling piece of burning thatch. One of the windows is blown out, and the flames brighten with the rush of fresh oxygen. It's eerie to be standing in the midst of it all, sensing the drama and intensity, but not being of it—not really being here at all. But I do not escape the feeling of horror at the spectacle.

The night air is suddenly cut by muffled screams and shouts coming from inside the house. A hush falls over the crowd. The men who are banging on the front door stop, apparently to listen, and then stumble backwards as the door is jerked inward. Terrified people begin to pour out. The crowd's mood has turned from carnival to slaughterhouse. First one person and then others of those fleeing the house are roughly dragged from the front of the door. I watch one older man—a servant perhaps—as he receives a single and apparently intentional blow from a horseman's sword across his collarbone. He shudders with the impact, staggers and falls. I have no doubt about his fate. What could this graybeard have done to deserve such treatment? Explosions ring out as muskets send their balls into the bodies of the terrified people who have run from the house. Others flee unmolested. Crumpled figures lie on the ground. Finally, a roar goes up from the crowd as one woman, a second and finally a third, all nightgown-clad, step from the burning house. Fear is written all over their faces. I recognize two of them as the ones I saw in the Stichen-Walling wedding, Jane and her daughter, Mary. I wonder where the women's husbands can be at this moment. Why aren't they standing there to defend their wives? And then I know without doubt the answer to those questions. The husbands are already in their graves. From what members of the crowd have shouted, those graves are probably still fresh in the Stichen-Walling churchyard. Pretty young Anne stands beside Jane and Mary. She is no older than her late teens. On her face is painted an expression of wordless horror. All around the three nightgown clad women, a pandemonium of bloodshed and shouting creates what must be the most terrible moment in their lives—and probably in the lives of all the others as well. Though the others may not realize the horror of what they're doing, at least not until tomorrow.

I also have never seen or imagined anything as awful as this or even dreamed about how a scene like this might feel.

I watch as the three women are dragged from the front of the burning house to one of the outbuildings where a long pole about six feet above the ground extends horizontally out the front. It is on that pole that newly slaughtered animals are hung to continue their transition from living creature to fire and table. Suddenly the crowd stills. For the first time, I can hear the flames of the burning house clearly as well as see them. Flames crackle and wood pops and breaks.

Another of the riders dismounts and removes a bundle from behind his saddle. He shakes loose first one then a second and finally a third length of rope. They have come with clear intent. A grim and determined look appears on his hardened face. I think I recognize him as one of the merrymakers in the wedding party. The leader of the horsemen remains mounted and passive as men drag the three women of Thirley Hall kicking, shrinking back and sobbing until they stand under the extended beam. A few isolated shouts cut through the night air.

"Bloody whores!"

"Kill the witches!"

"Give them as good as they gave."

One of the dismounted men rips the nightgown off Mary, then he moves to Jane and finally to the young girl, Anne. All three of the gowns now lie in rumpled heaps on the ground. The three women stand there naked, trying to cover themselves with their hands, and shivering from the chill in the air and the terror they must feel. A cheer goes up from the crowd. I'm too horrified by what is happening even to respond to their nakedness.

I look on helplessly as the dismounted horsemen bind the hands of each woman behind her back. The hush returns to the crowd as a length of rope is fixed around the neck of each of the three women and then the ropes are thrown over the butchering beam and the ends on to three still-mounted men. I want to look away and not watch what is about to happen, but I cannot. Young Anne begins to plead and cry. Jane is angry and defiant. Mary seems impassive. The stillness of the crowd is ominous. No one has any doubt about what to expect as the women stand there shivering, naked and humiliated. I look away and survey the burning house, the mesmerized mob, the restless horses, stomping and blowing in instinctive terror. Just as I spot the sad face of my Ghost in the crowd, a cheer arises from it. I look back toward the outbuilding with its extended pole. At one end of each length of rope horsemen sit rigid and straight in the saddle, holding the lengths of rope. Each one is wound once around the beam, taut against it. On the other ends dangle the three women; their feet swing only just clear of the ground beneath them. The three pale moonlight-bathed bodies dance and jerk, wrench and twitch. Finally, one at a time, they become still. Dark tongues protrude from their mouths. Unseeing eyeballs bulge in their sockets. Once-beautiful bodies sag and droop.

The still-mounted leader of the horsemen gives me one final, defiant glance. Why defiant? Have I become his judge? How does he, alone among all the others, see me?

I welcome the tearing feeling that signals the end of this nightmare. This terrible window into a past whose memory I now have no choice but to share. At the last moment I see the sad face of my ghostly companion peering out from the midst of that crowd.

chapter
twenty-one

Mary Beth stepped out of the elevator just as Brian arrived in the hotel lobby. She looked fully composed in a tailored white blouse, open at the neck and showing a tantalizing rise of flesh beneath. Black slacks, a tweed jacket in soft earth tones and, as on the previous day, a light raincoat thrown over her arm. It all looked carefully chosen. Her hair was a perfect tangle of short curls, her makeup immaculate. Clearly she had taken pains to look her best today. That only served to make him feel even more nervous than he already did. A quick embrace with glancing kisses on cheeks and they were out the door. He guided her in the direction of the busy shopping district along Oxford Street in search of just the right lunch place. Crossing the intersection of Tottenham Court Road brought them onto the busy boulevard where businesses and restaurants lined either side of the street. Red London double-decker busses and black taxis competed for road space while great schools of pedestrians swam across the street at every light change. They walked past an Oxfam shop, a Barclay's Bank, Fortum and Mason. Children's clothing stores competed with lingerie shops. Even a McDonald's was tucked in among other businesses. In the distance the dramatic classical facade of Selfridge's overshadowed John Lewis and the smaller department stores scattered along the street. Shop workers grabbed quick bites of take-away lunches. Snooty looking upper middle class restaurants filled with well dressed matrons and businessmen offered full course lunches at staggering prices. Brian and Mary Beth looked down the crowded side streets for a friendly pub.

"What about that one?" he said, pointing toward a quiet little place.

"Nobody else's there. The food must be terrible," she

said.

"I take your point. And how about that one? Lots of people there."

"Much too crowded. I don't want to wait all afternoon," she said, laughing out loud, apparently at herself.

"I'm beginning to feel like one of the three bears. So, where do we find one that's just right?"

She lay a hand on his chest and gave him a little push, as much as to say, Oh, go on now, and then confidently led the way into a busy little pub in a very narrow street. "This one isn't over busy," she ruled. "Just right." Inside, they ordered pints of Newcastle Brown Ale from the bar and waited in the standing-room-only crowd for one of the small tables to clear. Tobacco smoke and chatter filled the air.

Brian gradually slipped into a kind of funk.

"Don't you just love these greasy beery places?" she said.

"Yeah." He lifted one foot onto the bar's brass foot rail and made a point of looking around.

"Makes you kind of wonder how much thickness the beer-plastered dirt has added to the table tops, doesn't it?" She laughed. "A sort of veneer."

"Right."

"Oh, come on Brian, surely you can do better than that."

"Of course."

"And that's supposed to be an improvement?"

"Sorry. I guess I—I was just thinking." He hated feeling so awkward. "I don't know exactly about what. Partly about how odd it is for the two of us to be together here in a London pub after—after so long." What he meant was after all the pain and longing he had felt, but he didn't say it. "Ah, all the time that has passed. It kind of makes me introspective."

"But you still don't get to retreat inside yourself. Tell me about that project you alluded to yesterday. Something about a village mystery, I think. I didn't know historians got to solve village mysteries." This Mary Beth seemed more familiar somehow: taking charge; pulling him out of himself; using her extroverted good nature against his more introverted one.

"Actually, my particular mystery is four-hundred-years old." He decided to steer the conversation away from Stichen-Walling, partly because he wasn't ready yet to talk about last night's dream with anyone, and partly because he couldn't see himself talking to Mary Beth about any of it. He didn't know her well enough. How odd that he should feel that way about her of all people.

A table opened up and Brian placed their food orders at the bar: fish and chips for him and a Greek salad for her. The conversation suffered from Brian's reluctance to talk about the subject that, second only to Mary Beth herself, dominated his thoughts.

"I got here early on the train—left the car in Cambridge to avoid the traffic. So I spent a little time in the British Museum."

"What did you look at?"

"Sutton Hoo. This and that. Some illuminated Bibles. I'm a sucker for that kind of thing."

"Busman's holiday?"

"Sort of. What'd you do this morning?"

"I took a couple of taxis and wandered through Soho a bit. Poked around in the Leicester Square neighborhood, in and out of some antique shops and some bookstores. You know. That sort of thing. I even looked at the flashy new clothes in the shops in Covent Garden: Monsoon, Jigsaw, Accessorize. I even went in the Gap."

"Kind of like being at home?"

"Hardly. Buffalo isn't exactly Covent Garden." She smiled over her glass at him. Their knees touched under the table.

The food arrived, and they toyed with it, Brian sizing up how many individual chips the basket held. Neither of them ate much. Finally, they let the barmaid whisk away their plates. Brian bought them each a second pint.

"Probably enough carbs in these," she pointed at her newly refilled glass, "for any short-term energy a person needs." Was there something suggestive in her expression?

"I'll take that as a scientific assessment." He wondered if he looked as foolish as he felt.

Their eyes met and held for a long moment before they

recovered their composure. He felt his nose and hands go cold with nervous anticipation. The moment passed.

"I have something for you," she said.

"Really?"

She rummaged in her purse, pulled out a small package all tied up with a bow and handed it across the table to him. "I saw this in one of the bookstores this morning. It seemed to cry out, 'Take me to Brian.' So I did. Open it," she said.

He could tell that the wrapping covered a small book, and from the feel of its rounded and uneven corners, an old one. Excitement washed over him. He tugged at the ribbon-bound pastel-blue tissue paper wrapper. It came open on the table in front of him. Inside he found a Victorian edition of the English *Book of Common Prayer*, the basic 1661 version. This little cracked-leather volume had been signed and dated inside the front cover as a gift from E. T. Black, Esq. to "My Beloved Daughter, Caroline, on the occasion of her Confirmation, 14th April 1901." He held it to his face and sniffed, "Don't you just love the smell of old books? Leather, dusty paper, a lingering hint of ink and all?" Then he felt the crisp, flimsy paper of the pages between his fingers. A lump rose in his throat at this well-chosen gift from Mary Beth. Then he wondered about each person who had held the little book between the doting father and now. He felt connected to all of those people as he ran his fingers lovingly over the worn cover. "I—I don't know what to say. Thank you so much."

"You like it, then?" She smiled with what to Brian seemed an unusual shyness for the old Mary Beth, even today's Mary Beth.

"I love it." He held up the little volume and reached out his free hand and squeezed hers.

They walked out of the "Lion and Lamb," the little book stowed in his side jacket pocket, and strolled slowly along Oxford Street arm in arm. Crowds of shoppers passed around them unnoticed, making him feel like part of a small sandbar in the middle of a rapidly moving stream. His apparent calm was being worn away as if by the passage of the swift flow of humanity. Tension born of a mixed set of feelings gradually replaced the stillness.

"Shall we go back to my room?" she asked.

"Yes." Brian was reduced for a second time that day to monosyllables. Inside, his mind raced. So this is it, then? After all these years, it's just like that—"shall we go back to my room?"

As if reading his thoughts, Mary Beth squeezed his arm and smiled. She radiated confidence. Brian pulled his arm loose from hers, wrapped it around her waist and drew her against his side. He felt the trim firmness of her waist and rise of soft flesh over the bone of her hip. She pushed gently but firmly against him. Every second became elongated as if they had slipped inside an ethereal time tunnel. Storefront melted into storefront. Hawkers, annoying a moment before, blended as if into a chorus singing a Renaissance motet— passionate and earthy. It felt like those moments in movies when, for emphasis, the action goes into slow motion. But that wasn't quite how it seemed. Rather, he felt as if everything inside of him was rushing: blood dashing through veins and arteries, gastric juices pouring over meager quantities of solid food, intestines thrusting nutrients into a body that was asking for fresh energy, busy cells working at double their normal rate. All the while the world went on with its business, its constituent individuals falling into a synchronism as rhythmic as it was ordinary.

Brian found himself both anticipating and, oddly, dreading what lay just ahead. Would a new sexual experience equal the loss of the myth? Or was this to be the fulfillment of the myth? Its consummation was not in adventure and bloody struggle or heroic deeds and princesses rescued, but in completion. Was this the Grail, then: the bedding of one middle-aged mother of three? Did all of those years of longing and yearning come down to this leisurely dash along London's busiest shopping street toward what lay ahead?

They passed Tottenham Court Road for a second time that day and continued along New Oxford Street. Then, turning left, they threaded their way through small side streets towards Russell Square. The sounds of music school students practicing their instruments drifted on the air and didn't exactly create a cacophony, but blended together somehow and felt like a natural part of this place and time: faint strains of a difficult cadenza from a Mozart violin sonata; a flutist on a Baroque passage; a trumpeter practicing scales and trills as counterpoint to the bowed exercises of a double bass. They hurried along, probably looking like people who were late for an appointment. He felt smug. Why did this moment, one so long anticipated, make him feel smug? On Montague Street, the windowless stone side of the British Museum rose gray and majestic on the left. On the right a line of attached houses, long ago converted into small hotels, stood like a row of multi-colored boxes on a grocery shelf.

At Russell Square they drew together into the privacy of clustered tall shrubs. Their kiss, much the same as last night's in this same square, held more a feeling of inquiry than of a passion set aside long ago only to be hungrily picked up again. Their eyes met. He saw in her, as on the day before, an attractive stranger, today in tailored slacks and jacket. He suddenly became aware of his own near-cliché of the professor—tan slacks, blue button down-collared Oxford shirt, open at the neck, sweater vest, and a slightly rumpled blue blazer. They both carried raincoats and umbrellas against the threatening downpour.

So what is this? Would they, both calm and quiet, enjoy each other in bed like the two adults they were and then complete the day in companionable exploration of this sophisticated old city? Perhaps they would spend the night together in Cambridge as he had imagined. Would she take the lead and make the decisions as she had always done? They kissed again. She pushed her body against his. He pushed back.

They pulled apart and darted through the traffic in front of the Hotel Russell just as a cold gust of wind brought the first of what would soon become a heavy downpour from dark fast-moving low clouds. They ducked into the hotel entrance moments ahead of a skittering squall. Awareness of their timing left them laughing and high spirited to be inside and dry. They rode the lift to the fourth floor and walked down the hallway to her room. She touched him lingeringly and let her body glide against his. Her eyes and gestures made exaggerated promises. Inside the room tall windows dim from the heavy clouds outside left it lusterless but without the romantic ambiance that comes with darkness. He reached for her naturally and drew her to him. Her body yielded to his touch. His began to respond to her as he let his hand push against her rounded bottom. But before they could begin the ritual of petting and tasting and firing up libidos, the mood instantly changed.

"I have a phone message," she said. The flashing red message light seemed to shout at them. "It must be my kids. I have a nice woman watching them, but there might be a problem." She shrugged, smoothed her jacket and stepped over to the phone, turned on the bed lamp and checked the instructions on a laminated guide. Picking up the receiver, she punched in a short sequence of numbers and raised it to her ear. She listened for a moment, pushed more buttons, listened again and then disconnected.

"I have to call home," she said. "It's probably nothing, but . . ." She reached out and squeezed his hand.

"I hope everything's okay," he said.

"Let's see, what time is it in Buffalo? Eight o'clock?" She flashed him an apologetic smile. "He must've just called— Jason, my eldest. Do you mind?" She sat down on the edge of the bed.

"Of course not." Brian settled into the one chair in the narrow high-ceilinged room. The up-scale decor felt tawdry and artificial in this light and under these circumstances.

Mary Beth rummaged in her purse, "Oh, where is it?" she muttered and then finally pulled out her wallet. Another search produced a dark blue plastic card, which she held triumphantly in her hand and grinned. "Phone card," she said.

As she pushed the buttons on the phone Brian looked around the room at the flocked wallpaper and carved crown molding, wool carpet, and uneven plaster walls. It probably didn't actually look cheap and vulgar.

He felt cheap and vulgar.

Trying to shake off a petulant mood, he distracted

himself with other thoughts. He conjured up a mental image of the house on Lamb's Court in Bury St. Edmund's. Then he shifted to Julian of Norwich. Then to Carol Heppel. Anything and anywhere but right here and right now. The dead women of Thirley Hall rose up unbidden. Jeannie. He couldn't shake the gloomy foreboding that had dogged him all day. Where was all of that sexual energy that he had imagined Mary Beth would generate in him? What about the years of longing?

"Damn," Mary Beth said softly under her breath and then began to push the long sequence of buttons on the phone for a second time. "There you are," she said into the phone at last. "What's going on?"

He sat trying to remember times when he and Mary Beth had kissed and petted. There was the time in a grove of trees when they had come very close to making love. He remembered the soft pink skin of her nineteen-year-old breasts. He shifted his thoughts to this present moment, to the feel of her rounded bottom beneath his hand just a moment ago.

"I'm sure it'll be okay, Honey" Mary Beth said into the receiver. "Just get Mrs. Sanchez to write you a note. You behave, now." This time she graced Brian with her long-suffering-mother smile.

While Mary Beth greeted her other two children Brian continued to force his thoughts back and forth between this moment and their time together all those years ago. As his sense of the erotic and of the moment began to climb so did his impatience with this delay. He thought about the teenager he had once been. The one who had been so hopelessly in love with Mary Beth that he could barely think. That teenager still dwelled inside him somewhere. But so, too, also resided the toddler, the adolescent and the graduate student. His present self was a composite of all those previous selves. And more. He imagined how that was also true for Mary Beth. That girl-goddess was still there, only she, like his own teenage self, was covered over with layers of life and experience.

Finally, she hung up the phone with short I-love-yous for each of her three sons. She stood, sighed a bit and took off her jacket. Her white blouse retained its crisp ironed look even where it was drawn together at the waist and tucked carefully into her slacks. She reached out her hand for his and urged him to his feet with it. Standing there together, she first touched her hand lightly to his lips and brought her body close to his. Suddenly Brian received what he thought was a clear mental picture of what was happening here. He was standing in this hotel room with this woman, not exactly a stranger, but Mary Beth. The Mary Beth whose memory had tortured him. The same Mary Beth he had been obsessively fettered to for more than half of his life, even at the expense of his other relationships. Here she stood—an ordinary person with a bit of a controlling manner. An individual distinct from, but the same as, the memory he had held onto for all that time. A stranger he knew. Now the questions, the waiting, the wondering, and the longing were over, and he found that he lacked any strong desire toward this woman. He felt awkward and uncomfortable. He would have liked to flee had he seen any way to do so graciously.

Mary Beth seemed to read Brian's clumsy gestures as insecurity and a case of nerves, that he needed her to take the lead. So she led, being more aggressive sexually than Brian had expected from her. She kissed him in the attempt to stir up passion in them both. He wondered if she had ever been a particularly ardent lover. Her manner had always seemed to him to be cool, matter-of-fact and focused. Intentional. Still, she laid her hand on his chest and pushed her thigh against his groin. He began to feel slightly aroused. Yet his arms hung at his sides, limp and immobile. He remained disconnected and little moved. She shifted her body and gently rocked it side to side against his, rubbing his gentiles with her hip. He continued to stand there. She kissed him with apparent longing and passion, flicking her tongue against his, running it over his teeth and pushed her open mouth against his. Now his arms moved as he encircled her with them. He began to caress her backside again, remembering that it was the part of her anatomy that he had always found most sensual, especially in form-fitting slacks such as the ones she wore today. She felt at once firm and soft and rounded. Gradually he pushed his hand harder against her and pulled her against him.

But he was the dispassionate observer: analyzing and assessing, noting and cataloging, sorting and sifting. He did all of the right things and made all of his practiced moves. They were the ones that usually gave rise to passion in two people. Unbuttoning her blouse, he kissed her neck and shoulders, her cleavage. He cupped a breast in his hand. They kissed and nuzzled each other. But neither of them seemed to be getting really aroused. It felt to him as if she stood straight and tall, elegant and dignified. A statue. He seemed like a journeyman worker repeating practiced tasks in the mindless way he had done them hundreds of times before. Where had all of his former passion gone? She tugged at his blazer so he obliged her by pulling it off and throwing it over the chair. He pulled off his sweater vest. She began to fumble with the buttons on his shirt. He resumed unbuttoning hers. They were a matched pair of monuments, woodenly undressing each other without a compelling desire driving them. Their efforts would have made a poor porno flick. He didn't even find her naked body especially arousing. Somehow a figure that looked trim and elegant in clothing now looked thin and angular undressed. He averted his eyes, hoping that his imagination would be more effective in giving him energy for this encounter than his vision had been doing. Perhaps the problem came from it being daylight, a dreary gray daylight. Maybe if they had waited until night they might have felt more romantic. Or maybe there was something wrong with his eyes that kept them from seeing, really seeing, who stood before him.

Now she was lying back with invitation on the bed. She ran a hand between her breasts and down over her belly to caress the dark triangle between her legs. It was an erotic gesture. A practiced one? She motioned to him to join her, "Come, come here," she said, her voice husky.

For a moment Brian felt more aroused than at any other time this afternoon. But in the end the passion failed him, failed them both. Had the message and the phone call been the real culprits? Whatever the contributing factors, they went to bed together ultimately like robots, not as human beings who needed and desired each other. They pulled up the covers against the chill that had come into the air and went about the motions of making love in the practiced and experienced way of middle aged adults. None of that fumbling urgency of youth remained. His worry over maintaining an erection probably added to the problem and made the episode even less happy than it might otherwise have been. In the end, a cloud of failure seemed to hang over the bed. While he dutifully reached a climax, nothing at all seemed to happen for her. But he had no idea of what to do about that, and he didn't feel inclined to try.

They lay beside each other for a long time, both of them staring at the ceiling. Neither of them spoke. He had nothing to say. Neither of them slept. Finally, he got up and went into the bathroom, then came out to find her waiting for her turn. He began to pull on his clothes to the background of the flushing toilet. She returned and also started getting dressed. As he sat on the chair tying his shoes and she sat on the bed opposite him, they looked into each other's eyes. Hers seemed to reflect a combination of sadness and resignation.

At last he shook his head slightly and said, "Well, that didn't exactly move the world, did it."

"No, I guess it didn't."

Silence returned.

"I think I'll be getting back to Cambridge, then," he said.

"Yes, I guess so."

She stood and walked the three paces with him to the door. Their light kiss made for a formal goodbye, though neither of them admitted it to the other, and he didn't even acknowledge to himself just then how definitive the act really was. He couldn't get away from her fast enough.

Brian retraced his steps of the morning and picked up the Underground at Russell Square for the short ride to King's Cross. He kept going over and over in his mind what had happened since he and Mary Beth had met earlier in the hotel lobby. He didn't get it. He had felt ill at ease the whole time, and then being in bed together was a disaster. That had never happened to him before. Had there been too much anticipation? Were his expectations too high? Had he set both of them up to fail? Maybe no sexual encounter had a chance of success after so many years spent in such obsession.

Once he had climbed up out of the Underground station into the cavernous passenger hall at King's Cross he studied the big board and began to unravel the day's train schedule. Nearly two hours remained before a direct-service train to Cambridge would begin to board. A local service—one of the milk runs—was just taking on passengers and would actually get to Cambridge ten minutes ahead of the later express. Ten minutes was ten minutes after all. With a shrug he decided to take the slower train. On his way to Platform Eight to board, he grabbed a pint of Guinness and a Cornish pasty from a little station shop. He soon found a seat and sat down with his opened beer and his pasty, realizing how hungry he felt. As he sat eating and drinking and noting that the pastry, potato, onion, cabbage and beef combination tasted very good, he remembered the little book in his jacket pocket that Mary Beth had given him. He pulled it out and began looking at it as his thoughts returned to the time with her. What a humiliating experience he had just had. That was it. He felt humiliated. His spirits sagged. As he thumbed through the prayer book he happened onto the "Collects, Epistles and Gospels" section and wondered what was appointed in the book for this past Sunday. He pulled out his pocket calendar and calculated the church year. The twentieth Sunday after Trinity by that reckoning. The Epistle appointed was from Ephesians. It began, "See then that ye walk circumspectly, not as fools, but as wise, redeeming the time, because the days are evil." Hmm? He looked at the Gospel. It was from the ninth chapter of St. Matthew. A sick man had been brought to Jesus to cure, but instead of simply doing what was expected of him Jesus forgave the man his sins. Then and only then did he command the sick person to get up from his bed and walk away. Brian thought about those two readings. These present days certainly did seem like "evil days" to him, and he understood the implications of feeling oneself forgiven as the first step to health.

His thoughts shifted back to Mary Beth; the sense of having been humiliated returned. Closing the prayer book, he stuffed it back into his jacket pocket, and his mind shifted again, away from any interior examination. His eyes focused on passengers walking by the train, some getting on, others just hurrying on their way. Trains pulled in and out. Finally his historical mind clicked in to give him an even further respite from the present. He thought about how much more pleasant it must be in the station today in the age of electrically powered engines, than in the days of the old coal fired and steam driven or, for that matter, diesel powered ones. He looked out the window and up at the blackened roof of the station. It told the story of how sooty and dirty those earlier locomotives must have been. Instead, today the nearly silent electric motors ticked, brakes sometimes squealed, but no noxious fumes contaminated the air. Passengers were spared the din and throb of noisy engines.

He thought about his own life. Was it moving from its own smoky past into a much less obscure and less tortured present? Was that what was happening to him? Would Mary Beth no longer dominate his thoughts? The train finally jerked and began to pull out of the station. Shaking out of his reverie, he thought again about today, nursing his wounded ego. Something about the moving train made him feel safe and even began to give him some perspective on the day.

Mary Beth.

After all these years and all of the longing: the quest had ended. She was an ordinary woman after all, no more and no less. The Holy Grail had proved to be a human vessel after all, one unequal to the superhuman demands made of it over the years. Had spending time together and sort-of making love concluded the quest? No doubt he could have had sex with a total stranger more easily than with Mary Beth. With her the emotional expectations were too great, and the reality simply didn't match the expectation. Could it ever? Neither passion nor simple lust had arisen to energize what they both had been determined to do. Brian thought he understood his own reasons for being with her today in that hotel room. But why had she been so determined for them to have that experience? He couldn't fathom her motives. Moving beyond her divorce? Reaching back to recapture a piece of her adolescence? Wanting a genuine relationship with him? He had no idea what was in it for her. Maybe it was just an opportunity to have sex, a zip-less fuck as it were, while she was out of town. But, then, why had she contacted him in the first place?

And now what happened? They hadn't made any specific plans. He had told her about the B&B he knew in the Peak District with the implication that they would go there. But he couldn't imagine seeing her again anytime soon, let alone going off together for several days. What about the visit to Great and Little Milton? He'd have to make some excuse.

Suddenly he realized that he had not treated Mary Beth as a person, but as an object: an object of adoration to be sure, but still an object. Had he really cared about her feelings or her hopes for her life? This was no cardboard Madonna tacked to the wall for him to idolize. Perhaps this was why he had been so little taken with today's Mary Beth. This grown-up woman was not the substance of his obsession. His adolescent fantasy. That had been an illusion only existing in his mind. Instead, she was a real person. He wasn't interested in a real person. He only wanted the unblemished chimera out of his past, and that was not available to him. Now, what did he do about her tomorrow and the next day?

As usual Mary Beth had taken matters into her own hands. Back at his flat he found a message waiting from her on his voicemail. "Brian," her voice said out of the tinny little speaker. "I've been in touch with my kids again, and I've changed my flight plans." Her voice carried no emotion, but the clarity of her feeling still cut through the ordinariness of the message. She also had no illusions about their afternoon together. "I leave first thing tomorrow." A pause. "I'll be in touch when I get home. It's been great seeing you again." A nearly silent click punctuated the simple but definitive message as she broke the connection.

He sat down on the desk chair beside the answering

machine and replayed the message. The room was cold and dark. Gradually a half-smile broke out on his face. "Thank God," he said aloud to himself, feeling relief line up right beside the continuing emptiness. He stood up, pulled off his raincoat and bent over to turn on the electric fire. Then he went around the room and switched on all the lights.

As the bright room also became warmer and his spirits rose his thoughts shifted to Jeannie Mautner. "Sure, what about Jeannie?" he said aloud and reached for the phone. He tried all three of her phone numbers, but without success. Surely she would still be there for him. Oh, he would have to pass through a period of trial. He would have to deal with her anger. Maybe she would even feel hurt. But she'd soon get over it. She'll understand. This is Jeannie, after all.

Thinking about her, it occurred to him that maybe he was being optimistic. Could he really expect her to forgive and forget? But he had had to do this. Surely she'll be able to see that. He remembered that her planned visit was less than a month away. He began to fantasize all the things they would do together, the walks they would take, how her anger over Mary Beth would quickly evaporate and everything would return to the way it had been when she was here. He thought about her naked body against his; now that was a thought that got him going. Surely she will understand how important it was for him to get Mary Beth out of his system. And hadn't it worked? That very long shadow out of his past could now fade away into memory along with his Radio Flyer and his Hardy Boys collection. It would be a bright new time in his life. But why couldn't he reach Jeannie? He could hardly wait to tell her his news. He turned on his computer, and waited for the screen saver photo of Jeannie and Candy to come up. Just as the picture flashed on to fill his eyes with their bright smiles his mind's eye replaced it with the image of three dead women.

chapter
twenty-two

Brian tried with little enthusiasm to resume his work at the university library. On Thursday he came across an example of a purchaser of some former monastic properties in Sussex, one Anstel Sanderson. That was during the early 1540s. Typical of the period, Sanderson converted many of his financial holdings into landed respectability, thus taking a step up the social ladder. His grandson, also named Anstel, ascended to the next rung by purchasing the title of Baronet from James I, an honor created by the king to bring in revenue from the growing gentry class. That was in 1610. The title carried with it a hereditary knighthood; hence the purchaser became Sir Anstel and increased his family's respectability one more notch. It was a typical story in the redistribution of land at the Dissolution. It looked like a good example for Brian's book.

A few minutes later during a lull in the lunch conversation with Jeff at a little Thai restaurant, thoughts of the Sanderson family popped back into his head. What was it about that family name that nagged at him? Suddenly he thought he knew. With a fork-full of Pad Thai halfway to his mouth, he stopped his hand in mid-air and then dropped the fork back onto his plate with a clatter. He grabbed for the little spiral notebook he always carried in his jacket pocket and began to leaf through it.

"What's up, man?" Jeff asked.

"I ran into an amazing coincidence in my work this morning, and I just got it."

"Really?"

"Do you remember when we went to Bury St. Edmunds last week and I found out who had that estate after the deaths of the three women—before the Arnold family got it, that is?"

"Yes, of course I remember."

"Well, anyhow, I hadn't thought much about it." He looked down at his notes. "Yes, here it is." He looked up at Jeff again, "Here's the reference." He brandished the little book then flipped the pages closed and put it back in his pocket. "I ran into the same name today. I didn't recognize it at first."

"That's pretty fluky."

"In a way it brings the strands of my work together—the Dissolution and the Stichen-Walling business."

"I don't see what you mean."

"It's like this. I now know that the man who acquired Thirley Hall after Jane's death—according to the Arnold family papers—was the fifth or sixth generation of one of those rising gentry families that the period is famous for. They acquired monastic properties, and this particular Sir Anstel was also apparently ready to grab up the Thirley Hall estate." That memory, plus telling Jeff about it, was like a new revelation, a fresh avenue opening up to explore the continuing Stichen-Walling mystery and to place it within the scope of his official work. "I had also forgotten that the Sanderson family papers are in a collection in the British Library in London."

"So, you'll be off to London, then?"

"Yes, I imagine so." Brian felt his heart thumping in his chest.

That afternoon Brian found out a few more details about the second Baronet and the Thirley Green properties. When Jane died her land came into the hands of the crown for some reason that was never stated. Sir Anstel received it as a gift from King Charles I, apparently in gratitude for some service or other. Or money paid. Brian knew that Mr. Arnold's family acquired the land a few years later. But he found no explanations for any of these land transfers. There was nothing else for it: he would have to go into London and spend some time in the British Library—if, that is, he wanted to learn any more about Sir Anstel Sanderson and his dealings. He very much wanted to do that.

Brian attended daily Mass each morning at St. Bene't's and Evensong at the end of the day at King's. It felt like the natural thing for him to be doing. He had no dreams, no apparitions and no horrible spectacles to observe for an entire week, not even over the three days of All Hallows', All Saints' and All Souls' when he might have expected to be troubled by spooks and specters. Instead, October passed into November without disturbance from beyond the grave. He had begun to hope, even believe, that the dreams and visions had been about Mary Beth and his lingering obsession with her, and with finding out what happened to Thirley Hall and its three women residents. Now that Mary Beth had been exorcised from his psyche, in a manner of speaking, and he knew what had happened to the three women—and he believed that he did know, even if he didn't know fully why—he might reasonably expect the dreams to end. They seemed to have done just that.

He also kept trying to reach Jeannie by phone. She never answered his calls. It became clear after awhile that Caller ID was betraying him to her. She certainly was avoiding him. He left several messages, asking her to call him back, but she had ducked every one of them. In frustration he finally resorted to email. "Are you avoiding me? I guess you are. I wish you'd return my calls. Mary Beth has come and gone, and we found that we didn't have anything very much in common any more. College was a long time ago. So she left early on Tuesday without warning—except for a message on my voicemail. I can't tell you what a relief it is to have that reunion behind me. But enough about me. What's happened with you? Have you resolved the problems with Francis What's-his-Name?"

This wasn't being entirely honest with her, but that would keep. It wasn't as if he were hiding anything really important. Maybe she never needed to know about his pathetic efforts in bed with Mary Beth. He wouldn't lie to her. But then, maybe it would never come up. Why should it?

Jeannie's light-hearted and newsy reply made his day. He laughed out loud at her telling of how she dealt with Francis Cardham, the department head. Her sister Jannie had been the great heroine of a little drama. The sisters had gone to a departmental party dressed similarly in jeans and sweaters. "After a few drinks," she wrote, "Francis came on to Jannie pretty strong, thinking she was me. He even made vague references to my career. What a slime bag! Jannie played along without promising him anything. Just about then I wandered into the living room from the kitchen, and she caught my eye. I'll never forget the conversation that followed, or at least the gist of it. 'This nice man has been saying some really sweet things,' She said. Francis looked really startled. I loved it. He said something like, 'Well . . . I . . . you know . . . There are two of you! My God!' Jannie just giggled and cuddled up against his chest as if he were a long-time lover. She even gave him a little kiss on the cheek, 'He's asked me to go home with him.' Then she raised her voice, pretending to be a little drunk 'and he told me that your name is going before the tenure and promotion committee next week. He says you're a shoo-in for going on a tenure track . . . especially with his support. Isn't that right, Francis, dear?'

"Everybody in the room overheard this last part and gathered around to congratulate me. Of course, I had to be clear about which one of us really was me. I introduced Jannie to one and all and thanked Francis profusely for his support. He looked like someone had kicked him in the stomach. The first chance he got he made his escape. On Monday I had a note from him in my departmental mailbox telling me what he needed for the committee—vita, writing sample and referees, that sort of thing. It's all in. So I guess I'm launched at last. Good old Jannie. She really played him."

Despite the amusing tale the email held a hidden trap. "So the old girlfriend is gone?" she wrote. "And you didn't sleep with her, then?"

She would have to ask that question. What did he do now? It was one thing for him simply to let the whole thing slip away without ever bringing it up. But now it wasn't that simple. Pretending it hadn't happened was no longer an option. Instead, with a sinking feeling in the pit of his stomach, he packed up his laptop and headed for the library.

He would put the whole thing off. Maybe something would happen yet.

The blustery day had settled into a steady rain. A dark heavy overcast met Brian as he walked along the river looking for the black swan. He soon found him lazily floating beneath a tree branch, presumably receiving some protection from the rain. Did water foul need to find shelter when it rained? He looked around, wondering where the ducks and the white swans might be. Presumably they also had sought some kind of cover. He stood looking at the bird as it maintained its lonely vigil on that particular spot in the river.

Standing there with rain falling on his umbrella as he gazed absently at the swan, his thoughts turned to his dilemma with Jeannie. Much as he would have liked to avoid the showdown he decided that he had best try to level with her without delay. He searched for a simile that might help him put it all together and place the experience in perspective. Being with Mary Beth had been like picking up dirty laundry off the floor and putting it in the clothes hamper; like having his car serviced so that its rusty fittings wouldn't seize up; or like completing an especially troubling stack of freshman exam papers and finally turning in the grades so he could wash his hands of a semester. None of them was quite right, though each captured a piece of how he felt about the two days with Mary Beth. It was something he had had to do. But how did he say to Jeannie, "Oh, we slept together but it was kind of like grading papers, greasing the car, or picking up dirty laundry?" She would either think he was coming unglued or was so callous that not even the act of making love could move him to feel anything for his partner. That would make him seem like the worst kind of user, maybe even a classic predatory male. Perhaps all that he needed to do was to tell Jeannie the unvarnished truth: that a remnant of the teenage Mary Beth would probably always linger inside him, but he no longer felt any overriding emotional attachment to her memory.

Brian looked up from where he had been studying his feet, and the black swan was gone. The river had become vacant and lonely once more. He shrugged. Was the bird's disappearance a sign? Of what? He could think of no excuses for putting off the inevitable. He must come clean with Jeannie and without delay. He turned back the way he had come and walked with resolution to Lo-Host.

Inside again, he pulled off his raincoat and opened up his umbrella to dry. Shivering slightly from the cold, he lit the electric fire in the sitting room and sat down in front of his laptop. After congratulating her on her news and passing on some praise from Bobbie about her class, he moved on to his difficult confession. "Mary Beth and I had a pleasant day together on Sunday. It was good to have some company. But we sort of came to an unspoken agreement to finish what we had left incomplete all those years ago. Without any particular passion or ever actually saying we were going to do it, we understood that we were going to sleep together. Or at least that's how it seems now as I look back on it. We behaved like a pair of robots going through the motions. Then we couldn't wait to be away from each other. It's an understatement to say that we don't have a romantic future. Please do forgive me for this admittedly serious lapse. I won't use the unfaithful lover's lines and say, 'Oh, it wasn't important.' Or, 'It didn't mean anything.' Because neither would be true. It *was* important, and it *did* mean a great deal to me—but only in the sense of something that I had to get past, kind of like old business lying around unresolved. I feel as if my soul has been purged, and now all those years are over and finished. I don't expect you to understand, but this was something I had to do. There will be no repeat of it. Ever. You have my word. I know our relationship is very new, but I think you are the person I've been looking for all my life. I only hope you can find it in yourself to forgive me and give me a chance to show you how sorry I am and how completely over it is—all of it."

He sat staring at the note and thinking about how he had fretted over sending an early email to Mary Beth. As on that occasion he had tried to get up the nerve to click on the send button. He reread the note, changing a word here and a comma there. Finally, the moment of reckoning came. He could think of nothing else that might improve or soften the impact of what he had written; no different word choice that would avoid the simple truth that he had had sex with another woman. He knew that with her recent divorce from an unfaithful husband, this email was going to be hard for her to read. But there was nothing else for it. He couldn't lie to her. He had to tell her the truth. He sent the email.

He waited for a reply. No response came. It was likely that she was not on line at the moment; there wouldn't be any real-time writing. Or maybe she was so furious or hurt that she refused to respond. He would have to wait to find out the truth of it.

At that moment the last rays of the late afternoon sun broke through the otherwise heavy overcast and momentarily bathed his sitting room in pale watery sunlight. But the bleached sun gave off enough illumination in the otherwise shadowy room to highlight Bobbie's drawing of the Stichen-Walling church and yard. As if he had been pulled by a powerful magnet Brian stood in front of the picture. It seemed to beckon him to enter its world, the mysterious world of Stichen-Walling. He began to sway forward on his ankles and then back again, feeling mesmerized and fearing that he might at any moment lose his balance and be sucked into the image as if in a psychic maelstrom. The sun disappeared again without warning, and the room returned to its former gloom. Brian shook his head and stepped away from the drawing, glancing at it from across the room. The picture seemed to have lost, for the moment at least, its former power to draw him in.

He noticed beads of perspiration on his forehead and wiped them off. "That does it." He stepped over to the desk, picked up the telephone receiver, pushed speed dial number 8 and heard the double burrs in his ear as the phone began to ring. He knew from previous experience that he needed to let it go for a long time before giving up.

"Franciscan Priory," a voice finally said on the other end of the line.

"Father Jeremiah, please."

"Brother is already at St. Bene't's making preparations

for Evening Prayer."

"Thank you." He replaced the receiver in its cradle. Evening Prayer. He looked at his watch. Lots of time to get there. Today he would substitute the said service at St. Bene't's for the sung majesty of the Office at King's. Maybe Fr. Jeremiah would have time afterwards to talk with him. He shrugged back into his raincoat and hunched under his umbrella in the falling darkness of the early November evening.

Brian sat quietly after Evening Prayer had ended. A total of seven people had turned up for the service, about par for a Monday evening, even during term. At length the Franciscan came out of the vestry wearing his simple brown robe and sandals over heavy brown socks, what Brian had come to think of as his uniform.

"Good to see you, Brian. Everything go okay in London, did it?"

He quickly told Jeremiah about his time with Mary Beth.

"So the old flame has burned itself out?"

"Yes, you could put it that way," Brian said. "But let me tell you about my dreams."

"Your mystical visions?"

Brian just nodded and then told him about the horrible scene at Thirley Hall. "And I have no doubt that I saw more or less what happened."

"'More or less?' You have some doubts?"

He thought for a moment. "No, not really. It's just hard to accept that I can really see the details of the past in this way. Even after everything else that's happened." He stopped speaking and sat thoughtfully for a moment, remembering those earlier encounters with Erasmus and Julian of Norwich, poet George Herbert and the others. He realized that they had drawn him into the Stichen-Walling and Thirley Hall visions like lures before a lazy trout in a quiet pool. They had truly set him up. "Everything seems to lead to that climactic vision of violence and bloodshed," he said. "I know that my imagination could very well have conjured up all of these details out of what I've learned in traditional research. But that's not what I think has happened. I believe that what I've seen is true. All of it."

The Franciscan sat quietly for a moment. "But there's more, isn't there? That's why you're here tonight?"

Brian nodded his head and told Jeremiah about what had happened with Bobbie's picture. "I thought I could let it all go. After Mary Beth and all. Knowing about the women at Thirley Hall. But no such luck."

"It's not enough for you simply to gather information, then, is it? You know the facts. Just like the good historian you are. But you remain hungry for more. The mystical impulse keeps crying out to you to go deeper and farther. Perhaps, as we said before, you need to take some action and *do* something." Suddenly Jeremiah looked up from studying his hands and fixed his eyes on Brian's. "Are you going back to the village, then? To Stichen-Walling?"

"Why ever would I want to do that?"

"Isn't that the meaning of today's experience with the picture? That you should go there again?"

This time it was Brian's turn to study his hands. He rubbed them, pored over his knuckles, glanced at his wristwatch and then looked around the little church, sniffing the musty air. Finally, he said, "I suppose I do need to go back there. It's as if something is calling to me.

"Something?"

"Those dead women, then. But what do I do when I get there?"

"I think you'll know."

Brian tried to cope with a mounting restlessness. He felt distracted and ill-at-ease. Looking for something to do, he called up his email again. Still nothing from Jeannie. Should he phone her? Maybe being more direct would be better after all. He reached for the phone. But his hand never touched it. No, he just couldn't do that right now. He tried to shake off the anxiety he felt in the pit of his stomach. Instead, he went into the kitchen and cooked up a mess of eggs, sausages, toast and canned beans, which he managed mostly to eat without any real enthusiasm. He washed up his dishes, leaving them on the sideboard to drain.

What was he of all people supposed to do about those long-dead women?

On an impulse he reached for the phone and dialed the number for Jeff and Charlie. Jeff answered. "I'm planning to drive out to Stichen-Walling tomorrow," Brian said. "Would you be up for gong with me? I really would like your company. You might even find it interesting. I have the car until five o'clock tomorrow."

"Of course I'll go. In fact, I'd like to see the place."

"Good. I'll pick you up at ten."

"I'll be ready."

He hung up the phone and picked up the novel he had been trying to read, one set in the trenches and on the British home front during World War I. But instead of following the plot, he found himself fantasizing about conditions in the trenches and making up his own scenarios about people living through such brutalizing horror, coming time and again to mental images of the dead and maimed. Finally, he gave up trying to read and began to pace from one end of the flat to the other, thinking about its previous occupants, wondering what they had been like, and trying to call up memories these walls must harbor. Did any of the former residents have bizarre dreams or conflicted love lives? Certainly the latter. He walked up the short flight of stairs to the bedroom in the back and through that room to the window where he stared out at the Lo-Host garden through the dark rainy night. A single streetlight shone. Shaking off his nearly spellbound gaze, he stalked back out and down the stairs again and into the sitting room. He repeated it all once more, finally stopping at the telephone. Looking at his watch, he saw that it was past nine. That would be three in Chicago, not the most likely time to catch Jeannie at home on a Friday afternoon. Still, he picked up the receiver and punched in the speed dial number of her home phone. After what seemed like about a hundred rings the recorded message picked up. He hesitated for a moment, and then hung up without saying anything into the machine. He didn't know what he would have said to Jeannie herself, much less to her voicemail.

His restlessness, filled with flights of imagination, continued: dead women, ghosts, poets and philosophers, politicians and soldiers. Fiction, life and dream world mixed seamlessly together. Maybe a walk down to the Eagle and a pint of Greene King would settle him. He pulled on his heavy coat and wool cap and grasped his umbrella. Outside, broken clouds in turn obscured and exposed the moon, now in its second quarter. The wind felt very cold. Brian pulled up the sheepskin collar of his coat around his face and increased his pace. When he reached Silver Street, he had the feeling that someone else had joined him. He shivered in spite of himself, not entirely because of the cold, and looked around. As far as he could tell, he was the only one walking along that stretch of Silver Street at exactly that moment. Still, the feeling persisted.

Walking that ancient street—brick walls climbing up three and four stories on either side, Gothic spires and towers jabbing into the sky—his imagination began to explore what had recently become its expanded range. Suddenly he felt himself stepping into the black-and-white celluloid of a World War II movie. Was it a kind of extension of his earlier fantasies about the trenches of the Great War? It amused him to act as if he were walking the abandoned movie streets of wartime France, spies skulking around corners and the distant undulating wail of a mid-twentieth century siren slicing the air. He half expected to see George Raft leaning against a wall smoking a cigarette or Humphrey Bogart passing in and out of the light from a solitary street lamp. At any moment the Gestapo might appear under floppy-brimmed hats from around the next corner looking sinister and malevolent. What an imagination. Still, why not? Was that any weirder that what he had already seen and felt? At least he had control of this fantasy. At one point he even briefly ducked into a doorway as if perpetrating some skullduggery.

Finally he turned into the front door of the Eagle. The smoky air inside the pub carried the aroma of burning wood as well as the reek of stale tobacco smoke and the sweet smell of newly lighted cigarettes. He folded his cap, stuffed it into his pocket and stepped up to the bar to order a pint of the local beer. Finding himself a place near the fire, he pulled off his coat, returning the familiar smile of the young man picking up empties from deserted tables, and sat down. Being there gave him the sense of wellbeing that had eluded him in his flat. As a rule, he was content enough being alone, but sometimes a person needed the company of other people and the sound of voices laughing or raised in earnest conversation. He didn't really want to talk to anyone, but he liked having talk going on around him and picking up little pieces of the conversations: something about a former lover; a piece of an old joke that he recognized; someone imploring her partner about something—more grist for his flights of fancy. He recognized one or two of the other patrons and exchanged grins and "how-are-yous" with them. Fully warmed now by the fire, he finished the pint, went to the men's room, then picked up a refill at the bar and went back to his place beside the fire and sipped at his glass. It felt cozy and friendly there. He was content. Finally, he heard the bartender announce last call. Two pints had been enough, he thought, and, instead of getting a last refill, drained his glass and sat staring into the dwindling fire.

His thoughts turned to the Ghost, wondering if he would be there at Stichen-Walling tomorrow. Whatever his being there might mean. Stretching and masking a yawn, he decided to go back to his flat and explore the Bible he had picked up that afternoon. When had he ever spent time with a Bible? Never, that was when. He was actually looking forward to reading it. Perhaps something in it would clarify his mind about what was going on. He wasn't entirely sure why he thought that, but he did. Especially he hoped to discover some understanding of his ghostly companion's purpose. Maybe he would even get some sleep. He got up to leave and go back out into the dark cold November night, grabbing his umbrella, pulling on his cap and buttoning up his coat as he went.

Outside, the rain continued to fall. He shook out the umbrella and stood under it for a moment as the steady drizzle began to drip from its edges. Across the street the darkened churchyard of St. Bene't's beckoned to him as it had done on that other night back in August. No, he was not going to tempt a repeat of that. Instead he turned right in the direction of King's Parade, only to feel himself slipping into what had now become the familiar unreality of his mystical world. All of the familiar characteristics were there. Laughing voices from the Eagle were stilled and vehicle sounds ceased as an ethereal silence settled on the dark night. Only the rain continued.

I find it's not so easy just to walk away from St. Bene't's tonight. My wishes no longer seem relevant against the place's magnetic pull. I walk slowly across the street. No need to look for bicycle traffic, because none exists. Pushing against the black wrought-iron gate, I notice that the fence's fleur-de-lis tips pointing upward are like sentries on guard duty. For some reason they make me feel safe. The hinges sigh with the gate's smooth inward swing. I step down into the yard feeling comforted in the act, descending as if into a past where visions are understood to be the normal way of things and the bustle and shallow rationalism of the twenty-first century are banished. I walk over to the tall headstone, the one that had rolled and bucked before to my touch. I am feeling uneasy about it. Still, I reach out my hand and caress the cold wet stone. Nothing happens. I experience such an all-embracing feeling of relief that I begin to sit down on the wet bench beside the walkway, remembering at the last second how drenched with rainwater it must be.

Straightening up once more, I walk slowly along the pathway beside the squat Saxon tower and follow it along the Victorian south-aisle addition, surprised to find the gate there is open. Beyond the side fence I see the figure of a man standing quietly. His back is to me. I'm somewhat startled by his presence, though why anything might unnerve me when I'm in this misty state I can't begin to say. There's something familiar about him. Perhaps he's one of the men who regularly attends services at St. Bene't's, or perhaps he's one of the Franciscans who lives in this community and whom I have seen from time to time. His clothing could be

one of the Franciscan habits. It could just as easily be a
bulky raincoat. I feel sorry for the man, because no doubt
the bareheaded figure is becoming quite drenched in the
rain. Then he begins slowly to turn. Has he heard my step?

As the solitary figure comes around to face me, the
brilliance of a thousand light bulbs suddenly illuminates the
churchyard and the man's face—the face of my ghostly
companion. Why should I be surprised that he's the other
person with whom I share the churchyard just now? But I
am taken unawares. The familiar square-jawed face wears
a smile so wide that it seems perfectly normal when, as the
grin gradually fades, that the light should also be
extinguished. The churchyard slips back into darkness
again. My Ghost also disappears.

I stand frozen to the spot for what feels like a long time,
puzzled by the oddity of the moment, even in light of my
previous experiences. Gradually, feelings of confidence and
affirmation steal over me. I feel as if I have been given some
kind of approval. What is that supposed to mean? What, if
anything, have I done to merit such approbation?

Now come the nausea and the tearing feeling, and I
know that this vision in the St. Bene't's churchyard is over.

Brian shook his head both to clear it and in wonder and
turned and walked back the way he had come, reaching out
and patting the tall grave marker of the deceased church
warden as he passed it by. At the gate, he stepped up onto the
sidewalk and pulled it shut behind him. Just then a young
couple came out of the Eagle and walked, laughing, in the
opposite direction from King's Parade. Something in the
lightness of their mood reinforced Brian's new feeling of
hopefulness. He turned and walked briskly back toward his
flat, all his former feelings of restlessness and uncertainty
gone. He knew that he would sleep long and well that night
and that something, some resolution, would come to him in
Stichen-Walling tomorrow.

The next morning Brian awoke to find a new email from
Jeannie. He tried to ignore the hollow feeling in his stomach

as he clicked on the message and began to read, "I should have known better. Why would I have expected you to be more faithful to me than my husband was? Or more faithful than you've been to your wives?"

He winced at the truth of her accusation, though his unfaithfulness had never been more egregious than that of his spouses.

He continued, "Now you tell me that because the sex was bad, you and the old girlfriend have no future. What a relief that is! And I'm supposed to be grateful? Should I be comforted to know that I didn't wait on the sidelines for nothing? At least I know that as long as I'm good in bed, you'll stick around—unless, of course, something better turns up. This is the same-old, same-old. Why don't you grow up, Brian? Who needs it? Certainly not me." There was no signature.

Jeannie's interpretation of Mary Beth's short reappearance in his life felt harsh, but he had to admit as he sat with it that from her perspective it was probably fair. He had at least suggested that because the sex hadn't been good they had ended the affair right there. That meant, at least by implication, that if the sex had been great—or maybe even just okay—he would have developed a continuing relationship with her. Where, from Jeannie's perspective, did that leave her? It had to feel to her just like the unfaithful husband all over again. What else could he expect her to think? And how could he promise her that if during a time when their sex had been brand new and terrific he had slept with another woman that more of the same wouldn't happen in the future. But he felt different, and he couldn't exactly explain how or why.

He attempted to write a response, but couldn't find the words. Finally he just wrote, "I am so deeply sorry," and signed it simply "Brian." Maybe something more would come to him during the day, maybe even by the time she woke up.

chapter
twenty-three

So this is your famous Stichen-Walling?" Jeff sounded unimpressed. "Seems to me you've used up a lot of energy on rather a neglected-looking little place."

"It isn't much, I know. But see?" Brian pointed, "That's the old tithe barn. Early fourteenth century. That pub is Tudor, and so are some of the other buildings. There's the town hall." Brian realized that he was defending the village and sounding like he had a sense of proprietorship.

"Late Victorian institutional," Jeff snorted.

"Indeed. Over there, the spire in the distance? That's the Victorian church. The medieval one is just beyond." Unaccountably feeling a mounting excitement, he pulled the Rover up in front of the parish church. "Come on," he said, opening the car door, stepping out and pushing his unfurled umbrella before him to ward off the rain,

They followed the now-sodden path around the building, accompanied by music coming from inside the church. "The organist must be practicing for tomorrow's services," Brian said over his shoulder to the trailing Jeff.

Viewed from the path the rickety lychgate framed the old church and its yard with a look of total decrepitude—pitiful, neglected and forlorn. It had the same broken wall and askew headstones half masked by tall, bent and rain-soaked brown grass. The collapsing roof looked especially pitiful today. The whole place screamed abandonment. If anything it looked even worse on this gray wet musty day than ever before. Brian suddenly felt very sad for it.

"This is pretty grim," Jeff said.

Brian agreed but ignored the comment. They stepped through the lychgate. Its shaky condition seemed to make a fitting entry into the dismal site. "See the break in the wall? That's where those other graves are."

Jeff stopped and appeared to survey the scene before

him with an appraising eye. Finally he said, "It's as if those graves over there—the ones beyond the Pale, so to speak—were meant forever to sit yearning to be included. I wonder if someone thought this was some kind of twisted punishment. An eternal hell, so to speak. They would be doomed for all time to look longingly from the outside to the spot where the so-called decent people lay in some sort of bliss that's forever denied them. I don't even believe that crap, and yet the viciousness of it gives me the willies." He cleared his throat and seemed to shudder. Then he said, "Can we see inside the church?"

Brian walked over to the wooden door in the side porch only to find it locked. "Sorry. But this may be a good sign. Somebody cares enough about the place at least to lock the door."

"That's about as far as it goes, I'd say. Some serene spot."

"Come on. Let me show you those other graves up close." Brian tried to shrink beneath his umbrella for protection against both the rain and the feelings he had being there. He led the way to the wall's opening. Nothing had been disturbed.

Jeff studied each of the headstones. "I see where you removed the lichen. How long will it take to grow back?

"I don't know. It never occurred to me to ask. But they will look better when it does. Makes me feel a little guilty for disturbing them."

"Do you imagine that the place feels so abandoned because of some kind of ghostly revenge by these ones? The exiles?" Jeff flashed a toothy grin.

"What a curious notion," Brian snapped back. Then he thought about Jeff's flip comment. "I wonder . . .?"

Jeff gave him a hard look, then, becoming more serious, went on, "But, what a long banishment these poor people have endured, your three and the others." He paused while a questioning and thoughtful look passed across his face. "Does the church still have the same rules about burial in consecrated ground that it used to have?"

"You mean, does it deny church burial to some people? No, I don't think so, not really. Suicides were once prohibited from being buried in consecrated soil, I know, but they aren't any more—at least not in Chicago they aren't."

"Do you think these women committed suicide, then?"

"Not at all. I've told you what I think. Their burials outside the wall seem to me, as you say, more like the eternal kind of punishment for misdeeds, real or imagined." Brian thought about it for a moment, "Or maybe their murderers buried them here to justify their own actions and assuage their personal guilt. So far as I know the three women of Thirley Hall never had anything proved against them by their accusers. For witchcraft, I presume."

"Ah, I get it. Witches were not buried in consecrated ground." Jeff snorted. "Why didn't they just toss the bodies on the burning house?"

"I have no idea. I wish I knew."

"And why is the wall broken in just that spot do you think? You know, beside those graves."

"It never occurred to me to ask the question. I guessed it was the work of neglect, you know, weather and time."

Jeff's long face broke into another of his cynical smiles. "Maybe the ghosts of all these women, your three and the others—witches, maybe—just rose up and broke it down. The fury of women scorned. Big time!" He laughed.

"There you go again with your theories." Brian stood thinking for a moment before he said, "But maybe you have something there." It was Brian's turn to grin.

"I'm just joking."

"But still . . ." Brian turned serious again.

"If you think that's what happened and that it makes the place so malevolent feeling, then it's easy enough to solve. Why not rebuild the wall with the graves inside?" Jeff wandered away looking at headstones.

Brian stood staring vacantly across the open field beyond the graves, thinking about Jeff's sardonic suggestion. Perhaps the injustice represented by those graves had in some way led to the breach in the wall. Why not? Was that any harder to believe than his having visions? Besides, the three Thirley Hall women had apparently been killed for witchcraft—with or without trials. Could they have been guilty of practicing the dark arts? His rational mind reasserted itself. Impossible. There were no such things as witches: potions, spells, the evil eye, "bubble, bubble, toil and trouble." Harry Potter aside, it was laughable.

But what made him so sure? It was certainly easier for him to accept the women's guilt as murderers than to admit that they had actually been witches. The prototypical witch hunts had, after all, merely been grist for the mill of post-Reformation hysteria, religious bigotry and societal insecurity. He'd read all about it. Many people, mostly women, had been executed in the obsession with witchcraft, primarily because they were different, or maybe just old. There were the other excluded graves as examples—all apparently women. The Thirley Hall deaths fit the timing of the witch craze. Still, witchcraft? He thought about that for a moment only to ask once again why he might see visions, and yet other people couldn't be witches and practice some kind of magic, evil or otherwise. The rational explanations he had long held about the world no longer seemed sufficient. Although he had to stretch to find an explanation, he knew that the two weren't the same.

Maybe the whole problem with Stichen-Walling was about justice—the sacred power of creation straining to overturn human verdicts, in this case, on the lives of these women: rightly or wrongly condemned, but murdered nonetheless. Didn't the central truth of creation hold that life comes out of death and that nothing—either physical or spiritual—is ever lost? Perhaps in the same way no injustice ever goes away until the wrong is overturned. Enclosing the graves in the churchyard certainly beat having him skulking about in the dark of night to exhume those bones and rebury them. Why did he even think such a thought?

Brian could not imagine how these burial places mattered at all. Especially when considered in the larger scheme of things. But what would it hurt if he tried to follow Jeff's half-joking suggestion? Maybe he could help set right at least this one old wrong: the banishment of these graves. Maybe in that small way he might help to reclaim this tiny corner of the universe. Who could possibly object? One look at the place shouted out that nobody cared about it at all. But he cared. For some reason that he didn't begin to understand and couldn't explain, what happened in this forgotten spot mattered very much to him. Jeff was absolutely right.

"I think you've hit on it, Jeff," he called to his startled companion. "I need to rebuild the wall. I wonder how I might get permission to do that."

Jeff looked at Brian as if he were humoring a hopelessly idiotic child. "Permission? I imagine you just ask the vicar. What are you thinking?"

"Just what you said."

Jeff snorted derisively.

"I wonder where I'd find the vicar," Brian asked, as much to himself as to Jeff.

"I expect the organist would know."

"You're right. Let's go ask."

Jeff lagged behind again as Brian, energized by the prospect of taking some action, walked quickly back the way they had just come. Once he came within half-a-dozen steps of the building, he could hear the rumble and twitter of organ pipes as before. He slowed his pace and waited for Jeff to catch up, but he could barely contain his excitement. Inside, he strode purposefully through the chill and gloom of the Gothic nave and up the chancel steps to the organ console embedded in the dark wood of the choir stalls. A lone figure was hunched over the keyboard playing *Abbot's Leigh*: a man in his early fifties, thin, with a shaggy head of straight gray-streaked brown hair. He wore a heavy wool sweater vest and rumpled tweed jacket. He looked up at Brian standing beside him, finished the cadence and stopped.

"Hello. Is there something I can do for you?"

"I wonder where I might find the vicar."

"You've found him." A big smile broke out on the man's face as he raised both hands, palms up, in a gesture of availability. Perhaps he seldom had strangers seek him out here in this quiet church. "Just indulging myself here a bit. Not much of an organist, but I like to fool around a bit when nobody's around" He gave a sheepish grin. "I have this and two other village churches," he added. "But I live here."

"I was wondering . . . ah, you see, I've taken an interest in the medieval church." He pointed vaguely beyond the high altar. "Back there. And, well, I'd like to do something to repair it and help keep it up."

The vicar looked at him, an expression of disbelief on his face. "That would be lovely," he said at last. "There's no money right now even to have the weeds cut. It's not exactly a favorite spot in the village."

"So it seems. Well, I would be pleased to have the grounds tended and the lychgate repaired. The roof, too. Also, how could I get permission to rebuild the wall?"

"Permission? You have it," the vicar said, looking a bit puzzled, if agreeable. "I'm Mr. Biggs, by the way."

"Brian Craig." He extended his hand and had it grasped in a brief firm handshake. "This is my friend, Jeff, Mr. Biggs." He turned to Jeff and grinned. To the vicar he said, "It's as simple as that?"

"Exactly." He turned and shook hands with Jeff.

"And what about the graves outside the wall—you know, where the break is? Any reason not to include them on the inside, too?"

"Are there graves out there? I've never noticed. It would certainly tidy up the old place a bit. All part of the old glebe—owned by the church—you know."

"Don't you need to ask the bishop . . . or someone?" Brian's excitement climbed even higher.

"Whatever for? I learned a long time ago not to ask bishops anything that can be avoided. Besides, why would he object?"

"I can't imagine."

Mr. Biggs became thoughtful for a moment. "There's a lad in the parish, very handy, too, who would be glad of the employment just now. If you're serious. I know his work, and it's very trustworthy. This isn't really a very big job, is it?"

"No, I think not. And I *am* serious. This is something I very much want to do." No explanation of his motives seemed called for, and so he offered none. He wasn't sure in any case what he would have said if asked.

"Come on, then. The workman, Joey Jenkins is his name,

lives just over the street, and I happen to know he's at home today."

"I'm not sure just how this is going to make a difference," he said to Jeff on the drive back to Cambridge, "but I just know that it will . . . somehow." His excitement mounted with each mile he drove.

"At least you're doing something," Jeff said. "When I get frustrated I think of some action I can take. Even if it's small it often seems to make me feel better. Anything I can do to help?"

"I don't really know right now. There may be something down the road." Inside, Brian's optimism passed to thoughts about Jeannie and the impasse he had reached with her. Maybe if he could rebuild an old wall, he could also find a way to make up to her about Mary Beth, perhaps rebuild some personal walls. At the moment he felt so optimistic that he was sure most anything was possible.

He dropped Jeff and then drove the Rover to Cambridge Carriage Hire, feeling a bit sentimental about the clumsy old ride that had served him so well. At the last minute he extended his rental on the car for two more weeks. He wanted to go back to Stichen-Walling on Monday when Joey Jenkins got started on the work there. No doubt he would also like to turn up in the town regularly over the next couple of weeks. The car made that much easier than taking the bus.

First things first. To cover the costs of the work Joey would be doing, he would have to go online and shift some money from the investment account left to him by his father. Back in his flat, he booted up his computer and made the connection. Before he began the transaction, though, he called up his email and looked in his inbox in the hope that he would find a note from Jeannie. He was disappointed to find nothing.

He typed a quick note to Bobbie to tell her about what he was planning at Stichen-Walling and asked how she was doing in her classes, hoping in part that he might hear back something about her English Lit professor. What a wonderful thing it was to have a daughter. Then he turned his thoughts in earnest to Jeannie. What did he do now? Did he pretend that nothing was amiss and write enthusiastically about his plans for Stichen-Walling, much the way he had done to Bobbie? Did he grovel and plead? Did he try more to explain himself? He couldn't see how any of those possibilities might be right or even helpful. But he also knew that he didn't want to endure this painful silence any longer—anything but that. What about her planned visit over the Thanksgiving weekend? He decided on the simplest course and wrote a short note, "Just want you to know that I'm thinking about you. I miss you very much." He signed it with love. He couldn't bring himself to ask about Thanksgiving. He went ahead and sent the message. But he waited in vain for a reply.

On Monday morning Brian drove out to Stichen-Walling. Clear skies soon gave way to dark threatening clouds. Intermittent light rain had started by the time he got to the village. He pulled a bright yellow-hooded slicker over his heavy red-and-white sweater and tromped back to the old churchyard where he found Joey Jenkins already at work. Joey had his shirtsleeves rolled up on a plaid flannel work shirt, its tails tucked into jeans. He had a cloth cap on his head. Everything about him shouted English working class—self-deprecating manner, a mouthful of crooked teeth and rough oversized hands. Joey had been taking advantage of the mostly dry moment to begin work on the sagging roof of the little church.

"It's you, then," he said to Brian in a greeting that was friendly enough.

"Yes. I could barely wait to get out here and see the work started."

Joey whistled tunelessly as his strong hands removed the damaged slate tiles. A large black plastic tarpaulin lay folded on the ground, presumably to cover the hole Joey was making in the roof. It was fascinating to watch, but soon Brian began feeling useless. "Is there something I can do?" he asked. "I'd really like to *do* something, but I'm not very handy."

Joey seemed to think for a minute. "You could gather up

all the scattered rocks from the wall, couldn't you?" he said at last. "And maybe put them in some tidy piles along the line of the wall?"

"Yes I could do that. That's just about my skill level."

Jocy grinned at him and went back to whistling and pulling out the slates. Joey was a man of few words.

Brian set to work on the rocks, beginning first with the easy ones that were unencumbered by crumbling mortar or buried in tangles of weeds and grass. He laid out a line of stacked rocks that looked rather like the little pyramids of canon balls he had seen in woodcuts of eighteenth century battlefields. His thoughts returned over and over to the near-by gravestones lying outside the broken enclosure. He became absorbed in the work. After a time he noticed blood on his left hand. He didn't remember injuring it. Reaching into his pocket, he pulled out a tissue and wiped the spot. A nasty little scrape was the source of the blood. Then he noticed that the wind had begun to kick up. That was likely a prelude to increased rain. He was glad both for his sweater and the slicker. The rain resumed with some tentative drops then moved on to a steady downpour. The blood from his wounded finger soon washed away. He stopped to watch Joey place the tarpaulin over the hole he had created in the roof. Heavy planks were laid over the top to keep the plastic from blowing away. Soon Joey had joined Brian at the wall.

"You've gotten a good start here, haven't you?" he said.

"Thanks," Brian muttered as he began searching through the grass and weeds for hidden rocks.

"It's really good of you to be doing this. I'm right thankful to have the work. There's a new job next month—refitting a store in Cambridge. But right now . . . well, you know . . ." He took up a chipping hammer from a wooden toolbox and begin working away on the mortar that still clung to many of the rocks, confidently holding the hammer in one hand and the rock in the other.

They worked quietly side by side for a few minutes. Only the chipping sound of steel on stone broke through the sodden air. "I'll have to get me some more of these rocks for the extension of the wall," Joey said after a time. Brian noticed that the rainwater was dripping off the brim of his cloth cap. He seemed oblivious.

"Where exactly do you plan to put the wall line?" Brian asked from under his slicker hood.

"Just here," Joey answered and paced a line that marked out two sides of a shallow triangle.

"That looks good," Brian answered.

"There's lots of these rocks round here. I know just where to get 'em, too. You'll never guess they weren't always here."

Before long all of the scattered rocks had been gathered up and much of the old mortar had been removed. Brian stood up straight and arched his back to drive out the kinks. His hands felt rough and raw, and he noticed several other little nicks that the rain was keeping washed out. He felt good despite the cuts. Something about the physical work had given him a new sense of belonging and the feeling that he had the right to be in that lonely churchyard. He stood watching Joey chip away at the mortar and noticed a small red smudge on one of the stones piled at his feet. His own blood. In a way he would have found difficult to explain, that blood sign gave him an even deeper sense of connection to the place and the work being done in it. He watched the rain wash away the blood. Then he thought about those excluded graves and the women whose remains lay in them. A deep sadness passed over him. Suddenly he felt an overpowering urge to know more about the circumstances of their deaths and remembered with new resolve the unexplored lead at the British Library.

Stepping out of the crowded King's Cross Station onto Euston Road the next day, Brian unfurled his umbrella and lifted it against the steady drizzle. His small overnight suitcase dragged behind him through the rain, his computer bag over his shoulder. The sculpted red brick facade of the block-long St. Pancras Hotel and rail station, neither any longer in use, was on his right side as he walked. Both St. Pancras and King's Cross were remnants of Victoriana sitting side-by-side in contemporary London.

Brian continued on down Euston Road to the British Library where its vast collection of books and manuscripts created an enormous magnet for people like him. He crossed the courtyard and descended a short flight of stairs to the locker area, stowed his bag and put a pound coin into the key slot; he turned and removed the key. Several folios of materials were waiting for him at the reader's room desk. He settled in at one of the individual mahogany tables to work on the Sanderson family papers. Those particular archives were part of a collection assembled by Edwardian antiquarian Sir Henry Lyons. Tons of East Anglia materials had been given in a truckload to the British Library on his death in the early 1930s.

Brian untied the string, folded back the flap and opened the first of the brown Lyons Manuscripts folios. Gentle and almost reverent at holding them, he pulled out the stack of papers inside. The smell of dust and age was on them. Labeled by some unnamed archivist, perhaps Sir Henry himself, as "estate papers," the container held many kinds of documents. The Thirley Green estate hadn't passed into the Arnold family's hands until the time of the Lord Protector, Oliver Cromwell. That was sometime in the late 1640s or early 1650s. The deaths of Jane and the other two women of Thirley Hall had been in 1632. Sir Anstel must have had the property in the interim—or much of it. Exact dates remained unclear. The explanations he sought might appear in almost any category of papers, but the estate papers were as good a place as any to start. Working his way through the first three folios that same day, he found oblique references to Thirley Green, especially management matters about collecting rents and fielding tenants' complaints about needed repairs to cottages and the like. Mundane stuff, but a clear picture of seventeenth century country life emerged from it. The papers spoke of chickens and pigs, land violations and trampled crops. There was even an early complaint about foxhunters' disregard for agricultural land. Farmers in later centuries would have a great deal more to say about that growing issue in rural life. The only interesting item Brian found in those folios for his present purposes was a short entry on a loose page of financial accounts that listed payments received. Its heading said, "stonnes remoued frome Thirley Hous." No doubt this ledger recorded the sales of building materials from the burned building. It was customary to quarry old structures for new construction projects and for property owners to profit from the sale of the materials. Joey would acquire stones for the wall at Stichen-Walling in just that way. Sir Anstel Sanderson was the owner who profited from the destruction of Thirley Hall. At least Brian now knew what became of the remains of the house.

At the end of the day he returned to King's Cross Station and took the Tube to South Kensington. He had noticed several small Bed and Breakfast hotels in the neighborhood when he was there with Carol Heppel for the Proms concert. How unlike him to leave such details to chance. But surely he would be able to find a place to stay. Thoughts of a solitary night in London appealed to him—a quiet dinner, followed by a stroll through the busy streets of South Ken and ending with immersion in his current novel. It all sounded just right. Getting on the Underground train posed a momentary challenge in the rush hour crowds, but he managed it. Finally he unfolded himself from the packed humanity and located the colonnaded streets of uniformly designed houses in the Onslow Gardens neighborhood. Each house looked exactly the same as every other house—all in shimmering coats of glossy white paint. He soon spotted the generically named Onslow House and booked a room on the second floor. A small bunch of fresh flowers and a pile of frilly pillows gave the room a welcoming touch. The faint sweetness in the room's air seemed to carry a memory of the previous guest's perfume. He tossed his damp raincoat over the back of a chair, and put his suitcase on the dresser. All of his things stowed, he stepped over to the tall window that opened onto the street outside and looked out at the rainy darkness and at the uniform fronts of colonnaded row houses across the street. His watch read just before six o'clock. He took off his jacket, hung it up and kicked off his loafers. He stretched out on the double bed, pulled up a loose covering and fell instantly asleep.

I am walking briskly along the Cam. It's a bright night lit by a still-large moon on the wane, a dazzling site in the clear cold air. A hundred yards farther on I see a dark spot on the river, one that resolves itself into the shape of the black swan.

"Hello there, old boy," I call. "I guess it's just the two of us tonight." I look around to confirm that we are alone. The swan turns, arches its elegant neck and cranes its head to look at me. "What goes on inside that beautiful head of yours?" I'm vaguely aware that this is one of my dream/ visions.

The swan peers at me, as if to say, "What's it to ya?" I expect him to speak. That's not the first time I've had an anthropomorphic expectation of the creature. Instead, he shifts his gaze and looks across my right shoulder out across Coe Fen behind me. Suddenly he stiffens and begins to move on the water, becoming agitated, swimming back and forth, but keeping his head pointed toward the open fen. As if in confirmation of his agitation I hear the thuds of heavy footsteps behind me. Sounds of a running horse. A chill goes up my spine. I turn around. There, about fifty yards away and coming fast, is a solitary horse and rider. I can hear the rhythmic squeak of the saddle leather and the breathing of the straining animal. This mounted horseman is very real looking—and threatening. Now I can see his face. It's the same man who sent me careening off the road in the car that morning near Thirley Green, the one who led the band of riders and whose apparent orders resulted in the deaths of Jane, her daughter and granddaughter. Now he's bearing down on me with what feels like a murderous intent. How can that be? But it is.

I notice movement in the corner of my eye and hear a strange sound. I'm reluctant to look away from this imminent danger, but I steal a quick glance to the right. It's the black swan. He's flapping his enormous wings and making an eerie trumpeting sound. I'm not sure why, but I see what he's doing as an invitation. I turn and run the five or six steps to the bank of the river and jump in feet first. As I come up out of the murky water I see the horseman reign

*in his mount. It's the same roan I've seen him ride before.
Now they stand there beside the river. Horse and rider both
seem to be shaking with a combination of exhilaration and
rage.*

*I begin to feel sick, and I remember that this is a dream
and recognize the signs of its end. And none too soon. I'm
shivering, but it's not because I'm wet and cold as in the
dream. Indeed, I become aware that I'm sitting in the chair
in my London B and B. The only wetness I feel is the
rumpled raincoat against my back.*

Looking at his watch, Brian saw that it was coming on for
seven o'clock. The combination of his sleeping and the short
but terrifying dream/vision had taken up less than an hour.
Feeling groggy and shaken, he opened the door to the
bathroom where he bent over and splashed some water in his
face and patted it dry with the towel. What a terrible
experience the dream had been. It had a new and personally
threatening element. Suddenly his fear at seeing the horse
and rider bearing down on him returned. But why should he
have had this dream now? Why should he feel as if he were in
personal danger? But that was how he felt. No matter that he
had been right there in his room the whole time and had
been nowhere near either the black swan or the solitary
horseman. Who was that horseman? As soon as he thought
the thought and asked the question, he knew its answer with
a near-certainty. He shook his head in disbelief at his own
unfounded conclusion and the slowness by which he had
come to it. Umbrella in hand, he went down the two flights of
creaking stairs to exit the front of the house. Perhaps a
steamy Indian curry would revive him.

Chapter
Twenty-Four

how's Joey doing at the old church?" Brian asked Mr. Biggs in Stichen-Walling.

"Nicely, I think. The rain slows him down some, though."

"Yes, I imagine it does. Did you get my bank draft to pay for the work?"

"It came yesterday."

"I'm in London doing a bit of research. I hope the expenses are covered. At least until I'm back in Cambridge at the end of the week."

"Oh, I'm sure they are. Can we expect you at the weekend, then?"

"No, I'm sorry, truly I am. But I have commitments in Cambridge on Saturday and Sunday. Otherwise, I would be there." He thought about his obligation to attend a conference at Lords on Saturday and read a short paper on his current research. Considering what he was doing, that was an interesting challenge. He would have to get that paper written. Sunday lunch at Carol Heppel's house was much nicer, but he still ached to get back out to Stichen-Walling. Gathering up those rocks and putting them in little stacks had made him feel more useful than he had felt in months. "Joey would probably just as soon I stayed out of the way."

"Well, he is a bit of a loner. But I gather you were very useful the other day."

Brian laughed and, with a glance at his bandaged finger, said, "Thanks, but I have a realistic appraisal of my limitations." He adjusted the vase of flowers on the desk in his room.

It was Mr. Biggs's turn to laugh. "Then we can probably expect you on Monday?"

"Yes, definitely."

He folded up the phone, put on his coat, grabbed his

umbrella and headed for the Underground station. The crowd on the train was its usual abstracted collection of humanity, each person caught in private thoughts, mostly invisible to each other except as obstacles. Vivid memories of last evening's threatening vision rode along with him. He wondered what new horrors awaited him as he opened wider and wider this window into the past. Could it have been a warning? Just how did people dead nearly four hundred years gain access to his psyche?

Without a suitcase to stow he went straight to the reading room, got the next folio from the archivist and sat down at the same table as before, his pad of paper and pencil at hand. He was gradually enveloped by the no-nonsense feel of the British Library, still shiny in its comparative newness after its move to this location from Great Russell Street. Eventually he forgot to be anxious as he worked his way through the folios. Beginning with receipts, wills, property inventories, and then moving on to the letters and miscellaneous papers, he found bits of relevant information here and there about the Thirley Green property. He broke both for lunch and for afternoon tea in the BL's little coffee shop, a room with a glass wall on one side displaying level upon level of tantalizing leather-bound books. But the results of the day, though interesting in an abstract way, remained meager.

That evening Brian found a little French restaurant and had a leisurely dinner of salad and steak frites, all washed down with a half-carafe of quite acceptable red table wine. Thoughts of Jeannie were never far from his mind. At one point he popped into a café with internet connection and checked his email, hoping to hear something from her, but found nothing but spam and university messages. Back in his room after dinner, he turned to his laptop again. This time to write his paper for Saturday's conference, pleased to discover that it practically wrote itself. Eventually he fell into a deep sleep. There was no repeat of his encounter with the fierce horseman.

By the end of his third day at the BL Brian had learned a

great deal and was able to piece together much of Sir Anstel's life. He had even seen a notation by some unknown archivist that a miniature portrait of the man was part of the collection of the National Portrait Gallery just off Trafalgar Square in London. He would have a look at that before leaving the city.

Sir Anstel had been a Puritan. In that highly polarized era, religious confession and politics amounted to much the same thing. He had also maintained his strong family connections to the merchant community in London, cementing even more his adherence to the parliamentary party in the mounting tension leading up to the outbreak of the Civil War. King Charles attempted to rule without Parliament in those years. Many expedients were resorted to in the financing of the state. The king and his party took harsh actions against their critics and opponents, confiscating properties and selling them to the highest bidder, and trying every possible means, legal and otherwise, to keep the ship of state afloat. Sir Anstel was caught up in that struggle. His apparent outspoken and harsh words about the king and the Archbishop of Canterbury, William Laud, royal favorite Thomas Wentworth, and other government officials, resulted in his disgrace. Confiscation of many of Sir Anstel's properties soon resulted. That included the fields and tenants' cottages of Thirley Green. Three years later in 1642 Sir Anstel died fighting against royalist forces at Edgehill, the first major battle of the Civil War. Brian found no explanation for the deaths of the women of Thirley Hall. A mounting excitement that he might yet discover it kept him at his work every available minute, each new document sending his hopes soaring. He booked a third night at the Onslow House to give him one more half day on Friday to finish his work in the relevant papers before he had to get back to Cambridge.

That Friday morning, his last in London, and after he had checked out of the guesthouse, Brian was working in the last-but-one of the folios. There he came upon a small bundle covered front and back with pieces of thick parchment and tied up with some very old string that threatened to fall apart at his touch. Cautiously untying it, he smoothed out the crinkled papers inside. The top page said only, "The Papist Jane of Thirley Hall and hur daughter and hur daughters daughter." That sent him sitting bolt upright in his chair. At last. Here was what he had been looking for: papers specifically about the three women. But, "The Papist?" Jane and her family had been Catholics? The second page in the bundle was from a printed book. It had been charred around the edges as if it had been burned. In the Thirley Hall fire? Brian imagined how one page might miraculously have survived such a blaze. The words remained perfectly clear.

> 20. They shall sing the Mattines, laudes and the rest of the howers uppon the principallest Feasts of the yeare, kept either by the precept of the Church; or uppon Custome, uppon the Feasts of their patrones; patronesses, both of their Order and of their perticular Churches, and of the Feast of the dedication of the Same, alsoe they are to sing every day their conventuall Masse, except the Abbesse for just causes for a tyme ordayne otherways, both in these latter, as also in the former Solemnities Once every week a Masse of the holy Ghost is to bee sung . . .

The remainder of the leaf had been burned away. In the margin he found a notation in the same hand that had written the words on the previous page. It said, "Proof left after the Fyre." Brian was stunned. On the back he found where the archivist had left the notation, STC 17552. No doubt this referred to the Short Title Catalogue, a listing of books published in England and in English in the period. He could check that out easily enough. The page itself had apparently come from a Catholic publication intended to guide communities of Catholics in some form of monastic life. No doubt it was contemporaneous with Jane and the early Stuart period in England—a time when being a Catholic was a serious offense. Recusants—that is, Catholics who

refused to conform in any way to the Established Church—
were fined and subjected to a great deal of scorn, sometimes
personal danger. The wealthier ones often kept household
priests carefully hidden away. Death was the penalty for such
clergy if they were caught. Of special outrage to Puritans such
as Sir Anstel was the indisputable fact that there were lots of
Catholics at court in the reign of Charles I, beginning with
Queen Henrietta Maria herself. Such Recusants as these were
known to enjoy many privileges. Resentment engendered by
them often got leveled against local Catholics. But Jane and
her progeny were not Recusants. Their marriages were
solemnized in the Stichen-Walling parish church and
recorded in its Register. That would not have happened had
they been Recusants. Perhaps instead they were of the
category generally referred to as Church Papists—people who
conformed publicly to the Established Church, but privately
clung to the Roman one. Such people, like Recusants, often
had household priests or shared such illicit clerics with other
Catholic households. Like Recusants they might also have a
famous "priest hole" in their house where the cleric might
hide out in times of danger.

The next sheet of paper in the packet was the title page of
a book, also charred and burned around the edges. On the
margin the same hand had written "proofe positive of their
vile religione." The book had been entitled *Statutes
Compyled for the Better Observation of the Holy Rule of the
Most Glorious Father and Patriarch S. Benedict.* Below the
title began a statement of authorization that said, "Confirmed
by the ordinary Authoritie of the right honorable and Rever.
Father in Chr. The Lo MATTHIAS HOVIVS Archbishop of
Maclin and Primate of the Netherlands . . ." The remainder
was lost to the fire that had demolished the rest of the book.
Brian concluded that it was likely the title page of the book of
which the other sheet had been a part. He would check out
the digital version in Early English Books On-line—EEBO.
With the title page it should be easy enough to confirm one
way or the other.

He turned over to the next page in the packet. It was a
letter addressed to Sir Anstel and, signed by one Archibald

Lewis. "Thanks be to God," it read, "that those Papist whores have received their just rewaredes, and the priest kylled in the fraye. That was goode werk, God knowes. No reason to feare any reprisals from this quartere." Brian wondered what quarter that might be. At court perhaps? He made a note to look up Archibald Lewis. The remainder of the letter contained mundane matters of estate management, the movement of some cows and the collection of rents on certain of Sir Anstel's tenanted properties. Then in the concluding sentence, it read, "The finale disposition of Thirley Green its lands and cotteges appertaininge is assured. Mie cousyn at courte assures that you will recyve final commission of ownershipe in a fortnighte. Your lands wyle bee thusly all connected through the acquiryng of said property. Enclosures maye ensue. His Majestie lookes forewarde to your moste loyal support andetc." Enclosures? Possession of Jane's property would facilitate enclosing Sir Anstel's other properties? That seemed to bring together several motives for the killing of the three women: outrage against Catholics, the mysterious deaths of their husbands, and the combining of properties so that enclosure—a process going on since the late Middle Ages in rural England—might result. Landowners created a revolution in country life by dispossessing inefficient tenant farmers and introducing more efficient estate management, perhaps grazing, truck farming or grain cultivation. It was a kind of middle class business application to the use of land, especially inevitable after the sale of the monastic landed estates. This brought together Brian's two worlds: the one of his research on the lands of the Dissolution and the one of his dreams. But Brian found, even though he understood the historical forces at work in the man's life, that he liked Sir Anstel Sanderson less and less. A part of his old cynicism returned as, for a moment, he discounted the man's religious sensibilities. Then he remembered how easy it was for someone as ideologically driven as the seventeenth century English Puritans sometimes could be, simply to compartmentalize their economic motives from their religious ones. There was also an understanding among Calvinists that doing well financially was a sign of God's favor. A successful enclosing landowner would be understood in Puritan terms to be among the Elect of God: one of the good people.

Elsewhere in the folio Brian found a scrawled note to Sir Anstel. It took him half-an-hour to make it out. Dated 10 October 1632, it said simply, "Noe doubt remains. The Papist priest was seene to enter Thirley House and was warmlie welcomed there. The Papist whores must needs have their vile murthers and superstitiones avengyd. We are ready to followe you wherever you leade." The scrawled signature was impossible, at least at the moment, for Brian to decipher. Another find in the folio was a simple report of the incidence of a strange malady—probably influenza from the sound of the symptoms: breathing distress, abdominal pain and high fever, even death. This short-lived epidemic, apparently localized, came in the winter months of 1631-32. Brian suspected that this infection might very well be the cause of the deaths of all three of the women's husbands.

So this was it, then. The women had died as a piece in the mosaic of the history of their times: hated Catholics in a generally Puritan area who were apparently wrongly accused of witchcraft in the deaths of their husbands and whose lands were coveted by one of their enclosing Puritan neighbors. No doubt some resentment also existed over Jane's successful estate building through matrimony and her audacity at holding those properties in women's hands. The motives for their deaths were as mixed as the causes of the English Civil War itself, of which these events seemed a prologue.

Brian sat shaking his head in wonder over the human predilection for self-deception and the justification of narrow self-interest by religious prejudice all dressed up as principles. But he was also warmed by his newfound ability to see through such uses of religious extremism to the heart of the religious experience itself. Sex, religion and wealth formed a human trinity of the most powerful forces in history. At least sex and religion were capable of the greatest depths of compassion and love and, at the same time, the extremes of fanaticism and excess. He got up, made photocopies of the relevant papers and returned to his seat.

Leafing quickly through the remainder of that folio and the last one, he found nothing else connected to Thirley Hall. He decided he was finished there. One final stop at the National Portrait Gallery to gaze on the face of Sir Anstel Sanderson and he could be on his way back to Cambridge.

Brian climbed up into Trafalgar Square from the Underground. There he found the usual bustling crowds of people and flocks of pigeons around Nelson's Column. From his perch on top of the stone monument England's greatest naval hero kept perpetual watch down the Thames for the appearance of any enemy. Brian saw on his left through the Admiralty Arch onto the Mall and on down to Buckingham Palace beyond. Behind him Whitehall ran to Downing Street and beyond to Parliament Square and Westminster Abbey. On his right lay the Strand. Ahead stood the towering classical facade of the National Gallery, a site that seemed to reach out to him, inviting him to gaze on the beauty of its famous paintings. He decided to resist the urge to make that comfortable detour and instead to walk on past to the National Portrait Gallery around the corner. Dodging traffic, pedestrians and pigeons, he passed by Wren's modest masterpiece and the venue for much fine early music, St. Martin-in-the-Fields. He looked hopefully for notice of a lunchtime concert. No such luck. But he did remember that a quite good coffee shop and restaurant had been located in the church's undercroft. A thought accompanied by a rumble in his stomach. Lunch must be the very next order of the day, right after this final search.

He checked his suitcase and computer bag at the National Portrait Gallery and climbed the broad marble staircase to the exhibition rooms above, remembering from his last visit that the collection of seventeenth century miniatures would be in the third or fourth room past the entrance. He walked through the initial galleries and glanced at the portraits on the walls of some old historical friends: Henries VI, VII and VIII, Mary Tudor, Elizabeth I, Lord Burghley and his son the Earl of Salisbury, James I, Charles I, Archbishop Laud and Thomas Wentworth, and Oliver

Cromwell and his son, Richard. It felt like going to a cocktail party among a company of famous people—except that he didn't have a drink in his hand and, rather than a buzz of conversation, the hush of a museum greeted him. He would have welcomed a drink about now as he anticipated looking at the face of Sir Anstel Sanderson.

Finally he came to the display case with a mounting sense of foreboding. Sitting in the middle of the exhibition room, the glass-covered cabinet was stuffed full with miniatures: all Civil War figures, ones both familiar and unfamiliar—Fairfax, Cromwell, Prince Rupert, Charles I, and Prince Charles, the Stuart who would one day succeed his executed father on the English throne. There was no need to read all of the identifying tags, because he soon recognized the fierce-looking leader of the mounted men who had filled his dreamy world with so much mystery and horror. Sir Anstel Sanderson's unmistakable face looked much as it had looked in Brian's several encounters with him. The visage practically leaping off the display into Brian's mind's eye and sending a shiver down his spine.

After standing and gazing at the miniatures for a few moments, taking them all in at a glance, but letting his focus always return to Sir Anstel's portrait, he dared the triggering of one of his dream/visions. But nothing came. Or almost nothing. He saw, or imagined that he saw, just for a moment, a kind of shimmering iridescence hovering beyond the miniature case. But it was gone as quickly as it came. After a time he found his way to the gift shop where he obtained a slide representation of Sir Anstel's miniature. He paid for the slide, put it in a cardboard-protected envelope and, after retrieving his bags from the cloakroom, stuffed it in his suitcase.

Dragging bag and laptop behind him back onto the street, he walked to St.-Martin-in-the-Fields and descended into the crypt restaurant. Heavy medieval columns held up the floor above; there was a brass rubbing center in one corner alongside a gift shop; the serving counter had a large cluster of mostly-filled tables and chairs in front of it. It was a busy place. He picked up a pot of tea, a baguette sandwich and a bowl of peach crumble covered in custard sauce. As he sat there drinking and eating he realized that he had learned everything he had hoped to learn by this research visit to London. The mystery of the Thirley Hall women was solved. He had a clear identity for his mounted antagonist. It felt good that he had been doing something solid and real. Work that he understood and that was familiar to him. It felt like a return of the real Brian after all the wandering in the wilderness, wasted research hours on a subject he really didn't care about anymore, and the mumbo jumbo of his recent life.

Yet the more he thought about it, the more he realized that solving this particular mystery did not feel like an end in itself. He looked forward to the paper he would write about Jane and her progeny, Sir Anstel and his people, and life in a small Suffolk village and its environs during the years before the English Civil War. Maybe he would write a book about it. But that still didn't seem like quite enough. His thoughts returned to Stichen-Walling and the work that was going on there. Certainly that and his research conclusions would help to set at rest the souls of women so mistreated and brutally murdered all those centuries ago. Still, he couldn't escape the feeling that something more remained undone.

A full week had passed by the time Brian was able to get back to Stichen-Walling and catch up with Joey Jenkins. What he saw was downright depressing. Everything smelled musty and damp from the rain. Construction debris was piled around everywhere. The broken part of the church roof had all been removed; much of one entire side of the nave lay bare, covered by a plastic tarpaulin. A narrow foundation for the new section of wall had been poured, but the tidy piles of rocks Brian had stacked remained mostly untouched. A new heap of additional stones had been dumped outside the churchyard. Tire tracks leading to and from these new materials showed how they came to be there. But no work had started on the wall itself. The lychgate had been dismantled and lay beneath another of Joey's tarpaulins. Joey himself beamed like a proud father before his new child.

After standing around for a few minutes feeling useless, Brian left Stichen-Walling deflated and wondering if he would accomplish anything by these efforts.

It was a lonely time. Not a single word came from Jeannie. Only the black swan had been there to keep him company. He'd had no more dreams or visions since the one on his first day in London, nor had his spiritual companion appeared to keep him company over the weekend. Jeff and Charlie were in Paris. Father Jeremiah had been away attending to some family business. Each morning Brian went to the early Mass at St. Bene't's, hoping for the Franciscan's return. But day after day he was disappointed. Finally on Friday, a full week after Brian's return from London, Jeremiah turned up as the morning celebrant.

"You free for breakfast?" Brian asked when they greeted each other during the sharing of The Peace.

"Yes, that would be very nice? Everything all right?"

"More or less. But I have quite a lot to tell you."

Jeremiah flashed Brian a warm smile and went on to greet the remainder of the little congregation. Brian felt better than he had in days.

They walked to the Agora at the Copper Kettle restaurant on King's Parade a few minutes later and ordered up full English breakfasts, accompanied by steaming café lattes. Brian told the priest everything that had been happening. Jeremiah mostly listened, nodding and making little affirming sounds—my-mys, tut-tuts, and you-don't-says.

When Brian had finished his narrative, the priest said, "I know this sounds like a mundane matter to you right now, what with the work on the wall and all. But you may yet affect more than you imagine by your generosity. Perhaps returning a valuable ancient landmark to the village."

"You think?" Brian hungered for affirmation. He sipped his coffee. "No doubt the place will look better and be safer for visitors. Maybe a few tourists will find it attractive in the months and years ahead. But some kind of sweeping change? I don't think so."

"Maybe the restoration work is only a part of what's

needed. Are you planning anything else?"

"I don't know what you mean."

"A ritual or ceremony of some kind marking the occasion. Surely, you plan to do something." Jeremiah lifted his cup of coffee.

"I hadn't thought about that," Brian said. "What do you think?"

"Well, I've never encountered anything just like this before." He flashed his small white teeth at Brian. "But I imagine that the addition to the churchyard—the place where those graves were put outside the wall, you know—should be consecrated as sacred ground for Christian burial. That might be included as part of a Mass said in the old church, perhaps a requiem for the dead women. They certainly never received the ministrations of the Church. And, of course, there need to be prayers of special rededication or blessing of the whole site. Not exactly an exorcism, you know, but . . ." He grinned again and bobbed his head up and down. "But analogous," he continued. "Yes, analogous. Much the same result. The building and all its grounds must need to be reconstituted for sacred use. What you tell me about the place suggests that a kind of evil presence has grown up there. All rather arcane old rituals, I'll admit." His expression had changed from genial to serious.

Brian suddenly had a sense of unreality. Here he was once more, coming right up against ideas that he had long ago dismissed as medieval, at least as a part of that long-ago time period, if not pejorative. But he understood that beneath the easy going facade Jeremiah was very purposeful about his role as a priest and had to be taken seriously in his suggestion about administering these timeless esoteric religious rituals. What possible good could come from all that pre-modern ceremonial? It was all based on a very different worldview than what made sense today. Still, the locals did consider the place haunted. Maybe a rededication would at least convince them that the old church was okay. But he checked himself before he said anything cynical, and decided that in this, as in other things lately, he needed to be led by the priest. Brian tried to reorient his thinking to remember that not everything was as rational and explainable as he had always assumed it to be. After a time he said, "Would you be willing to plan and conduct such a service?"

Jeremiah laughed. "The vicar—what did you say his name was?"

"Mr. Biggs."

"Mr. Biggs, then. He's the one to do a service. It's his church, after all."

"I think Mr. Biggs would find this all a bit too . . . too Catholic for him. He's rather obviously evangelical in his views and probably finds the ritualistic practices in some quarters of the Church of England weird and maybe even dangerous." Brian laughed at the thought of Mr. Biggs swinging a smoking pot of incense. "But he's a very nice man, earnest and sincere, and I think he would be accommodating."

"I'd be pleased to help. But you need to contact the vicar right away for his agreement."

Brian talked to Mr. Biggs later in the day and told him of his research interest in the women of Thirley Hall and how he wanted to end the whole rebuilding project with a Requiem Mass. Mr. Biggs seemed pleased by the request.

"I've already talked to some of the parishioners about the project," he said. "I don't think any of them would have any objection. Some might even want to be on hand for the service. I'd be pleased to assist your Father Jeremiah. Didn't you say he's a Franciscan?"

"That's right."

"I'll get some of the people to help clean up inside the old church and move over some furniture from storage. Chairs and such like. Get it ready for a service, you know. I'd say the celebration of Holy Communion in the Old Church is long overdue."

Brian would arrange for a small brass plaque to go on the newly restored wall once it was completed. It said simply, "The repair of this wall is in memory of the women of Thirley Hall." The other occupants of excluded graves—Agnes of Stichen-Walling Common, Arabella Leighton and the anonymous graves—would benefit in the same way. If indeed it was a benefit. But their names would not be on the plaque. He placed the order for the small brass at a jeweler's shop on Sidney Street. He and Father Jeremiah met early the next week and spent quite a long time planning the service, talking and consulting reference books, the Bible, the English *Book of Common Prayer* and the contemporary worship book. Roles were allocated to Brian and his Cambridge friends, to Joey Jenkins and to Mr. Biggs. Finally, Jeremiah became very serious as he changed the subject.

"There's one other thing I need to raise with you now. Something I've been thinking about since our last meeting." He paused to take a breath and apparently to gather his thoughts for a change of subject. "You know, a basic goal of the Christian faith has been described by the Greek word *metanoia*, which loosely translated means transformation, sometimes rendered in English as repentance. It's about seeing the world differently. Maybe even, as the Buddhists say, shedding illusions."

"Yes, I've heard that term before. Hmm. *Metanoia*? Do you think something will actually change for these women even though they've been dead all these years? Just by someone knowing their story and the injustice done to them. That rebuilding the wall of the churchyard to include their graves will also do some good? What is it, shades of the old doctrine of Purgatory perhaps?" He laughed. He was feeling confident and optimistic again. The whole Stichen-Walling intrusion into his life would soon be over. "For their sins, they spent all these years outside paradise and now, in a manner of speaking, they will come inside?"

Father Jeremiah just sat quietly without commenting on Brian's facetious questions.

Finally, Brian said, "You mean *me*, don't you?"

chapter
twenty-five

id-November came and went without Brian hearing any more from Jeannie. That silence nearly drowned out everything else. Nor was there any word from Mary Beth; she seemed to share his desire to forget their whole reunion. Though his days were full and he felt productive, his evenings were often spent in lonely wanderings around Cambridge in the dark, which came earlier and earlier. Sometimes the rain fell so hard that not even his umbrella managed to keep him dry. Other evenings a moon-bright sky would invite long moments sitting under the stars, sometimes on one of the benches on Christ's Pieces or in isolated spots beside the Cam. He would gaze wonderingly at the heavens and then go on his journeys again. More and more the river was his focus, its timelessness and regularity speaking deeply to him. Evening after evening he sought out his alter ego, the black swan. Sometimes he watched the graceful bird feeding or just gliding on the surface of the river. Occasionally it would sit motionless in the water, little more than a dark shadow on the surface. Usually Brian carried a little bread to toss out on the water to the bird; there was no doubt that the creature had come to know him and perhaps even to await his appearance. Standing and feeding bits of bread to the swan gave Brian brief moments beyond loneliness. Their shared solitude strengthened him.

Brian had begun to accept the idea that he would never again hear from Jeannie and had stopped sending email or leaving voicemail messages for her. Then he opened his inbox one morning to find a short note from her. Feeling a mixture of elation and dread, he scrolled down to read it.

"I've thought a great deal about my planned visit to Cambridge this weekend for the Thanksgiving holiday," she wrote. "I already have my tickets and had cleared my calendar. Frankly, I've been back and forth about it. I really don't want to come. I don't want to see you. But I think I should. It does neither of us any good just to drop everything right where it is. I think we need to talk and to figure out where we go from here, and perhaps get closure. I just don't want to let it all sit and fester. But there's no way I'm staying with you. So if you will find me a hotel or something, maybe we can settle a few things between us. Even figure out what, if anything, comes next." There was no signature.

Brian felt a surge of elation replace his near-hopelessness. But that reminded him of his previous night's dream, an ordinary but disconcerting one. In it he had seen Jeannie with the department head, Francis Cardham. She had smiled at the man and invited him into her bed. No sooner had he gotten there than he promptly turned into a huge green toad. True to the fairy tale a kiss from her suddenly turned him into a handsome prince with a shining crown on his head. Despite this miraculous transformation he leered at her in a way that sickened Brian. Now shuddering at this typically sketchy memory of the dream, he typed a quick reply to her email, one that carried a newfound optimism that surprised even him.

"I'm so glad you've decided to come after all," he wrote. "I've been sick about everything. I know we have a lot to process, and I really want a chance to do that. Thank you." Feeling a little giddy, he told her about his Stichen-Walling plans and asked her if she might want to be part of it while she was there. He sent the message then stood up and stepped back away from the computer, trying to remember where he had seen an attractive little place with a B and B sign in front.

Brian paced the Arrivals Hall as he waited and watched for Jeannie to appear. Neither his excitement over seeing her nor his anticipation about the ritual that would happen at Stichen-Walling the next day entirely covered his anxiety. He had been there for an hour. It seemed like longer. He checked for the fiftieth time, and her flight still bore the label, "In the Customs Hall." His eyes ached from the strain of scanning the crowds for that one familiar face. Then he saw her. She was pulling a single suitcase and looking straight ahead. His heart jumped. But her expression of resignation was not the look of someone brimming with eagerness. Oh well, his enthusiasm would have to be enough for both of them. He threaded his way closer to where she would step out of this human stream. He imagined her coming into his arms, if not as lovers then like the friends they had once been. To be able to go back and begin again. But those days were gone forever. Then he thought about their last parting at this same airport. He nearly staggered, remembering the pain and worry of these last weeks. He ached to hold her, but he knew that wouldn't happen. At least not today.

She seemed not to have spotted him yet, so he had a moment to watch her unobserved. She was dressed in jeans and a sweater with a tan raincoat unbuttoned and open. A bright blue scarf around her neck set off her red hair and completed an image at once professional and casual. She looked terrific. The excitement he felt at seeing her rose from the bottoms of his feet to the flush in his cheeks.

Dodging and ducking his way through the swarming throngs, he caught snatches of diverse accents and languages ranging from East Asia to Jamaica, South Africa to Scandinavia. Finally he aimed toward the spot where she would emerge into the larger room. As he got closer to the opening in the rope barrier, he could see that the expression on her face had changed. It now held a mixture of interest in the crowd around her and a kind of fixed determination that Brian found hard to read.

What was she so determined about? To resist their emotional tug toward each other? Or was she preparing herself to go through a distasteful ordeal?

His pleasure over seeing her gave way to a wave of dread. Then he thought that maybe she was just nervous, too. He relaxed again. He could win her over. He would win her over. He longed to tell her all about Mary Beth, how for the first time in a quarter century thoughts of her no longer intruded into his mind and that he felt like a new man without her constant presence. But he knew that Jeannie had no interest in that conversation. How could he blame her for feeling that way?

She looked up and saw him. Their eyes met. Did he see a smile of greeting in hers? A large man wearing a turban stepped between them and broke the connection. When the sightlines had cleared, any suggestion of her being glad to see him had vanished. He wondered if he had been mistaken after all. She waved a hand rapidly back and forth in front of her face and flashed him a brief neutral smile. Then they stood in front of each other. She came stiffly into his arms and rather than offering her lips, she turned her face from him. He gave her a light peck on the cheek. She felt like the trunk of a slim but sturdy tree.

"I worried when I didn't see you at first," she said.

"Sorry. It's quite a crowd." He reached out and gently touched her arm. "Come, our exit's this way." He grabbed the handle of her one small suitcase and lightly touched her waist with his free hand, guiding her toward the exit passage. "I have this old car I've been driving for a few weeks now," he said, feeling stiff and awkward. He would be glad of the security he felt sitting behind the wheel of the familiar old Rover. "Actually, I've become rather fond of the homely old thing."

"What's that?"

"This old rental car I have."

"Oh, right."

They walked in silence across the busy street and into the parking garage.

"The drive takes a couple of hours with traffic and all," he said.

"I remember."

"If you like, I'll take you directly to the B and B where you can freshen up. Even take a nap if you want."

"Okay."

They got to the car. He put her suitcase in the back and unlocked the passenger's door for her to get in. The car started right up, and he retraced the circuitous route to the Motorway. They drove in silence.

Are you hungry?" he asked after awhile.

"A little. I hadn't felt like eating on the plane when they woke us."

"You slept, then?"

"Yes. A little. Dramamine helped."

"Well, we can stop somewhere along the way. At a Little Chef?" He grinned at the thought of actually trying one of the ubiquitous roadside eateries.

"I'm not sure we can find a decent lunch beside the Motorway."

"Sure we can. Whatever appeals to you."

"I'm not real particular right now."

They made their way around London's orbital system and caught the M11 north toward Cambridge, making occasional small talk between long awkward silences.

"And how's your move to a tenure track going?" he asked.

"The committee's positive recommendation passed the department and is on its way to the dean. Everybody says it's a sure thing." She sat quietly for a time and then volunteered, "I have been offered a book contract to write the early twentieth century volume in a reference series about literature in wartime. You know the war poets and all. About half of the book is collected readings. The other half will be my commentary and narrative. It's right up my alley—for a commercial press, yet."

"That's exciting. Have you signed?"

"No. I wanted to wait until after this trip. Until, well, you know . . ."

She left the unfinished thought hanging there, and Brian was reluctant to push her. For the moment they tacitly agreed to stay away from their shattered relationship.

He broke the silence, "I haven't had even a hint of one of those dreams. Or visions. Whatever they are. Since I finally figured out all the details of why the women were killed. The last one was when I was in London a couple of weeks ago."

"That's amazing," she said. "Then you really think it's all connected?" She seemed genuinely interested, which he took as a good sign.

"I'm not sure what to think." He paused. "No, that's not

entirely true. I do think it's mixed up together. "Father Jeremiah—I've told you about him."

"The Anglican Franciscan? Yes."

"We've been planning the requiem at Stichen-Walling to . . . well, to finish off the whole thing."

"I know."

They rode in silence for a few minutes while he drove the car. She looked out at the countryside and seemed to become mesmerized by some light snow flurries that had begun to fall. Dozing off for a moment, she started nervously at suddenly coming awake. Finally relaxing and curling up in the soft leather seat, she nodded off. Her breathing soon became deep and regular. Brian welcomed the quiet and her somnambulant absence for the diminished tension it brought. At the same time, he appreciated the companionable feel of having her sleeping there beside him. Alone with his thoughts, he negotiated the traffic and the falling snow, glancing over at her from time to time as she slept. Curly locks of red hair danced and swayed over her forehead as the old car bounced and jerked along the roadway. Her hair color highlighted both the healthy creamy look of her freckled skin and made her look at once vulnerable and available. He ached to touch her. In one of those quick glimpses stolen from attention to the road ahead he saw the familiar faint chicken pox scar on her right cheekbone and the line of lips and brows, the little upturn of her nose and the familiar curve of her chin. His anxiety gave way to a rush of feelings and of gratitude for having her there with him. Surely everything between them was going to turn out okay. A new and quiet confidence stole over him in that moment; a fresh self-assurance that he hoped would soon communicate itself to her and help to win her over again.

Jeannie slept until they reached the outskirts of Cambridge. When she did stir it was to sit for a few minutes before she said, "The number one thing in the entire world that I want right now is a hot bath." She flashed him a sheepish grin that set his heart to fluttering. But it soon settled down again when he touched her arm and she shook him off as if contact with him made her dirty.

"Shall I take you straight to the B and B?"

"Please."

Silence resumed. He drove into Cambridge and pulled up in front of the Hummingbird Guesthouse. "I'll be back in an hour. Would you like to go to the Eagle for lunch?"

"Sure, if you like." She treated him to a quick smile. "Thanks for understanding—about the bath, that is."

"No problem."

He passed the hour back at his flat checking email and worrying about what and when she would finally unload on him, imagining scenarios and how he might respond to her accusations, knowing that he deserved whatever she had to say. At the end of the hour he hoofed it back to the guesthouse, happy that the snow had stopped, despite the chill in the air. The landlady let him into the reception hall. Once more he was filled with the kind of anxiety he had felt earlier at the airport. But Jeannie surprised him with a cheerful smile as she came down the stairs.

"I feel about a million times better. Are you starved?"

"I am a little hungry."

She pulled on her coat and they went out the front door and onto the street. He put his arm around her waist. She stepped away from him

The Eagle felt warm — close and familiar. They shared an order of fish and chips and a salad and spent an hour over the distraction of food and drink. He slowly got used to the idea of them being together. He thought she did, too. They laughed when Brian spilled a handful of chips he was trying to slide from his plate to hers. They sipped at pints of IPA. They relived moments from her last visit to Cambridge with Candy in tow.

Jeannie was the one who finally brought up the subject of Mary Beth. "Something odd you said a few days ago on my voicemail sticks in my mind. About your old girlfriend. I think you described her memory as 'looming over you.'"

"I might have said something like that," he replied, caution winning out over his earlier confidence. "And, yes, it certainly does describe how I've felt."

"I'm trying to understand that. To be honest," she said. Her voice got very low, "I am real pissed at you."

"It shows."

She looked hard at him. Under her breath she said in tones just audible to him, "Fuck you. I'm only here to tie up loose ends. What the hell is wrong with men anyhow? What the hell is wrong with *you*? Jannie—she's my expert on the ways of men—says that men hanging onto attachments to their first love is not uncommon. So what?" She flashed a chilly little smile.

"I really don't know anything beyond my own experience," he said, his sense of caution rising even higher. "All I can say is that I think her memory has stayed with me and affected all of my relationships ever since I was a freshman in college. I've wondered so many times what my life might have been like had I never met her. Or if we had just burned out on each other naturally, rather than my being left feeling stupid and rejected."

"In other words, if you had slept with her you wouldn't have continued to carry a torch ever since?"

"Something like that. In a way. But . . . but, no it's—it's more complicated than that."

She didn't even take a breath. "And now, since you've had sex, it's all better?" She snarled the words relentlessly. "Kind of like a magic ritual, and the spell has been broken?"

"Kind of." As soon as the words had been spoken, he wished he hadn't said them. It seemed much too trivial, not credible. He didn't even believe it himself. Not really.

She sat quietly and stared at him. He had never before noticed how cold and hard those lovely blue eyes could look. Perhaps they hadn't been aimed at him before with such negative intensity. He averted his gaze and looked around, his senses taking in the atmosphere of the room, the historical memorabilia, the mingled odors of food and beer, the light conversation and laughter of the other people. No one seemed even mildly interested in them. He glanced down at the scratched tabletop. When he looked back at her again she still held him locked in that same icy stare. Her unblinking eyes glowed hard with a combination of disdain and disgust.

"That's crap," she said at last through bared teeth, scarcely containing the anger that she obviously felt. "Take me back to my room. I feel like being alone."

On the nearly silent walk back to the guesthouse he felt an agony of mixed emotions and confusion. Why did she refuse to get it? He had it all worked out. He *needed* to see Mary Beth; *needed* to experience all those old feelings again in order to move past them; *needed* to sleep with her so he could dump his denial that the relationship was dead once and for all. That's what he had told himself, and he had thought it was the truth, that he had not been kidding himself. He rehearsed in his mind all of his motives and self-justifications—the psychology behind his behavior and his carrying a torch for her all those years; his mother's death and the difficulty he had always had with intimate relationships; his ambition and workaholic habits; his shallow and often ineffectual commitment even to parenting his one daughter; and his gradual slip into cynicism about his work and his church membership. Why couldn't she see how it all fit together? Couldn't they just move on now and forget all about that time with Mary Beth? After all, it wasn't as if going to bed with her was in any way related to his relationship with Jeannie.

They trudged on through the chill afternoon air, silent and inside themselves. Overhead, the clouds began to return.

No, of course they couldn't just forget it. Because seeing Mary Beth *was* important. For him. Those few days had carried some long overdue justice. That was it. Justice. The forces of the universe had somehow come together to complete something that was incomplete, to give him that one success that had always been denied him—Mary Beth. His thoughts stopped abruptly. "Oh, my God." he said aloud.

"I'm sorry?" she said.

"Ah, nothing. I—I didn't mean anything. I just thought of something I forgot to do. That's all. Yes . . . that's all." He shook his head. "Here we are." He changed the subject as they arrived at the Hummingbird Guesthouse. "Can I come for you to go to Evensong at King's?"

"Yes, I guess so. What time?"

"About four. That gives you time for a rest if you want one.

"Will that get us there early enough to have the good seats near the choir?"

"Yes. No problem."

Jeannie turned on her heel and went inside without further comment. The door rattled with emphasis. Brian returned alone to Lo-Host for the second time that day, even more uncomfortable in his solitude than he had been before. In some ways it had been easier to be in denial about what he faced with Jeannie. Before that elephant in the room had been named. Now he had to come squarely to grips with all of those old feelings and self-justifications about Mary Beth. He had to adjust to that new awareness he'd had a few minutes ago. His lingering devotion to Mary Beth had really been more about adding her to his string of successes—his conquests, both intimate and professional—than any enduring emotional bond between them. Still, he couldn't deny all those years both of yearning and of smoldering anger. What were those feelings all about? He certainly hadn't spent decades having erotic fantasies about her. No, he had suffered a physical pain, a hollowness that came, he always told himself, from her absence in his life. That was how he had experienced it. But he had to face the fact that his devotion had been to an idealized memory and not to a real person. He should have been able to tell the difference, certainly on the Sunday they had gone to Oxford together, if not before. But he had pushed ahead, knowing full well that they would sleep together. He had justified it, in spite of Jeannie, in ways that now looked pretty shabby. Maybe Jeannie was right. Maybe it was all crap. What an unflattering realization. But there it was, and he had to do something with it. His former jovial optimism had crumbled in the face of this new perspective. His fragile equilibrium lay shattered at his feet.

Evensong at King's, a walk around Cambridge under cold threatening skies and dinner at Brian's favorite little Thai

restaurant on Green Street all managed to keep the subject of
Mary Beth at bay. He realized that Jeannie had no more
desire to pick up the former conversation than he had. Later,
as he was saying goodnight to her at the guesthouse door,
wishing she would invite him in but knowing she wouldn't,
he said some conventional things about the day and how
good it was to be with her again, concluding with, "I am
really very sorry for hurting and disappointing you the way
I've done. I would do anything to turn back the clock. I'm
beginning to get the picture: just how much I've been kidding
myself."

She looked intently at him for a moment. A breath of air
rustling her hair did not soften her expression. "We'll talk
some more." She turned to go inside.

"I'll come by for you at about nine-thirty in the morning
to go out to Stichen-Walling."

"That will be fine," she said and went up the three steps,
used her key to unlock the door and disappeared from sight
without looking back.

Not even the little clouds playing tag with the moon
lightened Brian's outlook. He took his time walking back to
Lo-Host. He felt deflated, sad, tired and lonely.

chapter
twenty-six

Brian blamed his restless night on anticipation of
the rites at Stichen-Walling the next morning. He
tossed and turned and wrestled with the
bedclothes. Surely all his troubles these last
months would end in that climactic ritual in the old church
and its graveyard. Something spectacular was bound to
happen. Would other people experience it too? Somehow
everything would turn out okay. He just knew it would. Even
Jeannie would be moved by the drama of the moment, and
their ruptured relationship would be put back on track. The
dreams would end once and for all. The village would have
back its ancient church. Justice would be done for the Thirley
Hall women. Life would return to an even keel.

But still he couldn't sleep.

In the end he sat down with his new Bible, flipping
through it and looking in search of inspiration or insight in
the same random way as he had done over the past week.
Thus far that method hadn't really produced anything much,
except for a growing superficial familiarity with both the
Hebrew and Christian scriptures that he had never had
before. Still, he played what he had come to think of as Bible
roulette. Like before, one phrase after another caught his
attention, but none of the passages led him anywhere in
particular. Surely there must be something better to do with
these ancient texts than that. Finally, he settled down with
the four Gospels. Their stories and parables always appealed
to him. He flipped back and forth, comparing the details of
Jesus' life and work as told by the four different writers.
Then, beginning with John, he checked out the endings of the
books, just because he had never done that before. The last
sentence in John seemed prophetic in an odd way, "But there
are also many other things that Jesus did; if every one of
them were written down, I suppose that the world itself could

not contain the books that would be written." He smiled and shook his head, wondering just how many books *had* been written about this same Jesus. Then he went to the next previous Gospel and read the last sentence in Luke. It followed immediately after the description of how Jesus ascended directly into heaven. It read, "And they worshipped him, and returned to Jerusalem with great joy; and they were continually in the temple blessing God." That seemed a bit unlikely. Would these simple men and women actually have been elated over his leaving them? In Mark, the earliest of the Gospels, he found a lack of agreement about just how the book was meant to end. Among the three possibilities offered, he decided upon the most abbreviated option since it was the most dramatic and, perhaps for that reason, the most authentic.

That text read, "So they went out and fled from the tomb, for terror and amazement had seized them; and they said nothing to anyone, for they were afraid." He found this scenario persuasive simply because it accorded with his sense of human nature: fearful and fleeing in the face of the unknown. Besides, the tomb reference fit his obsession with the Stichen-Walling graves. It also described how terrified and amazed he had often felt during the last few months. But he recognized that conclusion as more than a little self-centered. Finally, he came to Matthew, the first book in the traditional printing order of the New Testament. There he discovered something that stuck him with surprising force. That final sentence ended the Gospel with simple poignancy: "And remember, I am with you always, to the end of the age."

He puzzled over all four of the ending sentences, but that simple one from Matthew held him transfixed. Even after he turned off the light and tried at length to get some sleep, that metaphorical promise made by Matthew's risen Christ lingered. The meaning seemed unambiguous. Jesus promised to be with his followers always. Brian was unsure exactly what that meant, but he found the assurance oddly comforting. He thought about his Ghost. Where did he fit into all of this? Was he some kind of personal fulfillment of that generalized promise? And what had become of him? He seemed to have vanished. Holding these thoughts, at length he drifted off into a dreamless sleep.

It had taken a full three weeks and a bit more to complete the work at the old church at Stichen-Walling and for it to be ready for rededication and for consecration of the newly-enclosed graves. Even with that much time Brian knew that Joey Jenkins and Mr. Biggs had had their hands full getting it all ready on schedule. Brian had not been there in a week. So on that cold and rainy Friday morning his anticipation had reached a fever pitch.

Jeremiah drove the Franciscans' battered old minibus to the village. It was laden with passengers; the rear compartment held a vestment bag and a box of implements for the liturgy the priest would conduct. Brian would act as acolyte, serving at the altar and carrying the censor. Jeff promised to shed some of his cynicism and carry a bucket of holy water and the aspergillum for sprinkling, "But only if I get to wear a dress," he had said, laughing. The mental picture of gangly Jeff in acolyte's robes simply refused to come into focus for Brian. Charlie had brought along her viol to play period music. Carol and Jeannie would read scripture lessons from the King James Version of the Bible they carried with them, texts that would have been new and fresh at the time of the three women's deaths.

Mr. Biggs agreed to serve as deacon for Father Jeremiah, putting aside his Low Church sensibilities to accommodate his donor's desires and being the gracious and thankful host that he was. He had also arranged for a small group of parishioners to be on hand to join in the religious rituals. A beaming Joey Jenkins stood waiting impatiently in the porch of the Victorian church when they arrived, obviously anticipating with open pleasure the ceremony that would soon be performed over his handiwork.

Only the weather failed to cooperate. A gentle drizzle alternated with heavy cloudbursts to turn the earth into a marsh; it threatened to drench the unwary. At least the temperature had risen enough that the snow showers of the day before had passed. Brian alighted first from the minibus, greeted Joey with a handshake and led the way, barely able to contain his excitement. Once more he walked along the muddy path beside the parish church, beneath the bare trees and along the dripping shrubs to the newly restored lychgate. The entrance no longer looked dilapidated, but reappeared in its original form: unpretentious and unremarkable, but repaired and sturdy looking. Brian stepped through it into the old churchyard. There he almost dropped the box he was carrying in disappointment. The yard had been cleaned up and the wall rebuilt to be sure, but the work was so professional and smoothly done that he had difficulty telling that anything much was new at all. The wall itself was unusual in its jutting out to form two sides of its shallow triangle along that one perimeter. Still, it looked much as if it had always been that way. The grounds had a manicured look. The broken slates and sagging roof timbers had been replaced, but the church still looked and felt like a monument to better times. What was it about the place? Even after all of that work it managed to retain its abandoned and unloved feel.

"You've done such a good job, Joey," he said, knowing the truth of the words despite his feelings.

"You like it, then?"

"It looks as if it has always been like this," he said, still masking the disappointment that he would have been hard-pressed to find words to describe.

Joey beamed while Brian struggled to contain his melancholy reaction.

"Not much of a place, is it?" Jeannie said quietly to him behind her hand. "It feels, well—creepy." She appeared to shiver.

He repressed an instinct to glare at her for having the audacity to say something of what he himself was thinking. But she was right. After all the work and effort it felt no different.

The time had come to get on with the service. They all went straight into the little church for Jeremiah, Brian, Mr. Biggs and Jeff to pull on their vestments. Inside, the parishioners had wrought amazing results. Candles glowed on and around the altar and the pulpit, both of which wore sparkling white brocade hangings. More candles burned atop tall poles along the aisle that had been created by rows of wooden chairs arranged like pews on either side of the small nave. The church had never been outfitted with electricity or plumbing, but at that moment it seemed perfect in the flickering candlelight of the gray day. The piscina in a wall alcove had probably not had the Blood of Christ drained into it in more than a century, and certainly not within living memory. A single red rose lay across it. Brian later learned that Mr. Biggs had checked the Parish Register; no recorded liturgy had been conducted in the building since 1896. No wonder the place had felt so abandoned. It had been. Happily it had never actually been de-consecrated and turned over to secular purposes. That was something else that Mr. Biggs had learned in his check of parish records.

Father Jeremiah pulled out all the stops in celebrating the Requiem Mass, using texts that would mostly already have been in use in the early decades of the seventeenth century. He used the incense while Charlie played music by Thomas Tallis on her viol, going all around the small church, symbolically restoring it to its intended purpose and driving away what Brian cynically and laughing inside thought of as evil spirits. Jeff presented the Holy Water bucket and aspergillum to Fr. Jeremiah, who sprinkled the heads of the already damp congregation. That included elderly parish ladies in their best Sunday hats and old-age pensioners in raincoats, a couple of young women with babies in their arms and Joey Jenkins and his wife. Then they all sat for Carol to read a passage from I Corinthians 15, "Now is Christ risen from the dead, and become the first fruits of them that slept. For since by man came death, by man came also the resurrection of the dead . . ." Brian remembered from his preparations with Fr. Jeremiah, that in 1632, the readings, especially the Epistle, would likely have actually been at the gravesite. But there probably would not have been a Requiem Mass said either, and that was meant to be a part of today's event. Jeannie read psalm 40, "Lord, thou hast been our refuge from one generation to another. Before the mountains were brought forth, or ever the earth and the world were made: thou art God from everlasting, and world without end." Mr. Biggs read a passage from the Fifteenth Chapter of John's Gospel, "If the world hate you, ye know that it hated me before it hated you. If ye were of the world, the world would love his own: but because ye are not of the world, but I have chosen you out of the world, therefore the world hateth you."

As they read Brian was startled to see the candles in the little church burn brighter and brighter, lighting the space as if it had been illuminated by a surfeit of electric bulbs, but without losing the warmth of candlelight. He looked around at the others, and no one else seemed to be surprised or even to share that same experience with him. He noticed that Carol had even moved the Bible from which she was reading closer to the candle in order to see. She certainly didn't find the place almost painfully bright the way he did.

"I get it," he said to himself under his breath. Something was happening to him and only to him. A now-familiar shiver went up his spine. The brightness soon passed and the former look of the room returned.

Charlie played the viol. Even Jeff, who admitted to his Methodist upbringing, received Holy Communion. Finally, Brian swung the thurible as he had done as an adolescent in Peoria in wide smoky arcs. The congregation followed to the newly incorporated graves in a damp straggling procession. They stopped at the freshly rebuilt wall, and the priest proceeded to consecrate the new area and to dedicate the graves.

"O God, whose Son Jesus Christ was laid in a tomb: bless, we pray, these graves as the place where the bodies of your servants may now rest in peace." He ended with an antique absolution for the dead. "We therefore beseech thee, Let not the sentence of thy judgment press hard upon them, whom the reasonable prayer of thy faithful Christian people commendeth unto thee: but grant that by the succor of thy grace, they who while living were sealed with the sign of the Holy Trinity may be counted worthy to escape thine avenging judgment."

Throughout the dedication and consecration of the graves, rain continued to fall without letup. Standing there under an umbrella Carol held over his head, Brian realized that with this event and the article he had already mostly drafted, some measure of justice was finally done for these women. In as much as it remained possible for anyone to restore them in equity. Julian of Norwich, one of his dream figures, had captured an important truth when she wrote, "All shall be well, and all manner of thing shall be well." He knew that he had done everything in his power to make it all turn out for the better. Something very real had been attempted for the three dead women. But what of himself? He was unable to describe how much and in what ways any of it would make a difference to him. Despite all of Joey Jenkins' good work, the congratulations and the thanks of Mr. Biggs and the villagers and the moment of brightness he had experienced inside the little church, the whole place still felt unloved and lonely to him. No sudden transformation of it had occurred, no celestial trumpets had blown and no affirming rays of sunshine had broken through parting clouds. The day remained as dark and gray and wet as Brian's mood. Jeannie remained as distant and aloof as before.

He didn't know what he had expected to feel, but he had assumed he would feel something. Anything. But he didn't. Aside from a kind of satisfaction that the people in the congregation seemed to appreciate what had been done, the whole ritual left him empty inside. It did seem appropriate that the little church should be used again after all this time. But what of all the other things he had expected and hoped to experience? He saw no specters appearing before the gathered company; no vindicated women; no humiliated Sir Anstel Sanderson and guilty horsemen; and no spiritual companion. He dearly wished to see the familiar face of the Ghost and have the satisfaction of seeing a smile break out on his timeless countenance. Even worse he had no new insights. None of it seemed to matter. Jeannie thought the place felt creepy, and it was. He didn't know how he could reconcile this day with what had gone before: dreams, visions and a renewed sense of the role of spiritual ideals in his life,

Jeremiah's guidance—even the time with Mary Beth. Something was still missing.

After the service Mr. Biggs hosted a light luncheon at the vicarage. A variety of cut sandwiches, a cold vegetable salad, cakes and hot cups of tea and coffee awaited the damp worshipers. It put a festive end to the morning, and managed a light heartiness in place of the seriousness of the burial and consecrating liturgy. Carol had enjoyed getting to know her counterparts in the local church, and Brian saw her write down the name and address of one of them. He also overheard her tell Jeff that she would like to have him come to St. Bene't's. Even more surprising: Jeff had promised that he would. The buoyant mood stayed with the Cambridge contingent all the way back to town in the minibus. But Jeannie, who had been laughing and lively on the drive out to Stichen-Walling earlier in the day and had seemed to Brian to throw herself into the liturgy, had become quiet during the luncheon, spending much of the time in light conversation with Joey Jenkins and Mr. Biggs, as almost everyone else circled around Brian and Father Jeremiah. She remained quiet throughout the return drive. When Jeremiah stopped at her guesthouse to drop them off, she said goodbye to everyone and then turned to Brian after the minibus had pulled away.

"Would you like to come in? I think I can get Mrs. Jollif to serve us a pot of tea in the lounge."

"I'd like that," he said, allowing a moment's elation to break through his glum affect.

Inside they hung their damp coats on a hall coat rack, turned on the electric fire in the lounge and sat on two easy chairs at right angles to each other. Over cups of hot tea they relived moments of the day. Finally, Jeannie turned serious.

"How do you feel about today? All the work you have had done—and the service, all of it. I mean, how do you really *feel* about it?"

"I—I'm not sure what you mean?"

"You had high expectations about today, but I thought I detected—oh, it's hard to say what exactly—but maybe a bit of sadness or even disappointment in you. You still seem pretty subdued." Her blue eyes held a soft almost dreamy expression.

Brian sat in silence for a moment, reluctant to admit the truth out loud. "To be absolutely honest," he said at last, "I do feel let down. I have ever since we first got there this morning. I don't know exactly what I was expecting, but it wasn't what I got. The place looked, well, as good as it probably could look, I suppose. All of it—the service and everything—went perfectly well despite the rain. There was just a—how should I put it?—a lingering feeling of sadness about the place. I guess I expected something really big and important to happen. That being there would feel different. But in the end, well, it didn't. I did have a moment in the church when the candles seemed to burn brighter. Did you see that?"

"No, I'm sorry, I didn't." She sucked her little finger for a moment. "I thought as we were driving back that I was just picking up on your vibes—and maybe that's part of it—feeling the way I did. But the more I just sat with those feelings, the more I realized that I'm responding to how it felt to me to be there. It made me sad and melancholy. I'm glad to be away from that place."

"I'm sorry to admit it, but I feel much the same way. I wonder if my visions or dreams or whatever they were will start again. I have to admit that in a way I've missed them. I'd gotten used to having the Ghost around." He grinned and then looked down at his hands. "But I really *don't* want it all starting up again. I wanted resolution to come today, and for it all to be over. I want my life back. I want you back." Brian felt his eyes tear up with the truth of what he said.

She reached over with her left hand and placed it on top of his right one where it rested on the upholstered arm of his chair. She squeezed, but said nothing. They sat there saying nothing for a time. At last she cleared her throat, pulled her hand away and poured more tea into both of their cups, fussing with sugar and milk. He felt many things at that moment: a lingering melancholy over Stichen-Walling. And fearful that Jeannie would not come around and return what he felt so deeply for her at that moment. Beneath it all lingered his doubts about his previous understanding of what had happened with Mary Beth last month. He suddenly felt a need to get by himself for a while and to have some time to think.

"I have a couple of things I need to do," he said. "How about my coming back in a couple of hours so we can join Jeff and Charlie for our own bleated expatriate Thanksgiving dinner?"

"I'd forgotten about that. Where is it going to be?"

"The hotel restaurant at the Cambridge Arms. They're featuring turkey and all the fixings. American style. All weekend for the likes of us. It's a great old Victorian dining room: brocade wallpaper, crystal chandeliers and the like. We have a long-standing reservation since before I thought you might not be coming."

The hint of a smile passed over her face. "You know, I don't think I was ever *not* coming."

"I'm glad."

chapter
twenty-seven

What Brian wanted was to go to Evening Prayer by himself at St. Bene't's. There he could get some time out, some respite to think about everything. That little church drew him to it like some kind of energy field. He stopped by his flat for a quick bath and change of clothes before returning to the street and heading down the familiar route along Silver Street toward St. Bene't's. On a sudden impulse he made a detour to have a quick glance at the moorhens on their little rivulet of the Cam and to look for the black swan. He found the moorhens swimming about in their miniature world, but there was no sign of the swan. He stood and watched the tiny waterfowl dash and meander for several minutes, barely aware as he stood there that he was hoping to have his silent ghostly companion join him in this familiar spot. He found only the birds swimming through the lily pads and beneath the long grasses on the bank of the stream. Solitary walkers crisscrossed the Backs, mostly hurrying along to get out of the rain. Neither the swan nor the Ghost showed up.

He doubled back to Silver Street and passed over the Cam into the old city. Half an hour remained before the Evening Office would begin so he decided to keep looking for the black swan. Walking rapidly in the drizzle and fading light of the rainy afternoon, he scoured the usual areas of the riverbank downstream. Still no sign of the bird. He shrugged his shoulders and headed for St. Bene't's. Now he was ready for quiet time in the poky little church. The gate stood open as usual; he stepped down into the churchyard and out of the craziness and chaos of contemporary life. His life. He looked over at the once-mobile headstone. It stood there innocuous and unthreatening in the rain. In spite of himself, he looked around the corner of the church for any sign of his former companion, but saw nothing of that strong square face or the

Ghost's familiar figure. He went into the church. A row of six candles had already been lighted in anticipation of the Evening Office, but no other person had yet arrived. He sat in his usual pew: five rows back on the right. There he thought about the icon meditation he had attended in that space a few months ago. Such a lot had happened since then. Just for the fun of it he closed his eyes to narrow slits and looked at the candle-luminous altar to see if he might induce an icon effect. Nothing happened. Not that he really thought that it might. He felt sad and alone. He missed having Jeannie beside him. He missed the black swan.

The more Jeannie's no-nonsense attitude yesterday settled on him—especially her having pronounced his explanations about Mary Beth just *crap*—the more persuaded he had become that he had been kidding himself all these years about that first love. The changes he could feel in himself were much too complex to be explained entirely by a single sexual encounter with an old girlfriend. He remained the same person, and yet he knew he wasn't entirely the same. In some ways he felt as if he had acquired a heightened consciousness where other people were concerned. He thought about the women who had been his intimate partners, his two wives, Kathleen and Emily, and the girlfriend, Alison. He thought about Bobbie, the beloved daughter who had grown up largely in spite of him. He felt a genuine sadness for lost opportunities and missed chances. He thought about Jeannie. He did not want to look back one day and think of her as yet another lost opportunity.

He tried to dump all of his old illusions and to be entirely honest with himself. He sought to accept, finally, as the truth something that he feared he had been trying to hide from himself from the beginning. He had already known before he and Mary Beth went to bed together that the girl of his memory was not going to reappear magically and that the woman she had become stirred no particular passion in him. When he slept with her he was being self-indulgent pure and simple. Even the sexual desire had been forced and didn't carry the excuse of passion. Perhaps that was the worst kind of gluttony. It had been a conquest. And little else. He wanted to have her at least in part to settle an old score. So he had had her. Clearly, Jeannie understood that. This was why Jeannie wanted no explanations from him, no careful psychological arguments, no rationalizations about long-lost loves or justice finally coming to him after all these years. She wanted none of it. Even if a bit of his argument might still be true, and that his relationships had been twisted by memories of Mary Beth. As far as Jeannie was concerned it was all *crap*. He knew right then that all Jeannie really wanted from him, or would accept from him, was someone whose intimate life no longer relied on excuses or held back or made decisions that were either self-justifying or entirely egoistic. It was time he faced up within himself to his use of other people and learned to take himself seriously as a giving lover, parent and teacher.

An elderly woman he recognized from other services came in and sat down across the aisle from him. Then a man genuflected and entered the pew in front of him. Brian had also seen him there before. Finally, two of the brothers entered and took their places to begin the Evening Office. They were familiar, but he didn't know their names. He tacitly acknowledged some disappointment that Father Jeremiah was not there this Friday evening. A third brother rang three repetitions of three tolls followed by nine in succession of the church bell and then took his seat.

The Office began. Brian followed along, joining in the recitation of the psalm and was present to the ritual and the words without either concentrating on it or letting his mind wander away. Then the oddest thing happened. Though none of the concerns that had driven him to the little church this evening came to any kind of definitive resolution, suddenly the burden of them lifted from his shoulders, and he no longer felt so alone sitting there. None of it seemed to matter any more: his work, the old church at Stichen-Walling, his distress over his failed relationships. All that mattered now was Jeannie being in Cambridge.

More than merely not feeling alone he caught the sense that he no longer sat solitary in the pew. It was a comfortable sensation. As the lector read the last of the readings appointed for the service and the congregation stood to recite the text of the *nunc dimittis*, Brian's mind settled instead on the Bible passage from St. Matthew's Gospel he had read the evening before, "And remember, I am with you always, to the end of the age." And he understood why he no longer felt alone and why, similarly, he no longer saw the face of the Ghost as before. His personal spiritual companion was, indeed, always with him, visible or invisible, silent or chatty—nudging and directing him forward; sorrowing with him and affirming and celebrating his failures and successes; guiding and inspiring him to build upon the possibilities before him. He knew that these conclusions made no rational sense, but it mattered little whether they added up or not. In his mind's eye he could suddenly see the sad little church in Stichen-Walling and the graves that held those three women, the ones he had seen hanging from the butchering pole. He shifted into the language of traditional Christianity for an explanation of what he was feeling: the Christ had been with him, Brian Alexander Craig; had been with him throughout these past weeks and months; indeed, was with him yet, would always be with him. The Gospel promise had been fulfilled in him. He remembered the words of *St. Patrick's Breastplate,* "Christ within me, Christ behind me, Christ before me, Christ beside me, Christ to win me, Christ to comfort and restore me." He felt humbled. Brian had a sense that just for a moment the entire universe had opened before him, its secrets revealed and its truths laid bare. There were no trumpets—as, indeed, there had been none at Stichen-Walling earlier in the day. But in a sense the cloud of unknowing had parted just for a moment for him to grasp that glimpse of eternity.

One final, albeit complex, realization stole over him, much the way a solution to a vexing problem, unsolved by day could come at night during asleep. With surprising gentleness and subtlety he knew the truth about his life—his relationship problems, the restlessness, and the shallow feel of his work, his general dissatisfaction and his loneliness. None of his problems could be laid at the feet of any person but himself. Not even Mary Beth's. The point of everything that had happened to him during these last months and had come to a climax earlier today at Stichen-Walling was that he must take responsibility for his life. He thought about the black swan. Somehow the bird seemed to know all of this about him. But he had to face it: not all of the consequences of his actions in that little Suffolk village, and by extension everything else, were about him. The village received benefit; the women whose remains lay in those isolated graves grasped their belated share in justice; Jeff, Charlie, Carol, Jeremiah, Joey and even Jeannie might have come away changed by the experience he had helped to orchestrate. But all of these other consequences were about them and not about him. He had had a hand in it to be sure. Certainly as a facilitator. But it had never been only about him. He had felt a sacred presence with him in the form of a ghostly apparition, maybe even a kind of Cosmic Christ. That had given him the subsidiary result of appreciating the world and its beings: alive and dead, human and fowl—but on their terms, not on his. The black swan, like all the rest, had been living his own life, and had not existed for Brian. The loneliness Brian had suffered was not a result of his being alone on the planet, but the product of his reluctance to touch and be touched by the companions with whom he shared his world.

Brian suddenly noticed that everyone else had left the church and that the Franciscan who had conducted the Office was standing quietly beside the sacristy door. Waiting for him to leave. He got up from his pew feeling self-conscious and said, "Sorry. I lost track of time."

"Not to worry," the man replied, smiling and making a shallow bow. "I understand."

Brian walked out into the dark evening with his eyes set toward the Hummingbird Guesthouse. His thoughts focused on the evening ahead.

"Brian," Jeannie said. "I'm so touched by the way you've been these last few days."

He glanced over at her in the car seat beside him and then back at the road ahead. The A11 stretched out before them. They'd soon be back in Cambridge. "What do you mean?" he said.

"Oh, so attentive and thoughtful, different in lots of ways."

"I wonder," he said. He had been different?

Their Thanksgiving Dinner with Jeff and Charlie had been fun and lighthearted. Jeff even admitted that he was looking forward to joining Carol Heppel for church at St. Bene't's on some yet unnamed Sunday. After dinner Brian had walked Jeannie back to her B and B. He had been hopeful throughout the day that their relationship might genuinely be on the mend, but he had resolved not to push her. She had shown no inclination to be pushed. They spent Saturday mostly apart, Jeannie doing some Christmas shopping on her own and Brian pretending to do some work. Though his heart wasn't in it. In the evening they had taken in a play at the Corn Exchange and savored some hot Indian curry afterwards. There had been no more confrontational conversations, and it felt to him as if she were simply trying to get the sense of him. Perhaps just waiting out the time to go home. She had ended that evening with a light almost sisterly kiss. It was clear to Brian that she still didn't trust him.

They had started out early and driven to the North Sea coast east of Norwich to explore the little towns there and enjoy a bright clear day. After a late lunch they had started back toward Cambridge.

As Brian continued to drive along the A11 he looked over at her again, acknowledging to himself how nervous he felt. Finally the words burst out of him, almost without him knowing he was going to say them. "I've been trying to find a way to talk with you about what has happened to me over these last months and especially my obsession with Mary Beth. That's what it was, you know: an obsession." He concentrated on the road ahead, trying to sense her reaction to what he had said.

Jeannie sat quietly, looking over at him, but giving him no clues. She would not solve his problem for him.

"Anyhow," he said at last, "I have no excuses left. All of

the rationalizations aside, I know I behaved like a jerk. All I can say in my present defense is that I really don't think that anything like that will ever happen again. Maybe it's something about the dreams and all, but I feel, well, different in some subtle but important ways. It's something I sense in myself and in my reactions to—to various things. I honestly think I'm trustworthy now in ways I have never been before in my life." They drove in silence for a couple of miles. Finally, he added, "I only hope you can forgive me."

She remained quiet for a time, finally saying, "I don't know, Brian. I really don't know. Intellectually, I'm fine with it all. I even understand your rationalizations. Your word, not mine. But when I think about having you touch me in an intimate way, well . . . I feel a kind of involuntary revulsion. I'm willing to wait and see. I'm afraid that's the best I have to offer."

"I understand," he said, not knowing quite how to feel, but glad that the words had been said.

They drove again without talking as he negotiated the bypass and traffic around Thetford.

"How long would it take to drive to that village—to Stichen-Walling?" she asked as they passed a sign announcing the A134 to Bury St. Edmunds. "I'd like to have another look there before I go home tomorrow. Maybe without the rain this time."

"Probably at most an hour, I guess, plus the time we're stopped."

"We're not in any hurry are we?"

"Not so far as I know."

"Then, I'd really like to go. That seems important somehow."

"I'm glad about that. Frankly I'm aching to see it again myself." He made the mental adjustment and rethought his route, taking the turn for the A134 south.

"This all looks familiar," she said as they pulled into Stichen-Walling.

"Feels like a second home to me," he said, emitting a nervous laugh and glancing at the Wool Barn. Somebody had cleaned up the pile of rubbish that had disgraced the side of the building. Hmm.

"I imagine so," she said.

Why was he nervous? He stopped the car in front of the Victorian parish church and opened the door. "I can't say why, but I'm excited to come here again. It's only been a couple of days, but ..."

"I know what you mean."

They walked around the church and down the path through the small grove of bare trees. This time they walked in the warmth of the pale November sun, which by mid afternoon was already showing signs of slipping beneath the horizon. The watery blue sky, thin white clouds and gentle breeze made it nearly a perfect late autumn day. Finally, they saw the little stone church. Its grounds were trimmed and tidy and its wall looked as if it would withstand the centuries. Everything looked just as it had on Thursday.

But to Brian something about the place seemed different.

"Maybe it's because it isn't rainy and wet today, but this really isn't such a bad place," she said.

"I was thinking much the same thing."

"I'm sorry I was so negative about it."

"You were only expressing what I was also feeling. It seemed so depressing then. Must have been the rain."

"Can we go inside?" she asked.

"I don't see why not. I know where they hide the key." As he walked to the little porch and stood in front of the door to the church with the newly restored roof and grounds, he glanced over at the repaired section of the wall and saw the glint of the bright new dedication plaque. In what felt like perfect timing on her part, Jeannie took his arm. "It's undoubtedly the same place where we were on Thursday and which I've been visiting for months, but it doesn't either look or feel the same." He reached for the key in its hiding place.

"I agree." She released his arm.

He thought about Bobbie's drawing of this place and the way his reaction to it had gone through a metamorphosis, at first threatened and then invited. Now the place itself seemed to have traveled that same path. It had become different, appealing even. He suspected that he would spend much of the remainder of his life puzzling out everything that had happened to him here and in connection with this place. But through some odd alchemy neither he nor this ancient church and its graveyard would ever be quite the same again. Perhaps because Brian had come to care for both of them: the church and himself.

They looked around inside the church. It was less cheerful without the burning candles of Thursday, but it still looked loved and not abandoned. Going back outside, he locked the door and stowed the key again. They walked slowly the way they had come. Before stepping through the lychgate they turned around as one and stood looking at the little petrified pudding and its tidy yard. Brian suddenly felt Jeannie move over close beside him. He reached his arm naturally around her waist. She didn't push him away. They stood there together. He felt content in the moment, as if they were fully comfortable in each other's company for the first time since she arrived.

"I've decided to come back to Chicago for Christmas," he said. "That's really where I want to be."

"That will be nice," she answered. "And I mean it. Where will you stay? You are homeless, after all. At least on that side of the Atlantic."

"Actually, Bobbie has offered to let me sleep on her couch." He looked over at her. "Maybe we can have lunch? Do some things together like we used to?"

"Yes, we can have lunch." Her blue eyes sparkled in the last rays of the sun. "Maybe take a walk along the lake."

"A walk along the lake," he said. "I'd like that."

aBOUT ThE aUThOR

Gordon McBride was trained as an English historian, has a Ph. D. from the University of Cincinnati, and is an Episcopal priest. He is married to women's studies professor Kari Boyd McBride, and lives in Tucson, Arizona. *The Ghost of Midsummer Common* is his second novel. *The Vicar of Bisbee* is forthcoming from Windstorm Creative and is a sequel to his first novel, *Flying to Tombstone*.